SNEAK ATTACK

An explosion rocked the Chamber, flinging Leia into the air. She flew backward and slammed onto a desk, her entire body shuddering with the power of her hit. Blood and shrapnel rained around her. Smoke and dust rose, filling the room with a grainy darkness. She could hear nothing. With a shaking hand, she touched the side of her face. Warmth stained her cheeks and her earlobes. The ringing would start soon. The explosion was loud enough to affect her eardrums. . . .

The tone had truly been set for this Senatorial term.

And for that, the Empire would pay.

Also by Kristine Kathryn Rusch:

Fantasy novels:

THE FEY: THE CHANGELING
THE FEY: THE SACRIFICE
TRAITORS
HEART READERS
THE WHITE MISTS OF POWER

Horror novels:

THE DEVIL'S CHURN
SINS OF THE BLOOD
FACADE
AFTERIMAGE (with Kevin J. Anderson)

Star Trek novels:

SOLDIERS OF FEAR (with Dean Wesley Smith)
RINGS OF TAUTEE (with Dean Wesley Smith)
KLINGON! (with Dean Wesley Smith)
THE LONG NIGHT (with Dean Wesley Smith)
THE ESCAPE (with Dean Wesley Smith)
THE BIG GAME (as Sandy Schofield, also with Dean Wesley Smith)

Anthologies edited by:

THE BEST FROM FANTASY AND SCIENCE FICTION (with Edward L. Ferman)
THE BEST OF PULPHOUSE

THE NEW REBELLION

Kristine Kathryn Rusch

BANTAM BOOKS
NEW YORK • TORONTO • LONDON • SYDNEY • AUCKLAND

This edition contains the complete text
of the original hardcover edition.
NOT ONE WORD HAS BEEN OMITTED.

STAR WARS: THE NEW REBELLION

A Bantam Spectra Book

PUBLISHING HISTORY
Bantam Spectra hardcover edition published December 1996
Bantam Spectra paperback edition / October 1997

Library of Congress Catalog Card Number: 96-8073.

ISBN 0-553-57414-0

Published simultaneously in the United States and Canada

Bantam Books are published by Bantam Books, a division of Bantam Doubleday Dell Publishing Group, Inc. Its trademark, consisting of the words "Bantam Books" and the portrayal of a rooster, is Registered in U.S. Patent and Trademark Office and in other countries. Marca Registrada. Bantam Books, 1540 Broadway, New York, New York 10036.

PRINTED IN THE UNITED STATES OF AMERICA

OPM 10 9 8 7 6 5 4 3 2 1

This book is dedicated to four groups of special people:

First, to the old friends who sat with me in that darkened theater in Duluth, Minnesota, on May 25, 1977: Mindy Wallgren-Holte, Janine (Plunkett) McCusker, Kevin O'Neill, and Daniel W. Bergman. I miss you all and wish you well.

Second, to the nieces and nephews who, as children, helped me experience the excitement anew: Tim Rusch, Priscilla Wolfe, Kathy McNally, Kristine Hofsommer, Knute Hofsommer, and Aaron J. Reynolds.

Third, to the friends of the heart who have never lost their sense of wonder: Kevin J. Anderson, Paul B. Higginbotham, Nina Kiriki Hoffman, and Dean Wesley Smith.

And finally, to George Lucas, for giving me so many hours of enjoyment, and to John Williams, whose exceptional score still makes me shiver with delight.

Acknowledgments

Thanks on this one go to Tom Dupree, Lucy Autrey Wilson, and Richard Curtis for thinking of me in the first place; to Sue Rostoni, who answered all my questions; to Renee Dodds for keeping me on the straight and narrow; to Jenny Goodnough for understanding the depth of the Star Wars universe; to Dean Wesley Smith for reminding me to laugh in all the right places; to Kevin J. Anderson, Rebecca Moesta, Dave Wolverton, Steve Perry, and Barbara Hambly for their thoughts, theories, and advice; and to all the other *Star Wars* authors for providing me with the most enjoyable month of research I've ever had.

THE NEW REBELLION

One

He stood on the highest point on the planet of Almania, the roof of a tower built by the once-powerful Je'har. The tower was in ruin, the stairs crumbling as his boots touched them, the roof littered with debris from battles years gone. From here, though, he could see his city, a thousand lights spread before him, the streets empty except for droids and the ever-present guards.

But he was not interested in looking down. He wanted to see the stars.

An icy wind rippled his black cloak. He clasped his gloved hands behind him. The death's-head mask he had worn since destroying the Je'har hung on a silver chain around his neck.

Above him the stars winked. Hard to believe worlds existed there. Worlds he would control.

Soon.

He could have waited in his command, stood in the observatory specially constructed for his needs, but for once, he wanted no protective walls around him. He wanted to *feel* the moment, not see it.

The power of sight was so pitiful against the strength of the Force.

He tilted his head back and closed his eyes. No explosion this time. No bright flare of light. Skywalker had told him of the moment when Alderaan died.

I felt a great disturbance in the Force, the old man had said. At least, that's what Skywalker told him.

This disturbance would not be as great, but Skywalker would feel it. All the young Jedi would feel it too, and they would know that the balance of power had shifted.

But they wouldn't know that power had shifted to him. To Kueller, Master of Almania, and soon, lord of all their pitiful worlds.

✷ ✷ ✷

The stone walls were damp and cold against Brakiss's unprotected hands. His polished black boots slipped against the crumbling steps, and more than once he had to balance on a precarious ledge. His silver cloak, perfect for a brisk stroll across the city, did not protect him against the winter wind. If this experiment worked, he would be able to go back to Telti, where he would at least be warm.

The remote's metal casing was cool against his fingers. He hadn't wanted to give it to Kueller until the experiment was over. Brakiss hadn't realized, until a few moments ago, that Kueller would wait for the results here, at the site of his enemies' triumph and their eventual deaths.

Brakiss hated the towers. It felt as if something still rattled in their walls, and once, when he was in the catacombs below, he had seen a large white ghost.

Tonight, he had climbed more than twenty stories, and had almost run the first flights until it became clear that some of the steps wouldn't hold his weight. Kueller hadn't summoned him, but Brakiss didn't care. The sooner he left Almania, the happier he would be.

The stairs twisted and finally he reached the roof—or what he thought was the roof. A stone hut had been built to protect the steps, but the hut had no windows or doors. Only pillars, which gave a good view of the gravel inlay surface, and of the star-filled sky. Stones had fallen out of the hut and shattered onto the rooftop. The remains from bombs and blaster concussions formed little mounds on what had once been a level plane. Kueller had not repaired the tower or the other Je'har government buildings. He never would.

Kueller never forgave anyone who crossed him.

Brakiss shuddered and clutched his thin cape tightly around his shoulders. His frozen fingers barely got a grip on the material.

"I told you to wait below." Kueller's deep voice carried on the wind.

Brakiss swallowed. He couldn't even see Kueller.

The starlight fell across the roof, giving the dark sky a luminescence that Brakiss found eerie. He climbed the remaining stairs and stepped out of the hut. A gust of wind knocked him against the stone. He braced himself with his right hand, losing his grip on his cloak. The fastener tugged against his neck as the wind made the material flutter behind him.

"I had to know if it worked," he said.

"You'll know when it works." Kueller's voice was a live thing. It surrounded Brakiss, resonated within him, and held him at bay. Brakiss concentrated, not on the voice, but on Kueller himself.

And finally saw him, standing near the edge, overlooking the city below. Stonia, the capital of Almania, looked small and insignificant from this height. But Kueller looked like a powerful bird of prey, his cape billowing in the wind, his broad shoulders suggesting great physical strength.

Brakiss took a step forward when suddenly the wind died. The air around him froze and so did he. In that moment, he heard—felt—saw—a million voices scream in terror.

The terror rose in him, and he saw again that moment when Master Skywalker led Brakiss deep into Brakiss's own heart, that moment when he saw himself clearly and nearly lost his mind—

A scream formed in his own throat—

And died as the other screams exploded around him, filling him, warming him, melting the ice in the wind. He felt stronger, larger, more powerful than he ever had before. Instead of fear, his heart felt an odd, twisted joy.

He looked up. Kueller had raised his arms, his head tilted back, his face uncovered for the first time in years. He had changed, his skin filled with a knowledge Brakiss wasn't sure he wanted.

And yet . . .

Yet Kueller glowed, as if the pain of those million voices had fed something within him, had made him even greater than he had been before.

The wind returned, its frigid gusts knocking Brakiss against the stone. Kueller didn't seem to feel it. He laughed, a deep, rumbling sound that shook the entire tower.

Brakiss braced himself against the stone. He waited until Kueller's arms fell to his sides before saying, "It worked."

Kueller slipped the mask over his face. "Well enough."

Such an understatement for such a great moment. Kueller had to remember that Brakiss was strong in the Force as well.

Kueller turned, his cape swirling around him. He almost appeared to fly. The skull-like mask that adhered to his face shone with its own internal light. "I suppose you want to return to your paltry job."

"It's warm on Telti."

"It could be warm here," Kueller said.

Brakiss shook his head almost involuntarily. He hated Almania.

"Your problem is that you do not understand the power of hate," Kueller said, his voice soft.

"I thought you said my problem is that I serve two masters."

Kueller smiled, the thin lips on his mask moving with his mouth. "Is it only two?"

The words hung between them. Brakiss's entire body felt as if it were made of ice. "It worked," he said again.

"I suppose you expect to be rewarded."

"You promised."

"I never promise," Kueller said. "I imply."

Brakiss crossed his arms over his chest. He would not get angry. Kueller wanted him to be angry. "You implied great wealth."

"So I did," Kueller said. "Do you deserve great wealth, Brakiss?"

Brakiss said nothing. Kueller had put him together after Yavin 4, after the disastrous debriefing that had nearly cost Brakiss the rest of his sanity. But Brakiss had long since repaid his debt. He only stayed because he had nowhere else to go.

He pushed off the wall and started down the stairs. "I'm going back to Telti," he said, feeling defiant.

"Good," Kueller said. "But you will give me the remote first."

Brakiss stopped and looked at Kueller over his shoulder. Kueller had grown taller in the last hour. Taller and broader.

Or perhaps that was a trick of the darkness.

If Brakiss had faced any other mortal, he would have asked how Kueller knew about the remote. But Kueller was not any other mortal.

Brakiss held out the remote. "It's slower than the controls I built you."

"Fine."

"You have to set the security codes. You have to instruct it which serial numbers to follow."

"I'm sure I can do that."

"You have to link it to you."

"Brakiss, I can operate remotes."

"All right," Brakiss said. He braced himself as he moved inside the stone hut. It was warmer in there, out of the wind.

He didn't believe Kueller was letting him leave so easily.

"What do you want from me, when I return to Telti?" Brakiss asked.

"Skywalker," Kueller said, his voice thrumming with the depth of his hatred. "The great Jedi Master, Luke the invincible Skywalker."

The chill had reached Brakiss's heart. "What do you plan to do with him?"

"Destroy him," Kueller said. "Just as he tried to destroy us."

Two

*

Luke Skywalker was balanced on one hand, his fingers deep in the moist jungle earth. Sweat dripped down his naked back, onto his face, and off his nose and chin. His feet were bare, but he wore an old pair of tight pants that clung to his damp skin. Artoo-Detoo floated in the air above him, along with several boulders and a half-rotted tree. Some of Luke's students were gathered around him, half a dozen members of his youngest and most powerful class.

He had been in this position since the huge orange sphere of the gas planet Yavin had risen on the horizon of its fourth moon. Yavin was now directly overhead, and although Luke was sweating, he didn't feel tired or thirsty. The Force flowed through him like cool water, holding Artoo, the boulders, and the tree aloft.

The students were shifting, probably wondering how long they would have to continue watching. Perhaps he would lift them one by one, and then withdraw, leaving them to find the ground delicately or with difficulty, as their talents allowed.

Luke suppressed a smile. As much as he enjoyed teaching, he didn't always show that enjoyment. Sometimes the students believed he was laughing at their expense, which was not conducive to a good student-teacher relationship. Still, he had moments of pure pleasure, especially at times like this. Artoo didn't appreciate this aspect of the training, but it made Luke feel like a boy again.

Instead of lifting one of his students, he eased another boulder into the air. It hovered near the others, bobbing a bit before it found its place. The students watched, suddenly still. Luke scanned their feet, hoping for some sign of annoyance. The first one to look restless would be the first one into the air.

He had learned this method over the years as a way of teaching his students patience, and also as a way of showing them the powers of the Force. Like so many of the methods he used, it worked for some students and didn't work for others. Often he got an insight into a student's mind by the student's reaction to various aspects of training. These class members were still new enough to mimic each others' reactions. He hoped that mimicry would be gone by the end of the day.

Then a wave of emotion slammed into him—cold, hard, and filled with terror. The pain was worse than anything he had ever felt, worse than the near loss of his leg on the *Eye of Palpatine,* worse than the Emperor's electric blast on the Death Star, worse than the destruction of his face on Hoth. Mixed with the terror and pain was the shock of betrayal, a shock multiplied by the millions of minds who felt it.

Luke wobbled on his hand, struggling to keep the boulders and tree aloft, to keep them from falling on his unsuspecting students. Artoo screamed as he shot across the sky, the sound mingling with the screams in Luke's mind. Artoo landed with a metallic bang against the jungle floor, Luke's students scattered, and the rest of Luke's control fled.

His arm collapsed beneath him, and he tumbled to the ground, his breath gone from his body. He lay on his back, sinking in the soft dirt, the screams still echoing in his mind.

Then, as suddenly as they had appeared, the voices were gone.

"Are you all right?" one of his students asked. The voice was overlaid with his own, filled with the same trembly fear seventeen years ago. "What's wrong?"

Luke put his left hand over his face. He was shaking. "There's been a great disturbance in the Force." He wondered how they could fail to feel it, how he had failed to feel something even stronger, all those years ago.

As if millions of voices suddenly cried out in terror and were suddenly silenced.

"Ben," he whispered. "Another Death Star?"

But he expected no answer. Ben's comforting presence had left him before the Jedi Academy, before Grand Admiral Thrawn.

Luke closed his eyes, feeling for the location of the disturbance. He found a great emptiness where a moment before there had been life. The residue of pain, the deeply held surprise, the shock of betrayal, remained like an echo of a shout over a canyon rim.

"Master Skywalker?" The voice belonged to one of his most promising students, Eelysa, a young woman from Coruscant. "Master Skywalker?"

He waved his right hand at her. His back hurt from the force of his landing, his chest ached from the lack of oxygen, and his heart ached from the magnitude of the loss. Somewhere in the distance, Artoo whistled, a mournful sound.

He had to sit up, to show them everything was all right, even though it wasn't.

"Master Skywalker?"

Her voice merged and blended with the echoes in his head. He opened his eyes. In the shade of his shaking hand, he saw Leia's face, scorched and blood-covered. He reached toward her, and then she was gone.

It is the future you see.

The destruction did not come from Coruscant. He would know if Leia died. Or Han. Or the children.

He would know.

Artoo whistled again, impatient this time.

"Find Artoo," he said. His voice sounded haunted, shaky, preoccupied, like Ben's had after the destruction of Alderaan.

Feet snapped twigs around him as three students left in search of Artoo.

Or as they ran from Luke and his sudden, startling loss of control.

"What happened, Master Skywalker?" Eelysa was crouched beside him, her small, slender body hunched against an unseen enemy. She had been a surprise, a native of Coruscant, born after the Emperor's death, her Force abilities untainted by the poisons around her. She was young. So very, very young.

"A million people died a moment ago, all in great pain, and with great suddenness." He pushed himself up on his elbows. A vast evil had returned to the galaxy. That much he knew.

And it threatened Leia.

He knew that too.

For now, the days of teaching were over. He and Artoo had to leave immediately for Coruscant.

✷ ✷ ✷

Leia Organa Solo, Chief of State of the New Republic, adjusted the belt on her long white gown. She took a deep breath. Mon Mothma placed a hand on her arm. Leia smiled distractedly at her, much as she had as a young senator, facing Palpatine and his followers in the Imperial Senate.

She let the breath out. That was the emotion she was feeling, something she hadn't felt since she was a teenager. A sense of loss, of defeat, of the life changing without her permission or control.

Mon Mothma closed the golden carved door and turned the lock. They were in a small dressing room that had been added during Palpatine's days as Emperor, a room just outside the Senate Assembly Chamber. The room had been used as a secret communications area, but it masqueraded as a dressing room. The walls were gold leaf and delicate. A mirror covered one panel, floor to ceiling, reflecting both Leia and Mon Mothma. In some ways, Mon Mothma looked like an older, calmer version of Leia, although her short hair was now streaked with silver. Tiny lines webbed her skin, lines that had been there since her devastating illness at the hands of Carida's Ambassador Furgan six years before.

"What is it?" Mon Mothma said.

Leia shook her head. She smoothed her damp hands on her skirts. She didn't look much different from the girl who had walked into the Imperial Senate filled with hope and idealism, Princess Leia Organa of Alderaan, the youngest senator, the one who believed that persuasion and reason would save the Old Republic. The one who lost her idealism the moment she stared into Senator Palpatine's ruined face.

"They're members of the New Republic now, Leia," Mon Mothma said. "They were elected fairly."

"This is wrong. This is how it all started before." Leia had had this same conversation with Han since the elections. Several planets had petitioned the Senate to allow former Imperials to serve as political representatives. The argument was that some of the best politicians had kept their peoples alive by working with the Empire, as minor functionaries. They were petty bureaucrats who saved dozens of Rebel lives by overlooking strange troop movements, or unusual faces in the crowds. Leia had opposed the petitions from the beginning, but the arguments in Chamber had been fierce. M'yet Luure, the powerful senator from Exodeen, had finally reminded her that even she had once served the Empire in her role as Imperial senator. She had retorted that she was serving the Rebellion even then. M'yet had smiled, revealing six rows of uneven teeth. *These people were serving the Rebellion too,* he had said, *in their own way.*

Leia had disputed that claim. They had served the Empire and not fought against it, had merely looked the other way. But M'yet's argument was powerful, and because of it, the Senate had approved the petition. Leia had modified the election law with the help of her backers—no former stormtroopers could hold office, no Imperial of rank, no former Imperial governor—in short, no Imperial with access to power in the Empire could serve the New Republic. But still she felt this law was wrong.

"They're going to destroy all we've worked for," she said to Mon Mothma.

"You don't know that," Mon Mothma said softly.

Her words echoed Han's. Leia clenched her fists. "I do know that," she said. "Since we formed the New Republic, we have always known that our leaders have the same goals. We have the same philosophy of life. We have always worked in the same directions."

Mon Mothma's grip on Leia's arm loosened. "We have always fought the Empire. But the Empire is gone now. Only bands remain. Someday we must move beyond the Rebellion and into true government. Part of that, Leia, is accepting those who lived under the Empire but did not serve it."

Leia shook her head. "It's too soon."

"Actually," Mon Mothma said, "I think it isn't soon enough."

Leia tugged at her skirt. She had even worn her hair in the long-outdated style, braids wrapped around her ears, in defiance of the new Senate members—as a sign that Chief of State Leia Organa Solo was once Leia Organa, princess, senator, and Rebel leader. Han had kissed her roughly before she left their apartments and had grinned at her. *Well, Your Worship, does this mean I get to go back to being a scoundrel?*

She had laughingly pushed him away, but his words echoed even as Mon Mothma spoke. Perhaps Leia was the problem. Perhaps she was not willing to move forward.

Perhaps she was the one unwilling to let go of the past.

"All right," she said, straightening, a leader once more. "Let's get on with this."

Mon Mothma did not move toward the door. "One more thing," she said. "Remember that whatever tone you set at the opening remarks of this Senate will be the focus of the debate for years to come."

"I know," Leia said. She reached for the door when a wave of deep cold smashed into her. She froze. Voices screamed—hundreds, no—thousands of voices, so faint she could barely hear them. Then she saw a face form on the golden door, a white face with black, empty eyes. The face was concave, almost skeletal, like the death masks she had seen in a museum on Alderaan in her youth. Only, unlike them, this one moved. It smiled, and the cold grew deeper.

Then the voices ceased, and Leia collapsed against the door.

Mon Mothma hurried to her side, and grabbed Leia, staggering as she attempted to support her weight. "Leia?"

Leia was still cold. Colder than she had ever been on Hoth. Her teeth were chattering. She reached with her limited Force training and found her children in the apartments, just as they should have been.

"Luke," she whispered. Leia freed herself from Mon Mothma's hold, and headed toward the old communications control. She contacted Yavin 4, only to be told Luke was in his X-wing.

"Leia, what is it?" Mon Mothma asked.

Leia didn't answer. She waited to be patched into Luke's X-wing. Soon his voice filled the room. "Leia?" he asked, as if he had been worried too.

"I'm fine, Luke," she said, relief filling her.

"I'm coming to you. Wait for me."

But she couldn't wait. She had to know. "You felt it too, didn't you? What was that?"

"Alderaan," he whispered, and that was all she needed to know.

The image of Alderaan filled her mind, Alderaan as she had last seen it on the Death Star, beautiful and serene, in the seconds before it was smashed to bits.

"No!" she said. "Luke?"

"I'll be there soon, Leia," he said, and signed off. She wasn't ready for him to disappear so soon. She needed him. Something awful had happened, like the destruction of Alderaan.

And she had felt it.

"What happened, Leia?" Mon Mothma put her arms around Leia. Leia's shivering had stopped.

"Something terrible," Leia said. She reached out, touched the cool gold door, straightened, and stood. "There's death in that chamber, Mon Mothma."

"Leia—"

"Luke is coming here. He felt something too."

"Then trust him," Mon Mothma said. "He'd know if you were in immediate danger."

But he hadn't known. He had been as relieved to hear from her as she had been to hear from him. Her mouth was dry. "Send someone for Han, would you?"

Mon Mothma nodded. "I suppose you want to put off the opening session."

More than anything. But Leia straightened her shoulders, rubbed her cold hands together, and checked her braids a final time. "No," she said. "You were right. I have to be careful of the message I send. I'm going in. But let's double the guards this afternoon, and step up security on Coruscant. Also, get Admiral Ackbar to scan for anything unusual in nearby space."

"What are you afraid of?" Mon Mothma asked.

Alderaan flashed before Leia's vision at the moment of explosion, a flare of brilliant, horrible light. "I don't know," she said. "Maybe a Death Star, or a Sun Crusher. Something that could destroy us all."

Three

Han sat in the back corner of the smoke-filled room. He hadn't been in this casino since he won the planet Dathomir in a game of sabacc before he married Leia. The casino had changed hands at least fifteen times since then—now it was calling itself the Crystal Jewel, a misnomer if he'd ever heard one—but it looked no different. The air smelled of damp decay mixed with smoke and alcohol. A mediocre band played Tatooine blues with a decided disinterest. All around him, conversation rose and fell with the fortunes at the sabacc tables.

He clutched a pale blue Gizer ale, which he had snatched off a servo droid. Han's companion, Jarril, had disappeared a few moments ago, searching for the bar. Han wasn't sure if Jarril would be back.

Han was watching the sabacc game at the nearest table, where a Gotal was betting all it owned. As it slid the chips across the table, it shed piles of gray hair. Most Gotals had learned to control their shedding. This one had to be extremely nervous.

Its companions didn't seem to notice. The Brubb, a large brown reptile, was scratching its knobby hide, leaving scales all over the floor, its tail knocking the mechanical base of a nearby servo droid. The two-armed Ssty was counting her cards, her claws making indentations in each. The tiny Tin-Tin Dwarf stood on its chair, its rat-like features focused on the pile in the center of the table.

The dealer droids had been upgraded since Han's last visit. This dealer was bolted to the ceiling, but unlike its predecessors, it could slide down to table height and knock aside an unruly player. The dealer had done just that after Jarril left, and had riveted Han's attention. He had never seen such an aggressive droid before. Although he had to admit, they were needed in a place like this.

"The line was incredible." Jarril slipped back into his chair at the table. He had two drinks, both bright green. Neither looked appealing.

Han wrapped his hands around his Gizer ale. "I'd've waited if I'd known you were buying."

Jarril shrugged. He was a small man with narrow shoulders, and a face scarred from years of harsh living. Han had always envied Jarril's hands, though. They were smuggler's hands, with long, thin, tapered fingers, perfect for piloting, blasting, and those forms of gambling that required dexterity. "More for me," Jarril said.

The smuggler's credo. Han grinned. It'd been too long since he'd been in a place like this. He probably wouldn't even have answered Jarril's contact if it hadn't been for Leia. She had looked like that sharp-tongued princess he'd rescued back when he'd been an equally sharp-tongued scoundrel. Sometimes he missed that part of himself more than he cared to admit.

Han slid his chair back so that it hit the wall. He wore a blaster at his hip, having learned almost before he could walk that no sane man entered a place like this without protection. Besides, he didn't really know the reason behind Jarril's visit.

"I don't believe you came to Coruscant just to buy me a drink," Han said. He didn't bother to mention that the Jarril of old would never have bought anyone anything. A lot had changed about his old colleague, including the price of the man's clothes. Jarril used to wear shirts until they fell off him. This one was made of a dyed green gaberwool, a singularly ugly garment despite its obvious newness.

"I didn't," Jarril said. He downed one green drink, coughed, wiped his mouth, and grinned. His teeth glowed for a moment before he licked the liquid off them. "I came to tell you about an opportunity."

This was rich. An opportunity. For Han Solo, hero of the Alliance, husband, father, and family man. "I've got opportunities," Han said, and immediately wondered what they were.

"Yeah, sure." Jarril pushed a strand of hair off his pocked forehead. "I gotta admit you stayed legit a lot longer than I woulda thought. I figured six months with the princess and you and Chewie would be back on the *Falcon,* heading for parts unknown."

"There's enough to keep me busy here," Han said.

"Busy, maybe," Jarril said. "But it's a waste of talent if you ask me. You and Chewie were the best pirates I knew."

Han slid one hand to his blaster and rested his fingers against the trigger. "I haven't been away that long, Jarril. I still don't con easily. What do you want?"

Jarril leaned close. His breath smelled of mint, ale, and cream candy. "There's money out there, Han. More money than we ever dreamed of."

"I don't know," Han said. "I can dream of a lot."

"So can I." Jarril's voice was so soft Han could barely hear it over the band. "And I can't spend all I got."

"Congratulations," Han said. "You want me to propose a toast?"

"You're not interested, are you?" Jarril asked. He had a curiously intent look.

"Maybe I would have been years ago, Jarril, but I've got a life now."

"Some life," Jarril said. "Sitting around all day, watching the babies while the little woman runs her own private empire."

Han leaned forward and grabbed the collar of Jarril's shirt in one quick, practiced movement. "Watch it, pal."

Jarril grimaced in a vain attempt to smile. His eyes shifted from Han's face to his hidden hand and back again. Good. Han hadn't lost any of his reputation during the time away. "Didn't mean anything by it, Solo," Jarril said. "Just making conversation, you know?"

Han tightened his grip on Jarril's shirt. "What do you want?"

"I want help, Han."

Han let Jarril go. Jarril slammed back into his seat. He grabbed his second glass, gulped down the hideous green contents, and wiped his mouth. Han waited, finger still on the trigger. Smugglers never asked each other for help. Sometimes they conned their friends into assistance, but they never asked.

Jarril had been conning him. It just hadn't been working.

Jarril licked his teeth, and took another glass off the passing servo droid.

"Make it quick," Han said. "The little lady expects me home, dinner done, when she arrives." He tilted his chair back on two legs, his head resting against the wall. "I make a mean Smuggler's Pie."

Jarril held up his hands. "I'm not kidding you, Han. About any of it. The money—"

"You said you needed help."

"I think we all do." Jarril lowered his voice again. "That money comes with a price. I never seen so much money in my life."

"I got it," Han said. "You're rich. That brings its own problems. I know. I'm not in the mood for whining."

"I'm not whining," Jarril said, his voice rising in protest.

"Sounds like it to me, pal."

"No, you don't get it, Han. People are dying. Good people."

"I didn't think you knew any good people, Jarril."

"I know you."

"Are you saying someone's threatening me?"

"No." Jarril looked over his shoulder.

"Leia?"

"No!" Jarril scooted his chair closer. Han had to adjust the blaster angle. "Look, Han, anyone in the business with brains has made a fortune in the last few months. *Everyone* we know, and people you never met. Rich. Smuggler's Run isn't the same place anymore. There's more credits in the Run than the Hutts could spend in a lifetime."

"So?"

"So?" Jarril downed his last drink. "So it all seemed wonderful at first. Then a few Runners didn't come back. Stand-up folks. Like you and Calrissian."

Han suppressed a smile. In the old days, he and Lando had been considered odd because they occasionally helped another smuggler in distress. "Where were these Runners when they failed to come back?"

Jarril shrugged. "I didn't think nothing of it at first until I realized that the folks who were in the business for the adventure and for the money were the ones disappearing. It made me think of you, old buddy."

"Me?"

"Well, I was thinking, you know, maybe you and Chewie could see what's going on. Unofficially. Maybe."

"I've got a life," Han said.

Jarril bit his lower lip, as if he were struggling not to speak. Finally he said, "That's why I came here. You know people. Maybe you could find out what's going on. Unofficially."

"Since when does Smuggler's Run need legitimate help?"

"It can't be legit!" Jarril's stunned voice rose above all the other sounds in the casino.

The conversation halted. Han grinned at the faces that turned toward him, all of them pretending disinterest and hoping for blood. He was half-tempted to wave his blaster at them.

"You see something you don't like?" Han asked the Ssty who was peering over the back of her chair at him. She shook her angular fur-covered face.

He raised his eyebrows and scanned the rest of the room, silently asking the entire crowd the same question. One by one they turned away.

Han waited until the conversation rose before continuing. "If it can't be legit, why come to me at all?"

"Because you and Chewie are the only ones I know who can go between Smuggler's Run and the Republic, no questions asked."

"What about Lando? Talon Karrde? Mara Jade?"

"Karrde doesn't want anything to do with this. Jade's been with Calrissian, and you know about him and Nandreeson."

"Can't say as I do," Han said. He was lying. He knew of it, but he thought the matter had been settled years ago.

"C'mon, Solo. Don't make this hard. Nandreeson's had a price on Calrissian since the days of the Empire."

"It couldn't have been a big price. Everyone knows where Lando is."

"Calrissian's good at making friends," Jarril said. "But he doesn't dare go into the Run."

"And you think the problem is in Smuggler's Run?"

"I think some answers might be there."

Han sighed and let his fingers relax on the blaster trigger. "How come you don't go after this yourself, Jarril?"

Jarril shrugged. "There's no profit in it."

"Jarril," Han said, his voice low and menacing.

Jarril took a deep breath and leaned as close as he could. "Because," he said, his voice just above a whisper, "I'm in too deep, Han. Way too deep."

✶ ✶ ✶

See-Threepio stood outside the nursery, recovering. He had spent the morning with the twins, Jacen and Jaina, and their brother, Anakin. This morning had been particularly difficult for Threepio. The children had planned their assault the night before. They had not done their homework on the origins of the Old Republic, and to distract Threepio, they had staged a small food fight.

The distraction had succeeded. Threepio, covered with salthia beans and curdled milk, tried to discover how the food fight had started. He kept asking how food got into the nursery, although as the fight progressed, he bemoaned the children's lack of discipline.

The lack of discipline became most evident when Mistress Leia and Master Solo left. They were indulgent parents. Winter, who had helped raise all three children from infancy, at least understood the value of discipline.

Fortunately, she had arrived before Anakin located his slingshot.

She had eased Threepio out the door and told him to

rest. He had tried to inform her that droids did not need rest, but she had smiled at him knowingly. Long after she had shut the nursery door, he still stood outside it, perhaps confused by the order to rest, or perhaps unwilling to leave the scene of the latest disaster.

The entry to the nursery belied the chaos within. The room was octagonal, with chairs resting against each small wall. It had once been a listening chamber off an important meeting room. The room was rarely used as more than a hallway. No one sat in the chairs, and the children did little more than skate across the marble in their stocking feet. The cleaning droid assigned to this wing had complained of streak marks more than once.

A clatter in the hallway made Threepio look up. The clatter resolved itself into whirring footsteps. The door slid up, and a nanny droid glided in. Her four hands were clasped over her aproned stomach. Her silver eyes glowed and her mouth turned upward in a permanent look of good humor.

"See-Threepio?" Her voice was modulated for warmth. "I am TeeDee-El-Three-Point-Five. I am here to replace you as the children's nanny."

"Oh, dear." Threepio looked over his shoulder at the nursery door. "I was not informed of this."

"It is," the nanny droid said, "an unusual situation, after all. A protocol droid caring for children? You have no synthetic flesh, no hug circuitry, and, quite frankly, my dear, you are out-of-date. A few upgraded protocol droids have the programming to handle such a difficult assignment, but—"

"I assure you," Threepio said. "I have served these children well."

"I am sure you have." The nanny droid was clearly humoring him. "And I am sure you will be well rewarded for your service. But I am here to replace you."

"I have heard nothing of this replacement," Threepio said.

"Droids are never informed—"

"I have a special place in this family. I cannot be dismissed like a—a—"

"A rusting sanitation droid?" The nanny droid clucked at him. "Certainly we overrate our importance, don't we?"

"I do not overrate my importance!" Threepio said. "I daresay I am the most humble droid I know."

"As you have told me quite often." Winter leaned against the doorjamb, her tall frame filling it.

Jaina peeked out of Winter's skirts. "How can he be humble if that's all he talks about?" Jaina asked.

"Hush, child," Winter said.

"Mistress Winter," Threepio said. "I do believe protocol demands that if you're to replace me, you inform me first."

"You're getting rid of Threepio?" Jacen asked. He came to the door, his seven-year-old face a replica of Master Solo's. "Really, Winter, you should know better. We pick on him, but that's only because we like him."

"I wasn't planning to get rid of him," Winter said. She brushed a strand of her snow-white hair away from her face. "And neither were your parents."

"I was ordered specifically for this nursery," the nanny droid said. "I am TeeDee-El-Three-Point-Five, and I am here to replace See-Threepio according to instruction code Bantha Four Five Six."

"*Bantha?*" Winter asked. "That's not a family code."

"It's not my fault!" Anakin yelled from the other room.

"I don't think he liked it when you decided he was too old for *The Little Lost Bantha Cub,*" Jacen whispered to Threepio.

"Really," Threepio said. "That story outlived its usefulness years ago. Why, just last week, I heard Master Solo express relief that none of you children wanted to hear it anymore."

"Threepio," Winter said, caution in her voice. She stepped beside him. "Forgive us, TeeDee-El-Three-Point-Five. Apparently one of us was exploring areas of the shopping net that he wasn't supposed to."

"All the more reason for proper supervision," the nanny droid said. "Under my charge, children behave with the utmost decorum. An outdated protocol model like the one you have guarding the children obviously cannot control them. You need experience—"

"Yes, you do." Winter crossed her arms over her chest. "Have you ever reared Force-sensitive children before?"

"Children are children," the nanny droid said. "No matter what their special talents. In my experience, oversensitivity can be related to a lack of discipline—"

"I thought you hadn't," Winter said. "Threepio has done well with the singular challenges these children have presented him. All in all, I believe a nanny droid would be a disaster, both for the children, and for the adults."

"Are you dismissing me?" the nanny droid asked.

"You were ordered here by a child," Winter said.

"That was someone else!" Anakin yelled from inside the room.

Jaina put her hands over her mouth. Jacen went back into the nursery. "Anakin, no sense lying about it. The code gave you away. And now we can't use it anymore."

"I should say not," Threepio said. "Imagine children with access to the shopping nets. What will they think of next?"

"Something equally outrageous," Winter said, her gaze still on the nanny droid. The droid hadn't moved.

"TeeDee-El-Three-Point-Five, you have no place here. I am dismissing you."

"Forgive me, Mistress," the nanny droid said. "I do believe you're making a mistake."

"How exceptionally rude," Threepio said. "Mistress Winter has charge of these children—"

"I'll handle it, Threepio." Winter was smiling now. "I will make note of your complaint," she said to the nanny droid. "It will go into the file."

The nanny droid made a soft sound of disgust. Then her body swiveled, and she rolled out of the anteroom, the door sliding shut behind her.

"File?" Threepio asked. "I didn't know you kept files."

"I don't," Winter said.

"What were you thinking?" Jacen asked, his voice carrying through the open door.

"The holo was pretty," Anakin said.

Winter smiled at Threepio, then started for the nursery to settle the building dispute. "Anakin's life was once saved by a nanny droid, you know. He might have been simply wishing for the security of his babyhood."

"I am not—" Anakin started and then stopped as if his voice caught in his throat. Threepio hurried into the nursery. Anakin's face had gone white.

"What is it?" Winter asked.

Jacen and Jaina had frozen in place. Their eyes widened, and then, in unison, all three children began to scream.

Four

Kueller strode across the hangar, his boots clanging on the metal. Technicians prostrated themselves before him, their gloved hands extended on the webbing. He walked so close to the group on the left that the hem of his cape brushed their skulls. The death's-head mask adhered to his skin, giving him comfort, giving him power.

"I need a ship," he said, his Force-strengthened voice echoing in the large room. It was empty except for three TIE fighters in various states of repair.

"Prepared, milord." His faithful assistant, Femon, rose to her feet. Her long black hair hid her unnaturally pale face. With a flick of her head, she flipped the hair aside, revealing kohl-blackened eyes and blood-red lips. She had made her own face into a death mask that looked less realistic than his.

Kueller nodded. No one else moved. "Brakiss?"

"Gone, milord."

"He wasted no time."

"He said he had your permission."

"You didn't check?"

Femon smiled. "I always check."

"Good." Kueller caressed the word. Femon straightened beneath his praise, as she always did. If she weren't so capable, he would . . .

He let the thought fade. No distractions, not even of the pleasant sort. "Any reports from Pydyr?"

"One thousand people are imprisoned in their homes, as per your command," she said.

"Destruction?"

"None." The word hung between them.

He allowed himself to smile, knowing that the expression chilled even his hardest followers. "Excellent. Loss of life?"

She clasped her hands behind her back, taming her silver cape and outlining her willowy form. "One million, six hundred and fifty-one thousand, three hundred and five, milord."

"Exactly as planned," he said.

"To a person. You'll be investigating?"

"I always check," he said, throwing her words back at her.

She smiled. The expression softened her face despite her attempts otherwise. "Permission to accompany you?"

For a moment, he hesitated. She had been with him from the beginning. This part of the plan had been as much hers as his. "Not yet," he said. "I have need of you here."

"I thought we would wait for Phase 2."

"Oh, no," he said, purposely gentling his tone. "The wheels are rolling. Better to maintain momentum than to lose advantage. Remember?"

"Vividly." In the shaking of her voice, he heard the residue of each and every nightmare he had sent her, sometimes as many as five a night.

"Good," he said, and with his leather-gloved fingers he stroked her face. "Very, very good."

✱ ✱ ✱

The chamberlain pulled open the door to the Senate Hall as the heralds announced Leia. All this pomp and circumstance had seemed unnecessary until Leia's discussion with Mon Mothma. Now, after the strange event in the dressing chambers, Leia was glad for the ceremonial diversion. It gave her a moment to collect herself, to set aside the terror sent across space on a wave of frigid cold.

She entered, head held high, two guards at her side. The stepped-up security was obvious: guards at all the doors of the amphitheater, and defense droids scattered among the protocol droids stationed near the non-Basic-speaking senators. Representatives from all species and planets in the New Republic sat in their assigned seats, watching her expectantly. Mon Mothma had been right; Leia's actions on this day would determine the course of the Senate in the future.

Reporters from dozens of worlds crowded the visitors' balcony near the fragmented crystal segments in the ceiling. The segments caught and reflected sunlight in a rainbow effect, illuminating the center of the room. The Emperor had designed this little trick to strike awe in those observing him. Leia was glad for the sun and the rippling light. It would distract the new representatives, who had never seen it before.

She started down the stairs. The smell of bodies, human and alien, filled the Chamber, already too warm from the proximity of so many beings. Leia studiously looked ahead, noting, as she passed, M'yet Luure sitting beside his new colleague from Exodeen. Both Exodeenians had six arms, and six legs. They barely fit in the regulation chairs that Palpatine had built in the days when nonhumanoids were considered to be among the less important species. By looks, it was impossible to tell the former Imperial Exodeenian from his rebellious fellow senator. Indeed, she couldn't tell any former Imperials by sight, only by reputation.

Like Meido, the first and only senator from the planet Adin. Adin had been an Imperial stronghold, and Leia still wasn't certain if Meido's election had been fair. She was quietly having some of her people investigate him. She had memories of his seamed face from her Rebel days, but she couldn't place him.

Finally she reached the front of the Chamber. The chamberlain announced her as she took her place behind the spotlit podium. The senators applauded, or did the nearest equivalent. The Luyals pounded their tentacles on the desks. The eel-like Uteens had their droids applaud for them. She rested her hands on the podium's wooden surface, careful to avoid the computer screen. She had no prepared speech, a fact that relieved her now.

The Senate Hall doors closed and the guards moved in front of them. The applause was loud and favorable. Leia smiled, nodding toward old friends and ignoring the new faces. She would deal with them soon enough.

"My fellow senators," she said over the din. The applause slowly faded. She waited until it was gone before continuing. "We begin a new chapter in the history of the Republic. The war with the Empire is long over and finally we have extended the hand of friendship—"

An explosion rocked the Chamber, flinging Leia into the air. She flew backward and slammed onto a desk, her entire body shuddering with the power of her hit. Blood and shrapnel rained around her. Smoke and dust rose, filling the room with a grainy darkness. She could hear nothing. With a shaking hand, she touched the side of her face. Warmth stained her cheeks and her earlobes. The ringing would start soon. The explosion was loud enough to affect her eardrums.

Emergency glow panels seared the gloom. She could feel rather than hear pieces of the crystal ceiling fall to the ground. A guard had landed beside her, his head tilted at an unnatural angle. She grabbed his blaster. She had to get out. She wasn't certain if the attack had come from within or from without. Wherever it had come from, she had to make certain no other bombs would go off.

The force of the explosion had affected her balance. She crawled over bodies, some still moving, as she made her way to the stairs. The slightest movement made her dizzy and nauseous, but she ignored the feelings. She had to.

A face loomed before hers. Streaked with dirt and blood, helmet askew, she recognized him as one of the guards who had been with her since Alderaan. *Your Highness,* he mouthed, and she couldn't read the rest. She shook her head at him, gasping at the increased dizziness, and kept going.

Finally she reached the stairs. She used the remains of a desk to get to her feet. Her gown was soaked in blood, sticky, and clinging to her legs. She held the blaster in front of her, wishing that she could hear. If she could hear, she could defend herself.

A hand reached out of the rubble beside her. She whirled, faced it, watched as Meido pulled himself out. His slender features were covered with dirt, but he appeared unharmed. He saw her blaster and cringed. She nodded once to acknowledge him, and kept moving. The guard was flanking her.

More rubble dropped from the ceiling. She crouched, hands over her head to protect herself. Small pebbles pelted her, and the floor shivered as large chunks of tile fell. Dust rose, choking her. She coughed, feeling it, but not able to hear it. Within an instant, the Hall had gone from a place of ceremonial comfort to a place of death.

The image of the death's-head mask rose in front of her again, this time from memory. She had known this was going to happen. Somewhere, from some part of her Force-sensitive brain, she had seen this. Luke said that Jedi were sometimes able to see the future. But she had never completed her training. She wasn't a Jedi.

But she was close enough.

An anger flowed through her, deep and fine. She let her hands drop. The tiles had stopped falling, at least for the moment. She beckoned Meido and anyone else who could see her. If she couldn't hear, they couldn't either. And they all had to get out.

She glanced up once. The blast had made several holes in the ceiling—big, jagged, gaping holes in the crystal inlay. All of the tile put in by the Emperor had come loose and was falling like hail across the Hall. Other senators were standing. A few ancient protocol droids were lifting chunks of debris and pushing them aside, apparently in an attempt to get someone underneath free. M'yet Luure's junior senator was already halfway up the stairs, his six legs and long tail blocking the exit for half a dozen other senators. Of Luure, she saw no sign.

The guard took her arm and gestured forward. She nodded, shook him free, and kept moving. She expected more blasts and got nervous each time one failed to happen. This attack was unlike any she had ever felt. Why hit the Senate Hall once and then quit?

She slipped on broken tile, almost fell, put out her left hand to brace herself, and found it in something squishy. She turned, and saw that her hand rested on one of M'yet Luure's six legs. It had been blown away from his body. She scrambled toward him, hoping that he was alive, shoving aside rock, tile, and marble as she searched—

—and then stopped when she found his face. His eyes

were open and empty, his mouth half-closed over his six rows of teeth. She ran a bloody hand along his torn cheeks.

"M'yet," she said, the word rumbling in her throat. He didn't deserve to die like this. She hated his politics, but he was a good friend, a decent friend, and one of the best politicians she had ever met. She had hoped to convert him to her ways. She had hoped he would work with the Republic in a leadership position one day, outside the Senate, where he would be a strong voice for change.

The doors opened. Blinding light filled the Hall. Leia braced herself and propped her blaster on a nearby rock. Then she saw her own security people hurrying in. She got up and ran to them, struggling on stairs and debris, trying not to trip.

"Hurry!" she said as she reached the top. "We have wounded below!"

One of the guards spoke back to her, but she couldn't hear him. Instead, she surveyed the damage from above. Each seat was covered with debris. Most of the senators were moving, but many weren't.

The tone had truly been set for this Senatorial term.

And for that, the Empire would pay.

Five

The boom made the glow panels dim in the Crystal Jewel. Then the ground shivered. Droid dealers all over the casino wailed as they shook on their moorings. Han's precariously tilted chair fell. He slipped off it and caught it with one hand. Jarril toppled against the table, spilling the remaining drinks.

"What the—?"

"Groundquake?" someone asked.

". . . falling . . ."

". . . Look out!"

The screams and shouts drowned out any attempt at conversation, not that Han was going to try. He'd lived through enough over the years to know that that was no groundquake. That was an explosion.

He tapped Jarril on the shoulder. "Let's get out of here."

"What is it?" Jarril yelled.

Han didn't answer him, at least not directly. "We're underground, pal. If we don't get out now, we might not get out at all."

Jarril probably hadn't thought that through. These dives never felt as if they were six feet under, although they were. His scream joined the others as he stood. Han was already shoving his way to the door, his blaster in the face of anyone who tried to stop him. Along the way, he helped a Cemas to its feet, dodged the teeth of a freed nek battle dog, and pulled a wingéd Agee off a crumbling section of ceiling.

The crowd at the door was huge, all scrambling on top of one another, all trying to get free. Then Han realized some idiot had pulled the door shut.

"Let us out of here!" he shouted.

"You don't know what's out there!"

"I know that whatever it is, it's a lot better than dying in here."

Voices rose with his, all agreeing with his protests. He managed to shove his way to the front. An Oodoc, a species known for its size and strength but not its intelligence, stood before the door, its spiked arms crossed in front of its massive chest.

"It's safer in here," it said.

"Listen, toothpick brain," Han said. "The roof's about to cave in. I would rather take my chances with whatever's out there than die with you in here."

"I wouldn't," the Oodoc said.

"Then you don't have to go." Han shoved him aside and blasted the lock on the door. The ricochet caught the Oodoc in its spiny back. It growled and lunged for Han as the door swung open.

A tide of seamy creatures flowed into the corridors beyond, gathering Han and sweeping him away from the Oodoc. He pulled free, reached the turbolift by himself, scanned for Jarril, and didn't see him. The lift stopped a level below the surface and Han went up the stairs two at a time, braced for the next blast, which seemed to take forever in coming.

The crowd reached the doors, bursting through them.

The screaming and shouting stopped when people reached the surface.

Han reached the top and stopped so suddenly that the Gotal behind him slammed into his back. The Gotal shoved him as it pushed away, then it, too, stopped and looked up, its double-cone-shaped head pointing toward the sky.

Han stepped away from the entrance, his mouth dry.

Coruscant looked the same. Nothing had touched the city. Nothing at all.

The sunlight was bright, blinding, and warm. The afternoon was as beautiful as it had been when he went below.

"It couldn'ta been underground, could it?" asked one of the gamblers from the Crystal Jewel, a man who looked vaguely familiar.

Han shook his head. "Something happened somewhere."

"Not from above," the Gotal said. "If it had come from above, we'd see the effects."

"We'd be ducking and running, hoping nothing else hits the city," the gambler said.

Han put a hand up to shade his eyes as he looked for movement. Finally he saw it: a contingent of guards and medical personnel heading toward the Imperial Palace.

The palace.

The children.

Leia.

He took off after the guards at top speed, nearly mowing down that nek battle dog, which was scampering away from its master. Han dodged in and out of building columns, through streets, always keeping the guards and medical staff in sight.

It was the medical personnel who worried him.

People had been hurt.

They avoided the main entrance to the palace and instead ran along its side. He felt a moment of relief until he realized where they were going.

The Senate Hall.

His breath was coming in sharp gasps. A stitch had formed in his side. He was in shape, but it had been a long time since he had run at top speed anywhere. And he had been going at top speed for a long time now.

No more blasts.

Odd. Very odd.

He rounded the corner and the sight before him made him run harder. Senators were scattered across the lawn, covered with dirt and several different colors of blood. A black ichor trailed from the senator from Nyny. All three of his heads were tilted backward. If he wasn't dead, he was close.

Mon Mothma was bent over another senator, talking carefully. Han stopped long enough to tap her shoulder.

"Leia?" he asked.

Mon Mothma shook her head. She looked ten times older than she had that morning. "I haven't seen her, Han."

He dodged the wounded, even though she shouted his name again. He knew what she would say. Exactly what Leia would say in this instance: Don't go inside. Let the trained personnel deal with it. But his wife was missing. He'd find her himself.

The large marble entrance was filled with dust, blood, and more bodies. Some were stacked against the wall like cargo. As he passed he realized those were droids. They weren't even full droids, only pieces: arms in one corner, legs in another. He saw dozens of golden body parts and didn't want to think about the possibility of Threepio being among the shattered.

The blood and dirt had made the floor slippery. He slid across part of the floor, finally stopping when he reached the entrance to the Hall itself.

All the doors were open, the emergency glow panels were on, and dust hovered in the air like a sandstorm on Tatooine. From inside, he heard wailing, moaning, and voices crying for help. Other voices mingled in the din, calling for assistance or giving orders. The medical personnel he had followed were already inside, as were dozens of guards and security people.

A huge bomb had to have gone off here to do this kind of damage. Bigger than anything he had seen outside of a space battle. And this bomb couldn't have come from space. The outside of the building was fine. This one had to have come from within.

Then he saw Leia, drenched in blood, her white gown, white no longer, ripped and stuck to her frame. One braid had come loose and hung down her back. The other was half-undone, her beautiful brown hair tangled and matted as it fell along her face. She had her hands beneath the secondary bumps on an unconscious Llewebum. Two guards supported its feet. She limped as she moved backward, favoring her right leg.

Han hurried to her side, placed his hands beside hers on the Llewebum's ridged skin. "I've got it, sweetheart," he said, but she didn't seem to hear him. He bumped her slightly with his hip, and she let go. The weight of the Llewebum made him stagger. He didn't know how she had supported it. He put the Llewebum beside one of its comrades, near a medical droid that was tagging all the cases according to degree of emergency. Then Han went back to Leia.

She had started into the Hall again, but he put his arm around her waist and gently held her back.

"I'm getting you medical care, sweetheart."

"Let me go, Han."

"You've helped enough. We're going to the center."

She didn't shake her head. She didn't even look at him when he spoke. One entire side of her face was bruised and her skin was covered with scorch marks. Her nose was bleeding and she didn't even seem to notice.

"I've got to go in there," she said.

"I'll go in. You stay here."

"Let me go, Han," she said again.

"She can't hear you," one of the medical droids said as it passed. "A concussion of that size in an enclosed space damaged everyone with eardrums."

She couldn't hear? Han gently turned her toward him, trying not to let his fear for her show on his face. "Leia," he said slowly. "Help is here. Let me take you to the medical center."

Beneath the dirt, her skin was pale. "It's my fault."

"No, sweetheart, it's not."

"I let the Imperials in. I didn't fight hard enough."

Her words chilled him. "We don't know what caused this. Come on. Let me get you help."

"No," she said. "My friends are dying in there."

"You've done all you can."

"Don't be stubborn," she said.

"I'm not the one—!" He bit back the words. He couldn't stand here and argue with her. She couldn't hear. She'd win. He scooped her into his arms. She was light and warm. "You're coming with me," he said.

"I can't, Han," she said, but she didn't struggle. "I'm fine. Really."

"I don't want you to die because you don't know when to quit," he said as he stepped past the wounded.

Either her hearing was coming back or she could read lips. "I'm not going to die," she said.

His heart was pounding against his chest. He cradled her close. "Lady, I wish I were as sure of that as you are."

✳ ✳ ✳

Jarril stopped running when he reached the hangars. He had seen activity all around the flight bases, but he figured it wouldn't reach his ship yet.

He was right.

Although he probably didn't have much time.

He had left the ship, the *Spicy Lady,* in the far corner of the hangar, behind two larger ships. The *Spicy Lady* was small but distinctive. Brown, shaped like the *Millennium Falcon* crossed with an A-wing, she was of Jarril's own special design. She was built for carrying cargo, but if things got difficult, he could jettison the storage unit and let the fighter ship move on its own. The fighter could be remote-operated; he could lead a pursuer on a wild-goose chase with the fighter while in reality he was on the storage ship with all the cargo. He had only had to use that scenario once, and fortunately he'd been able to recover the fighter part of the ship later.

He was never so relieved to see anything in his life.

He had to get off Coruscant before they put a clamp on space travel. And they would, once the source of that explosion was located. He had to get back to the Run before anyone noticed he was missing. He was afraid someone already had.

This part of the hangar appeared to be empty. Odd. If he were in charge of Coruscant, he would close down access to and from the planet immediately. But the New Republic did things democratically, not logically.

He only hoped he had piqued Han's interest enough. They wouldn't have another chance at a conversation.

He hurried across the platform to his ship. Then he dropped the ramp and climbed in. It felt strange to enter an empty ship. Usually he traveled with Seluss, a Sullustan. They had started in the business together. Seluss was supposed to cover for him while he was gone.

The *Spicy Lady* smelled of cool processed air. He had left the interior pressurized, a mistake he didn't usually make. This time it didn't matter, though. It would be easier for him to leave.

He would pilot out of the storage section. Safer. If the Coruscant command gave him any troubles, he would separate the sections and let them worry about the fighter while the storage unit escaped. He had just slid into the pilot's chair when he heard something behind him.

He stiffened but did not turn. He might have been mistaken about the sound.

No. There it was again. The hollowy inhale of someone breathing through a mask.

Jarril swallowed. As he turned, he put his hand on his blaster.

Two stormtroopers faced him, blasters already trained on him. "Where do you think you're going?" one of them asked. The voice was unrecognizable through the helmet's mouthpiece.

Then Jarril realized they weren't stormtroopers. They were wearing his cargo. He recognized the battle scorch on the helmet on the right.

They must have come on the ship wearing other clothing. They had put on the stormtrooper uniforms to scare him? He wasn't afraid of stormtroopers. At least, not stormtroopers wearing his own haul.

"I think it's high time to leave Coruscant, don't you?" Jarril asked. He wished he knew whom he was addressing.

"We plan to leave," the other trooper said, "after you tell us your business here."

"I was visiting an old friend," Jarril said.

"Strange time to be visiting," the first stormtrooper said.

"Strange time to be helping yourselves to my equipment," Jarril snapped.

"It's ours ultimately," the second stormtrooper said.

"You don't want to get caught wearing those on Coruscant," Jarril said.

"We won't get caught," the first stormtrooper said. He nodded his helmet toward Jarril. "Put down the blaster."

Jarril shrugged and let go. "I wasn't going to use it anyway."

"Tell us again why you're on Coruscant."

"Why are you?" Jarril said. "Did you have anything to do with that bombing?"

"We'll ask the questions," said the second stormtrooper.

Jarril swallowed. His head was woozy from exertion on top of too many drinks. It was his ship. He should be able to find a way out of this. "I was following a lead."

"A lead," said the first stormtrooper. "I thought you were visiting an old friend."

"Where'd you think I was going to get the lead?"

"From Han Solo, husband to the leader of the New Republic?"

They had followed him. He wasn't going to be able to talk his way out of this one. He grabbed the control console, but too late. A well-placed blaster shot hit his hands. He screamed as pain burned through him.

He clutched his hands to his stomach and looked at the troopers. "What do you want with me?" he asked, voice shaking.

"To silence you forever," said the first stormtrooper.

And then they did.

Six

Luke had seen the medical center near the Imperial Palace this full only once before, and that had been in the days after the Empire attack that had forced the New Republic leadership to lead. A long time ago now, but it felt close, with all these wounded around him. Wounded waited in reception areas just like guests, while medical personnel found beds for them, or moved them to more-specialized wings of the medical center.

Luke walked among them, feeling more shaken than he had when he learned of the attack.

Familiar faces, some gray with pain, others so scarred he could barely recognize them, looked away from him. The attack had to have been horrible. He had been worried when he approached Coruscant and all the defenses were up. He had had to get special clearance from Admiral Ackbar—no one could raise Leia—and it wasn't until he had spoken to Mon Mothma that he had known why.

As he strode through the hallway to the recovery areas, something grabbed him around his booted leg. He looked down to see Anakin clinging to his thigh.

"Uncle Luke," Anakin said, his face upturned, his blue eyes tear-streaked, his eyelashes gummed together.

Luke bent down and picked up the boy, even though, at six, Anakin was getting too big to be held in this way. Anakin clung to him so tightly that Luke could barely breathe.

"Is your mother all right?" Luke asked, not sure he wanted to hear the answer.

Anakin nodded.

"Then what is it, little Jedi?" Luke kept his voice soft, soothing. And suddenly he knew. His own words had brought it clear to him. But before he could say anything, he heard his name. Jacen and Jaina were running toward him, looking as ravaged as Anakin.

"Hey, guys," he said, gathering them around him.

"Uncle Luke," Jaina said. "Daddy said you could talk to us."

He didn't know if they had felt the cold and heard the screaming. Many of his students hadn't. But his students weren't as talented in the Force as the children. Or maybe the children had felt some impact from the explosion. Whatever had happened to them, though, had traumatized them in a way the other adults weren't able to deal with yet.

"Come on," he said. He led them to a bench alongside the metallic wall. A medical droid passed without giving them a second glance.

"Did we do it?" Anakin asked.

"Do what?" Whatever he had expected, it wasn't this.

"Hurt Mama."

Luke set Anakin back on his lap. Jacen and Jaina squeezed beside him. They had obviously discussed this. Luke suppressed a sigh. Raising Force-sensitive children was more a trial than anyone had thought. Each time something new came up, he found himself wishing he could talk with his aunt Beru. She had managed with him despite his uncle Owen's hostility, on a planet so far away that no one knew about it.

Except Ben.

She had probably talked with Ben.

"How could you have hurt your mother?" Luke asked.

All three children started to speak at once, hands moving, arms waving, voices raised in concern.

"Wait, wait, one at a time," Luke said. "Jaina, you explain it, then you boys can add if you want."

Jaina glanced at Jacen as if for support. The movement always made Luke's heart ache. Would he and Leia have been like that if they had been raised together? They would never know.

"Something came into our nursery, Uncle Luke," Jaina said. Her small face was a replica of Leia's, round and beautiful, sincere brown eyes, and small, purposeful mouth. "It was cold and it yelled with a thousand voices. And it hit us all at once."

As he had suspected. They had felt the deaths. Just as he had. As Leia had. He resisted the urge to close his eyes. When Leia was better, he had to talk with her. They had to realize that the children, though young, felt everything as strongly as others trained in the Force did.

"So we joined—" Jacen began.

"I'm telling it," Jaina said. "We joined hands and beat it back."

That caught Luke by surprise. "You what?"

"We made the room hot," Anakin said. Jaina shot him a malevolent glance, but he ignored it. "It was my idea."

"It was not," Jacen said.

"Was too."

"Anyway," Jaina said loudly, "we pushed it out of the room, and then a little while later, the whole . . . the whole . . ." She took a deep breath. "The whole . . ."

"The whole building shook," Jacen said, clearly finishing for her. "And Mother nearly died."

"And sometimes," Anakin said softly, "when I don't plan it, something I do hurts somebody."

Luke nodded. A lot of things he had done had inadvertently hurt someone. If he hadn't bought Artoo and Threepio, his aunt and uncle would still be alive. But if he hadn't, he wouldn't be sitting here now, with these precious beings beside him. But he couldn't explain that. It would sound patronizing. Ben hadn't tried when Luke returned from the ruined farm. Luke shouldn't try either. They would learn it on their own.

"What you felt," Luke said, "was something pretty terrible. Somewhere in the galaxy, thousands, maybe millions, of people died at one time. I felt the same thing, that deep cold, and all of their pain."

"Did Mom feel it?" Jaina asked, her voice still quivering.

Luke nodded. "And a few of my students on Yavin 4 felt it too. That's part of being a Jedi. When something destroys life on a grand scale, we feel it as if it happened to us. Because, in a sense, it did. It ripped the fabric of the Force for just an instant."

The children's faces were serious. Jacen's mouth was set in a thin line reminiscent of Han's when he was angry.

"Sending heat to that cold place was brilliant," Luke said. "I wish I had thought of it. It's like sending love to a place that's only known hate. We can't go back in time and make those lives reappear, but we can help the people who have felt the loss heal."

"Or make the people who caused it pay," Anakin said.

The bloodthirsty one. Luke put his hand on his nephew's, knowing that he would always have to give this boy special attention. He understood what Leia had been doing in naming Anakin after her father—she had been trying to reclaim a good part of her past—but the name made Luke give extra attention to the recklessness behind Anakin's fierceness. Recklessness that Anakin shared with his uncle at times.

"If we're not careful, Anakin," Luke said, "that kind of vengeance will make us turn to the dark side. Then we are no better than those who fail to value life."

Anakin looked away, a slight flush staining his cheeks.

"Look at me, children." Luke spoke firmly. He wanted their full attention for this next. "You did the right thing creating warmth. Your actions had nothing to do with the explosion that hurt your mother. Nothing at all."

"You promise, Uncle Luke?" Jacen asked. His voice was quivering too. He tried to be tough, just like his father, but beneath he was one of the most sensitive hearts Luke had ever met.

And that, too, was like Han.

"I promise," Luke said. He gathered the children close and hugged them. They squeezed him back. He held them, letting his own warmth comfort them, as he thought about the conversation.

The children were on to something. But they had it backward. The deaths happened, and then, a short time later, an explosion occurred in the Senate Hall on the opening day of the new session. If the events weren't related, then that was a startling coincidence.

And the older he got, the less Luke believed in coincidence.

"Come on," he said when the children started squirming. "Let's go see your mother."

The children slid off the bench, and he let them lead him to a large room. Leave it to Leia to insist that she was not given any special treatment. Five other senators filled beds in the room, with curtains between them. Leia's was at the far end. Her curtain was open. Han sat beside her, while Chewbacca stood at the foot, holding his paws together, as if this were a state function and he didn't know how to dress. A medical droid placed medication on Leia's bedside table, then disappeared through the pulled curtain beside her.

Winter was sitting in a chair beside the wall. When she saw Luke, she smiled. Sometimes he wondered if she had special powers besides her fantastic recall. She rarely let the children out of her sight, and yet they had found him at exactly the right moment.

"Luke," Han said as he stood. "Leia's been asking about you."

She turned her head then on its pillow. Her face was a mass of bruises and cuts. Even though she had clearly been in the bacta tank, she still wore bandages on her hands indicating serious injuries that needed several more tendings.

"Oh, Luke." Her voice was unusually loud. "I'm glad you're here."

Luke sat beside the bed. "Me, too."

She frowned slightly.

"I don't think she understood you," Han said. "She can't hear."

Luke glanced at Han. He seemed remarkably calm.

"They say her hearing will come back in a few days. It was the strength of the explosion." Han smiled tightly. "It's been rather humorous, actually, watching the medical staff deal with a hundred deaf patients. No one is following instructions."

His tone implied there was no humor in it. In any of it. Luke had already gotten the statistics when he landed. Twenty-five senators dead, a hundred more wounded seriously, and another hundred bruised. That didn't count the support personnel or all the destroyed droids.

"Any idea what happened?"

Winter stood. "I think, children," she said, "we've been here long enough today."

"Daaaad," Jaina wailed. She took his arm. "They always make us leave when the conversation gets interesting."

"I'm not going," Anakin said.

Chewie growled at him. Anakin ran to his sister's side.

"That's telling 'em, Chewie," Han said, but it sounded more like a reflex response. "Go with Winter, kids. I'll be back to tuck you in."

They hugged their mother good-bye, and left without further protest, which made Luke wonder if they wanted to stay as much as they pretended. The last day or two had been very stressful for them. He would have to talk with Han about their fears before he left.

"Leia believes the new Imperials in the Senate caused this," Han said. "I'm not so sure."

"I am," Leia said. She had obviously become adept at lipreading since the explosion. Some of her abilities probably were Force-enhanced. Luke would have to test that theory later.

"What do you think happened?" Luke asked.

"An old buddy of mine surfaced at a convenient time," Han said. "I was with Jarril in the Crystal Jewel when the explosion happened."

"A decoy to keep you away?"

"Maybe," Han said. "Or maybe he was trying to warn me and was too late. I tried to find him afterward, but he was gone."

"Any idea where he went?" Luke asked.

Han shook his head. "His ship was gone too, and no one saw it leave, which I find odd. Jarril's ship is distinctive. He took the *Falcon*'s design and crossed it with an A-wing."

"I saw that ship," Luke said. "The defenses were up when I got here. It took me a bit of convincing to get in, but when the shields lifted, a ship like that shot out, as if it had been waiting for just a moment like that. I notified Space-Traffic Control but they didn't even register it as a blip on their equipment. It's not often I get told things are a figment of my imagination anymore."

"Some figment," Han said.

"This means nothing," Leia said too loudly. Luke wasn't sure how much she followed. "It was the Imperials."

"You have less proof than I do," Han said. "Your people don't even know what kind of bomb hit the Senate Hall."

"*My* people?"

Luke put a hand on Leia's arm. "What makes you think it was the Empire?"

"They have new members in the Senate. It would be just like them to destroy something they had gained." She had turned her head toward him so that she could see him clearly. "First rule in investigation, Luke. Look for the changes. The answer lies in the changes."

"You have no proof either," Luke said. He suppressed a sigh. "Let's see what the experts turn up. Maybe once we know what hit the Hall, we'll be better informed."

"The other thing you look for is money," Han said. "Jarril told me a lot of smugglers are getting rich, and then dying."

"But he could have been lying," Luke said.

Chewie growled. He clearly agreed with Han.

"I'm not dismissing him, Chewie," Luke said. "I just don't want us to make suppositions before we have information."

He hadn't expected to arrive and be the voice of reason. The stress was taking its toll on the whole family. He had seen it in the children, and now in Han and Leia.

"He said I could find out more at Smuggler's Run," Han said.

"It might be another diversion," Leia said.

"Or it might be unrelated," Luke said.

"Or it could be something we need to know," Han said.

Chewie mumbled his agreement.

"You can't leave now, Han," Leia said. She clearly knew her husband. "The children need you."

Han smiled, but he seemed distracted. "They need you too, sweetheart," he said. "The whole Republic needs you. And we almost lost you."

Luke cleared his throat. "Let me do a little investigating of my own," he said. "I may turn up something none of us expects."

✶ ✶ ✶

See-Threepio followed Artoo-Detoo's rounded frame through the permacrete corridors. Ancient oil stains mingled with skid marks and other stains of unknown origins all over the floors and walls. The glow panels flickered, as if they didn't have the same access to power as the rest of Coruscant. Artoo led with purpose, his silver body tilted back, his wheels outstretched.

"I don't know how you always get me involved in these things, Artoo," Threepio said as he hurried, hands raised for balance. "You've only been here a few hours and already I feel as if we're in trouble."

Artoo whistled, then blatted at him.

"You *did* invite me," Threepio said. "You said you believed they were doing something to Master Luke's X-wing and we needed to investigate."

Artoo tweebled.

"All right, then. You *knew* they were doing something to Master Luke's X-wing, and you said *you* were going to investigate. But *you* told *me*. That's like an invitation."

Artoo speeded up, chirruping and twittering as he glided forward on the filthy floor.

"I will not stay behind," Threepio said. "Over the years, you've gotten us into too much trouble going off on your own like this. Besides, as I told you upstairs, Master Luke's X-wing has been scheduled for upgrade for more than a year."

Artoo blatted again. His head swiveled as he investigated a portal in the wall. Apparently it was not the one he wanted.

Threepio didn't even look at the portal as they passed. "I think it's arrogant of you to believe that Master Luke will tell you all of his business."

Artoo bleeped loudly.

"All of his business concerning the X-wing, then. It's not as if you own the machine. You're a droid."

Artoo warbled.

"Really, Artoo. Another astromech droid could run the X-wing," Threepio said. "It's not as if you're that special."

Artoo gave Threepio a raspberry.

"Maybe they should have wiped your memory. Your so-called exploits went to your head after the Battle of Endor. I don't know why I continue to put up with you." Threepio's patter stopped when they reached the closed maintenance-hangar doors. "How odd. Doors in the maintenance area are supposed to remain open at all times."

Artoo didn't respond. Instead a compartment opened on his side, and a thin metal service arm extended. He jacked into the door panel, and beeped softly to himself.

Threepio peered through the small square transparisteels. Ships and parts were scattered all over the floor. Droids worked carefully, supervised by Kloperians. Kloperians were short, squat gray creatures, with a series of tentacled limbs running along their sides like filaments. They had hands at the ends of many of the limbs. Their necks could extend as well. Their physical makeup and their talents around all things mechanical made them among the best mechanics and engineers in the Republic.

Artoo bleeped.

Threepio turned away from the transparisteel. "Of course it's a routine maintenance order," Threepio said. "I don't understand why you're so surprised. All of the X-wings have been upgraded in the last few months."

Artoo bleebled some more.

"I'm sure Master Luke did know of it," Threepio said. "I'm sure they notified him. Really, Artoo. You get upset about the strangest things."

Artoo whistled repeatedly and rocked on his two wheels.

"I will not ask Master Luke down here," Threepio said. "We don't even know what they're going to do to the X-wing."

Artoo whistled louder, a piercing shriek that echoed in the enclosed space.

"Artoo!"

The clank of his rocking treads added to the shrillness.

"Yes, I understand that you have a bad feeling about this," Threepio said. "But Master Luke didn't, and he is the expert on feelings."

At that moment, the maintenance doors opened. A Kloperian stood behind them, six of its tentacles crossed over its squishy chest. "You want to explain to me why you're illegally jacked into our computer system?" it asked.

Artoo removed his jack and pulled his service arm inside its case. "We meant nothing," Threepio said. "Our master had sent us here to check on his ship. We couldn't get in and my counterpart here was trying to open the door."

"That's the door panel," the Kloperian said, pointing with a seventh tentacle at a small panel on the other side of the maintenance doors.

"Oh, dear, Artoo," Threepio said. "I told you not to touch anything."

The Kloperian's bulbous eyes narrowed. "All right, you two. Get inside. We're going to check your hardware."

It grabbed Threepio and Artoo with four of its tentacles and pulled them in the maintenance bay. The metal doors clanged shut behind them. Fifty Kloperians stared at them. Dozens of droids stopped work to watch.

"Artoo," Threepio whispered. "I have a very bad feeling about this."

Seven

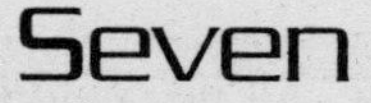

Kueller stood on the sandstone streets of Pydyr, his legs spread, hands clasped behind his back. The air was warm and dry with a touch of salt, reminding him that an ocean loomed over the artificially created hills. In the arid heat, the death's head felt like a mask. He was sweating beneath it, destroying its delicate calibration with his skin.

He couldn't remain on Pydyr long. The mask, a finely tuned instrument, only worked properly in certain environments.

This wasn't one of them.

He hated to think of what it was doing to his face.

But if he was uncomfortable, the troops were as well. The stormtrooper uniforms, cleaned up and repaired, looked fine. Menacing. The memories of the Empire were embodied in the white suits and the elaborate helmets, memories of power he hoped to arouse.

Image was everything, as Pydyr once knew.

The empty streets spoke of wealth. The sandstone blocks wore down after only a few days. The Pydyrians had a special droid designed specifically for street care, another designed for building wash. Pydyr's wealth was the stuff of legends, its aristocratic class the inspiration for stories told all over this section of the galaxy.

Almania had envied Pydyr for generations.

But no more.

Pydyr was his.

The quiet was eerie. All he could hear was the sound of booted feet brushing against sandstone. The troopers were investigating each building, making certain no one remained.

He had half-expected the stench of bodies decaying in Pydyr's harsh sun, but Hartzig, the officer in charge, had been thorough. Pydyr's aristocracy was dead, its bodies disposed of within hours. But the moon's wealth remained.

And he needed it. His timing couldn't have been better. He tried to smile, but his skin slid beneath the mask. The lips still adhered, though.

He whirled on a booted foot and walked into one of the buildings the troopers had already investigated.

Pydyrian architecture was bold, with heavy brown columns and large, square rooms. Each surface was covered with decoration, some hand-painted by famous artists long dead, and others studded with tiny seafah jewels. In addition to the wealth accumulated over centuries, Pydyr had its own source. Seafah jewels were formed in the ocean in the shells of microscopic creatures. Kueller had ordered the seafah jewelers spared; it took a trained eye to locate most of the jewels on the seabed. A trained Pydyrian eye. The aristocratic Pydyrians had tried for generations to create droids that could locate the jewels, but no matter how good the droid, it couldn't tell the jewel from centuries of hardened fish dung.

He walked to a column and ran a gloved finger over the ridged jewels embedded in the baked surface. The jewels were bright spots of swirled color, some blue and green, some black and red, some white and orange, some a startling, lusterless yellow. Each jewel, no wider than the seam on his fingertip, had formed over the centuries from tiny seafah bodies discarded on the ocean floor.

The column alone held two years of materials cost for him at the rate he had been spending it. He would probably increase his spending now. He had some large ships that needed rebuilding quickly. Unlike the Pydyrians, he was not one to hoard his wealth. He would have plenty more within a few months.

"It feels as if someone just left." Femon's soft voice boomed in this empty place. She had apparently finished her tasks on Almania and decided to join him.

"Someone did." Kueller did not turn. His mask was slipping more than he liked. The mouth no longer moved with his. "They haven't been dead very long, Femon."

"It seems so strange. I was in the eating wing, and there were still dishes on the tables."

"But the food was gone," Kueller said. Cleaned up by the droids, as was anything organic and likely to decompose.

"Of course." She walked up behind him. He could feel her warmth against his back. He did not move, even though he wanted to. She was getting too presumptuous of her own power. He would have to remind her who controlled whom, and soon. "I don't understand why the Emperor didn't do this. He was so destructive."

Kueller remembered the delicious feeling of all those screams, all those lives, all that fear filling him. "He hadn't found a clean way yet. Maybe he didn't look for one. Sometimes I think Palpatine was less interested in power than in destruction itself."

"But you're interested in power."

She seemed to be making a statement, but he thought he heard a question beneath it.

"You have an opinion?" he asked in a way that made it sound as if she had no right to one.

"It would seem to me," she said slowly, "that if we are going to conquer, we should do so now. Everything is in place."

"Only on Coruscant," he said.

"But that's where it's needed."

He brought his hand down. Her questions were interrupting his fine mood. "It's needed on all the designated planets. The secret to control is thoroughness."

"So we do Coruscant first. Everything else will be in place in a few days."

"Timing is everything," Kueller said. "I will wait."

"If you get rid of the leaders—"

"Others will rise in their place." He resisted the urge to turn, to glower at her through the mask. The mask wasn't working, and he didn't want her to see his face. Sweat dripped off his chin onto his linen shirt.

"Is that why you're trying to get rid of Skywalker?"

He hesitated, unsure how much he wanted to reveal himself to her. Then he said, "Skywalker's sister leads the Republic."

"How do you know she survived the attack on the Senate Hall?"

"She survived," he said softly.

"So go after her."

"I am." He clenched his fists, careful not to let his temper show on such a fine, successful day. "I most assuredly am."

✷ ✷ ✷

The ship hung in space. Lando Calrissian peered out the cockpit on the *Lady Luck*. He was alone on this trip, having dropped Mara Jade off at the Minos Cluster to run some errand for Talon Karrde. Lando didn't like their continued association, but he had no real right to complain—and he wasn't sure he wanted that right.

Still, the last few weeks with Mara in the floating cities of Calamari had been delightful. He hadn't seen her in a long while. He had enjoyed her company, and only a few times had longed for solitude.

He had the solitude now, but he no longer wanted it. At the moment, he'd give anything to have someone to consult about the ship spinning slowly in front of him.

It looked familiar. At first he had thought it was the *Millennium Falcon.* Then he realized that the Arakyd concussion-missile tubes weren't just missing. They hadn't been there at all. Something had been built to fill the area and that something was long gone. He had only seen one other stock light freighter that so closely resembled the *Falcon,* and that had been the *Spicy Lady.* Although the *Spicy Lady* had a modified A-wing where the missile tubes had been.

An A-wing that could fly on its own. A separate ship, for escapes and escapades.

Lando hailed the *Spicy Lady,* his heart pounding. "*Spicy Lady,* this is *Lady Luck.* Are you in distress? Over?"

No response. The ship looked abandoned. Only he had never known Jarril to leave the *Spicy Lady* for long. Jarril had invested his personal fortune in her, and used her to make more money. He never let her drift. Even when he was in the A-wing, he made certain she looked powered-up so that no one would board without major preparation.

"*Spicy Lady,* this is *Lady Luck.* Over."

Lando swore under his breath. This was supposed to be a simple trip. He didn't like flying solo. He had a new astromech droid that Mara had bought with profits from their most recent shared venture, but even with the modifications, the droid wasn't a lot of help in a situation like this.

He scanned the *Spicy Lady* for life signs. None. She was dark. Life support wasn't even functioning.

He sighed. He couldn't board her. He didn't want to leave the *Lady Luck* without good cause. Instead he checked to see if the *Spicy Lady* had slave circuitry. He doubted it. Most smuggling vessels avoided slave circuits, which allowed remote control of the ship from other ships. But business had changed since Lando entered it. A few suppliers were requiring slave circuits. And Jarril was still hip-deep in the business. He might be dealing with some of those suppliers.

The *Lady Luck*'s computer beeped at Lando. The *Spicy Lady* not only had slave circuits, she had fully rigged slave circuits.

"First break I've had all day," Lando said.

He linked the *Spicy Lady*'s internal holocams to the *Lady Luck*'s and surveyed the interior of the ship.

It looked like an Imerria Windstorm had gone through the public sections. Supplies floated in the zero-gravity environment. Blaster scars seared the couches in the rec area. The oxygen masks were broken, the emergency equipment destroyed.

Lando panned through the public areas. He knew that Jarril wouldn't allow holocams in the storage compartments. Lando's mouth was dry. The discomfort he had felt when he first saw the ship was growing.

Except for the blaster scars in the rec room, he saw no signs of battle. No real destruction, only the kind made when someone—or several someones—searched a ship. Still, the tension in Lando's shoulders was growing.

Finally he brought the *Spicy Lady*'s cockpit up on his screen. And then he let out the breath he had been holding.

Jarril floated, his body bumping against the controls, the viewport, the ceiling, the floor. Judging from the hole in his chest, he had been hit with a weapon at very close range.

Lando closed his eyes and rubbed the bridge of his

nose with his thumb and forefinger. An old friend shouldn't die like that. Especially not in the rear-end of nowhere with no one to guard his back.

Then Lando frowned. Jarril usually had a Sullustan with him. Seluss. Had Seluss taken the A-wing? For help? That made no sense. He would have been back.

Unless he was followed.

But Lando had seen no other vessels in this corner of space. Very few ships went back and forth here. There was nothing to smuggle. Lando himself wouldn't have been here if Mara hadn't had to meet Karrde. The Republic had little interest in the primitive planets nearby and the Empire had abandoned hope of uniting such diverse peoples.

The Empire had long ago abandoned hope of anything.

Something nagged at the back of Lando's mind. He had seen something in that debris. Something that didn't belong.

He opened his eyes as he panned away from the cockpit, searching, searching, scanning the debris at close range until he found what he was looking for.

In the galley, banging off one wall and ricocheting into another like a puck in null hockey, a stormtrooper helmet floated.

A helmet so clean it reflected the emergency glow panels.

Stormtroopers. This far out. Perhaps Lando had been wrong about the Empire.

With a flurry of movements, he rigged up the rest of the slave circuitry. He'd tow the *Spicy Lady* to his mining operation on Kessel and then inspect the interior himself. Maybe he could see what Jarril had been into.

Lando had a hunch he wouldn't like what he was about to find.

Eight

The surviving senators filled the Emperor's Audience Room in the Imperial Palace. The senior senators, the ones who clearly supported the Republic, were mingling with one another, and talking about substantive issues. Leia stood beside the buffet table that lined one wall. She wasn't interested in her colleagues. She was watching the junior senators, many of them former Imperials, argue. Her hands still hurt from the burns she had sustained in the blast, but otherwise she felt fine.

Except for her hearing.

She wished it hadn't returned.

The arguments rose around her, so loud that one voice would quickly cover another.

". . . decide who's in charge now that . . ."

". . . *never* would have allowed such chaos . . ."

". . . glad we're here. The New Republic can't afford such lax . . ."

She didn't need to hear more than a few snatches of conversation to know what was happening. Here, at least among the junior senators, the blame for the destruction of the Senate Hall was going to fall on her government.

She shouldn't have listened to Han. She should have been up and around the day of the explosion. Two days away had allowed this situation to get out of hand.

Leia took a vagnerian canape and ate it quickly, hoping its sweetness would give her energy she still lacked. The doctors said she needed time to recover, that she had nearly died, but she had made it through serious wounds before. This time, she suspected, part of the problem was her attitude.

She wiped her hands on her pants—she wore a loose, flowing pair that resembled a skirt, with a blouse over them, deciding to be dressy but comfortable at this meeting—and stepped into the crowd of junior senators.

Their conversation ceased. She smiled at them, as if she had heard nothing, and clapped her hands for attention.

"I want to thank you all for coming on such short notice," she said. "We are currently preparing the ballroom as a temporary home for the Senate, but it won't be completed until tomorrow. In the meantime, I thought we would hold this informal meeting. I wanted to get you all up-to-date on the investigation."

"What investigation?" asked R'yet Coome, the junior senator from Exodeen. His voice, filtered through his six sets of teeth, sounded so much like that of his colleague, M'yet Luure, that Leia started. It was even a question that M'yet would have asked.

She glanced at R'yet as he preened his six arms against his side. If she hadn't known M'yet was dead, she would have thought she was speaking to him.

"We've had an investigation running simultaneously with the rescue effort," she said. "The rescue effort took top priority for a day. We had to make certain—" Her voice broke.

"We had to make certain that no one else was trapped in the rubble," said ChoFï, one of the senators who had been with her since the beginning of the New Republic. He stood just behind her, his seven-foot length protecting instead of dwarfing her.

She nodded, grateful for his support. She hadn't seen him when she came in. He must have been eavesdropping, as she had been.

"You should have taken the precautions up front," R'yet said. "I don't know how I'll tell the people of Exodeen that one of their most beloved figures is dead."

"We have the best security of any place in the Republic," Leia said. "Obviously, it wasn't good enough."

"Obviously," R'yet said.

Meido, vibroblade-thin, his crimson face covered with tiny white lines, put a two-fingered hand on R'yet's first arm. Leia was astonished that Meido knew Exodeenian etiquette. A touch on the first arm was a signal to stop speaking. A touch on the second would have been a challenge to fight.

"The Chief of State has had a difficult week," Meido said.

"As have we all," some senator in the back said.

Meido ignored him. "We must give her the benefit of any doubt. Of course, we had to see if anyone remained in the ruins of the Hall. Now the investigation can begin in earnest."

His support made Leia suspicious. Meido hadn't been supportive since his election.

"Thank you, Senator," she said. She took a deep breath. "The damage to the Hall was extensive. The bomb, if we might call it that, was detonated inside the Hall. There was no exterior damage at all. We are currently investigating all personnel who were in the Hall at the time of the explosion as well as people who had access to it in the days before."

"Does that include senators?" asked Senator Wwebyls, a tiny humanoid from Yn.

"It includes everyone," Leia said.

"Even the dead?" R'yet asked, his lower hands perched on his secondary hips.

"Even the dead," Leia said softly. "We can't overlook anyone or anything here."

"So you're being investigated as well," Senator Meido asked.

Leia started. Of course she wasn't being investigated. She knew she wasn't involved.

"She said everyone." ChoFï spoke without judgment as he reminded them to listen, and as he got Leia off the hook.

Kerrithrarr, the senior Wookiee senator, growled from the back of the room.

"My Wookiee colleague has a good point," ChoFï said. "The best way to survive this crisis is to work together."

"We can't work together when we're being investigated," said another junior senator.

"We're all being investigated," said Nyxy, a senator from Rudrig.

"We have to work together," said Senator Gno. He had been a senator in the Old Republic, and then a member of the Rebel ring in the Imperial Senate. He was one of the few Old Republic members who hadn't retired. "Have you ever thought that whoever set off that bomb did so for precisely this reason? If we fight among ourselves, we no longer focus on outside threats. We cannot tear this government apart from within."

That thought hadn't occurred to Leia either. She had been concentrating on finding the perpetrators, and on discovering if they were the source of the Force-vision she had shared with Luke. She hadn't forgotten that feeling of impending doom, not just for the Senate, but for the government itself.

She couldn't tell this body, though, about the new

weapon. Not without a greater proof than her feeling, and Luke's.

"It seems to me that this government is already being torn apart," R'yet said. "We need leadership. Good leadership would have prevented this attack."

"We don't know that," ChoFï said. "We won't know anything like that until we discover what caused the destruction."

"The teams are working on that now," Leia said. "We have some experts digging through material removed from the building, as well as searchers still in the Hall. We'll know more by later today."

"Will we know then whether the attack was aimed at the Senate or aimed at you?" R'yet asked.

He had the right to ask that. Leia knew he did. But that didn't stop the flare of anger within her. She had had enough. He was acting as if he had attained a moral high road through M'yet Luure's loss.

"Senator Coome," she said, rising to her full height. "If the attack was aimed at you, at me, or at any of our colleagues, then it was aimed at all of us. We are a body, a group, whether you like it or not. The attack occurred in the seat of government, and affected all of us equally—"

"Not equally," R'yet said. "Some of us are dead."

"Equally," Leia said, "at least for the survivors. Now you can work with us and help the New Republic."

"Or?" He had stepped forward despite Meido's restraining hand. "Are you threatening me, Leia Organa Solo?"

"That wouldn't be good for unity, now, would it?" Leia asked.

"It certainly wouldn't," Meido said smoothly. "Perhaps it would ease my colleague's mind if we had a separate investigation going, as well as the official investigation. With two teams, we might get better results."

"Or we might confuse the issue," Leia said.

"So you're opposed to a separate investigation?" Meido's tone implied that she had something to hide.

"Of course not," Leia said. "I just don't like expending unnecessary resources. The New Republic is not wealthy, either in credits or in available labor."

"I think that anything that enables us to trust one another again would not be a waste," Meido said.

Again? Leia thought, but did not voice it.

"She obviously doesn't like the idea," R'yet said.

They had forced her into this. She should have expected it. She took a deep breath. "We're a governing body," she said. "Let's vote."

"I thought this was an informal meeting," ChoFï said. It was an admirable ploy to delay the vote.

"An informal meeting is still a meeting," Meido said.

Leia suppressed a sigh. They had outmaneuvered her. It would be hard to take a vote without their consoles, without the electronic count, or computer backup. But a voice vote would work, if someone counted the votes, and tallied them to the proper senators. It also had the added benefit of making each voter accountable in front of the others.

She sent one of the pages to get an official tally sheet. When the page returned, she scanned the sheet, her gaze stopping each time it hit a dead or seriously wounded senator. She would remember that day in the Hall for the rest of her life. In its own, less devastating way, it had shaken her as the destruction of Alderaan had. She had thought the Hall a completely safe place. Perhaps that was why she fought the introduction of the former Imperials. Perhaps she wanted to protect one of the few havens left in the galaxy.

It only took a few moments to get the system set up. Time enough for each senator to think of a response.

"The question we are putting to the vote is this: Should we have an independent investigation team? Your vocal response must be 'yes,' 'no,' or 'abstain.' " She took a deep breath, then called on the first senator.

Both she and the page recorded the vote as it occurred. A protocol droid also listened, double-checking the tally. She had expected the vote to go in her favor. At the least, she expected to break the tie on a close vote. But as she ran through the list, skipping the missing and the dead, she realized that her voting block, which had been the majority, was now in the minority. Most of the uninjured were the junior senators. The senior senators, those with long ties to the Republic, had somehow received the brunt of the blast.

By the end of the list, Leia's throat was dry and her eyes burned. Her shoulders were stiff from tension. Fifteen senators voted against the independent investigation. Fifteen. The rest abstained or voted in favor. The measure won by an overwhelming majority.

Across the room, she met Kerrithrarr's gaze. The Wookiee senator believed, as Leia did, that the former Imperials would destroy the Senate. Kerrithrarr's hair stood on end, and when he noticed Leia, he shook his head in despair.

Leia checked her results against the page's. Then the droid confirmed their numbers. "By a clear majority," Leia said, "the measure to provide for an independent investigation passes."

The junior senators cheered while the rest of the room looked on in astonishment. Leia picked up a wooden cup and pounded it on the buffet table as she called for order. As the room quieted, she said, "I realize that we are not meeting in the Hall. Due to the informal setting, I will let this breech of etiquette pass. In the future, though, any senator showing undue partisanship will be expelled from the room and his vote will not be counted. This rule is in the Senatorial bylaws. I suggest you read them."

Her voice echoed back to her, and she could hear the thread of anger below it. Usually she prided herself on her restraint, but her patience was wearing thin. Didn't these so-called leaders understand the effects of their actions? Didn't they know that this kind of partisanship would divide the Republic?

Faces were turned to hers expectantly. She nodded toward them. "Since it was your idea to have an independent investigation, Senator Meido, I would like you to compile the team. We will need the names of the investigators for our records."

Meido smiled. His teeth were pale pink against his crimson skin. "Gladly, President."

She didn't like his expression. It made her feel vulnerable. It made her feel as if she had walked into a trap.

"Tomorrow we will meet in the ballroom at the normal time. Until then, we are adjourned." Leia pounded on the buffet table. As she did, the conversation rose around her. The junior senators were pounding one another on the back and laughing.

ChoFï was staring at the list. "You know," he said so softly that only Leia and Senator Gno could hear, "their report won't be the same."

"I know," Leia said. "But I had no real choice. I couldn't appoint one of our people to pick the investigative team. They outmaneuvered me. If I had been thinking when I came in—"

"It's not your fault, Leia," ChoFï said. "If they didn't approach you on that issue, they would have done so on another. You were running the Senate as it used to be instead of as it is. It is no longer a uniform body. Now we have factions."

"I don't like it," Gno said.

"Like it or not," ChoFï said, "the factions exist and we have to live with them."

"I will not live with them," Gno said. "This is how the Empire took over the last time. Small disagreements became major. Major disagreements were ignored, until the government was so factionalized it didn't work at all."

"That won't happen here," ChoFï said.

Gno smiled. "I used to believe that, all those years ago."

Leia picked up the voting record, wincing at the pain in her hands. "We can't be afraid of change, Senator," she said to Gno. "We have to remember that there is one major difference between then and now. They don't have a leader like Palpatine."

"At least not yet," Gno said.

✳ ✳ ✳

Sunlight poured through a hole in the collapsing roof of the Senate Hall. Against the sky, the black-clawed hand of a construction droid awaited orders to remove the rubble and rebuild.

Luke stood in the double doorway, and peered into the Hall. The sunlight illuminated only one corner. Emergency glow panels revealed more destruction.

Most of the voting desks were covered with stone and shattered crystal. The floor was a mass of debris. Freight droids, maintenance droids, and repair droids waited in the back. No one had started the cleanup yet. Leia wanted it to wait until the investigation was underway.

Luke had decided to do some investigating on his own.

Several things bothered him: Leia's insistence on the involvement of former Imperials; Han's strange conversation with the missing smuggler; and, most importantly, the disturbance in the Force that Luke, Leia, and the

Solo children had felt to varying degrees. Luke agreed with Han; he doubted the direct involvement of the former Imperials. If they had all known, they would have found an excuse to be away from the Hall at the time. Leia had a point too. Most of the junior senators were uninjured. If she was right, and a former Imperial or a group of former Imperials were involved, what greater way to turn away suspicion than to be in the Hall during the explosion and "miraculously" escape injury?

Luke stepped inside. Dust motes rose in the circle of sunlight. He had been in so many places of destruction, seen so much devastation, and still it didn't prepare him for this. This Hall was the working Chamber. It had housed the Old Republic's Senate, and even Palpatine's redesign hadn't affected that feeling of ancient and irrevocable law. It had been Leia's favorite room.

She had been below, at the podium, when the blast hit.

The podium was shattered. The circle on which it had stood was littered in ceiling rubble. The repair crews outside had warned Luke that the building was unstable. They weren't going to let him in without an escort, but he insisted. He had to see this, and he had to see it alone.

A chill pervaded the air. It was the same kind of chill he had felt on Yavin 4, the chill of quick, sudden death. So many lives, senselessly taken.

He stepped in deeper. Beneath the chill was that odd sense again, that sense of betrayal. Betrayal was probably a common response to sudden death, but this sense felt different. It felt—personal, like the betrayal Luke had felt when Kyp had joined forces with Exar Kun. As if all in this room had died at the hands of someone they once trusted.

Personal death. A bomb was an impersonal death.

He closed his eyes, let the Force flow through him,

and felt for the pockets of coldness. Voices swirled around him, remembered voices, calling for help, shouting instructions. Shouts for friends, wails of the dying.

Pockets of cold.

He opened his eyes.

Not one large explosion. Several small explosions had detonated all at once in this room. And the senators sitting closest to the detonations died.

Several planned executions?

A warning?

Or a destruction of the Hall that went awry?

He couldn't tell. But now he had something to tell Leia's investigators. They should stop the search for one big cause, and search for several small ones.

Rubble fell from the ceiling, clattering onto the ruined floor. He turned and accidentally stepped into one of the pockets of coldness. The sunlight grew dim, and he felt the taint of a presence.

A former student.

A man.

Brakiss.

Nine

The closet the Kloperian had placed the droids in had a stained permacrete floor, metal walls, and a metal ceiling. The walls were unadorned, and there wasn't even a knob on the inside of the door. It was pitch-black after the door was closed.

Artoo whistled softly.

"You're right, Artoo," Threepio whispered. "I hear footsteps as well. And they're coming our way."

The computer lock on the door's knob clicked and beeped. As the door opened, the closet flooded with light. A different Kloperian from the one that captured them stood outside, work orders clutched in one tentacle, a special key code in another.

"Oh, thank the maker," Threepio said. "I am See-Threepio and this is my counterpart, Artoo-Detoo. We belong to President Leia Organa Solo, the Chief of State, and to her brother, the Jedi Knight Luke Skywalker. We have been falsely imprisoned—"

"You were trespassing," the Kloperian said.

"On the contrary," Threepio said. "We—"

"I don't care," the Kloperian said. "If it were up to me, I'd put you in recycling with all the other out-of-date droids. But we ran your serial numbers and you are who you say you are. Next time you come down here, your owners need to give us official notice. We can't have just any old droids down here. This is a dangerous area, and some of my assistants are overly enthusiastic. They might think you're scrap and use you for parts."

"Parts!" Threepio said. "I assure you, sir, we are anything but parts. Why, my counterpart and I might even be considered—"

"You are a protocol droid at least three models behind, and an astromech droid sixteen models out of date. If you were part of our team here, we'd definitely recycle you."

Artoo blatted.

"As it stands, we'll let you see the X-wing. Then you have to leave." The Kloperian crossed two tentacles. "Follow me."

Threepio hurried out of the closet, Artoo at his side. The Kloperian slithered forward at a fast clip. Threepio dropped back a few paces, just out of the Kloperian's hearing range.

"You see, Artoo. I told you that they wouldn't hold us once they knew who we were."

Artoo bleeped.

"Well, it doesn't seem odd to me," Threepio said.

Artoo blurbled.

"All right," Threepio said. "I admit they could have checked our serial numbers quicker. But the point is, Artoo, that they did. Although I do admit, things could have gone badly. Recycling! And I thought the scrap heap for out-of-date droids was just a legend."

Artoo's head swiveled as they walked, and the tiny holocam in his unit flickered. He was filming.

"I don't believe you have permission—"

Artoo bleebled so loudly that the Kloperian turned.

"Is there a problem?" it asked.

Threepio glanced at Artoo. "There is no problem," Threepio said. "No problem at all." And he put his hand heavily on Artoo's head for good measure. The clang of metal against metal echoed in the hangar.

They passed dozens of X-wings in various states of disrepair. Through open hangar doors were Y-wings and A-wings that had been disassembled. And in a final hangar, new craft glistened, cleaning droids polishing the luminescent metal.

Finally they stopped. The Kloperian pointed to a battered and scarred X-wing in pieces on the hangar floor.

Artoo moaned.

Threepio approached the pieces. "Oh, dear," he said. "Master Luke relies on this craft."

"We'll have it reassembled for him in two days," the Kloperian said.

Artoo whistled and beeped.

"My counterpart wants to know why it had to be dismantled in the first place."

"Orders," the Kloperian said. "These old X-wings have too many problems to fly across the galaxy without an occasional overhaul."

Artoo cheebled.

"My counterpart says the ship was in perfect condition."

"Well, he's wrong," the Kloperian said. "Amateur upkeep is no substitute for a major revamp."

Artoo shrilled.

"Artoo!" Threepio said. "I'm so sorry, sir. He was close to the X-wing. He's afraid you've damaged it permanently."

"I haven't touched it," the Kloperian said. "And now that you've seen it, you can report on its condition to your master. The exit is through that door."

Threepio nodded. "Come along, Artoo. We must talk with Master Luke."

Artoo gave a warbling sigh. He stopped beside the X-wing and leaned precariously over it.

"Artoo!" Threepio said. "We've seen enough."

"You might want to tell your master to purge that astromech unit's memory. The R2 unit is seriously dated as it is, and with the new changes in ship design it will be obsolete in a matter of months."

A cylindrical arm extended from Artoo's left side, the side away from the Kloperian.

"I will certainly inform Master Luke," Threepio said. "This little R2 unit has been trouble from the day he bought it."

"They all have," the Kloperian said. "Now you two get out of here before I take you out myself."

"Yes, sir! Come along, Artoo."

Artoo's arm slid back into its compartment. He put his third wheel down and rolled toward the exit.

"Thank you, sir, for showing us the X-wing," Threepio said as he scurried after Artoo. "I will most certainly speak to our master about you—"

And then he stopped as the bay doors closed behind them. Artoo let out a long, pitiful wail.

"I think you're overreacting, Artoo. The X-wing isn't dead. It's merely disassembled." Threepio hurried down the corridor.

Artoo beeped as he kept up.

"Erase its memory? But Master Luke gave specific instructions that the X-wing's memory shouldn't be touched."

Artoo bleeped an affirmative.

"But that doesn't mean there's a conspiracy, Artoo. Organic beings are subject to error."

Artoo whistled and shrilled.

"Very well, then," Threepio said. "You can believe what you want. But you'll tell Master Luke yourself. I'll have no part in such flights of fancy."

Artoo grunted.

"Still," Threepio said as they left the hangar and entered the upper level of the docking bay, "I will inform Mistress Leia of that being's attitude. If we were imprisoned over such a trivial thing, imagine what would happen to droids with less important owners. It's a disgrace. Such a thing should not be allowed on Coruscant."

Artoo blurbled.

"I am not thinking about myself," Threepio said. "If I were thinking of myself, would I have mentioned other droids?"

✶ ✶ ✶

Leia's long hair flowed down her back. She was brushing it steadily, her newly healed hands looking perfect in the soft light. The last dip in the bacta tank had done it. She would be fine.

Han sat on the edge of their bed, wishing she would face him. She had picked up her brush the moment the conversation had grown serious.

"Look, sweetheart, I'm only asking for a week."

"We're in the middle of a crisis, here, Han." She hadn't missed a stroke. "And you want to go off and play with the boys."

"I don't want to play, Leia. I think Jarril came to me for a reason."

"I'm sure he did. From what you said about the conversation, he couldn't understand what happened to Han Solo, gadabout adventurer."

Han pushed off the bed. "I think Jarril's visit is connected to all this."

"And I don't."

He crouched beside her. She stopped brushing her hair, and placed both hands in her lap. The scratches were gone from her face, but she still looked drawn and pale.

He put his hands over hers. Her skin was cold and she was shaking. Time for honesty. For both of them.

"Leia," he said, "I'm useless here."

"Not useless," she said, looking at his hands protecting hers. "You're never useless, Han."

He put his head against her shoulder, felt the silky smoothness of her hair against his forehead, smelled her faint perfume. He didn't know how to explain something she usually understood. He was a man of action. He needed to act.

Then she sighed. "You want to contribute."

He nodded.

"And there's nothing you can do on Coruscant."

He sat back on his heels. He was squeezing her hands tightly. The bristles of her brush dug into his fingertips. "I've already done what I can do, Leia. I've followed Jarril's trail. He left with the last wave of ships in all the confusion. Then escaped when the shields went down for Luke to enter. Jarril apparently talked to no one but me. He didn't even have any friends here except me."

"He might have had nothing to do with the attack."

Han nodded. "I know. In that case, the investigators you've assigned are following all the possible leads."

"What if there's another attack, Han?"

"It hasn't come. I've been waiting for days but it hasn't come."

"That's strange, isn't it?" Leia said. "I've been thinking it's very strange."

"So have I."

She smiled at him then, the quirky half-smile she got when she knew she should fight with him, but didn't have the heart to.

"I'll stay if you need me," he said.

She shook her head. "I don't need anyone, you big oaf."

"I know that, Your Worship," he said, grinning. Then he let the grin fade. "But I mean it. If you need me—"

"We're better if we work as a team, Han."

He knew that too. He'd been trying to say that all along.

"My only concern is the children." She slipped a hand out from underneath his, and put the brush on her dressing table. "What if the next attack is on them? What if R'yet is right? What if the attack was meant for me or my family?"

"If it was meant for you, it was meant as a warning," Han said.

"Like Jarril's visit."

He nodded.

"Winter says the base at Anoth has been rebuilt. Maybe we should send them there with her."

"A visit to their babyhood homes?" He got off his haunches and stood. "Can you do without them, Leia? I'll be gone, and they'll be gone, and then you'll have the political crisis to deal with."

She took a deep breath. He could see the struggle in her face. He knew how much she relied on her family, how important it all was to her.

"I'll work better if I know everyone is safe," she said.

"That's why you want me to stay, isn't it?"

She didn't look at him. He pulled her hair back and kissed the nape of her neck.

"I can take care of myself, Princess."

"I know," she said, still not looking at him.

"You're the one in the greatest danger. Maybe you should go with Winter and the children to Anoth."

She lifted her head, finally looking at him. "I can't do that. I have duties here. I have to take the same risks as the rest of the government."

He knew. He had to take risks too. Protecting him

and forcing him to remain on Coruscant would be as bad as making Leia go to Anoth.

He waited, watched the realization dawn on her face as she understood what he had done.

"You've manipulated me," she said.

He nodded.

She stood and wrapped her arms around him, pulling him close. In the last few days, she had lost weight. She felt thin and fragile. He held her tightly, knowing that more strength lay within her slender form than he would ever have. He had to trust in her abilities, just as she had to trust in his.

"Don't you wish that, just once, we could live calmly and comfortably like normal people?" Her voice was soft, almost a whisper.

"No," he said. He stepped back just far enough so that he could see her face. "Because if we had been normal people, we would never have met. Your Highnessness."

She laughed, and he kissed her. Deeply. Passionately. As if he would never be able to kiss her again.

Ten

✷

Jarril's ship was a treasure trove of unusual junk. Lando had towed the *Spicy Lady* to Kessel, and had spent half a day exploring his old colleague's cargo. The body remained in the cockpit. Lando wasn't certain yet what to do with Jarril. He supposed he'd have to go through the records, looking for next of kin.

He wanted to save that until last.

Jarril hadn't been carrying any cargo when he was killed. Or so it seemed. But someone could have cleaned out the cargo while the ship listed in space.

Still, Lando found numerous abandoned items. Taken separately, they were explicable. But together, they were inexplicable.

He found a blaster handle, a single stormtrooper glove, a laser cannon, and pieces of a Carbanti signal-augmented sensor jammer. He found power cells and the schematics for cannons designed for the all-terrain armored transports. He found bolts for a repulsorlift, and, most disturbing of all, a case of needles made specifically for an Imperial interrogator droid.

But no credits, no jewels, and no spice.

Either Jarril had been involved in something sinister, or he had stumbled on something.

Lando liked to believe Jarril had been in the wrong place at the wrong time.

But what Lando wanted to believe and what was true were probably two different things.

So he almost decided to take the *Spicy Lady* back into space and set her free. Lando was halfway back to his ship when he remembered Jarril's laugh.

It had been a hearty, deep, almost choking laugh. Lando had thought Jarril was going to laugh himself to death the day he smuggled Lando out of Smuggler's Run. Right under Nandreeson's nose.

I owe you, Lando had said.

Jarril grinned. *I know, pal. And someday I'll collect. Big.*

But he never had. And now it was too late. Ever since he'd seen Han Solo slide into the carbon freeze in Cloud City, Lando had placed a higher priority on old debts and friendship.

The old Lando would have walked away, sent the *Spicy Lady* back where he had found her, and forgotten the whole thing.

The new Lando sighed, bypassed the main hatch, and walked to the cockpit.

The cockpit on the *Spicy Lady* was an exact replica of the *Millennium Falcon*'s. It comfortably fit four humanoids, and was tall enough to accommodate a Wookiee. Blaster scars had left rips in the seats and had charred one of the viewports. When Lando turned on life support, Jarril's body had fallen between the pilot's seat and the wall, crumpling like discarded clothing.

Lando bent over the body. Blaster at close range, just as he had thought. Jarril's eyes were open, and filled with terror. Lando gently closed them. Too many times he had been afraid he would die that way, alone, attacked in space by someone he'd crossed. Or someone he hadn't.

"Let's see what we can do for you, Jarril," Lando said. He sat in the copilot's chair, as far from Jarril's body as he could get. Then he logged on to the *Spicy Lady*'s computer. This part of the computer was not tied to the slave system.

When Lando logged on, a cargo manifest floated on the screen. It had been left there by whoever had gone before. The manifest was dated for a week before—and it was empty.

It had clearly been erased.

Lando searched the backups, but whoever had erased the manifest had been thorough. There were no backups of any of the manifests. In fact, all he could find were the ghosts of the files: the names and the dates of issue.

Jarril's cargo had been so secret, he hadn't even kept personal records of it.

Lando left the cargo manifests and went to the address files. The hailing codes for all of Jarril's contacts had to be here. With a few keystrokes, Lando opened the files.

He recognized all the names as smuggling contacts except for three. One was on Fwatna and hadn't been used in more than three years. Another was on Dathomir, and the third was on Almania. He looked up the Fwatna address first. It was for a contact named Dolph, and Jarril had noted [NAME RETIRED] in the hidden-words section. From Lando's cursory examination of Jarril's system, it seemed that Jarril deleted unusable information. Lando made a note of the name, the out-of-date address, and continued searching.

The address on Dathomir had no name attached to it. Instead, it had notes that appeared to be directions, along with stars marking it as a Big Find. The address was new enough that Lando suspected Jarril hadn't had a chance to exploit the Big Find, hence its continuation in the records.

He opened the file on Almania to find that Jarril had sent a message there on the day the manifest was erased. The message had been deleted as well, but Jarril had based the *Spicy Lady* on the *Falcon.* He had followed all the schematics for the cockpit—the schematics that Lando had—and had bragged about it. Which meant that he had put in all of Lando's back doors.

Once erased, not always erased.

Jarril had never been a brilliant man. He not only put in Lando's back doors, he had used the same codes. Or perhaps that was bright. Who would think that two such diverse ships had the same coding system?

Except, of course, Lando.

It only took a moment for Lando to find the message. He put it on speaker, only to have the computer tell him the message was coded.

And written.

Stranger and stranger.

Lando uncoded the message and brought it onscreen. The message had no addressee and it was unsigned. Typical smuggler. That way no one who intercepted it would know who it was for.

CARGO DELIVERED. FIREWORKS SPECTACULAR.

It was followed shortly thereafter by another message.

SOLO KNOWS. WE CAN COUNT ON HIS INVOLVEMENT.

Then nothing. Those were the last messages Jarril had sent.

Lando copied them to his own computer. He glanced at Jarril. Jarril had known something, told Han, and now Jarril was dead. Which meant that someone was after Han.

Someone who had taken the A-wing and left the *Spicy Lady* to drift.

Lando got out of the copilot's chair. He had a call to make to Coruscant, and he couldn't make it from here.

✷ ✷ ✷

Brakiss. Luke sat on the rubble-covered stair. He wasn't willing to leave the Hall, not yet. Not until he had gotten all the remnants of emotion and knowledge he could get.

Brakiss. One of the failures. One of the students who had turned to the dark side. Luke remembered each student who left Yavin 4 before completing training. Some had left because of family crises *(Decide you must how to serve them best),* and those crises always came at the wrong point in the training. *(This is a dangerous time for you, when you will be tempted by the dark side of the Force.)* He remembered Ben and Yoda; he always let those students go although he gave them the same admonition Yoda had given him: *Mind what you have learned.* And in his mind he always added the next sentence: *Save you it can.*

Some did. They returned for more training. Others disappeared. Luke hoped that they too would return someday.

But none of them had left in the same spectacular manner as Brakiss. Brakiss was one of the handful of Imperials who had tried to infiltrate the Jedi Academy. Unlike the others, Brakiss had a true talent for the Force. Luke decided to see if he could keep Brakiss away from the dark side.

The training went well. Brakiss softened, and Luke thought it time to give him the equivalent of the dark cave on Dagobah. Luke sent Brakiss on a journey in which Brakiss had to face himself. Brakiss emerged, terrified and angry. He left Yavin 4 and went back to the Empire.

Luke knew that one day he would see Brakiss again. He had feared it would be like this.

"Master Luke! Master Luke! Oh, thank heavens we found you!" Threepio's voice cut through Luke's reverie. Luke glanced over his shoulder. Threepio stood in the door with Artoo at his side. They started to come in.

"No!" Luke said. "It's too unstable in here. Meet me outside."

"But Master Luke—"

"I'll be right there, Threepio."

"I hope so," Threepio said. He walked away from the door. Artoo bleeped at Luke and then followed Threepio. It had to be something serious, then. Artoo sounded distressed.

Luke stood. He got no more of Brakiss than that initial sensory impression. And it bothered him. He wasn't used to such superficial feelings. But all he had felt around this blast had been strange.

He climbed out. One of the workers in the outer corridor looked at him. "Those your droids, Master Skywalker?"

Luke nodded.

"They seemed agitated."

Luke smiled. "Threepio always seems agitated. I'm sure it's nothing."

He continued outside. Threepio and Artoo stood on the dirt-covered lawn. They were facing the door. Threepio turned and said something to Artoo when Luke appeared.

"What's so important?" Luke asked.

"Master Luke, Artoo and I had a dreadful experience in the maintenance bays. Artoo insisted that we go down there and we were taken prisoner by this horrible Kloperian who seemed to have no idea who we were. I wouldn't have brought this to you, sir, but Artoo insisted. He said you needed to know—"

"What were you doing in the maintenance bays? Those are off-limits to all but specialized droids."

"Artoo insisted," Threepio said. "He's been behaving quite badly. In fact, the language he used in front of the Kloperian—well, it made my gears freeze if you get my meaning, sir. And—"

"Artoo?" Luke asked.

Artoo bleebled, then a compartment opened near his base and a small tube arm emerged. Luke held out his hand, and Artoo dropped several tiny chips into it.

He crouched and examined them. "These are the X-wing's memory chips."

Artoo moaned, a mournful sound.

"The X-wing is in pieces, sir. If I had known that Artoo was going to steal parts—"

"In pieces?" Luke said. He closed his fist around the chips. The X-wing and Artoo had been flying together so long that their memories were linked. They had their own special language. The X-wing was as much of a person as a ship could be. "Who authorized this?"

"Why, I thought you did."

"I authorized routine maintenance." Luke stood. "This would have to happen the moment I need the X-wing. How bad is the damage?"

Threepio said, "There is no actual damage."

Artoo beeped and squawked.

"Aside from the pieces," Threepio said.

Luke's grasp on the chips was tight. "It sounds more like they're rebuilding the X-wing. Why else remove the memory chips?"

Artoo whistled an affirmative.

"I know nothing about technical matters, sir," Threepio said. "It just seems to me that routine maintenance is routine maintenance, at least on Coruscant."

"Which is why they imprisoned you?" Luke shook his head. "I don't like the sound of any of this."

"We didn't exactly appreciate it either, Master Luke. Why, if I hadn't told them that we belonged to you and Mistress Leia, we would still be in that closet. Or"—and Threepio's golden body shook in an imitation shudder—"we'd have had our memories wiped and our bodies sold for scrap."

Artoo moaned.

"Good thinking on your part, Threepio, and yours too, Artoo." Luke gave the memory chips back to Artoo. "Keep these safe. I'll see about the condition of the X-wing. We'll get it back together in no time."

But he wasn't as sure as he sounded. Routine maintenance did not require the disassembly of the X-wing. He should have been more cautious in his instructions when he arrived. But he hadn't thought there would be a threat to him, his droid, or his X-wing on Coruscant. Even with the bombing and the strange feelings he had had.

Someone was watching them. He glanced over his shoulder. They were alone on the street.

But someone was watching him. He had had that feeling since Yavin 4. Someone was watching, planning, and outguessing him.

It was time to regain control.

"Come on, Artoo," Luke said. "Let's get our X-wing."

"With all due respect, sir," Threepio said, "I would prefer not to return to that den of iniquity. I think it better if I return to my duties."

Luke nodded. "Threepio, tell Leia about your adventure, and tell her about the X-wing. Tell her that—" Then he stopped. Better to tell her in person. In person he could communicate the depth of his unease. "Tell her that I will speak to her before I leave."

"Very good, Master Luke," Threepio said, and toddled off toward the Imperial Palace.

Luke disagreed. It wasn't very good. But it was the best he could do.

For now.

Eleven

The Inner Council met in the Ambassadorial Dining Area. It was another large, gold-leafed room, filled with decorations that dated from the Emperor's reign. Leia couldn't wait for the investigations to end so that she could rebuild the Senate Hall. The temporary offices only reminded her how much she missed it.

The room had an antiseptic smell, probably from a recent cleaning. She had decided on this room as a meeting place at the last moment, and planned to continue random room choices until the murderers were caught and the Senate could return to normal business. She didn't want anyone to have days to plan another attack.

Leia sat at the head of the table, and the other members of the Inner Council surrounded her. Three of her most valued friends had died in the attack. One had died in the medical center. She missed them. Han had been right about the gaps in her life. She had sent the children and Winter off that morning to Anoth. Han was gone, and she knew it would only be a matter of time before Luke left too. She could work well on her own, but with her family spreading to all corners of the galaxy, and with so many friends injured or dead, she felt as she had in those first few days after the destruction of Alderaan. All alone with only herself to rely on.

"The news has reached the Outer Rim," Borsk Fey'lya said. His melodious voice contained his concern. The fur near his face was shorter than usual, where the medical personnel had cut off the singed areas. "The Rim Worlds are agitating for revenge."

"Vengeance isn't the issue," Leia said. "Stopping another attack is. I hope you've all let your people know that the investigations are underway."

"They don't care about the investigations," C-Gosf said. She was petite, even for a Gosfambling. They were delicate furred creatures, intelligent and soft-spoken. Her whiskers curled around her face as she talked. Leia had to lean forward to hear her. "It is the loss of representation. With so many serious injuries, and so much loss of life, the Senate is unable to vote on any but simple-majority declarations. We barely have a quorum."

Leia leaned back. She had been fearing this.

"The term is just beginning," said Gno. "If it were near the end, Leia, I would suggest closing the session with the representatives we have. But we are looking at three years and more in which certain planets will be underrepresented."

"Exodeen lost its senior senator and its secondary senator," said ChoFï. "Now it is only represented by R'yet Coome. That's not good for any of us."

"Don't let your political biases interfere, ChoFï," said Garm Bel Iblis. His craggy face had a look of exhaustion. "We have to get used to the former Imperials."

"I worry that we'll invite even more of them by having emergency elections," Leia said.

"Or we give the ones already in the Senate more power," Fey'lya said. "Leia, the Senate is based on the will of the voting republics. They have chosen former

Imperials as their representatives. We cannot argue with that."

Leia smiled sadly. "I suppose we can't."

"And we have to trust them to make the right choices in the future," Fey'lya said.

The Bothan trusted no one. Even Leia knew that. "And what does your elaborate information say will happen if we hold elections now?"

Fey'lya's fur rippled, the only sign he showed of distress. "Nothing would happen to the Bothans. We were surprisingly lucky in this."

"If we hold the election quickly," ChoFï said, "no one new would have time to mount a campaign. The losers of the last election would probably take office."

"You can't predict like that," C-Gosf said. "My people would not elect someone who lost. Such a person can never run again, nor can that person ever hold a position of power. Once a loser on Gosfambling, always a loser."

Leia glanced at C-Gosf. She hadn't realized what her colleague had risked in running for the Senate.

"So what would happen on Gosfambling?" Leia asked.

"Someone who is already in power would be promoted," she said.

"It's a problem we've grappled with all along," Gno said. "Imposing an electoral system on different cultures."

"We have rules," Fey'lya said.

"Yes," ChoFï said, "and you should know perhaps better than the rest of us how cultures manipulate those rules."

"The Bothans haven't done anything untoward."

"You mean illegal," ChoFï said.

"It does no good to fight among ourselves," Leia said. She sighed. "Gno is right. As much as I don't want to, we have to hold emergency elections in those places where the representative was killed or is too injured to carry out official duties. And we have to do it soon, otherwise any legislation we enact will have the onus of being decided by a diminished council. We have enough troubles uniting the various members of the Republic. We don't need additional problems."

"You realize," Bel Iblis said, "that we could create problems by having this rapid election."

"You mean gain more former Imperials than we want?" Gno said. "We have to take the risk. Leia is right. The Senate is diminished already by the attack. To operate underrepresented would be a clear signal to those planets whose representation was lost that they are unimportant."

"We can't be afraid of our colleagues forever," C-Gosf said. "We voted to allow former Imperials into the Senate. We have to accept them now."

Leia nodded. She agreed, even though she didn't want to. "Let's set up the elections for one week from today," she said, "and bring the new officials in as soon after that as they can come. No later than one month from now. Agreed?"

The members agreed. Leia called an official vote, and then moved to other business. But as she did, she couldn't stop a chill from running up her spine.

Perhaps this was what her unseen enemy wanted. A rapid change in the Senate. Disorientation, destruction, and a sudden increase in new faces would cause fragmentation.

Fragmentation existed as Senator Palpatine took over the Old Republic Senate.

It would be up to Leia to prevent such a takeover from happening again.

✷ ✷ ✷

Femon sat in her office on Almania. Death masks from a dozen different cultures covered her walls. Red, gold, blue, some with mouths open in agony and others looking serene, they all shared an eerieness that she had once found comforting.

She did no longer.

She had almost wiped the makeup from her face upon her return from Pydyr, but that would have been a clear sign that she no longer believed in Kueller. His hesitation in continuing the fight would be their downfall. He had said he wanted to replace the New Republic with a government of his own. She had believed him from the moment she met him.

The New Republic was weak, he said. They allowed too many threats to their own people. They spent too much time legislating things that could not be legislated and too little time effecting change.

Femon's family had died six years ago, when the *Eye of Palpatine* swept over their planet. The Imperial starship operated on an old computer program whose mission had been established by the Emperor himself. Femon's family had been killed in the crossfire as they tried to save others being lured onto the ship. Sure, the New Republic eventually stopped the *Eye of Palpatine,* but too late to save Femon's loved ones.

The New Republic allowed too much Imperial equipment to remain on conquered planets. Several times, the Republic had allowed former Imperials, trying to reestablish their government, to threaten peaceful worlds. Too many times. The New Republic had never gone for the kill, had never executed those directly involved, had never done all that needed to be done to establish their own government firmly.

Kueller had said that the New Republic's inability to destroy its enemies was the sign of a fatal weakness. He said it didn't matter who ruled the galaxy as long as that rule was accomplished with an iron fist.

Now he was exhibiting the same weakness he had once attributed to the New Republic.

Femon could no longer support him.

She had pushed, on Pydyr and before, for him to strike swiftly and decisively. He had the power to do so. But he wanted to toy with Skywalker and Organa Solo.

He acted like a man who wanted revenge, but for something she didn't completely understand.

It didn't matter anymore. He was going to spend two more days on Pydyr, cataloging his wealth and meeting with his spies. Two days was more than enough time for her to take the decisive action he had failed to make.

She had the knowledge, the equipment, and the codes. She even had the ability to get rid of Kueller.

He had left himself wide-open on Pydyr.

By tomorrow, Kueller's death mask would be real.

Twelve

The oily, metallic smell of the maintenance bay reminded Luke of days spent repairing his uncle's speeder on Tatooine. He used to love hunching over equipment, looking for the small variances that would improve speed or accuracy.

Another world. Another time.

Artoo moved silently behind him, inching closer the deeper they went into the bay. The Orders and Requisitions area had told Luke to come down here; all they had been able to confirm was that his X-wing was receiving routine maintenance as requested.

The main bay was empty except for several disassembled X-wings. Artoo wheeled his way toward the double maintenance doors and whistled.

"All right, Artoo," Luke said. "I'll go there if I can't find anyone. But let's wait."

His patience was rewarded a moment later when a young blond man—a boy, really—in mechanic's clothing sauntered out of the back. He was wiping his hands on a formerly white cloth when he saw Luke.

"This is a restricted area," the boy said. He wasn't

much older than Luke had been when his aunt and uncle died.

"I know," Luke said. "I was sent by Orders and Requisitions. Apparently you have my X-wing down here."

The boy shrugged. "If we do, we're working on it. It'll be done as soon as we can get to it."

"It's not supposed to be here."

"You'll need to take that up with Orders—"

"Look." Luke stepped into the light, his Jedi cloak flowing behind him. "I don't have time for this kind of runaround. I need the X-wing this afternoon. I was told it's in pieces—"

"Then you won't get it until it's done. I'm sorry. Orders should never have sent you down here."

"Perhaps not," Luke said. "But they did. Let's see if we can resolve this, shall we?"

The boy looked up. Apparently he hadn't expected Luke to be reasonable. Artoo moved closer. "Your astromech unit shouldn't be here either, you know."

"I know," Luke said. "But I need my X-wing today. Artoo works it with me."

The boy pursed his lips as if the idea disgusted him. "You really didn't plan to have your X-wing here, did you?"

"No," Luke said. "Just regular maintenance, as I always do when I come to Coruscant."

"Didn't you see the memo from General Antilles?"

Wedge? What had Wedge to do with Luke's X-wing? "Apparently not," Luke said.

"Routine maintenance includes upgrading all X-wings to current clean fighter status."

"That sounds costly," Luke said.

The boy frowned. "Where did you say you came from?"

"I didn't," Luke said. "Where can I find Wedge?"

"General Antilles?" The boy gasped at Luke's forwardness. "I don't know. I've never spoken to the man. Do you know him?"

Luke grinned. "A bit. We were in the same squadron at the Battle of Yavin."

The boy dropped his rag. "Forgive me, sir. I had no idea. I—uh—I can leave a message for him on the system."

"I can contact him myself if you just lead me to my ship."

"Sir, the area is restricted."

"We've been through this before," Luke said. "My name is Luke Skywalker. All I want is to see the state of my X-wing and—"

"Luke Skywalker?" The boy's voice squeaked. "The Jedi Knight? Why didn't you say so in the first place, sir? I would have pulled some strings."

"It's not the Jedi way to take unfair advantage," Luke said, although that wasn't precisely true. "Let's check on the X-wing, shall we?"

The boy punched up some codes in the computer, then wiped his hands on his brown mechanic's pants. "If you'll follow me, sir."

Luke crossed the main bay. Artoo followed.

"You might want to leave your astromech unit here, sir. The equipment in the new X-wing bay isn't droid-friendly, at least for R2 units."

"Will he be in any danger?"

"No, sir, but the Kloperians don't really like R2 units."

"He noticed that the first time he was down here. Apparently he was imprisoned for a while."

"Imprisoned?" the boy glanced over his shoulder. "Forgive me, sir, but you can't imprison a droid."

The boy thought Luke was being dramatic. Luke folded his hands over his robe, rather like Ben used to do. "He's more than a droid," Luke said. "Just like my X-wing is more than a tactical fighter."

The smell of X-wing cleaning solvent was strong inside the new bay. More X-wing pieces were scattered about some already-reassembled ships. The new ships were streamlined. The long nose cone remained the same, but the area in the back that housed the astromech droids was gone.

The hair tingled on the back of Luke's scalp. "Tell me about General Antilles's order."

"It came down last year, sir, after the prototype of the new X-wing arrived here. The new design works better in battle. It combines the computer system and the astromech unit into one complete system."

"But that was tried a long time ago, and they discovered that if the unit broke down, the pilot was in grave danger."

The boy shrugged. "They've overcome that bug, sir. The changes in droid and computer technology just in the last six months have been astonishing. We can do things that we've never been able to do before. Where've you been that you didn't know about this?"

"Yavin 4," Luke said, suddenly feeling old and out-of-touch. "I teach there."

"Hm," the boy said. He led them around another disassembled X-wing to the back of the bay.

"You're overhauling all X-wings in this way?" Luke asked.

"Yes, sir. We've also combined some similar systems on other starfighters." The boy's enthusiasm was charming. Luke remembered feeling that way about new technology himself once.

"How can the Republic afford this?"

The boy shrugged. Clearly, financing was not his business. "I don't know, sir, but we've been doing it for more than a month now. Keeps us all busy, I'll tell you. I haven't had more than a day off since the changes began."

He stopped in front of a maintenance platform. The X-wing on it was almost unrecognizable as a starfighter. Artoo moaned softly as though mourning for a dying friend.

Luke bit back his irritation. "How long will it take to reassemble the ship?"

"Sir?" The boy sounded startled.

"I need it this afternoon. Is that possible?"

"They just started on the computer system, sir. We can't have it to you for the next day, maybe more."

"I don't want the changes made," Luke said. "How long to reassemble it as it was?"

"I'm afraid we can't, sir. General Antilles's orders. He says the old X-wings aren't stable enough for space use."

"Mine's fine," Luke said. "I'd like it shortly."

"I'm sorry, sir."

"Forgive me," Luke said, feeling the inevitable wave of frustration he felt whenever he had to pull rank. "I'm going to be leaving on diplomatic business for my sister, Leia Organa Solo, the Chief of State. I would like to use my X-wing. I need it this afternoon."

The boy peered into the workings of the ship. "I'm really sorry, sir, but they've already taken out the memory and the astromech hookups. The socket is still there, but we have nothing to hook it to. If they're running true to form, the pieces have been recycled already."

"I have the memory chips. My R2 unit picked them up earlier."

The boy wrung his hands together. "Sir, if you'd look at the interior . . ."

That had been precisely what Luke *hadn't* wanted to do. He was afraid he'd see an old friend gutted and nearly destroyed. He climbed onto the edge of the bay and peered in. The entire astromech area had been pulled and disassembled. Even though Luke hadn't worked extensively on an X-wing since the Battle of Endor, he recognized a mess when he saw one. The X-wing was already half-converted.

He patted the ship's sides, and Artoo moaned again. "Put her back the way you found her," Luke said to the boy.

"But, sir—"

"I'll deal with General Antilles. You just fix my X-wing."

"Sir, we can't have it for you when you need it."

Luke nodded. "I realize that. Get me an older X-wing, one you haven't upgraded, and I'll put the memory chips in that. It'll have to do for this mission."

The boy looked chagrined. "I'm sorry, sir. We disassemble the X-wings when they arrive. It's quick and easy. We don't have any that you can use."

"Surely there are some on Coruscant. . . ." Luke's voice trailed off at the boy's expression. Nothing in the New Republic ever ran smoothly. When something finally did, it turned out to be a problem.

"I can give you a substitute X-wing," the boy said, "but it will be one of the new ones. Your chips won't work, and neither will your astromech unit."

"Will Artoo fit in the new X-wing?"

The boy shook his head. "It's strictly a one-person vehicle."

Luke sighed. He didn't like his choices. He wanted to be in a starfighter so that he had speed and the ability to enter into planetary defenses unnoticed. He could take a bigger ship—Leia would probably let him have the *Alderaan*—but that meant he had to take a support staff larger than Artoo. It also meant that he would be noticed as he traveled across the galaxy, and it meant that he would have to explain why Leia wasn't with him. Han had already left with the *Falcon*. And all the other ships had the New Republic insignias.

"You'll work with my astromech unit," Luke said. "Artoo-Detoo knows that X-wing better than anyone. I want it fixed by the time I return."

Artoo bleeped and moaned.

Luke put a hand on Artoo's head. "I'm sorry, old friend. I don't think this can wait. I trust you to make sure the X-wing is repaired."

Artoo whined.

"And I'll let Leia, Threepio, and Wedge know you're here. Nothing will happen to you." Then Luke looked at the boy. "Will it?"

"He's an outmoded R2 unit, sir. They—"

"No," Luke said firmly. "He's a hero of the Rebellion. Neither Leia nor I would be alive without this little guy. You will treat him as you would treat me."

"Sir—"

"What's your name, son?"

The boy took a deep breath. "Cole Fardreamer."

The name made Luke start. "You're from Tatooine?"

The boy nodded. "I grew up hearing stories about you, sir. How wonderful you are, and how you were once just a moisture farmer. I came here because of you."

Luke had no real sense of himself as an inspiration to anyone. He resisted the urge to step back. "And now you work on X-wings."

"It's a place to start."

Luke nodded. "That it is." He took a deep breath. "Take good care of my X-wing and my R2 unit, Cole. See that nothing happens to either of them. When I come back, I want them both intact, ready to use."

"If you want, sir, I can have the X-wing for you by this time tomorrow."

Luke studied the boy's face. He had no doubt Cole would give the repair of the X-wing his all. But that wouldn't be enough. "I'd wait if I could," Luke said softly. "But I have a feeling that time is running out."

✷ ✷ ✷

Smuggler's Run hadn't changed. The Run was an asteroid belt that had, over the years, become the hideout for hundreds of smugglers. The entry into the Run was complex: Han was surprised he had remembered it after all the years.

But he had. He landed the *Falcon* on Skip 1, the thirty-fifth asteroid in the system, and the one first settled. Skip 1 had always supported human life the best and was extremely well-protected.

The hideouts were deep inside the Skip, carved centuries ago by creatures that Han didn't even want to think about. As he and Chewie made their way down the old, familiar passages, he remembered the feeling of claustrophobia distinctly. He'd always associated it with the feeling of being on the run. But he wasn't on the run these days, and the feeling remained.

Chewie growled.

"Yeah," Han said. "You'd think that they'd have controlled that stink by now."

The corridors smelled of sulfur, rancid meat, and rotting flesh. The stench had always been a part of the Run. Chewie complained about it each and every time they came.

The source of the odor was a greenish-yellow ooze that ran down the center of the corridors and into the main trading areas. When Han had first arrived on the Run, he'd witnessed the first and only attempt to block the ooze. Some Bothan got it into his brain to plug the ooze at its source. He did, and Skip 1 was instantly rocked by the biggest groundquake in its history.

"The place has gas," the Bothan later explained. "Either we let it stink around here, or Skip 1 will explode."

The smugglers chose to live with the stink. They hadn't found a better hiding place in the entire galaxy.

Or a better-defended place. Han knew that the *Falcon* was being watched from the moment of her approach. What he hadn't expected were the armed guards at the end of the corridor.

Five of them, all old friends.

Chewie roared in indignation. Han put a restraining hand on his friend's furry arm. He scanned the group. Kid DXo'ln, bald now, had taken Han on his first run to Kessel. Zeen Afit, his craggy face even more lined than Han remembered, had first brought Han and Chewie to the Run. Sinewy Ana Blue, looking more beautiful than ever, had run the sabacc games in which Han won a lot of credits. Wynni, the Wookiee who had tried to seduce Chewbacca on his first visit to Skip 1, looked exactly the same. And Seluss, the Sullustan who usually traveled with Jarril, clutched his blaster as if he couldn't wait to use it.

Han held out his hands. "Is this any way to greet an old friend?"

"You're no friend, Solo," Sinewy Ana Blue said.

"So how soon until your friends in the New Republic show up to arrest us?" Zeen Afit asked.

"Have you done something illegal?" Han asked.

Wynni growled.

"A guy can ask a simple question," Han shot back at her.

"Not if he already knows the answer," Kid DXo'ln said.

Chewie's arm tightened. Han kept his grip on Chewie's fur.

"If the Republic was going to go after Smuggler's Run, it would have happened a long time ago."

Seluss chittered, his mouse ears wiggling forward as he spoke.

"Oh, yeah, right," Han said. "As if there is a list for you guys to finally rise to the top of. You're overestimating your importance, Seluss, don't you think?"

Wynni roared. Chewbacca roared back.

"Stop it, Chewie," Han hissed. "No need to bring personalities into this."

Chewie grumbled. Han understood Chewie's frustration: Wynni had never acted according to Wookiee code —she had abandoned her family and two life debts to pursue her smuggling career—but Han didn't want an old wound to fester into something ugly. Especially when Han and Chewie were outgunned.

"Personalities are already in this, Han," Kid said. "You left us a long time ago. You have no right to come back here."

"I have as much right to be here as you do," Han snapped. "And when did it become a privilege to be on the Run? I seem to remember when most of us here were struggling to leave."

"The Run's a different place," Blue said.

"Sure smells the same," Han murmured.

They moved closer to him. Zeen poked Han with his blaster. Chewie growled again. Wynni waved her bowcaster at him.

"What? Are you going to push me all the way back to the *Falcon*? Or shoot me right here?" Han grabbed Seluss's blaster, and pulled the short humanoid toward him. "I'm here on the invite of your partner, buddy. You want to bring him over here?"

Seluss let go of the blaster and chittered, loudly and angrily. Han raised his left hand—the one without the blaster—in self-defense.

"Hey, how was I to know he's not here? I figured he was coming right back."

Seluss shoved Han, still chittering. The shove was surprisingly hard, considering that the Sullustan only came up to Han's waist.

Chewbacca growled and grabbed Seluss by his collar, lifting him off the ground.

"Put him down, Chewie. He's upset."

"He's got a point," Zeen said. "Jarril went to see you and never came back. Now you're here."

Seluss kept chittering. He was swinging wildly with his arms and legs. Chewie held him an arm's length away —Chewie's arm. Seluss looked like an angry pinwheeling mouse.

"You guys know me. I don't double-cross people and I don't murder them in cold blood." Han was beginning to get angry now. "I came here because Jarril said there was trouble."

"You came here because Jarril told you about the money," Kid DXo'ln said.

Wynni moaned a caution.

Han raised an eyebrow. "First I'm an enemy of the Run, and then I'm after your money? Which is it?"

Chewie barked softly.

"I think 'paranoid' is too mild a word," Han said. "What are you guys hiding?"

"See?" Zeen said. "I told you he was here for the New Republic."

Sinewy Ana Blue elbowed Zeen. "It's a legitimate question. Put Seluss down and we'll talk."

Chewie shook his head. Seluss tried to swing at him, and succeeded only in making Chewie's hold on his collar tighter.

"Put him down, Chewie," Han said.

Chewie yowled.

"I said put him down." Han didn't want to fight everyone.

Chewie held Seluss over the ooze, and dropped him. Seluss screamed, an ear-piercing whistle that had the

Wookiees covering their ears. Seluss landed, splashing ooze everywhere, doubling the stench. Han backed up, while the other smugglers angrily wiped greenish-yellow goo off themselves.

Seluss sprang out of the ooze and yanked his blaster out of Han's grasp.

"Hey!" Han shouted.

Chewie grabbed for the blaster, but it was too late.

Seluss fired.

Thirteen

Lando waited most of the night, and it felt too long. He tried to sleep, but his mind kept feeding him dreams. Dreams he didn't like. Memory dreams, mostly, of Han in the carbon-freezing chamber. *What's going on . . . buddy?* Han asked over and over. Lando tried to tell him that Vader had betrayed them all. But Lando couldn't speak. And then the dreams would shift to Chewbacca's hands on his throat, repeating over and over in Wookiee that Lando could have prevented this.

Lando could have . . .

. . . prevented . . .

He sat up on his cot, the thin gold thermal blanket gathered around his thighs. He was cold despite the perfectly adjusted temperature. This particular nightmare hadn't come to him in a long time, but he remembered its effects vividly.

It always left him cold, shivering with the most intense cold of his life. And the chill came from within. He felt as if—

—as if he'd been shoved in carbon freeze and left to die.

Lando glanced at his screen. No responses from Coruscant. He'd left messages for Han, Chewbacca, Leia, and finally for Winter. Repeated messages of urgency, and he received no response at all. Usually someone got back to him.

He had also tried Yavin 4, figuring Luke would know where everyone was, but all he got was Streen, who made certain the academy ran smoothly in Luke's absence. Streen said Luke had left rather suddenly for Coruscant, but didn't know why.

Lando had left Luke several messages after that. One keyed to his X-wing, which got bounced back to Lando over the vagaries of interspacial communications, another at Coruscant, and another at the Imperial Palace.

Then he tried Mon Mothma, Admiral Ackbar, and Wedge Antilles. He'd even left a general message for any member of the Coruscant Inner Council.

None of those was answered either.

Someone should have answered him by now.

The hair stood up on the back of his neck. His teeth were chattering. He got out of bed, slipped on his thickest, warmest robe, and poured himself a cup of hot Aitha protein drink. He wrapped his fingers around the cup to gain additional warmth. Then he sat in front of the computer, trying to quell the low-grade panic his dream had left him with, and called Mara Jade.

She answered with such immediacy that he was startled. He had half-expected her to have disappeared as well. She was in the cockpit of Talon Karrde's ship, *Wild Karrde,* his vornskrs partially visible behind her.

She grinned as she answered his hail. "Can't be away from me even a few days, huh, Lando?"

"Each moment seems like years, Mara," he said, knowing he had to keep up his side of the banter, even though his mood was anything but light.

"You can do better than that," she said, suddenly serious. "What's wrong?"

"I've been trying to raise Han and Leia for almost a day now, and I can't," he said. He no longer tried to keep the worry from his voice. He braced his wrists on the desk so that she couldn't see his hands shaking. "In fact, I can't raise anyone on Coruscant."

"That's not a surprise," she said.

His spine stiffened. She wasn't smiling.

"You've been busy with something, haven't you?" she asked.

Big news, then. News he should have heard.

"Don't toy with me, Mara."

"I'm not, Lando. It's been the buzz of this sector, at least."

"What has?"

"The bombing. Of the Senate Hall." Her lips formed a thin line. Behind her, Karrde came into the cockpit and paused as he saw Lando on the screen. "Don't worry. From all I heard, Organa Solo only had minor bruises, and Han wasn't anywhere near the Hall."

"And Luke?"

"Wasn't on Coruscant at all when it happened. But a lot of people died and even more were injured. It's played havoc with the communications array." She glanced over her shoulder. Karrde sat down beside her.

Lando's mouth was dry. It was, as he had expected, something bad. How bad yet he wasn't sure. "I thought you said the destruction was at the Senate Hall?"

She nodded. "But everyone's been trying to contact Coruscant. From political problems to inquiring about relatives. The volume of calls actually knocked part of the array off-line."

"It's been a mess with business," Karrde said.

"I expect it has," Lando said. "But traffic is getting onto Coruscant?"

Karrde nodded. "Not the place I'd want to go now, Calrissian. From what I hear, they're all waiting for another attack."

. . . could have prevented . . .

FIREWORKS.

SOLO KNOWS.

FIREWORKS.

"You all right, Lando?" Mara was giving him her concerned look from clear across the galaxy.

"You said Han is all right?"

She nodded.

"Who did this?"

"If they knew," Karrde said, "Coruscant wouldn't be in such an uproar."

"Lando?" Mara asked.

Lando frowned. "Talon, what's Jarril been up to these days?"

Karrde leaned back in the chair. Then he glanced at Mara. She shrugged. "I haven't worked with Jarril in two years, maybe more."

"You're not answering me," Lando said.

"I think you should make a trip to the Run," Karrde said.

"I can't go to the Run," Lando snapped. "I thought you knew that."

"What's Jarril got to do with this?" Mara asked.

"Ask your friend there," Lando said.

"Talon?"

"The Run's a different place these days," Karrde said. "Not a place I enjoy discussing, Calrissian."

And not on an open line. Karrde's message was clear.

FIREWORKS.

Jarril had just been to Coruscant.

SOLO KNOWS.

And now Jarril was dead.

"Thanks," Lando said. "I'll be in touch soon."

He signed off before they could say anything else. His dreams had been right.

He couldn't risk sending a message that wouldn't get through.

He had to go to Coruscant.

He had to warn Han, before it was too late.

✶ ✶ ✶

Kueller shoved open the door to Femon's office. His guards flanked him, but he waved them back. He wanted them to observe, not to act.

Femon had taken her death masks off the wall. The room looked odd without them. But that wasn't the only change. She was different too. She had scrubbed her face clean. He had almost forgotten what she looked like without the makeup. The years showed. But she was still a striking woman, with her alabaster skin and dark blue eyes.

She didn't seem surprised to see him.

But the fifteen guards who had accompanied him seemed surprised to see her. Even with their faces hidden in their stormtrooper helmets, he could sense their shock at her appearance.

"I didn't order anyone to stand ready," he said.

She got out of her chair. "I did. You're too bent on revenge, Dolph."

He started at the name, but he didn't allow it to show. His mask was working again, ever since he had returned to the artificial environment on Almania, and it gave him more control of his movements than a normal person had.

"We aren't ready," he said. "To do this your way would invite disaster."

"To do it yours loses our advantage." She was nearly as tall as he was. Her eyes sparkled with fury. He had never expected her to cross him, but he should have foreseen it. She was more passionate about the mission than about anything else in her life, even him. She needed this to succeed. She needed to control everything around her so that nothing bad would happen again.

His understanding gave him no compassion, only a muted pity that her needs had driven her to oppose him.

He turned to one of his guards. "Rescind the orders. Tell everyone to stand down."

"I wouldn't do that," she said to the guard.

The guard, to his credit, turned to Kueller, nodded, and said, "I shall do as you wish, milord."

"No!" she shouted.

"Thank you," Kueller said to the guard. Then he walked closer to Femon, his black cape swirling about him. Her body odor was sharp in the close room; she was nervous, no matter how she presented herself.

He tilted his head and looked at her from the corners of his eyes. She lifted her chin, defiant to the last.

"You think I'm bent on revenge," he said.

"I know it." She kept her arms free, but he saw no weapon. She had to have something planned. A woman like her would leave nothing to chance. "You and Brakiss talked often about repaying Skywalker."

"And I intend to."

"Do it after we take over the Republic," she said. "We have everything in place now."

"Not everything," he said.

"Enough."

He shook his head. "Impatience is the downfall of most megalomaniacs, Femon."

"I am not a megalomaniac."

He smiled. "Neither am I."

The guards were watching, clearly unable to understand the conflict. They edged closer to him.

"I have studied the history of this galaxy, Femon," Kueller said softly. "Have you?"

"History is old, dusty, and unimportant," she said.

"I'll take that as a no." His smile grew. He kept his voice low, infusing it with as much charm as he had. "History, Femon, provides lessons. Lessons in living, lessons in dying. Lessons in the way this galaxy works."

"I know how it works," she said.

"Do you?" He put a slight threat into his tone and she almost flinched.

Almost.

Then she nodded. "I do."

He reached out and tucked a strand of her long black hair behind her ear. "Then you know," he said tenderly, "why I fight Skywalker."

"Revenge," she said. "He did something to you and Brakiss long ago. I don't need history for that."

"Ah, but you do." He let his hand drop. "I've had my revenge. Conquering Almania was my revenge. I know clean ways of killing, Femon. Why do you think I spent a week torturing the leaders of the Je'har?"

"Information." Her voice was husky.

He shook his head. "Revenge, sweet. My revenge for their slaughter of my family and the destruction of the place I loved. I thought the Je'har should have a small taste of the pain they caused. I think you should notice that I have not tortured anyone since."

"You found better methods," she said.

He tugged at his black gloves, looking at his hands. His powerful hands. "I knew better methods then. I simply did not believe the Je'har deserved them. I am a reasonable man, Femon. You should have remembered that."

"You've been trying to be fair?" she asked. He suppressed a smile. At that moment, her certainty wavered. She had lost, and she hadn't even realized it. "You've been baiting Skywalker to give him a chance to defend himself?"

"Skywalker needs no favors." He was speaking now not just for her, but for his guards. He had brought them as witnesses, so that tales of her treachery would be muted by tales of his response to it. "Skywalker is the most powerful man in the galaxy."

Femon laughed. "I thought you were, *Dolph.*"

"I will be." His voice was still level. He felt remarkably calm, even though treachery usually sent him into a fury. His training had been good. He gave a mental nod to *Master* Skywalker. "When I defeat Skywalker."

"So it is a power struggle."

Kueller laughed. "You are so simplistic, Femon. You lack intellectual complexity because you have not studied." He glanced at the guards. They were watching intently. One of them had loosened his grip on his blaster. Kueller reached over, grabbed the guard's hand, and tightened his grip.

Femon made her move then. She reached for the control panel. The fail-safe. The security he had installed. The one that slid the initiator down a passage while everyone else in the room suffocated.

With a quick movement of his left hand, with a slight draw on all the Force within him, he stayed hers. Then he tightened his grip, holding her entire body in thrall to him. All except for her neck and head.

"What you don't know," he said calmly, as if he were not controlling her at all, "is that the history of this galaxy is a history of the Force. The Old Republic was guarded by the Jedi Knights, who believed in decency and honor. But they became complacent and allowed Palpatine, who had found a dark power in the Force, to overtake them. He ruled as Emperor and, over time, forgot the lesson of his own life. So, when faced with the youthful power of Luke Skywalker, Palpatine believed he could defeat him. And Skywalker, who had unusual talent in the Force, killed the Emperor instead."

"And you will kill Skywalker, to live up to some noble idea of history?" She spat out the words. He admired her spirit, however misguided.

"I kill Skywalker, first, because it is my destiny," Kueller said. "And secondly because I cannot rule this galaxy as long as he is alive. That is the lesson of history. I must be the strength in the Force. I must be the sole king of the Force. To do that, I must defeat the Jedi. I must defeat Skywalker."

"You are a fool, Kueller," she said.

"No, I am a patient man." He smiled. "I also—"

He reached out with his right hand, stopped neck-high, and clutched his fist—

"—control—"

She gagged, unable to get air, her eyes widening. She couldn't even claw at her throat. Her body shook as she struggled to break free of him.

"—the Force—"

He squeezed his right hand as tight as he could. The snap of her neck echoed in the closeness of the room. Then he let her go and she crumpled to the floor, a person no longer. Only flesh, bone, and memory.

He stood over her. "I will rule this galaxy," he said. Then he looked up at all the stunned guards. "Best you remember that."

Fourteen

The shot ricocheted off the blaster-resistant walls. Han leaped out of the way, but not quickly enough. The shot nicked his buttock, then bounced off the wall in front of him. All the smugglers yelled, and everyone dived for cover. The red beam of dangerous light missed Chewie, brushed Wynni, and scraped Zeen, until it finally slammed into the ooze, where it died in an explosion of foul-smelling steam.

Han's skin burned. His nose and eyes were running from the smell. He got up first, pulled Seluss upright, and shoved him into the scorched wall.

"Where did you learn how to shoot?" Han snarled. "Didn't anyone tell you these walls were blaster-resistant? Haven't you learned yet that firing in an enclosed space is dangerous? You could have killed all of us."

Seluss raised his tiny gloved hands, chittering piteously.

"I don't care how worried you are about Jarril. You *shot* me," Han said.

"Han—" Zeen said.

"I don't like getting shot," Han said.

"Han—" Blue said.

"In fact, I hate getting shot," Han said.

Seluss's chitters rose above the pain threshold again. He crouched and covered his round face with his arms.

"You better hide," Han said, "because when I get done with you, you'll wish you never saw a blaster."

"Han—" Kid DXo'ln said.

"You'll wish you never knew what a blaster was," Han said.

Chewie grabbed Han's arm and pulled him away from Seluss.

Han shook him off. "Leave me alone. Can't you see I'm getting vengeance here?"

Blue laughed. "Not very effectively," she said. "But you have convinced us you're the same old Han. Forgive us. So much has changed around here, we figured you had too."

Han was stalking Seluss. He stopped when Blue's words penetrated. "He shot me," Han repeated.

"And anyone else would have blasted him back, no questions asked." She grinned, revealing the blue crystal tooth that had given her part of her name. "But Han Solo never shoots his friends, no matter what they've done to him."

She stuck a finger in the long slash the blast had left in his pants. "I must admit, though. This is a nice look for you."

He pushed her hand away. "Leave it alone, Blue."

"Oooh." Her grin got wider. "We are married though, aren't we? Some things have changed."

"Just my taste," he snapped, his good humor completely gone.

"From smugglers to princesses," Zeen said. "Can't argue with that."

Blue drew herself to her full height, showing her slender, magnificent body to complete advantage. "Some of us don't need a pedigree to prove our worth," she said. "I've been quality from the beginning."

"That you have, Blue," Kid DXo'ln said.

Seluss moaned and slid down the wall, his head completely covered by his arms.

"I think Seluss was caught up in the heat of the moment," Blue said, looking at him. "I don't think he meant to hurt you, Han."

"I hope not," Han said, unwilling to give Seluss any comfort. Han's skin burned. He tried to twist around to see the damage.

Chewie chuckled.

"It's not funny, furball. It hurts."

"Come on," Blue said. "I got some salve that'll work wonders."

Zeen put his arm around Han's shoulders and propelled him forward. "Then we can sit down and chat."

Seluss whistled softly.

"You can come too," Kid DXo'ln said. "But you'd better keep your distance from Han."

"And take his blaster away, would you?" Han said. "I'm not in a very charitable mood."

He shoved his own blaster into the holster at his hip. It hurt to walk, to stretch the skin, but he would rather spend a cold day on Hoth than show anyone the pain he was in. Especially Chewie.

They followed the ooze into the entry chamber on Skip 1. As Han entered, three dozen smugglers pointedly holstered their own blasters. He resisted glancing at Chewie. Things had changed on the Run.

Drastically.

Usually personal fights remained personal. But they didn't seem to anymore.

The entry chamber on Skip 1 was as far as some renegades got. Bones were stacked in a pile in one corner, most of them trophy bones. The bones all belonged to beasts and creatures, but a number of newcomers were told that this was what happened to anyone who let the secret entry to the Run slip.

Beyond the bones were sabacc tables, half a dozen of them, staffed by talents like Blue, who rarely lost. They were designed to trick the newcomer as well—to clean him out and send him, unhappily, on his way, never to return. On the other side of the sabacc tables was a glass bar, built against the rock. Bômlas, the bartender, believed the customers needed to see his vast store of liquor from all over the galaxy. Bômlas was a three-armed Ychthytonian—he had bet and lost his fourth arm in a particularly savage sabacc game—yet he was the fastest bartender Han had ever seen.

Closing off the cavern was the hokuum station for those smugglers whose tastes went to nonliquid stimulants. Han had seen his first spice users there, as well as his first glitterstim users. He hated the hokuum station, although the Run swore by it. Users on its stimulants often killed each other within three days.

The food court stood in the center of the cavern, as far from the ooze as possible. When Han was first here, the chef was known galaxy-wide. She was killed in a hot-grease duel with another chef. Han's palate still missed her.

"Who's cooking these days?" he asked.

Blue wrinkled her nose. "The former cuisine artist at the Court of Hapes."

"Ze foood, it must have a delicate flaavor, no?" Kid said.

"They don't talk like that on Hapes," Han said.

"He does," Zeen said. "He claims he was the favorite chef of the queen mother."

Han grinned. "Did he have a recommendation from Isolder?"

"What?"

Han shook his head. His old rival for Leia's hand had proven yet again to be a man of action and good taste. He had gotten the best of the queen mother once more. "I hope people are checking the cuisine for poison."

Blue shrugged. "He works with many poisons. We don't care. Only newcomers eat there, anyway."

Chewie roared.

Zeen laughed. "No, Chewbacca, we haven't got rid of the real food. It's two caverns back."

Han glanced at his old friend. Chewie looked as if he were about to gnaw the furniture. "I think we'd better go there first."

"I think we'd better tend to your wound first," Blue said with a suggestive leer.

"Lay off, Blue," Han said.

"Testy, testy." She moved ahead of them, leading the group into a thin passage that wound around Cavern 2 and led directly to Cavern 3. "You were a lot more fun when you were younger, Han."

"You weren't interested when I was younger, Blue."

"You were so naive, untested, good-hearted. I like a man with a bit more experience, Han."

"And a wife," Zeen said.

"That's not true," Blue said.

"All right, then," Zeen said, "you prefer men who have other attachments."

"She's a smuggler of the heart," Kid said.

"Cute, boys," she said as she ducked through the opening in Cavern 3. Han followed her. The cavern smelled of roasting meat, garlic, and onions overlaid with Wookiee warm won-wons and Sullustan stew. The cavern was humid. The walls were coated with liquid and an extra layer or two of blaster resistance.

"I don't remember this place," he said.

"It belonged to Boba Fett and five other bounty hunters. Most of Boba Fett's friends died six years ago, and we decided to make it into a gourmet area for those of us who frequent this place," the Kid said.

Han shuddered at the mention of Boba Fett. That little bounty hunter had nearly cost Han his life. He was glad to hear that Fett's associates were dead.

The cavern showed no signs of having once been a bounty-hunter den. Han counted eighteen cooking stations, with several more disappearing down the back. Each station was set up with a booth that suggested the home planet of the cuisine. The Wookiee station, right near the door, was nestled into a fake (at least he hoped it was fake) wroshyr tree. Chewie let out a delighted roar and hurried over to the Wookiee station. Han searched for—and found—the Correllian booth. It looked like something out of Treasure Ship Row, a bright red, green, and purple tent with an equally gaudy Correllian roasting meat on a spit outside. Han didn't recognize her, but she recognized Han. That wasn't a surprise. Most Correllians had heard of him, it seemed. And he didn't like it. He liked to know who he was talking to.

"Slumming, Solo?" she asked as she carved him several slices of meat.

"Dining," he said, holding out his hand for the plate. The food smelled wonderful. He hadn't had a Correllian meal in—well, since before the twins were born, at least.

She added some Correllian greens mixed with charbote root, and a scoop of mounder potato rice.

"Sixteen credits," she said.

"Sixteen?!" He almost choked on his saliva. "This would cost half a credit on Correllia."

She grinned. "Been a long time since you've been home, hasn't it, Solo?"

He let the remark pass. "A half-credit," he said again.

"Fifteen," she said.

"Two," he said.

"Ten," she said.

"Five," he said.

"Done."

He paid her, repressing his grin. It had been a long time since he'd bargained for a meal. He took his plate to one of the center tables, where Chewie was already digging into a plate of won-wons. He had five round, greasy won-wons hooked to each claw, and was sliding them down his throat like a delicacy.

Han had had won-wons. They tasted like granite slugs, only slimier. At least won-wons smelled appetizing. He sat next to Chewie—

—then leaped to his feet exclaiming in pain. His wound hurt even worse when he put weight on it.

Blue laughed. She was carrying a plate of Exodeenian pasta. "Told you to put salve on that, Solo."

"Funny, Blue."

"There's an emergency med station over there." She nodded toward the left with her head. "You might want to buy some salve there."

"I'm going to put it on myself," Han said.

She smiled prettily. "I wouldn't suggest otherwise."

Kid came over, carrying a cup of steaming Vayerbok. "What, no longer heart smuggling, Blue?"

She shook her head. "No sport in it. Experience hasn't changed the man. He's still too good-hearted for me."

"I would think a good heart is a valuable heart, Blue," Kid said.

"Probably," Blue said. "But it's also the kind that gets all mushy and romantic. Still treat your wife to candle-light dinners, Solo?"

"Of course," Han said. "The rewards are worth it." He winked, then sauntered to the med station.

A battered medical droid worked the side. It perfunctorily examined Han's wound and said to the burly man behind the counter, "Blaster scorch."

"I could have told him that," Han said.

"No, you couldn't," the droid said. "You're a smuggler. It takes specialized knowledge to have a medical opinion."

"I'm sure it does," Han said. "You weren't a protocol droid in a previous life, were you?"

"Absolutely not," the droid said. "I'm an FX droid. I have never been nor do I want to be a protocol droid. It goes against my programming."

"Obviously," Han said. He moved away from the medical droid and leaned against the counter.

The burly man slapped a jar of salve on it. "Fifty credits."

Han grinned. "You have to have a high demand for blaster salve here. I'll give you five credits."

From under the counter, the burly man pulled out a blaster and aimed at Han's chest. "You want me to make the salve really necessary?"

Han took a startled step backward. "I'll just pay you, how's that?"

"Fifty credits for the prescription," the burly man said.

"And fifty more for the diagnosis," the droid said.

"Nope, no way," Han said. "I *remember* the blaster shot. I didn't need your expert opinion."

The droid turned its silvery face toward the burly man. "It never works," the droid said, sotto voce.

"Timing's off," the burly man said.

Han frowned and yanked his salve off the counter. Then he ducked into the small booth beside the counter and applied the salve, nearly groaning with relief as the jelly relieved the burning.

He came back out, half expecting the burly man to charge him for the use of the booth. But the man didn't.

Han returned to his chair. Chewie was done with his won-wons, and the other smugglers had returned. Someone had picked at Han's mounder potato rice. He didn't care. He'd always hated the stuff.

He sat—gingerly—and ate. The food was delicious, better than anything he'd had in a long time.

Or maybe it was just the atmosphere, the humid cavern, the voices swearing at each other in a hundred different languages.

"You said you were here on Jarril's invite," Kid said.

Han shrugged. "He said there's money to be made."

"The husband of a princess doesn't need money," Blue said.

"He does if her kingdom was blown up."

"That was seventeen years ago, Solo," Zeen said.

"Was it?" Han said. "You apparently don't get news here."

Wynni rumbled.

"All right," Han said. "So you've heard about the bombing on Coruscant."

"The Senate Hall isn't an entire kingdom," Kid said.

"You gonna buy her a new one?" Zeen asked.

"Like you bought Dathomir?" Blue said. She was grinning.

"It worked, Blue."

"Yeah, I heard how well it worked, Solo," she said.

He shoved his plate aside. The meal had been good, but he was full.

"So why are you here, Solo?" Zeen asked.

Han glanced at Chewie. Chewie was sucking the remains of the won-won off one claw as if the conversation didn't concern him at all.

"Jarril disappeared right after the bombing. In fact, he got out of Coruscant's shield at the last moment. That, and the things he said to me about easy money here, made me wonder if he knew more about the attack than he was saying."

Seluss stood on a chair at the far end of the table and

chittered angrily at Han. The Sullustan was shaking his blaster emphatically.

Han put his hand on his own blaster. "I told you to take that weapon away from him," he said to Blue.

"He knows better—"

"Take it."

"Han, he's got a point—"

"Take it."

Seluss chittered louder. With his free paw, Chewbacca slapped the blaster out of Seluss's hand. The blaster skidded across the floor and slammed into the medical droid. It screamed.

Seluss jumped off the chair as if to go after the blaster. Han raised his weapon above table height. "I wouldn't do that, chubby cheeks," Han said. "Sit back down, slow and easy."

"Han, he's just distraught," Blue said.

"And my butt hurts," Han said. He hadn't taken his gaze off Seluss. "Sit down."

Seluss did, looking like a chagrined child.

"Now, in the course of this conversation, I may say things you don't like. You will listen like an adult, and refute what I have to say, like an adult." As he spoke, he realized he was using the same tone he took with the children when they'd been particularly wild. "If you don't like this agreement, if you plan to defend Jarril's honor with firepower only, tell me now so that I can shoot you and be done with it."

"Han, he's an old friend," Blue said.

"Yours, maybe. Not mine."

Seluss stared at him, lips pursed.

"I haven't trusted this twerp since he stole the blueprints for the *Falcon.*"

Seluss chirped indignantly.

"I stand corrected," Han said. "Since the day Lando told me this twerp stole the blueprints for the *Falcon.*

The details don't matter, pal. The fact remains that you're not honest."

"None of us is," Blue said.

Chewie roared.

"Oh, please," Blue said. "Save it for someone who believes it, Chewie."

"Leave him alone," Han said. He leaned forward. "I don't want Seluss shooting at me again. If you can't handle that, spice brain, I suggest you exit the conversation now."

Seluss stood and started for the medical station.

"Without the blaster," Han said.

Seluss chittered at him, but left the cavern.

"You didn't make him happy," Zeen said. "He could tell you more about Jarril than any of us."

"Somehow I doubt that," Han said.

✶ ✶ ✶

Brakiss's last known address was on Msst. Msst was a small planet near the Rim Worlds that had once been a major Imperial stronghold. The Empire had theoretically abandoned the place after the truce at Bakura, but Luke knew for a fact that many Imperials still used Msst for rendezvous.

But not recently.

Luke landed unassisted in the milky-white mist that had given the planet its name. The new X-wing had superb guidance powers, but they didn't make up for the loss of Artoo.

The landing strip on Msst was in one of the few areas where the constant milky whiteness burned off by midday. Although somehow it hadn't this midday. Luke hated to think that this might be what the records meant by "burned-off."

The mist was pale, waist-high, and damp. The dampness sent a chill through him. Most of Artoo would have been lost in the murk. This was where the new X-wings had their biggest failings. Luke flew well enough alone, but landing here, on a planet he had never seen before, without any companionship, seemed wrong. He felt oddly defensive, as if he had no one to watch his back. He hadn't realized how much he counted on Artoo for the little things: wry observations, quick fixes, and companionship.

Cole Fardreamer had better have the old X-wing in tip-top condition when Luke returned.

A group of buildings rose out of the mist, tall and gray and steely. They had an Imperial seal on them, but time had worn the seal down, made it less ridged, which made it less threatening. The buildings looked abandoned, but he couldn't be certain.

He half-hoped he would find Brakiss here, but he had no sense of the man. And by now, he would have. He would have known, through the Force, about the presence of someone else with such a natural talent.

Luke thought often about Brakiss—at odd moments, really—and strangely, at times when he thought about Ben. Ben had had a wistfulness, a touch of regret, to him when he spoke of Darth Vader, as if Ben had a certain responsibility in losing Anakin Skywalker to the dark side of the Force.

I don't want to lose you the way I lost Vader.

Those words had reverberated for Luke as Brakiss ran to his ship, as he escaped Yavin 4, as he tried to flee himself.

I was amazed how strongly the Force was with him. I took it upon myself to train him as a Jedi. I thought that I could instruct him as well as Yoda.

I was wrong.

The chill Luke felt echoed the frigid cold he had felt on Yavin 4 when all those voices were silenced. It mirrored the cold he had felt in the destroyed Senate Hall when he felt the taint of Brakiss's presence.

Luke had tried to bring Brakiss into the Jedi way. He had tried to turn him away from the dark side, thinking that once Brakiss saw the good in himself, he would understand that being a Jedi was so much better.

I was wrong.

Instead, Brakiss had fled, and early reports showed he fled here, to the officers who had sent him to infiltrate the Jedi Academy. Luke hoped to find some trace of Brakiss on Msst. He had actually hoped that Brakiss had gone on to live a quiet life, much as Obi-Wan had in his years on Tatooine, guarding Luke Skywalker.

But Luke got no sense of Brakiss at all.

Although something on Msst could be dampening Luke's Force abilities, much as the ysalamiri did on Mrykr. But Luke had felt a physical effect from the ysalamiri, and he felt none here.

None at all.

Except the cold, damp mist.

And that, in itself, was odd.

His files on Msst had shown that the Empire had done its usual planetary abuse on Msst. They had ripped out essential plant life, made the natives work in the crystal swamps, and had a large colony of slave laborers constantly building buildings that were not needed. But he had no records of them destroying the local wildlife.

Which meant that something else was keeping the wildlife at bay.

And that something else had to be him.

He touched his lightsaber, then glanced at the X-wing. Its upper-level wings were visible above the mist. It looked undisturbed.

What he needed was the emergency kit. It had a fog light, and some rations. Those would carry him to the buildings.

He turned—

—as large pink bubbles floated out of the mist in front of the wing. The bubbles had no faces. Long strands of floating pinkness descended from the base of the bubbles. The bubbles didn't seem to notice him. They bumped against his X-wing, like hands feeling in the darkness.

Luke remained motionless. If they were sentient creatures, they would have some way of reacting to stimuli. The pink strands were a clue, as was the bubbles' bumping behavior. They probably responded to movement. If they responded to heat, they would have found him first, not the X-wing.

But the X-wing hadn't moved in quite some time. Either they had been coming for it since it landed, or something else about it attracted them.

Its energy stores?

He couldn't tell. But he couldn't let them keep bumping it. The X-wing was his only way off the planet.

He gripped his lightsaber tightly in his right hand and started toward the bubbles.

With a large sucking sound, the mist around him disappeared. A bubble three times the size of the X-wing rose from the ground to hover over Luke, its pink strands stinging him, sending rivulets of pain through him. His body instinctively reacted, forcing him to his knees, his arms wrapped around his head.

The attack was eerily quiet. Except for the disappearance of the mist, he had not heard a sound. Even when the little bubbles bumped against the X-wing.

Each touch of the strands left his skin numb. This was not a solution. He kept his head protected, but shifted position so that he could peer through his arms. Above him floated the giant bubble. It appeared hollow inside.

The strands continued to stab him, constant coordinated movements designed to numb him inch by painful inch.

The edges of the bubble were jagged, and the strands came from the inside, like strings hanging from the inside of a tent. The jagged edges were—

Teeth! They were teeth!

The bubble stung its prey until it couldn't move, and then raised it into the hollow part of the bubble and chewed.

Luke's lightsaber hummed on with a rush of power. He swung his arm upward, slicing off half a dozen strands. They fell around him like live wires, stinging him each place they touched.

His muscles felt odd, as if he hadn't used them before. But he kept slashing, moving as quickly as his wounded body would let him.

The bubble's only reaction was to sting him harder. Each touch of a living strand sent more pain into him. He jolted. His body was cold and burning at the same time. He could barely get his breath.

But he concentrated all of his energy into his arm, into swinging the lightsaber. More strands fell around him, slapping the hard ground in the eerie quiet.

The gaping mouth got closer. Its breath was chill and white—the source of the mist. It accented the cold he felt, made the numbness spread. It was all he could do to keep moving, keep fighting. His shoulder ached, his hand barely closed, and he had no feeling left in his neck and face. He could see the strands stinging him, but he could no longer feel them.

What an odd way to die. Here, alone, no Artoo. No one even knowing—

I feel cold, death. His own voice echoed in his mind, along with the memory of Yoda's.

That place . . . is strong with the dark side of the Force. . . . Your weapons . . . you will not need them.

And little Anakin's:

We made the room hot.

Luke envisioned all the heat within him flowing upward and out, into the center of the bubble creature. The creature started to float away, but Luke sent more warmth, and more.

Then, with a great, ear-deafening pop, the creature exploded, followed by a dozen other pops as the little bubbles exploded as well.

Pink globs rained around him, sizzling as they hit the ground. Some hit him, making the numbness complete. He tried to build a shield around himself with the Force, but it was too late.

His body collapsed onto a pile of pink stuff. He watched, horrified, as the pink goo ate into his flight uniform, and headed for his precious, frozen skin.

Fifteen

Leia sprawled on the center of her bed, flimsies spread before her. She wore an old pair of fighting pants, and one of Han's shirts. Her hair was loose except for two braids in front to keep it from falling in her eyes.

The bed, a large, soft mattress, piled high with pillows and blankets, was the safest place in their quarters. She and Han spent much time in the chamber, and she felt his presence strongly there. No one else came into the room without invitation, not even the children.

Sometimes she felt as though it was the only place she could be herself.

On this afternoon, she was there because it was the only place she could be completely alone and undisturbed. She also felt that she needed Han's presence, however superficially, while she studied the hard copies in front of her:

The election results.

From Gno's expression when he had called that morning to let her know they had arrived, she had known the news was bad. She had asked for hard copies, and then retreated to her rooms. If she had remained in her office, she would have been bombarded by well-wishers, worriers, and gloaters. She needed time to process the information on her own.

The elections had been held quickly, just as she had planned. A few places complained that they didn't even have enough time to mobilize the electorate (*Exactly what we want,* Gno had said), and others requested permission to grieve for the lost senators before replacing them. That request was denied. The swifter the business of government moved, the better. Sometimes even funerals were places for politicking of the kind that Leia and her supporters had hoped to avoid.

Leia's hands shook as she sorted through the information before her. She checked the planets represented by critically injured senators first. Most had decided to follow the senators' wishes and allow them to vote by proxy. Those places that hadn't, where it was uncertain whether or not the senators would be able to function in public again, voted in politicians whose records seemed, at least on the surface, to mirror those of the officials they were replacing.

The trouble rested in the hundred other planets whose senators had died. Despite the haste, despite the precautions, only fifteen percent elected someone with the same political cast. On all the rest, former Imperials were voted into office.

Thanks to the bombing, former Imperials held a simple majority in the Senate.

Enough to defeat any proposal that required a voice vote, but not enough to win in each instance.

Just because these people had lived within the Empire didn't mean they would all vote the same.

Or at least, she hoped they wouldn't.

But if they did, she would have to fight for each and every important vote. The Senate had become a political body now, not a place of colleagues.

That night, she would have to respond to the results, and do so in her most diplomatic manner. She couldn't alienate the new representatives by assuming they would oppose her, and she had to reassure her own supporters at the same time.

She put her head down on one of the pillows, crumpling half the flimsies beneath her weight. More and more she longed for the days of the Rebellion, days when most crises found an answer in the unplanned use of a blaster, in the ingenuity of the fight, in the strength of the fleet and the feeling of fighting for truth, goodness, and justice.

She was good at subtlety. Luke had told her that. Han had told her that. She knew it. She had proved it a hundred times.

But she had always been a direct woman. She preferred directness in herself, in her friends. The business of setting aside that directness for the correct thing to say left her exhausted.

Especially now. She could see the future of her government, and directness was not a part of it. As the former Imperials gained power, the Rebels would have to tone down their language for fear of insulting their colleagues. The history of the Rebellion would be changed slightly to show that the leaders of the Empire were the only ones who were corrupt. And with each subtlety came a small lie. The lies would accumulate until the truth was lost.

She sat up and pushed the flimsies away. She wouldn't stand for this. Her speech tonight would be a warning that the policies of the Empire would never replace the policies of the New Republic. She would remind everyone whom they served now, and how important the ideals they had fought for so hard, and so many times, were.

Have you ever thought, sweetheart, that you're the one who's being unfair?

She frowned at Han's imaginary voice, just as she had frowned at him when he said that. The Empire had been their enemy; always would be.

But the Empire was dead.

Then who set off the bomb?

It angered her that the investigations were going more slowly than the elections had. She had hoped that the criminal or criminals would have been brought to justice by now. But it seemed the more she studied this, the more out-of-control she was.

The secret to using your powers, Leia, is to let go of what you know. Let the Force guide you. Luke's voice was as clear as if he were in the room. Several giddy times, in his exercises, she had parried all the attacks of the seeker remote while blinded. She had fought in a number of battles, feeling the Force flow through her and guide her. Luke claimed that she had done the same in diplomatic situations, although she had not felt that way.

Perhaps she would have to do that now.

She pushed herself off the bed. Letting go of those emotions was harder than anything she had tried. Since she was eighteen years old, she had fought the Empire. It had destroyed her home, murdered her beloved father, and given her a twisted birthright from an evil man, a birthright she had tried to cleanse by naming her youngest son after that evil man's good side. She had been tortured, shot, and wounded in explosions. She had lost friends over and over again to the Empire.

And now she was expected to coexist with them.

Someday we must move beyond Rebellion and into true government. Mon Mothma's words. Perhaps Mon Mothma was the person to move them to true government. She had laid the foundations. Her strengths were in persuasive abilities, and in her talent at looking long-term.

Leia rubbed her hands on her torn military pants. She was unwilling to give up any symbol of her Rebellion. The Rebellion had replaced all that had existed before. The Empire had destroyed her home and friends. The Rebellion had given her a new home, new friends. The Empire had murdered her family. The Rebellion had given her a new family.

She couldn't abandon that. She couldn't let go. For if she let go of her hatred for the Empire, she might lose the love she had found in the Rebellion.

Mon Mothma had the ability to set those passions aside.

But that had been part of the reason she had stepped down.

Our leadership must be strong and dynamic. We need someone like you, Leia.

Strong and dynamic. Full of passion.

Full of anger.

Fear, anger, and hatred belonged to the dark side. How many times had Luke told her that?

And where was Luke? Chasing some phantom. Just as Han was. Her children were on Anoth, Winter with them. Whenever Leia needed guidance, the people closest to her were gone.

The house computer bonged.

Her irritation flared. "I told you that I didn't want to be disturbed."

"Just so, madam," said the house computer, using Han's voice but not his syntax. Leia's irritation fled in the face of her amusement. Anakin had been messing with the controls again. "But you have a persistent visitor who claims that he is here with a dire emergency. He threatened to disassemble my circuits if I did not contact you."

"Really?" she said, unable to reconcile the words with the voice. "Does our mysterious visitor have a name?"

"He claims to be one Lando Calrissian." Anakin not

only had tampered with the computer's voice, he also had tampered with its memory. The computer should have recognized Lando's name at least. Good thing the little mechanical whiz wasn't home, or he'd get a hearing from Leia. Of course, he would just blame Jaina, who often wasn't completely blameless in all of this. The difference was that Jaina meticulously covered her tracks.

"Let me see a visual," Leia said.

A holographic projection of a man hovered before her face. He wore his trademark cloak, his dark smuggler's boots, and a flashy satin shirt. His black hair was cut close to his head, but that was the only change Leia saw. Except for the frown not hidden by his carefully trimmed mustache.

"Send him in," she said.

She left the bedroom and went into the living suite. Lando's practiced flirtations were, for the most part, a thing of the past, but Leia scrupulously avoided any situation that would give him an excuse to flirt with her.

The main area of the living suite had been redecorated on Jacen's whim. He had complained that none of the chairs was comfortable—something Han had agreed with—and the two of them scoured the Imperial Palace for more suitable seating. Now none of it matched *(Comfort is more important than looks, Mom),* but it was all well-used. While she waited for Lando, Leia stood in front of the puce couch that Winter mercifully had covered with a white duvet.

He burst through the door and glanced around, almost as if he didn't see her.

"Where's Han?"

No "Hello, Leia, how's the galaxy's most talented princess?"; no "You're looking beautiful today." If she hadn't seen that expression before, she would have thought this Lando was an impostor.

"He's not on Coruscant. Can I help you, Lando?"

Lando shook his head. "We've got to find him, Leia. It's critical."

A frisson of fear ran along her spine. "Tell me, Lando."

"I've been trying to reach you for days."

"The communications array has been overloaded since the bombing."

"I know." Lando put his hands behind his back and paced the room. His expression was as dark as it had been in the carbon-freezing chamber that horrible, horrible day when Han had nearly died, and Lando learned that Vader had betrayed him. "Where's Han?"

"You tell me what the problem is first."

He stopped pacing, and glanced at a painting Jaina had done when she was two. Even though he was staring at it, he didn't seem to be seeing it. "I found a smuggler's ship that belonged to an old colleague of ours. It was abandoned, and had clearly been sabotaged. The smuggler was in it. He'd been slaughtered."

The fear that had run along Leia's back had moved to her stomach.

"He had just come from Coruscant. And when I checked his logs, I found these messages."

Lando gave her a small hand-held computer. She tilted it toward the light.

CARGO DELIVERED. FIREWORKS SPECTACULAR.

SOLO KNOWS. WE CAN COUNT ON HIS INVOLVEMENT.

She handed the computer back, careful not to show her sudden shakiness. "Whose ship did you find this on?"

"A smuggler named Jarril. Did you know him?"

"Han left a few days ago looking for him." Leia sank into the puce couch, letting its softness enfold her. "Why do you think this is an emergency, Lando?"

"Jarril was killed because of this message, and Han is mentioned."

"You think Han might be next?"

"What do you think, Leia?"

"I'm concerned about the 'fireworks.' "

"Han would never be involved in something like that."

She lifted her gaze to Lando's. He thought "fireworks" related to the bomb, then, too. "I know that," she said. "But maybe Jarril didn't."

"Jarril knew Han. Everyone did. His ethics were a subject of bitter complaint among the smugglers. He got more of us into trouble because of his conscience than anyone would like to admit."

"And saved more of you because of it, too." She bit her lower lip while she thought. "Han thought Jarril was connected to the bombing. He was right."

"Han's hunches are usually good."

She nodded. And she hadn't believed him. Jarril, though, was dead. A pawn, nothing more. Like Han? "That second message is really unclear," she said. Subtle, even. "What if it signals the opening of a trap?"

"That's what I figure. Jarril wasn't exactly left in a busy area of space. No one was supposed to see that message. In fact, it had been deleted. If I hadn't known his ship's codes, we wouldn't know this at all."

"Where was it sent?"

"A place called Almania. Have you heard of it?"

Leia shook her head.

"It's on the farthest reaches of the galaxy. It makes Tatooine look close. It's so far out that neither the Empire nor the Rebellion claimed it during the recent conflict."

"You think an Imperial base is there now?" Leia asked.

"I found a stormtrooper helmet on that ship. And some odd Imperial equipment. But this doesn't seem like the Empire's style. They always destroyed first, asked questions later."

"The Empire isn't run by Palpatine anymore. Or Vader." Or Thrawn or any of the other pretenders who had arisen in the last seventeen years. "Someone new might have a new style."

A subtler style. One that blended better with the politics of the present. Destroy the belief in the New Republic. Implant some of your own people in the Senate—and take over, as Palpatine had done all those years before.

Leia shuddered. "We have to reach Han. We have to warn him."

Lando nodded. "You send him a message, if you can. I'll go after him. Where'd he go?"

"Smuggler's Run."

Lando sank into the couch beside her.

"What's the matter, Lando?"

He took a deep breath. "I can't go to the Run. A rather nasty character named Nandreeson has a price on my head."

Leia felt the air leave her body. If Lando couldn't go, she'd have to send someone else. But whom? From Han's description of the Run, no one but a select few people knew how to find it.

Then Lando pushed off the couch, his cape flying behind him. He almost looked as if he were flying. "But that shouldn't stop me, should it?" he said as he reached the door. "What's a few credits between friends?"

"It's not necessary, Lando," she said softly. "We can find someone else."

"Not quickly enough," he said. "And not someone I'd trust to help Han. No. I have to go."

"Lando—"

He held up his hand to stop her from saying any more. "You can't change my mind, Leia," he said. "On Bespin I nearly killed Han through my own greed and recklessness. I'll never forget that."

"You helped rescue Han. You've worked well for the

New Republic. I think you've more than made up for that moment."

"I'll never make up for it, Leia," he said, looking more serious than she had ever seen him. Then he grinned, the wide rogue's grin that someone must have taught every shady character who once visited Smuggler's Run. "But no one can stop me from trying."

✶ ✶ ✶

Cole Fardreamer had never reassembled an old X-wing before. And he certainly had never done it while supervised by an outdated R2 unit. This little unit seemed to have a mind of its own. It bleeped at him every time he moved away from the X-wing. If it had had arms, they would have been crossed in front of its silver-and-blue barrel-like chest.

He had tried to bring in a Kloperian to help, but the little R2 unit had rocked on its wheels and squealed so loudly that Cole rethought the idea. Skywalker had said the R2 unit had been "imprisoned" by the Kloperians. An odd choice of words, but the R2 unit's very human reaction gave them credence.

This part of the bay was empty. Whenever coworkers approached, the R2 unit would whistle. Cole would greet them, and if they were curious about what he was doing, he would report that he was working on a special project. No one questioned him further—except his supervisor, who, upon learning that the project and the X-wing belonged to Luke Skywalker, left Cole alone.

He was glad Skywalker hadn't waited. This job had already taken longer than Cole had expected. The R2 unit had commented on that—at least, Cole thought that was what the R2 unit was giving the raspberry to when Cole mentioned his difficulty with reassembling the X-wing. Cole couldn't really understand the R2 unit, but the unit was so expressive that at times he felt he didn't have to.

What had Skywalker called it? Artoo. As if the designation of type were a nickname. Thinking of the droid as the R2 unit seemed like a mindful. Cole grinned at it. "Now we get to work on the socket for the astromech unit, Artoo."

The droid whistled and rocked, but Cole didn't know if that was in response to Skywalker's nickname for it, or to the action Cole had just outlined. He thought it might be both.

He climbed behind the small cockpit and removed the bolts holding in the upgraded astrogation and hyperdrive computers. Five new computer outlets had been installed in the X-wing. Cole had already removed three. Once he removed these two and set them aside, he would have to reattach the astromech socket and its ejector seat. Then he would have to reinsert the chips the droid still held and reprogram the flight and sensor computers. He had done that sort of thing on Tatooine, trying to build X-wings out of damaged equipment he had managed to find before the Jawas, but he had never been completely successful.

Cole was sprawled on his stomach, leaning into the small bay where the socket used to be. The position made his back ache, and the metal lip of the bay dug into his stomach. He had to hold his arm at an odd angle to work the rotator wrench.

As it hummed, he watched the bolts come out. Imagine him working on Luke Skywalker's X-wing. He had seen Skywalker a few times on Coruscant, but had only heard of him on Tatooine. He was a well-known figure in Anchorhead—and everyone, if the tales could be believed, had been his friend.

Cole had mentally collected stories about Skywalker, half hoping to follow in his footsteps. Somehow he hadn't put it together that Skywalker's heroics were tied to his Jedi talents. Someone pointed that out to Cole, ending his dream.

He shook the bolts off the rotator wrench's magnet and they clattered on the ground. The R2 unit watched them, as it did everything he removed from the ship, as if it were afraid he would again remove something important.

After that, Cole had wandered around Anchorhead, doing odd jobs. It wasn't until someone who had known him—and who thought his loss funny—had taunted him *(Whazzamatta, Fardreamer, can't become a hero by repairing other people's machines?)* that he realized his talents were just as valuable as Skywalker's, only in a different manner. A lot of people in the galaxy, a lot of beings, important beings, had no Force capabilities, and yet they contributed all sorts of things to the New Republic.

He had left on the next transport to Coruscant, and offered his services as a mechanic to the government. They had started him with meaningless work, work a droid could have done better, including sorting bolts by size, hoping to drive him away. But he couldn't be driven. And when he showed more expertise in hands-on assembly than their best Kloperian, he was finally allowed to do the kind of work he loved.

The kind of work that, ironically, brought him to Luke Skywalker.

The last bolt rotated out. Cole slipped his fingers under the panel and yanked. He wasn't strong enough to pull it out. He didn't have the proper leverage.

The R2 unit moaned.

Cole tried again. The panel should have slipped out, but it didn't. He climbed off the X-wing and brushed the dirt off his clothes.

The R2 unit bobbed and whistled.

"I'll get back to it," Cole said. "It just doesn't want to come off."

But his response didn't quiet the little creature. It continued to make noise. He watched it with a stunned expression on his face. Maybe its systems were malfunctioning. Maybe—

Then it bumped him aside and approached the X-wing. A small metal arm emerged from its cylindrical body. At the end of the arm was a mechanical claw. The claw attached to the panel, and the R2 unit pulled.

"Hey!" Cole said. The droid could break the panel, the very thing Cole didn't want because then he would have to replace it out of his own salary.

But the droid didn't stop. The panel popped away from the fitting, leaving a five-centimeter gap. Then the droid swiveled its head 180 degrees to face Cole.

The droid jabbered something, clearly trying to communicate.

Cole wondered if Skywalker could understand everything the creature said. Probably. He had the Force to help him.

"Okay, okay," Cole said. "Let me check it out."

He balanced precariously on the platform beside the X-wing—there was barely enough room for him and the R2 unit—and peered behind the panel.

A green-and-blue Imperial insignia stared back at him.

He whistled, and glanced at the droid. It looked at him wisely. No wonder Skywalker valued this little being.

He pried some wires and chips away from the insignia, and went cold. The insignia was part of the new computer system, buried within the internal workings, unseen except by those who assembled the system.

Cole couldn't tell if the device was unique to Skywalker's X-wing or not. It would take some research to find out. Research he would have to do.

Because he recognized the device in the computer system. He had seen it in some of the remains on Tatooine, had watched one of his friends die by switching it on.

The Imperial symbol hid a detonating device of unique capability. The device remained inoperative until a certain command code had been spoken or entered into the attached system. Then, without skipping a beat, the energy polarity in the system would reverse, overload, and the detonator would go off, creating the largest possible explosion with the equipment at hand.

Cole's hands were shaking. Skywalker had been right not to take this X-wing. If he had, he would have died.

Sixteen

"Skin . . . you will . . ."

Luke thought he heard Yoda's voice. He listened very carefully, but the words kept fading in and out.

". . . lucky . . . are . . ."

Just as his consciousness faded in and out. He was warm for the first time in what seemed like forever, but he couldn't feel anything against his skin. It was like floating in zero G, only without the movement. He was stationary and touching nothing. How very, very strange. He had never been without the sense of touch before.

". . . know you . . . I . . ."

His eyelids were closed, but the texture of the darkness had changed. Instead of seeing nothing but blackness, he now saw that light brown color he would see when he closed his eyes in Yavin 4's bright sunlight.

". . . feeling . . ."

Smells, too, were fading in and out. He thought he caught the scent of the meat stew his aunt Beru used to make when ships brought meat into Anchorhead. The meat wasn't all that fresh, so she stewed it for two days and dished it out as if it were as precious as the moisture they farmed.

". . . in time . . ."

The voice had the same qualities as Yoda's, but wasn't his. The same deep, androgynous quality existed, but the twisted syntax that marked Yoda was missing here. The speaker knew the language well. Luke's ears simply weren't working. They kept skipping words like a malfunctioning droid.

He concentrated, reached for the Force, found it, and heightened his senses.

Bubbles.

Sizzling.

Pink goo against his skin.

He forced his eyes open, his heart racing.

A woman in her late seventies looked down at him, her wrinkled features breaking into a smile. She had been beautiful once; still was, if truth be told. Her hair was silver and her eyes were the brightest blue he had seen since—

Since—

The memory failed him.

"Don't worry," she said. "You'll be all right."

Actually he heard her say "don't," "be," and "right" and parsed out the rest by reading her lips.

"Not many people survive the mistmakers, and I've never seen anyone live who was as covered in their slime as you were. It was touch and go for a while there." Her smile softened. "You're lucky I have a bacta tank."

He came fully awake then. The bacta tank was across the room, its water still holding traces of the pink slime. That stuff had to be really potent for it to last in a bacta tank.

The room had other medical equipment from several different cultures. Through an open door, he saw a regular living area, complete with kitchen. Another door led into still another room that he couldn't see.

All of this he noticed without turning his head. He

still could feel nothing around him. With an incredible effort, he twisted his neck slightly and saw that he floated several feet above the bed. Air cushions. He had seen them in Imperial medical centers, but had never really been on one. They were reserved for burn patients who had lost most of their skin.

Luke shuddered. He tried to raise his hand to see if he had any skin left, but the woman shook her head.

"The more you try, the longer it will take you to recover. You can't feel anything because mistmakers numb their victims before eating them. The numbness will wear off soon. An hour, maybe less. Then we can eat. I've been afraid to feed you like this. Didn't know if you'd drown in food or not."

It was an odd way to listen, hearing half the words and deciphering the rest.

"I know you have questions. It's better if you don't say anything." The woman grabbed a chair, pumped its base so that the chair rose to Luke's height, and then she climbed in. "I'll answer what I can."

He blinked, conveying, he hoped, his gratitude.

"You're lucky I heard you land. I was hoping—" She caught herself, shook her head as if she were self-censoring, then said, "Never mind what I was hoping. I came to investigate and saw the mistmakers floating around the ship. I was about to turn around when that mistmaker exploded."

Her eyes widened with the memory. Luke heard the sound, reverberating in his head, the amazing *pop!* that had saved his life.

"Nice work, that," she said. "You'll have to tell me how you did it. Those things are even resistant to blaster fire."

His hearing was slowly coming back. He could make out more words. He also thought he could feel the air currents blowing on his back.

"I ducked. Slime went everywhere. Good thing I was far away, or I might have gotten covered. When I stood again, I saw you."

"Thank you," he whispered, or tried to. His lips didn't work.

"Shush," she said. "I'd've left you there if I weren't already wearing my protective gear. Would've been nothing I could've done. By the time I'd've gotten my gear and come back, you'd've been dead. Luck. That's all it was."

And she was trying very hard not to take any credit. He would ask her about that later.

"Lessee. What else would you want to know?" She frowned and tugged at a silver ring on her right hand. "You've been here the better part of a day, and your X-wing is fine. Some small stains on the hull where the slime hit it. Nothing more."

He cleared his throat. Feeling definitely was coming back. He felt as well as heard the sound.

She shrugged. "And me, I suppose. You'll want to know about me." She waved her left hand at the room. "Stole most of this stuff when the Imperials left. I should've left a long time ago myself, but—" Her pause was too long. That self-editing thing again. "—it's home. No matter how terrible, there's no place like home, right?"

He didn't know. He was glad he didn't have to answer that. Tatooine was home, but he would never live there again. Although he wasn't certain if his answer would have been the same if Aunt Beru and Uncle Owen had lived.

"All this stuff has come in handy," she said. "I can take care of myself, for the most part. Never had a run-in with the mistmakers like yours, though. Never seen anyone else do that and survive."

The air currents were warm. That was what he had

felt as he had first woken up. Because he wasn't wearing anything else. Not pants, not a blanket, nothing. He tried to cover himself, but his hands just flopped beside him.

She laughed. "Don't worry, son. I've seen it all and more. I had to uncover you to get you in the tank. And I thought it might be better if we waited for modesty until we were sure you were healed."

His mouth was dry. Parched, as if he had been in the desert instead of in the mist. He licked his lips. "Water?" he whispered.

This time the word came out. And, he realized, he had feeling in his mouth, of all places.

"Nope." She sounded positively cheerful as she denied him sustenance. "Worst thing you could have until all the feeling comes back."

He licked his lips to ask again, and she waved a hand.

"Trust me on this," she said. "It interacts with the poison the mistmaker put in your system. You don't want any."

Although he did. Desperately, now that he had feeling back in his mouth. He strained his mind, reached through the Force again. Strengthened himself as much as he could.

Pain shot through his toes, up his legs, and into his hips. Feeling, he reminded himself. He was feeling things.

And his lips could move.

"I came here—" he said slowly.

"Oh, I know," she said. "And it wasn't the brightest thing you've done, now is it? When you get your feeling back, you crawl into your X-wing and fly away home. Back to your family. You'll be better off."

"I'm looking for someone." His voice wheezed out of him, like an old man's voice.

"Well, you found someone." She lowered the chair, got off it, and turned up the knobs on the bacta tank.

"Sometimes," she said, as if she were speaking so that he couldn't, "I miss droids. But only sometimes. Won't have them anywhere near me now."

She had said that to provoke him, because in this galaxy, avoiding droids was not only odd, it was difficult. You had to live on a planet as far away as Msst even to attempt it.

"I'm looking for a man who was here when the Empire was."

The pink slime had faded from the tank. She shut off some of the other equipment, then walked into the main room as if he hadn't spoken at all.

Luke sighed and concentrated. Feeling in his back, in his legs, in his face. He worked on his chest and his arms. If he closed his eyes, he could make his hands tingle as if he had slept on them wrong. The tingle spread along his skin into his shoulders.

Slowly, cautiously, he raised his right arm. Except for slime trails that shimmered under the glow panels, his skin looked normal. He knew better than to sit up on an air cushion. He would have to float off or find the switch.

The switch was below him. Using the Force, he turned the knob so that the air cushion died gradually. He landed on the regular cushion and suppressed a scream as pain, sharp as needles, shimmered through his back.

He could stand it. He had to stand it.

He sat up. The pain shifted with the pressure points. He eased his legs off the bed and saw his clothes, stacked neatly in a pile on a nearby chair.

His lightsaber was on top of them.

He dressed. Even the light touch of fabric against his skin caused him agony. But he could endure it. She had said it would only be temporary.

Then he hobbled into the main room.

She was seated on a pile of cushions, her back to the

door. A cup of liquid steamed beside her. The room blazed with light, but none of it was natural. Heavy black sheets blocked the windows, almost as if she didn't want to see outside.

"I can walk," Luke said, his voice breaking like a teenager's. "Does that mean I can drink?"

He had hoped for a laugh. Instead she whirled, her face filled with shock.

"You shouldn't be up," she said.

He managed a small smile. "The pain is an amazing experience, but I assume it will fade soon. I'm not making anything worse, am I?"

She hesitated a moment, then shook her head. Then she sighed and got up. "Sit, Luke Skywalker. Let me make you a meal."

He started at her knowledge of his name. A thousand rationalizations came to mind—she might have probed his X-wing; she might have recognized him from long-ago news holos—but he suspected none of those reasons was right.

"You know why I'm here."

She nodded, her expression miserable. "My son told me you'd come."

This time Luke did sit down, ignoring the pain that shot from his thighs to his chest. She was Brakiss's mother.

And she had saved Luke's life.

"He wasn't a bad boy once, Luke Skywalker. Really he wasn't. He was this bright, wonderful baby. He fairly glowed with life." She stepped into the kitchen, her hands busy as she spoke. It was as if talking about her son made her restless. "Then they came."

"The Empire."

She nodded. "They came into my home, looked at my boy, and they could use him. Him. A baby. And they took him from me."

Luke stood, about to go comfort her, when she started moving again.

"They let him come back for visits. But he never smiled after that. Not really. Not the kind that reached his eyes." She turned on the hydroprocessor. It made a quiet whirring sound. "They took something from him." She turned, leaned on the counter, and looked at Luke. "You tried to give it back to him, didn't you? At that academy. You tried to bring my baby back."

Luke was chilled. The Empire had taken Brakiss away as a baby, knowing that he was Force-sensitive. No wonder Brakiss couldn't face himself. The loss of self, of goodness, of warmth, was deeper than Luke could ever have guessed.

"I tried," Luke said. "I failed."

"He came here after that, but he didn't stay." The wrinkles on her face seemed to have grown deeper. "He told them at the Imperial site all that you did, and it ate at him. I'd never seen him have a conscience before. It angered him."

She spoke the last softly. Angering a man like Brakiss could be deadly. "And then they had no more use for him here. So he left. He said he had skills he could sell. I didn't hear from him for a long time after that. Until recently. When he said you would come here, looking for him."

The pain was subsiding. So was the thirst. Luke stood.

"He wants you to find him, Luke Skywalker." She twisted her hands in front of her. "I think you should go home. Forget him. Nothing good can come of this. Whatever was good in my boy died a long, long time ago."

"No," Luke said. "It didn't die. It's just buried real deep." And would be harder to get to than it would be with almost anyone else, because Brakiss's foundation in the dark side was never his choice, as it had been with

Anakin Skywalker. The choice had been made for him, before he even had conscious thought. "You know where he is, don't you?"

She nodded. "He told me. He wants you to come. But you're a nice man, Luke Skywalker. I can't send you there. My son wants to kill you."

"I know," Luke said. "I've been in danger before."

"Not like this," she said. "Oh, Luke Skywalker. Not like this."

✳ ✳ ✳

There were always abandoned sleeping quarters on Skip 1. But they were abandoned for a reason, and the reason was never a good one.

Han shoved the door open for the room he would share with Chewie. Chewie roared.

"Stop complaining, you big furball. There's nothing I can do about the stench." Han put his traveling duffel on the mildewy cot. The greenish-yellow ooze slid down the walls in this chamber and went through a drain in the floor. The main floor was flat and untouched by the ooze.

Blue had assured him that this was the best room available.

If it was the best, he didn't want to see the worst.

Chewbacca growled and moaned, then wailed.

"So sleep on the *Falcon* if it'll make you feel better. You know that's the best way to get beat up and have the ship tossed." Han lifted the blanket. The mildew went all the way down to the mattress. Maybe Chewie's idea about the *Falcon* wasn't a bad one.

Chewie yerled.

"Yeah, I know you've slept on the *Falcon* before. But that was on Skip 8. And do you remember how I found you?"

Chewie shook his shaggy head and mumbled.

"If you could've gotten out of it, you would have done

it long before I showed up. You don't need false bravado with me." Han sighed. "You got your sleeping bag? I wouldn't lie on that mattress otherwise."

Chewie nodded and pulled his bag from his pack. He laid the bag on the mattress and it fell off both sides. Chewie growled softly, but didn't address his remarks to Han. Han ignored him anyway. On principle. One night, maybe two, in this place. Then they could leave.

But he didn't want to stay on the ship, partly because other smugglers believed that a guarded ship was a valuable one, and partly because no one would approach him on the *Falcon.* Now that his presence was known on Skip 1, he might see some interesting visitors.

"Okay, Chewie, let's settle in," Han said. He loudly pulled his bag out of his duffel while Chewie searched beneath the cots for listening devices. He collected three before looking at the walls.

Pitifully.

His fur would get coated with the ooze. Han would have to help him clean it off. Either way, Han would have to touch the stuff.

"All right, you big baby," Han said. He tossed his bag at Chewie, who folded and unfolded it, making the plastic rustle noisily.

Han stood on the nearest cot, half-closed his eyes, and stuck his fingers in the ooze. It felt as disgusting as touching the evil Waru on Crseih Station. The ooze was warm and viscous. He knew it would take days to get the stench off his fingers. As he carefully searched the walls and ceilings, he found four more listening devices, some of them rusted.

He still pulled them free. Then he made Chewie hand him the other three. Chewie mimed stomping on them, but Han shook his head.

He took the devices into the hallway, and threw them into the next room. That way, the devices would get some ambient sound, and Han wouldn't have to search through the ooze again before they left.

He washed his hands in the well down the hall, paying particular attention to his fingernails.

As he went back to the room, he was startled to see the door still open. He pulled his blaster before going inside.

There, Chewie had his bowcaster pointed at Seluss. The little Sullustan had his gloved hands in the air. He was quiet. His wide eyes were shiny with fear, and his big ears were bent forward in defensive position.

"Nice work," Han said to Chewie as he came in and closed the door. "You know, Seluss, it's easier to assassinate someone *after* he's fallen asleep."

Seluss chittered pathetically.

"Yeah, right. I'll believe you're on a peaceful mission when my butt stops hurting." Han kept his gaze on Seluss, and leaned against the door. "Want to tell us why you're here?"

Seluss nodded. His chittering was rapid, and Han hadn't had much use for Sullust since the Battle of Endor. He glanced at Chewie and saw that Chewie wasn't getting it all either.

"I'm not going to kill you until you're finished," Han said. "It's in your best interest to slow down."

The folded flesh above Seluss's mouth wiggled. His lower lip protruded. He continued to speak, but much slower.

Much slower.

This time, Han caught it. Or he thought he did. "Let me get this straight," he said. "Jarril told you to shoot me when I arrived so that everyone would think we're enemies? That way, no one would follow you, and no one would notice that you were talking to me? Do you buy this, Chewie?"

Chewie growled for some time.

"The language is a bit harsh, but his meaning is clear, I think." Han nodded. "It was a stupid idea. Try again, Seluss."

Seluss took a step forward, chittering as he moved. Han's blaster whipped into place, his finger very tempted against the trigger.

"Stay where you are, pal. I'm short-tempered today."

Seluss froze, then raised his hands again. He chittered —slowly—and Han began to listen.

I'm in too deep, Han. Way too deep, Jarril had said.

Seluss was confirming that, in his own panicked way.

"What did you say they're smuggling? Imperial equipment? That ruined junk that the Jawas gathered on Tatooine?" Han frowned. That made no sense, certainly not at the prices Seluss was quoting him. "I don't understand why you and Jarril are complaining when it's making you rich."

Seluss glanced at Chewie.

Chewie shrugged.

"Okay, I agree," Han said. "Not even that kind of money is worth dying for. But how do you know the deaths are connected?"

Seluss chittered fast, then chopped his arm in the air three times. And then he moaned.

"All three of the dead guys had spoken out about this? They didn't have anything else in common?"

Seluss half-growled, a puny sound when compared with Chewie's growl, but a threat nonetheless. Chewie moved in closer, but Han waved him back.

"I'd hope you'd be this worried about me if I didn't come back from that kind of mission, Chewie." Han righted his blaster, made sure his aim was still on Seluss. "I need to think about this."

Seluss had essentially confirmed Jarril's story, but he had added some details. Most of the folks on Smuggler's Run were selling junked-out Imperial equipment at outrageous prices. And, both Jarril and Seluss claimed, some were dying because of it. Han still didn't know how that tied into the bombing on Coruscant, but he knew it did. Somehow.

The fact that Jarril hadn't returned added some veracity too. As well as the stupid plan Seluss had made. Jarril was always doing things like that to mislead others. Seluss had attacked Han so that everyone would think they were enemies, and wouldn't realize they were talking together. It did make a curious kind of sense.

Han lowered his blaster.

Chewie moaned.

"It's okay, Chewie," Han said. "I think we can trust the little guy. For the moment."

Chewie lowered his bowcaster, but kept a tight grip on it all the same.

"What do you think I can do?" Han said.

Seluss chittered softly.

"I think you have a better chance of discovering who's paying for the equipment than I do."

Seluss shook his head, speaking all the time.

"Resources? You have all the resources here. You're the ones dealing with the buyers. Just take it a step further."

Seluss shook his head really hard now, speaking so fast that Han almost lost the thread. Almost.

"All three of them had tried to go beyond the buyers? And all three turned up dead?" He whistled between his teeth. "And Jarril tried to trace the source, too?"

Seluss bowed his head. His chitter was soft, almost hesitant.

"Jarril came to me." Han sighed and lowered the blaster all the way. Now Jarril was missing. Han didn't like the sound of this. If Jarril had died for coming to him, then whoever had killed Jarril would be gunning for Han next. "Wonderful."

Seluss chittered apologetically.

Chewie looked somber. Things were worse than they had known. A lot worse.

"All right," Han said to Seluss. "What's the plan?"

Seluss glanced at Chewie, then at Han. Finally, the Sullustan chittered.

"You don't have a plan?!" Han swung his blaster in disgust. Seluss ducked. Han didn't have his finger on the trigger. He didn't understand the Sullustan's overreaction. "You don't have a plan. No one ever has a plan. How come no one ever has a plan?"

Chewie roared.

Seluss, cowering near the mildewy cots, chittered.

"You thought *I* would have a plan? I just found out about this, pal. Chewie, you make the plan."

Chewie shook his head.

"Great," Han said. "Just great. I come here as a favor to a man who has disappeared and he doesn't even leave me with a plan."

Seluss chittered softly.

"Thanks a lot," Han said. "But somehow I believe this has more to do with Jarril's poor management skills than his faith in my brilliance."

Or maybe it had to do with Jarril's very real fear on the day of the bombing. Maybe Jarril couldn't plan any further ahead.

Seluss was watching Han through gloved hands. Chewie was pretending to check his bowcaster.

"Of course I'll come up with a plan," Han said. "Don't I always?"

Chewie growled.

"I don't guarantee quality, fuzzball. I don't even guarantee it'll work. I just guarantee movement." Han glared at both of them. "And for now, that'll have to be good enough."

Seventeen

Cole backed away from Skywalker's X-wing and hurried to the nearest completed upgrade. The R2 unit was beeping at him, as if it was chastising him for abandoning his post.

"Listen, Artoo," Cole said. "If we're going to work together, then you're going to have to trust me."

Had he just said that to a droid? He shook his head slightly and climbed the work platform to the reconditioned X-wing. Its computer was attached with bolts and he had forgotten his wrench.

Artoo came up behind him, the wrench in his outstretched claw. A few of Cole's other tools hung from Artoo as if he were part of an Artesian space collage.

"Thanks." Cole grinned at the little unit. "Guess I'll have to trust you too."

Artoo beeped in agreement.

Cole removed part of the panel on the reconditioned X-wing, then leaned back on his heels, whistling softly under his breath. This X-wing had a detonator too.

And so did the next reconditioned X-wing, and the next.

Artoo cheebled urgently and Cole nodded. They were

thinking alike. If the reconditioned X-wings had this problem, did the new ones have it too?

That would be a bit more difficult to discover. Cole wasn't authorized to work on the new X-wings. It didn't matter. If he got caught, he would report his findings.

To whom? What if someone in the maintenance bay had authorized these systems? Maybe Skywalker hadn't been so far off when he claimed that his little droid had been imprisoned.

Cole looked at Artoo. Artoo moaned softly.

"Yeah. This is a tough one," Cole said. But before he panicked too much, he would examine the new X-wings. Maybe the problem was only in the reconditioned models.

He stood on the platform and scoured the room, hoping to see a new X-wing. There was only the model in its pristine booth. And since he was working late, he was the only person in the area. The maintenance droids were in the main X-wing assembly area. He hadn't seen any Kloperians, and all the humans had gone off-shift.

Except him.

He hoped.

"Can you stand guard for me, Artoo?"

The little droid beeped twice in a rather offended tone, although how Cole knew the droid was offended was something he didn't want to examine. The beep code was something they had worked out that afternoon, almost unconsciously. Clearly the little droid was used to working with people.

"Okay. Let's go, then."

Cole got them both off the platform and headed toward the new X-wing. He turned back once to check on Artoo and saw the little droid pick up a few more tools, ones that Cole had forgotten he would need. No wonder Skywalker had been upset about leaving the little creature behind. He was valuable.

"Hurry!" Cole hissed.

He went to the display area and punched in the code to open the door. The computer asked his reason for entry. He typed some gobbledygook about a uniform malfunction on all the new X-wings, and the computer let the door slide open. His hands were shaking. He didn't know how long it would take before the guards or some of the supervisors would show up.

If they did, he would just explain the nature of the problem, show them the devices, and hope beyond hope that no one on Coruscant was involved with the remains of the Empire.

Because chances were, that was who would respond to his computer notation first.

Cole slid into the cockpit of the new X-wing. These X-wings were configured a little differently from the older model, the T-65C-A2. In the new model, the T-65D-A1, the new computer system could be reached from the cockpit itself, giving the pilot more maneuverability—and more options—while in space.

Still, it wasn't built for doing maintenance. In fact, the computer was difficult to work on in any position. Cole wedged himself into a corner of the cockpit and detached the light pins. His hands were shaking. He had never done anything he was forbidden to do before.

At least, not on Coruscant. On Tatooine he had occasionally worked on fighters he wasn't supposed to work on, trying to see how they operated. But on Tatooine, he had been learning, and his supervisors had known that. Here he was investigating the very people who had hired him.

The computer panel fell off into his hands. He peered behind it at circuitry more sophisticated than any he had ever seen in an X-wing. Artoo leaned in as best his cylindrical body would allow. A light came on. Cole looked up. Artoo was shining a light attached to his head into the opening behind the computer.

"Thanks," Cole said.

He squinted and looked through the circuitry, careful not to touch anything. For a moment, he thought he would find nothing.

The white and silvery Imperial insignia winked in the light. Cole leaned his head against the metal lip of the computer. These X-wings were designed to blow. Each and every one of them. He didn't want to think about all the ships he had reconditioned, all the X-wings already flying through space, floating bombs, waiting for the pilot to hit the wrong lever, push the wrong button.

He peered up at the little droid. Artoo shut off his light. "Can you find out quickly how many X-wing accidents have happened after ships left Coruscant?" Cole asked.

Artoo beeped an affirmative.

"Let's do it, then," Cole said. He grabbed the edge of the computer, about to replace it, when he heard something crunch.

Artoo eased down onto his wheels. The droid beeped softly, and the sound felt like a warning.

The hair on the back of Cole's neck rose.

"So the notification was right," a deep male voice said. "We have a saboteur. Show yourself."

Artoo moaned. Cole set the edge of the computer down carefully, leaning it against the pilot's seat, making sure the internal workings touched nothing.

"Show yourself!"

He rose slowly, hands up. Half a dozen security guards surrounded him, their blasters pointed at his head.

✷ ✷ ✷

Nandreeson leaned back in his baquor-lined couch. The top half had not been properly slimed. It felt damp and cold against his skin. His legs were warm, though. They were underwater. There the couch was covered in algae. That part, at least, had been tempered right.

He had left Skip 6 for three days to investigate the loss of one of his men in the Outer Rim. When he returned to Smuggler's Run, someone had replaced his old couch with a new one, and had failed to condition it properly. When he was rested, he would check the rest of his quarters to see what other mistakes had been made.

So far things seemed fine. The air was so humid that it was almost visible. Tiny gnats gathered in a cluster, and Eilnian sweet flies swarmed on the far wall. The sweet flies were nearly ripe enough to eat. His mouth burned, just thinking about it.

The lilies had bloomed on top of the pond, and someone had scraped the algae to one side, probably for later conditioning. Bubbles rose in the middle, exploding into the air with the stench of sulfur.

Home. It felt good to be here. In a little while, he would go for a swim through the caverns and see if anyone had disturbed both his egg clusters and his treasure hordes.

First, though, he had business to take care of. He had sent all of his people to their pod beds, except for Iisner. Like Nandreeson, Iisner was a Glottalphib, only his snout was six inches shorter, and his teeth had worn to small nubs. His eyes rested over his snout like small beetles. His small hands floated on top of the water, and his tail was wrapped around the base of the couch. A strand of algae hung from his right nostril, remains of his underwater trip through the pond, making certain no one had poisoned it, bugged it, or rigged it harmfully in any way.

His gills were still opening and closing, as if he couldn't get enough air.

Nandreeson would have to replace him someday soon. Iisner was getting old. His scales were already falling after two or three days without water. He had built a slime pond into his quarters on the *Silver Egg* so that he wouldn't lose too many scales during a long space voyage.

"Word is," Nandreeson said, "Han Solo is on Skip 1." A tiny flame emerged from the left side of his snout. He was hungrier than he had thought.

"Yes," Iisner said. "He has quarters there. Jarril sent him."

"Jarril." Nandreeson dipped his snout into the warm, slick water. That cooled some of the burning. He didn't feel like going to the sweet-fly wall and looking for the ripe ones yet. Maybe, when he swam, he would take a caver egg and eat it raw. "Jarril paid his debt to me last week. Thirty thousand credits. I was not pleased."

"He has come into money, then."

Nandreeson shook the water off his snout. "Everyone has come into money. I have not made a substantial loan in months. Jarril is one of many who have paid me off. I will have to go into another business if this doesn't change."

"Perhaps we should get off the Run," Iisner said. "It's changed too much for my tastes. I don't like rich smugglers. They are no fun."

Nandreeson smiled. "The challenge is gone, I'll admit. And if I knew of a better place to go than the Run, I would. But this place still serves us, for now."

"What about Glottal?" Iisner said.

Nandreeson frowned. His home planet, with its ponds and pads, its fronds and sweet bugs, its dark forests and its sticky, humid air, held a great attraction for him. But on Glottal, he would be one of a thousand rich 'Phibs.

Here, he was the only rich 'Phib, and one of the most powerful crime lords in the galaxy. The second title would mean nothing on Glottal.

"I am not ready to go to Glottal," he said. He would go there when he was going to die. He would spawn, and leave his fortune to the surviving offspring. "No. I need a new business. And a new diversion."

"You could start dealing in Imperial equipment."

Nandreeson swiveled one eye and used it to stare at Iisner. "I prefer credits and glittering treasure. The equipment is a limited market. As soon as the buyer finds what he is searching for, or gets his own factories up and running, this sudden wealth will cease. And a whole group of overextended smugglers will need money again." He smiled. "Perhaps we are jumping too soon at the vagaries of the market. Patience, my boy. Patience is the watchword of the wise."

Iisner slipped deeper in the water and swam to the far side of the pond. The hump of his spine rose above the surface, and scales flaked off into the algae. "You've never struck me as particularly patient," he said from the safety of his new position.

Nandreeson's tongue shot out and scooped a mouthful of gnats. He roasted them with his breath and swallowed, a small, appetizing bite. He would need a large dinner.

"I'm patient," he said. "I'm very patient. And the patience often pays off. Witness Calrissian."

"Calrissian hasn't been near the Run in seventeen years."

Nandreeson swallowed the last gnat. His stomach rumbled. "But he will be here soon."

"You don't know that," Iisner said.

Nandreeson swiveled his other eye. Iisner slipped into the water until only his eyes and the top of his head showed. "I do know that, and although I appreciate your counsel, I do not appreciate your doubts. Calrissian will be here because Solo is here."

Iisner blew water through his nostrils. The piece of algae soared through the air and landed on the moss-covered rocks beside the pond. Then he rose enough to speak. "Solo and Calrissian are not partners. They have never traveled together. Before he married, Solo only traveled with the Wookiee."

"You do not pay attention." Nandreeson sank deeper into the warm water. The back of the poorly conditioned couch gave him a chill. "Since Calrissian lost Cloud City, he and Solo have joined forces during each Imperial threat."

"So?"

"So?" Nandreeson popped a sulfur bubble under the water. It formed several other smaller bubbles that rose to the surface. "So, my dear Iisner, what has changed on the Run?"

Iisner's mouth opened wide enough to swallow a whole shore of lily pads. "The Imperial equipment."

"Precisely," Nandreeson said. "And who in the New Republic knows how to find the Run, besides Solo and his Wookiee?"

"Calrissian." Iisner breathed the word as if it were sacred. "You have a plan, don't you?"

"Of course," Nandreeson said. He smiled, and tongues of flame licked out of the corner of his mouth. "Although, in this case, I may not need one."

Eighteen

Lando slowed the *Lady Luck* at the edge of the asteroid belt that housed Smuggler's Run. If he went any farther, he would be within scanning range. They would know he was nearby. His burst of heroism suddenly seemed like an exercise in stupidity. He had avoided the Run for more than a decade. What made him think he could stroll in there now?

Alone.

All the good intentions in the galaxy wouldn't save him from Nandreeson. And neither would an apology, or a promise to pay the Glottalphib back. What had seemed a point of pride years ago now seemed like pointless posturing. So he had managed to steal a cache from Nandreeson's private storeroom. So he had braved the humid, stinky air, the slimy water, the treacherous lily pads. So he had held his breath for nearly four minutes, and pulled out, in the pocket of his wet suit, enough riches to fill his own stash for years.

The last of the money had disappeared when Vader forced him from Cloud City. Lando's own definition of derring-do had changed since then, as well. It had meant more to him to succeed at the Battle of Endor than it had to best Nandreeson.

Since Lando had made a home among the Rebels, he had learned that his acts of pirate courage meant nothing when compared with Leia, for example, who had lost her home and her family and still managed to go on, without taking a breath. Or when compared with Luke facing evil in himself over and over again.

Or Han, thrusting himself into situations greater than he was, and always emerging victorious.

He might not emerge this time.

Lando stood, and paced through the cockpit. He had brought droids with him, half a dozen, all of various uses. Leia had forced credits on him as well so that he could buy information in the Run.

And he had brought a small arsenal, hidden in the secret smuggling compartments of the *Lady Luck*. The smugglers might find his weapons, and they might not. Lando hadn't gotten where he was without gambling.

He paused, leaned forward, and looked out the cockpit transparisteel at the Run. From this distance, it looked as if an artist had swept a glitter-filled paintbrush across the blackness of space. The asteroids sparkled in the light of a nearby star. Debris formed a milky trail from asteroid to asteroid.

The Run had existed for a long, long time. The entrance was tricky to anyone who didn't know the way. More Imperial ships had been marooned in the debris trail than any others. The Emperor had tried to find the Run several times, thinking he could recruit its denizens. Those ships that didn't slam against rock were blasted out of space.

Smugglers didn't work for anyone except themselves.

The Emperor had never learned that.

Lando knew that, though.

The chill that had followed him since he had first discovered the *Spicy Lady* was more pronounced here. For the fifteenth time, he checked the environmental controls. They were working perfectly.

If he backed out now, and something happened to Han, this incident would burn in his memory worse than losing Han to the carbonite. A man couldn't betray a friend twice. Han, despite the difficulties the two of them had had, would figure out a way into a dangerous situation to save Lando.

Lando had to do the same.

Impressions of the Run rose in him; the dank, smelly chambers in Skip 1, the gambling tables, the constant scams. The duels that had forced him to watch his back, and the friendships that he still had.

Or that he thought he still had. Nandreeson could buy anyone for the right price.

Anyone except Han.

All Lando had to do was find Han, warn him, and get out. The first two might not be difficult. The third would. But Lando's mission would be accomplished, and that was all that mattered.

Still, a man was foolish if he didn't allow himself a back door.

He punched in a coded message, sent it to Mara, and sent a duplicate to Leia, with instructions to forward it to Mara. That way, his back door was assured.

Then he sat back in the pilot's chair, strapped himself in, and aimed the *Lady Luck* at Smuggler's Run. He burned the engines high, giving the ship tremendous speed. As it headed toward the Run, he bent under his console, took his all-purpose laser wrench, and removed the panel. He pulled three chips, pocketed them, and watched as the power to all the ship's vital areas failed.

The *Lady Luck* was disabled, and hurtling toward the Run.

He punched the communications console, and sent

the Run a copy of the *Luck*'s legitimate cargo manifold—a smuggler's equivalent of Mayday.

✱ ✱ ✱

Luke landed the X-wing on a wide metallic strip on the northern face of Telti. Domes rose around, metal domes on a barren, sandblasted landscape. When he had first read about Telti, he had thought it would look like Tatooine, a desert planet, but as he landed he realized he was wrong.

Tatooine was full of life. Creatures lived in the sand. Even the suns had a presence.

But Telti was a moon. It had no atmosphere and no life of its own. The dirt covering the ball floating through space was just that—dirt. And yet the moon was littered with domed buildings and metal landing strips. His computer showed him, as he landed, that a series of tunnels connected each building underground.

He was reaching for his breath mask when the landing strip started to move. He glanced over his shoulder, an old reflex, to see Artoo's reaction.

But Artoo wasn't there.

Luke had never felt more alone. He hadn't spoken to a living being since he had left Brakiss's mother. She had given him directions to Telti, all the while warning him away from her son.

Luke's entire communication with Telti had been computer-to-computer. The metallic moon had even sent his landing coordinates directly into the navigation unit. Luke had tried to reach Brakiss, and on each instance was told that voice communication with the moon was blocked. Purposely.

Visitors seldom came to Telti, and were not welcomed.

Even though that message had been sent, however,

Luke had had no trouble with his own entry. He hadn't really expected it. Brakiss was waiting for him.

Luke wanted to know why.

Something was going on here, something bigger than a failed student-teacher relationship. Brakiss was working for someone—the Empire, probably—and his duty was to lure Luke Skywalker into a trap.

Luke would be lured.

He wouldn't be trapped.

The landing strip continued to move forward, conveyor-belt style, inching slowly toward a nearby building. Luke could lift off at any point. This movement was not part of the trap, but part of Telti's day-to-day operations.

One side of the dome ahead of him rose, flattening against itself like a fan. There were no lights inside, just as there had been no lights on the landing strip.

But Luke could sense a presence.

Brakiss.

Not inside the dome, but on Telti.

Waiting.

If Luke could sense Brakiss, it would only be a matter of moments before Brakiss could sense Luke. If he didn't already know of Luke's arrival.

Then, perhaps, Luke would have some answers.

He certainly hadn't received any when he had called up information on Telti. New Republic sources claimed that Telti was an abandoned mining colony, its wealth completely destroyed by Imperial exploitation. A factory remained. It apparently did some business with the New Republic.

The most information Luke had received on the moon had come from Brakiss's mother. She had said that Brakiss finally had real work. She had been afraid that Luke's presence would destroy any chance for Brakiss's future.

Luke had thought she meant that he might kill Brakiss.

Now he wasn't so sure.

He turned on the X-wing's front running lights. They worked as a spot illuminating the interior of the dome. It was empty, but it looked like a bay big enough to house dozens of ships. Landing platforms were recessed into the floor. Beyond those was an open door.

And no movement. None at all.

The sensation of barrenness continued. Except for Brakiss, Luke felt no other life. No plant life, no animal life. Nothing. Not even insect life.

He breathed deeply, running through a few mental calming exercises he taught at the academy. Clearly his expectations had been different. Clearly he had expected more life here than just Brakiss.

That should have reassured him, but it didn't.

The metal runway pulled the X-wing into the building, and with a loud grinding, the door closed. Luke did not look back. He had made his choice. He would continue with it.

As the door closed, lights came on all through the bay. Some illuminated the platforms from below, others from above. A bank of glow panels lit on the ceiling, and a hissing told him that the atmosphere had changed. He checked his monitors. The air was breathable now.

He pushed up the canopy of the X-wing. The air was warmer than he had expected, and smelled faintly of metal, rust, and grease. The rust surprised him. He would have expected nothing like that.

As he levered himself out, he felt as if he had been in this room before. Then he realized that he had been in one just like it on Anchorhead as a boy, back when Jabba the Hutt had tried a few legitimate businesses. He had sold landspeeders, and Luke had gone with his uncle Owen to buy one.

Jabba's lackeys had put the landspeeders in a large room and placed display lights on them, lights that shone on the clean patches only, and hid the dents and dirt and flaws. Uncle Owen had not bought anything that day, saying that all the speeders had had their ID numbers sanded off. It was years later that Luke realized the speeders had to have been stolen.

Weeks later, Luke and his uncle had returned. Jabba's business was gone. All that remained were the platforms and the lights.

It bothered Luke that no one approached him. A normal droid factory would have sent a sales representative by now.

Brakiss again.

Both he and Luke knew this would be no normal visit.

Before Luke dropped to the metallic floor, he closed the X-wing's canopy and set the safety seals. They wouldn't do much good against a determined saboteur, but they would deter a droid.

Brakiss had other ways of tampering with Luke.

Luke patted his lightsaber, its slight weight a comfort at his hip. He wore only a loose shirt and tight military pants. His cloak remained in the X-wing. He wanted no diversions here, and with this much equipment, a flowing cloak could easily snag on a metallic edge.

His mouth was dry. He had expected a confrontation. He hadn't expected no greeting at all.

But Brakiss was still Empire. He liked games. He always had.

Luke took a deep breath, and headed for the open door. He was probably being watched. Brakiss would note each of Luke's movements, from the patting of the lightsaber to the sealing of the X-wing. He would know that Luke was uneasy in this place.

At the mouth of the door, Luke paused. The door's frame should shield him from any holocams. He reached out through the Force, sending tendrils of inquiry across it, searching for Brakiss.

Brakiss's presence was strong here, but diffuse. Luke couldn't pinpoint it. That didn't surprise him; Brakiss's mother had said Brakiss was expecting Luke. Which meant Brakiss had had time to prepare.

He knew many tricks, some Luke had taught him, others that he might have learned from the Empire. Any gifted Force-sensitive being could scatter his presence through a finite area. The fact that Luke could feel Brakiss at all meant that he was close.

Luke stepped through the door and into the next room. And stopped.

Thousands of golden hands hung from the ceiling. The right hands faced palm-out, the left hands had the knuckles showing. The thumbs all went in the same direction. They gleamed in the light. More hands lay on conveyor belts. All those hands were in partial assembly. Some had open forearms revealing equipment not unlike the equipment in Luke's right wrist. Unattached fingers lay beside the conveyor belts, and golden arm sockets waited attachment to golden shoulders.

Threepio might have started life in a place like this. Somewhere in one of these domed buildings, the domed heads of the R2 units were assembled. Hard to believe such ignoble beginnings might have led to the personalities that had become so important in Luke's life.

The room was eerily silent. The belts were off, the atmosphere controls made no noise, and there was no movement. The hands hung like stalactites, stalactites with a hint of life.

Luke glanced at the ceiling. The arms were resting in metal runners, and were not attached to anything.

His relief was palpable.

"Hello?" he said.

His voice echoed off the metal around him, returning in tiny, tinny sounds to him.

"Hello?"

He had no idea where to go from here. He wouldn't follow the ghosts of the false Brakiss in search of the real one. Brakiss probably wanted to lead him through room after room like this, one filled with legs, another with torsos, to make some kind of point.

A point Luke would only learn when he reached Brakiss himself.

"Hello?" Luke called again. He would remain here, near the open door to his ship, until he got a response.

Even though it felt as if one would never come.

Nineteen

Brakiss tracked Luke four ways: with the surveillance equipment he had installed all over Telti; with the computer system; with a group of specially designed gladiator droids that silently flanked Luke; and with the Force. His Force sense was the most reliable. Luke's presence felt as if someone had tossed a boulder into the calm pond of Brakiss's world. Although Brakiss had known Luke was coming, he still wasn't prepared for the strength of the disturbance.

Brakiss stood in his communication center, in the dome of the protocol-droid building. Experimental droid parts hung from the rounded ceiling: eyes that listened; hands that saw; mouths that grasped. The eyes were his favorites: They didn't need a droid at all. They tracked everything that happened in a room, and they sent all communications forward. They also had the added benefit of spooking most creatures that used their eyes for sight. Brakiss wasn't certain how to use the eyes yet, but he would figure something out.

He was good at this. Telti had brought forth his creative powers. If only Kueller had allowed Brakiss to work the factory without using his Force abilities. Kueller had promised that Brakiss would have nothing more to do with Almania. But Kueller's promises never held, especially with Brakiss. Kueller felt that Force-experienced warriors were rare, and he aimed to use each one in his power. The most talented one he had was Brakiss.

So Brakiss got to lure Skywalker into Kueller's trap.

Brakiss sat. The chair molded to his shape and braced him. On the screens before him, he watched ten Luke Skywalkers shout hello into an empty room. Empty except for the overstock droid hands. Even the mighty Skywalker had looked surprised at that.

He hadn't changed. And he should have. It had been years. Brakiss had heard that Skywalker had almost died on board the *Eye of Palpatine.* Yet he looked the same. His scarred face still had a boyishness, his body was lean and powerful, and he had the same assurance he had always had.

The assurance he had had when he forced Brakiss to face the darkness.

Brakiss swallowed. Even thinking of that moment, alone, with only himself and the evils Skywalker had thrown at him, sent trembling explosive shivers through him. If Brakiss thought about it too much, he felt as if his brain would shatter. Brakiss had run from that test, run as fast as he could, and when he returned to his mother, he found her living in the shadow of the Empire. He had had to report, and he had, on the condition that they let him go.

His information had been valuable enough, and his mind damaged enough, that they had let him go. He had run until Kueller found him, and Kueller had put him together again.

For a price.

Skywalker.

Brakiss leaned forward and flicked the communicator. Kueller answered immediately, forming a small holo image on Brakiss's holopad. This Kueller looked tiny enough for Brakiss to crush with his fist. Even so, the power radiating from the small image made Brakiss slide his chair back.

"He's here," Brakiss said.

Kueller's death mask smiled. "Good. Send him to me."

Brakiss licked his lips. "I was thinking . . . I thought . . . maybe I should kill him. I owe him. He—"

Kueller waved a hand. His skeletal grin grew. "By all means. Kill him."

A chill ran down Brakiss's back. His victory was too easy. "But I thought you said you would have to kill him."

Kueller shrugged. "I doubt you can kill him, but if you do, my response is simple. I will have to kill you."

Kueller spoke with such confidence and calm that Brakiss backed away even farther. "I thought we were working together," Brakiss said.

"We are," Kueller said. "But the person who kills the great Jedi Luke Skywalker becomes the strongest in the galaxy. If you kill Skywalker, you take that honor, and leave me no choice but to take that honor from you."

"But the Emperor wanted Vader to kill Skywalker."

"The Emperor has been dead a long time, Brakiss." Kueller's smile had faded. "It would do you good to remember that."

Brakiss nodded.

"And remember, Brakiss," Kueller said. "I will know if Skywalker dies."

Kueller's image winked out. The air around the pad glowed for a moment, then the strength of Kueller's presence faded as well. Brakiss put his fist over the vanished image and pounded the pad. Pain shot through his palm. He was no match for Kueller yet. But someday he would be.

It would only be a matter of time.

He cupped his fist against his chest and stared at the screens. Skywalker had stopped yelling. He was looking toward the dome and frowning, his lips parted slightly, his eyes glazed like those of a man sensing only with the Force.

Had he felt Kueller's presence?

Nonsense. No one could feel over so great a distance. Not even Skywalker.

Could he?

Brakiss whirled. He snapped his fingers and a protocol droid strode in. This droid, C-9PO, was a newer model that Brakiss had modified for his own needs. The final memory wipe, done two months ago, combined with the language augmentation, made this droid useful in ways that went beyond language.

Skywalker might never learn that.

Then again, he might.

"See-Ninepio," Brakiss said, "we have a guest."

"I know, sir." The droid stood the requisite two meters in front of him, its golden eyes radiant with inner light.

"Bring him to the assembly room, and have him wait for me."

"But sir, guests do not go to the assembly room."

He glared at See-Ninepio. See-Ninepio continued to give him an implacable stare. Some things remained the same in protocol droids no matter how many memory wipes they had.

"This one is not a buyer."

"Then what is he, sir, that I may learn who goes to the assembly room?"

What is he? Brakiss smiled, but the smile had no amusement behind it. Skywalker was impossible to fit into a category that the protocol droid would understand.

"He is a Jedi Master, Ninepio. He is not here on factory business."

"Ah," See-Ninepio said. "Then it is personal. I understand." He turned and minced out of the room. The small feet on the C-9's were not an improvement over the normal-sized feet of the C-1's through C-8's. Not an improvement at all.

He would have to remember that.

But even focusing on the droids was not enough for him. It usually cleared his mind, and it did no longer. Skywalker's presence surrounded him.

The sooner he got Skywalker off Telti, the better.

✶ ✶ ✶

They took the *Millennium Falcon* to Skip 5. Seluss wanted to take one of the Skippers, but Han reminded him that Han was in charge of making the plans.

Han wasn't going to go ten meters without the *Falcon*.

He had decided that he needed to see this outrageous operation for himself. Something felt wrong. Smugglers always moved *valuable* products. Now they were getting paid ten times more than usual for junk—junk any resourceful crime lord could find on dozens of worlds.

The Empire, or what was left of it, was no longer making equipment. The New Republic had seen to that by shutting down each factory it could find. The prototypes and designs were taken and destroyed. If any factories remained, then this crime lord had to be paying them, too, in order to get modern Imperial equipment.

Or was there something about the old stuff? Something different?

Han felt that if he looked at the stuff the smugglers were selling, he might discover it. For the first time in a long time, he missed having Threepio at his side. The Professor could tell him about the differences in Imperial equipment, and if Threepio didn't know, Artoo did.

It felt odd to travel without his resources.

When Han had been a regular at the Run, Skip 5 had been abandoned. The caves of Skip 5, while huge, were lined with sunstone, and the ambient temperature inside was about forty degrees Celsius, unbearable for humans most of the time, deadly for many of the larger species that inhabited the Run. A decade before Han arrived, a gang of human smugglers had lived in the caverns for months. They ended up killing each other in a fight some said was sparked by the heat.

Han had never been to Skip 5. He had only heard about it.

He was unprepared for its size, and for its level of development.

The landing pad in the caverns at the edge of Skip 5 was large enough for six luxury liners to rest comfortably. Han hadn't seen a landing pad that big outside of Coruscant in years. The *Falcon* looked small next to the dozens of freighters that waited, their cargo doors open, for the binary load lifters to finish placing boxes inside. Some of the boxes were as large as the *Falcon*'s cockpit.

Han glanced at Chewie, who moaned in astonishment. Seluss, who had been sitting behind them, chittered excitedly.

"Boxes could carry anything, Seluss," Han said. "I want to see what's inside."

Seluss chittered again.

Han ignored him. He knew that no one would voluntarily open a box for him, especially now that he was perceived as legitimate. But he wanted to see the packing rooms and the work stations. He still didn't entirely believe that smugglers had voluntarily pooled their efforts to supply this mysterious customer. He had a hunch that only a few worked together. The rest made a play at it, and delivered the real goods personally. He would discover who was working Skip 5, and who wasn't. Then he and Chewie would follow the ones who were conspicuously absent. He hoped one of those smugglers owed him an old debt. Then he could solve the mystery of the client without a personal meeting.

"You two stay here," Han said to Chewie. "I'll be back."

Chewie growled.

"We've been through this," Han said. "I'm not going to leave the *Falcon* unguarded here. And I'm not going into the Skip with Seluss alone."

Seluss chirped.

"Just because your explanation's plausible doesn't mean that I should trust you," Han said. He slipped out of the pilot's chair. "If I'm not back soon, Chewie, get out of here."

Chewie roared.

"I mean it, Chewie."

Chewie shook his furry head and moaned.

"Yeah, I know. A life debt," Han said. "So why doesn't that mean you'll listen to me?" He grabbed his blaster. "Protect the *Falcon,* Chewie. I'd rather rely on my own wits than be trapped on Skip 5 forever. Got that?"

Chewie mumbled under his breath, but he turned back to the control panel. Seluss grabbed Han's shirt and chittered.

"Yeah, I know you know what you're looking for, mouse brain," Han said. "That doesn't mean I'm looking for the same thing."

He shook Seluss's hand free and left the cockpit. Chewie already had the ramp down, and Han disembarked.

The heat was so intense it felt as if he had hit a wall. Sweat broke out all over him, plastering his clothes to his body. He wished he had brought water rations, but he didn't want to return to the ship for them.

He wouldn't be gone that long. He could last.

Besides, he'd been in this kind of heat before, weaker and with no protection. The worst time had been on Tatooine when he had hibernation sickness. Blind, in the blazing sun, a battle going on around him. He'd been amazed he had survived that.

Still was, if truth be told.

The deep breath he took stalled in his lungs. He tried again, and then hurried down the ramp.

Smugglers watched him from their cargo bays. Blasters followed him. Two binary load lifters stopped as he went by. Near the droids and the running spacecraft, the heat intensified. And this was a relatively open space. Inside it would be worse.

He slipped through the door and into a narrow corridor. The sunstone walls here were sealed with a coolant cover and the temperature dropped several degrees. Han took the moment to wipe the sweat from his face and to breathe deeply. He also checked his blaster, uncertain how well it would work in the heat.

It checked out fine.

"Plan to use that?"

Han looked up. A slender human with golden curls falling past his shoulder sat on a desk built into the wall. He wore mesh pants and no shirt. His chest was covered with tattoos. His hand rested on the desktop. Han couldn't see the man's fingers. They probably covered a blaster.

"Just making sure it worked in case I needed it," Han said.

"That your ship outside?"

"Yeah." Han kept his tone neutral. He wasn't sure if the man was friend or foe yet.

"Awful small for a cargo ship."

"She's a great freighter," Han said.

"Sure," the man said, his tone full of disbelief.

Han made himself take a breath. "You have a problem with my ship?"

"No," the man said. "It's just this bay is usually used for larger ships. Ancient equipment goes to the other side of Five."

"Well, no one explained the rules to me until now," Han said. "Next time I'll go to the other side."

The man lifted his blaster and rested it sideways on his knee. "There won't be a next time, pal, until you tell me your business."

"A friend sent me here to inspect the cargo. He hired my ship to take his stuff off the Run."

"Your friend got a name?"

Han lowered his blaster into position as well. "Seluss. He's a Sullustan whose partner disappeared on him, with their ship."

"Heard about that," the man said. He still hadn't moved his blaster. But he hadn't moved his finger near the trigger, either. "Been happening a lot lately."

"Smugglers disappearing?"

"Not coming back." The man shrugged. "Guess they make their killing and get out of the business."

"I thought there was no out of this business," Han said.

The man tossed his hair over his shoulder. "Ah, people get out. They retire, they leave. It's normal. Smugglers just like to be romantic. And they hate to think about getting old. It's just not as much fun as it was when they were young. And now that there's some money flowing, well, who can blame them."

"You don't look that old," Han said.

"I'm not retiring, either."

"Then what are you doing here? I've never seen guards on Skip 5 before." Of course, he'd never been on Skip 5 before, but the man didn't have to know that.

"Never said I was a guard." The man slid off the desk.

"Just thought maybe your ship was too close to mine. Wanted to see what you were about before I loaded up."

"Which ship is yours?" Han asked.

"The one you parked beneath."

Han glanced over his shoulder. He had parked beside the only bulk freighter on the landing pad. The freighter dwarfed the other ships, with its square armored build. The *Falcon* had slipped right under the freighter's rear hold. "How'd you get that thing into the Run?"

"I didn't," the man said. His tone didn't invite any more questions. Han didn't need to ask any. Jarril was right; the Run was a different place these days. In the past, no smuggler would have stolen another's vessel. Now, it seemed, that was something to brag about.

Han was happier than ever that he had left Chewie on the *Falcon*.

"So," he said. "You going to let me through here or not?"

The man shrugged. "I never tried to stop you."

"You did a good imitation of it," Han growled, and slipped into the corridor. He was getting rusty. He was so used to Coruscant that he had never once questioned the man's role as guard. Smugglers didn't use guards, unless they were their own. He had to clear his mind, get back into the old habits, the old ways. The new ways might get him killed on the Run.

The corridor wound down in near darkness. The coolant cover also blocked the radiant light of the sunstone. Even so, the air was dry here, unpleasantly so. He missed the sound of dripping water, and he almost missed the stench of Skip 1.

Almost.

His boots scraped along the cover. His hand slipped on his blaster, the sweat on his palms making it difficult to hold anything. Gradually his eyes adjusted. Various-sized footprints messed the sand on the sloping corridor.

Below, he heard the sound of large equipment, and the titter of voices, speaking a language he hadn't heard in a long time. Then the stench drifted up to him, grease, oils, cleaning solvent, and something foul, like a gondar pit.

Jawas.

But it couldn't be. Jawas remained on Tatooine. The only time he knew of Jawas leaving were the ones Luke had encountered on the *Eye of Palpatine,* and those hadn't left by choice.

Maybe these hadn't either.

Han kept his back to the corridor wall, and moved slowly down the slope. Bright light illuminated the far wall, and heat rose, making the stench worse.

Down here, the covers were off the sunstone.

He swallowed, licking his lips to keep them moist. He promised himself one quick look, and then he would return to the *Falcon.* His grip tightened on his blaster. Jawas were not his favorite creatures, even in the best of times.

The sunstone blinded him as he rounded the corner. The heat enveloped him like a lover. He remained in one place until his eyes had a chance to react to the light. Then he crept forward, careful to remain as quiet as he could.

The corridor opened into a large cavern. Its ceiling was several stories high—high enough for the sunstone to mimic the sun—and all the walls from the second story down were coolant-covered. The effect somehow made this cavern, in the center of Skip 5, look like Tatooine.

Parked in the middle of the cavern was a sand crawler. Its wedge-shaped doors were open, and Jawas moved in and out. Their eyes glowed red from beneath their hoods. Their robes were tattered on the bottom, and they kept a continual conversation going as they loaded pieces of stormtrooper uniforms onto the sand crawler. Jawas inside were cleaning the uniforms, and others were repairing droids, making them usable. Buried in the sand were more pieces of stormtrooper uniforms, some blasters, and parts to an Imperial shuttle.

Han forgot his discomfort. He leaned as far forward as he could. He saw shadows of other caverns through the openings, and sand-crawler tracks leading away. After a few moments, a Jawa raised a small hand, gave an order, and the Jawas carried the remaining uniforms on board. They apparently hadn't seen the shuttle pieces. The crawler moved forward on its giant treads, leaving even more tracks. As it rumbled past Han's hiding place, he leaned against the wall so that no one would see him.

As if anyone were looking.

After the Jawas were gone, he crept forward and crouched. The sand was hot, as he had expected it to be. He grabbed a handful, then let it filter through his fingers. He watched the tiny rocks slip away until he saw a bolt in the pile. He shook the sand off the bolt and examined it. Imperial issue, about twenty-five years old. Usually used on cargo ships.

He tossed the bolt aside and dug through the sand, uncovering more and more pieces of equipment, until below, he found more coolant covers.

The sand had been placed here on purpose.

And so, apparently, had the Imperial equipment.

It made no sense.

He remained hunched for a moment, thinking. There was a clue here, and he had had one earlier. An important clue.

The heat was intense on his back. The rumble of another sand crawler made him look up. In the cavern beyond, a different sand crawler was closing its doors.

If Skip 5 was as big as Skip 1, the Jawas could drive through the caverns for days without seeing one another.

They could almost imagine they were on a small, isolated section of Tatooine. And as long as they had equipment to find and repair, they would be happy.

As long as they had a place to trade it.

Or some way of getting paid.

Jawas loved to barter, but they never took many credits. Credits meant little to them. It was the act of scavenging and reselling that made their lives worthwhile. What a great, easy way to get equipment cleaned and repaired at almost no cost. Whoever was behind the setup of this part of the operation was brilliant.

A fishy stench swept over him, and he pulled his hand out of the sand. Between the Jawas and the ooze, his experience on the Run had been one of awful smells. Who could guess what was in this sand? He wasn't sure he wanted to know.

He wiped his hands on his pants, and turned. Chewbacca was standing behind him, back to Han, bowcaster aimed up the corridor.

"I thought I told you to stay at the *Falcon*."

Chewie waved a paw for silence. Han gripped his blaster tighter. Seluss was nowhere to be seen. If Chewie had left that little mouse on the *Falcon*, he would never live it down. Ever.

Finally Chewie put his paw down. He spoke softly in Wookiee, in a series of growls and low moans, his paws moving eloquently as he did. All the while, he kept his gaze on the corridor, as if he expected someone to come through it.

Han listened, his frown growing deeper. Chewie had watched Han disappear, then had seen three men follow him down the corridor. When Chewie had come in, Han was alone.

And that wasn't all. Most of the ships on the loading bay weren't loading. They were *un*loading.

No one unloaded on the Run. It was an unwritten rule. It was also unwise.

"I'm missing something here, Chewie," Han said. "Where's Seluss?"

Chewie nodded toward the corridor.

"He's up there? You gave him a blaster?"

Chewie shrugged, then growled softly.

"You have a point. I would have been very unhappy if you'd left him alone on the *Falcon,*" Han said.

Chewie moaned and wiped a paw over his nose.

"You're going to have to stop complaining about the stench, fuzzball," Han said. "Between the heat and the Jawas—"

"Between the heat and the Jawas what, General Solo?" The voice came from behind him.

Han whirled, blaster out. Six Glottalphibs stood behind him, their big feet buried in the sand. They all stood taller than Chewie. Five of them held swamp stunners on him, the stub-nosed weapons covered with mud and dried algae. Han had been hit with a swamp stunner once, and the pain had been so intense, he never wanted it to happen again.

"You should lower your blaster, General Solo," said the unarmed Glottalphib. Smoke curled out of his snout as he spoke. He was as tall as the others, but his scales were a motley gray-black color instead of the normal yellow-green. His tiny green hands were clasped over his elongated chest. "Else someone might think you were threatening us. You wouldn't threaten us, now, would you, General Solo?"

Han didn't glance over his shoulder, but he knew from experience that Chewie had his bowcaster down and was facing them. Han had never fought six Glottalphibs before. Even with a Wookiee on his side, the odds were poor.

"You have me at a disadvantage," he said. "You seem to know who I am, and I have no idea who you are."

"Nonsense, General Solo. How many Glottalphibs have you encountered in your career?"

"Enough to know that you all look different, pal. And I've never met you." He was stalling; they both knew it. The only Glottalphib of any repute was Nandreeson, who had a stranglehold on Skip 6.

"I rarely make such a serious oversight, General Solo." The Glottalphib smiled, and as it did, a tiny lick of flame emerged from its nostril. "My name is Iisner. I work for Nandreeson. He's heard that the concubine of the great Princess Leia is on the Run, and he would like to meet you."

Han's finger edged toward the trigger. The comment was supposed to make him angry. He knew that. And he was even angrier that it had. "I'm no one's concubine," he said, unable to stop himself.

Chewie growled a warning.

"I'm her husband."

"Ah, yes," the Glottalphib said. "Human customs are so perverse. I have never understood the proprietary needs of your people. Better for the gene pool to leave eggs where any wandering male can fertilize them."

"You didn't pull swamp stunners on me to discuss mating habits." Out of the corner of his eye, Han glanced at the cavern beyond. The sand crawler's door had closed. It would be coming toward him at any moment.

"No, I came to invite you to Skip 6."

"An invitation made with five swamp stunners isn't an invitation," Han said. "It's an order."

The Glottalphib's smile grew. Another lick of flame, longer this time, extended from its right nostril. "I suppose you would see it that way. Our customs differ so much. But we do ask out of kindness and polite interest.

We get so little news of the New Republic. It would be nice to hear some directly from the *husband* of one of the great leaders."

Chewie's growled warning grew louder. This time, Han bit back the angry response. Leia was a great leader.

"Put down the swamp stunners, call off your goons, and maybe I'll come with you."

"Ah, General Solo, I can't make such drastic changes on the strength of a maybe." Flame arced out of the Glottalphib's left nostril. Each fire blast added to the heat in the cavern.

The sand crawler was nearly to the cavern door. The floor was shaking. The Glottalphibs didn't seem to notice.

"Okay," Han said. "Put down the swamp stunners, call off your goons, and Chewie and I will follow you to Skip 6."

"We have no landing pads for conventional ships, General Solo."

"Then maybe Nandreeson should come to me. I have rooms in Skip 1." Han backed up slowly. "Now, if you'll excuse me, I have business to finish."

"Not so quickly, General Solo," the Glottalphib said. "No business is as important as ours."

The sand crawler entered the cavern. The Glottalphib turned toward it, as if it surprised him.

Han pushed against Chewie. "Run!" he said.

They both started up the slope. Blue light from the swamp stunners hit the sunstone walls and radiated heat. Chewie roared. Han pushed Chewie's furry back. Suddenly they were in darkness. Then flames burned the sunstone where they had been standing a moment before.

Han fired back. The blaster fire went wildly, through the opening to the corridor, but hitting wide. Chewie's padded feet were slipping on the sand covering. Han had to keep pushing. The Glottalphibs were getting way too close. Another roar of flame seared the wall next to him, burning off the coolant covers. The air was searing hot.

"This way!"

Han glanced up. One of the coolant covers had been pulled back. The long-haired blond man from the entry was peering out of it.

"Hurry up!" the man said. "We only have a moment."

Chewie roared in protest.

More flames hit the wall beside them. The coolant covers stayed on this time, but radiated red with the intense heat. They would never make it up the corridor, not quickly enough to stay ahead of the flames and the swamp stunners. Han didn't know who this guy was, but anything was better than being Glottalphib fricassee.

"Go, Chewie, go!"

Chewie protested again, and Han shoved him into the open coolant cover. The man pulled Chewie in, and Han crawled in after him, landing in a pile of fragrant Wookiee fur. They were in a narrow crevice, lined with sunstone and extremely bright. The man reached around Han and pulled on the coolant cover.

"Let's get out of here before we get fried alive," the man said.

"You'll get no argument from us, pal," Han said. Together they helped Chewie up. He couldn't stand upright in the crevice. The man hurried through a nearby opening, and Han followed. Chewie crouched and slid in.

Then roared.

He was stuck.

The coolant cover suddenly glowed red. A blast of flame must have hit it. The heat magnified. Han's throat was raw, and his shirt was soaking. He should have gone back for that water.

At least the coolant cover didn't come off.

He put a hand out and pulled on Chewie's furry arm.

"Let him go," the man said. "We've got to get out of here."

"All three of us go or none of us goes," Han said, although he wasn't sure how to make good on the threat. "Crouch lower, Chewie."

Chewie roared again.

"Then tell him to shut up."

"You shut up," Han said to the blond man.

Chewie crouched, but his knees banged the crevice wall.

"Okay," Han said. "I got it. Slide one leg out either side, crouch, and lever yourself out."

Chewie muttered some select Wookiee curses, the graphic ones that Han always pretended to misunderstand, and then did as Han told him. His bowcaster hit the wall, and the sound of ripping fur filled the crevice. But he crouched and slid toward Han, and was suddenly free.

A mat of Wookiee hair stuck to the sunstone crevice walls. Chewie moaned again. A patch of fur was missing from his back.

"Your friend sure whines a lot," the man said. He hadn't moved from his post farther in the crevice.

Chewie growled.

"He's a Wookiee, pal," Han said, "and I wouldn't make him mad."

"I can handle Wookiees."

Han grinned. "Anyone who's said that has never met a Wookiee."

"You want my help or not?" the man said.

"I don't know," Han said. "What do you get out of helping me?"

"Satisfaction, General. Now come on." He slipped through another narrow opening and then ran down a wider hall before Han had a chance to answer. The man knew who Han was.

Had known it all along.

That made Han decidedly uneasy.

Han peered through the crevice. The hall looked nature-made, just like the crevice did. The sunstone was bright.

And hot.

"Think you can make it, Chewie?"

Chewbacca nodded.

"Think we should trust him?"

Chewie shook his head, then moaned.

"You're right. It might take forever for those covers to cool. Then we're here, in the heat. Nothing can be worse than that, right?"

Chewie shook his head, as if he couldn't believe Han had said that. Han couldn't believe it either.

"You go first, furball. That way I can shove you if you get stuck."

And fight off anyone who tried to enter from the coolant side. Han didn't know why Nandreeson was after him, but he wasn't going to wait around to find out.

Chewie maneuvered his way through the second crevice without leaving much fur behind. Han followed. The hall that the man had run down was wide and tall. Chewie could stand upright.

The heat had lessened in the wider space. Han wiped off his face. He was a mess. The man was gone, but his footsteps led down the hall.

As if they had a choice. There were no other openings.

They followed the footsteps, weapons out. Cool air was flowing in from another passage. The man was waiting for them. He was sitting on a pile of unused coolant covers, his blaster on his knee.

"Thought you weren't going to make it," he said.

"Sometimes the enemy we know is less dangerous than the one we don't," Han said.

"So you think you know me." The man smiled.

Han shook his head. "We almost stayed back there to wait until the coolant cover cooled."

"You'd face Nandreeson's boys over me?"

"I don't know what you want," Han said. "Or who you are."

The man held out his hand. "My name's Davis."

"Names mean nothing," Han said. "I don't know you."

"I don't know you either, General. Not really. But I know of you."

"That gives you a distinct advantage."

"You don't trust people, do you? I'm trying to help you."

"That remains to be seen. Where're we going?"

"These passages will take us to a side entrance on the landing pad where your ship is."

"And where Nandreeson's men wait," Han said. "They know I'll be back for the *Falcon.*"

"You propose to leave it?"

"I just don't plan on being predictable." Han let his blaster drop to his side. "Tell me what the Jawas are doing here."

"Now?" Davis asked.

"Now," Han said.

The blond man sighed. Then he holstered his blaster as well. "A bunch of the smugglers brought the Jawas in to clean and repair equipment."

"For free?"

The blond man shook his head. "Jawas never work free. But they do work cheap. It's a lot easier for the smugglers to do it this way than to do the work themselves. Or to hire it out."

"So they leave their equipment in the sand and let the Jawas pick it up, fix it, and sell it back to them?"

"It works," Davis said.

"Depends on your definition of what works," Han said. "Jawas never repair things very well."

"But they do sort the working equipment from the useless stuff, and even that is valuable to the folks around here."

"So who's buying this junk?" Han asked.

"Don't know," Davis said. "And it doesn't pay to ask." He glanced over his shoulder. "I really don't think we should stay here much longer. They've probably killed your Sullustan friend by now, and are searching the corridors for you."

"Seluss can take care of himself," Han said. "And I thought they'd be waiting by my ship."

"There were a lot of them. They might be spreading out."

"How'd you know how many there were?"

"I watched them go in, Solo. I knew they were after something."

"They didn't come down the corridor."

"No, they didn't."

"Then they know the tunnels."

"There are other ways to the sand, Solo, beside one corridor and a warren of tunnels."

Chewie growled agreement.

Han took a deep breath. He hated Skip 5. The heat was unbearable, even in the tunnels. "There's only six of them," he said. "And three of us. I think we can get past them and onto the *Falcon*."

Davis shook his head. "They're Nandreeson's boys. You start firing on them in the loading area, and most of the smugglers nearby are going to shoot you."

Chewie yarled.

"You have a better idea, fuzzball?"

Chewie growled and gestured for a moment.

"Might work," Han said. "It might work."

"What?" Davis asked. He clearly didn't understand Wookiee. For some reason, that relieved Han.

"These tunnels open onto the sand, don't they?"

Davis nodded. He was frowning.

Han smiled. "Great," he said. "It's been a long time since I've done business with a Jawa."

Twenty

At first, Luke didn't see the droid approaching him. The droid's golden form blended into all the gold in the room. The hands reaching down, the unattached fingers, the bent arms scattered everywhere. He heard the droid before he saw it, its feet clanging on the metal floor.

Then it appeared, its eyes glowing in its pointed face. It looked like a droid god emerging from the golden sea, striding with all the power of a leader when actually, all it had was its normality. It was assembled, the others were just parts.

"Jedi Skywalker?" it said as if it already knew the answer. Its voice was modulated on the same frequency as Threepio's, but it lacked the slightly frantic, slightly nervous edge that Threepio always seemed to have. It wasn't the same model as Threepio, either. Luke could see that right away. Its face was narrower, its chin pointed, and its nose more pronounced.

"I am Luke Skywalker," he said.

"You are to come with me."

Luke nodded. He clasped his hands behind his back and followed the droid. The movement felt good. For a moment there, he had felt another presence, one both familiar and unfamiliar at the same time. Almost as if a friend had become someone else. Traces of the friend remained, but the person was different. If Luke were on Yavin 4, he would have taken the time to sift through his feelings, to find the threads of the person he had known. But he hadn't the time, or the peaceful setting. He would have to let his subconscious work on it. His conscious was busy.

Brakiss was nearby.

And Brakiss was frightened.

The droid led Luke past the stalled conveyor belts. It seemed unconcerned about the unattached limbs lying all around it.

"What is this place?" Luke asked.

"This is the protocol hand-and-arm-testing facility. We're working on new hands that will give the fingertips sensitivity and the knuckles greater flexibility. We have made startling innovations in droid technology in the last year, innovations that will serve any function for which a droid can be used." The droid's speech sounded like a spiel, as if it were designed to sell droids to a buyer.

"Do you normally handle sales?" Luke asked.

"Oh, no, I'm just a protocol unit, Jedi Skywalker. I do escort guests through the facility from time to time and have been programmed to answer questions."

"How long has Brakiss been here?"

The droid swiveled its golden head toward Luke. "I don't know, sir. My memory has been wiped many times."

Luke suppressed a shudder. Memory wipes had always seemed a barbaric custom to him. He would lose two good friends if he allowed Artoo and Threepio to be wiped. This droid might have had more of a personality, once.

At least it confirmed that Brakiss was here.

The droid led Luke through a door, and into a room filled with golden legs. None of the feet had been attached. They were sitting on the floor like unused shoes, small poles sticking up for attachment to the ankles. The legs were hanging from the ceiling, much as the arms had, and they had a frighteningly mobile quality to them. It felt as though the legs would go marching off on their own if someone attached the feet.

"This is the leg-and-foot-testing facility for protocol droids," the droid said.

"I can see that," Luke said. "You don't have to give me the regulation speech. Just answer a few questions as we go."

"As you wish, Jedi Skywalker."

Luke ducked beneath a set of low-hanging legs. "How big is this facility?"

"The protocol unit occupies this building, Jedi Skywalker."

"No," he said. He tapped a leg with his finger. It felt cold and hard and lifeless. "The droid-manufacturing plant."

"The plant encompasses the entire moon, Jedi Skywalker. We make each and every type of droid. Is there one you would like to see in particular?"

Luke shook his head. "This part of the factory seems empty."

"We have just received a large order for MD-10's. Most of the units are occupied in the medical-droid centers."

"Tens?" Luke asked. "I've only seen MD5's."

"The fives are an older, less efficient model. MD-6's were used briefly by the Empire. MD-7's through 9's were prototype droids, used only in small sectors. When the MD-10's came about, they revolutionized the medical-droid areas. We manufacture 10's exclusively now."

Again part of the speech. The droid led him through

another door. This opened into a room full of heads. Golden heads with dark eyes. The heads were stacked one on top of the other, like rubble. Their mouths were partly open, as if they were trying to speak.

Or to scream.

A number of the heads were hollow, the backs removed. Chips, droid brains, and on-off switches hung in packs from the ceiling.

"Doesn't this place give you the creeps?"

The droid swiveled its head toward Luke. "Jedi Skywalker, we have made innovations in droids, but none that would give a droid human emotion. You know as well as I that human emotion in a droid would ruin its usefulness."

Luke remembered the arc of Artoo's very expressive scream and Threepio's nervous chatter. He found them extremely useful.

"Besides," the droid continued, "we must all accept where we come from."

That much was true. His own struggle in accepting Darth Vader as his father was a case in point.

He didn't like the subject matter. Or how far he was getting from his X-wing. "Where are you taking me?"

"We are going to the assembly room. It is quite an honor for you to see the room. Most of our guests never do."

Luke wasn't sure if he felt honored or not. He could still sense Brakiss, though. Brakiss was closer, and he was getting his fear under control. Luke couldn't quite tell if the fear was of him, or someone else. Brakiss had never been afraid of him in the past.

"How far is the assembly room?"

"Not far, Jedi Skywalker, but we shall be leaving the public areas. You must not touch anything as you pass it from now on."

Luke nodded. That wouldn't be hard. He almost felt

as if he were walking in a droid graveyard, seeing the skeletal remains of friends long gone.

The droid avoided a main door, and opened a door beside it. Luke hadn't even noticed that door until the droid touched it. The door had blended in with the metallic walls, and some heads were stacked near enough to it to hide the door's knob.

They stepped inside. The lighting was thinner here. The air smelled of hydraulic fluid. The walls were unfinished. Shelves rose from floor to ceiling, holding smaller droid parts, all painted golden for the protocol droids. Fingertips, knuckle joints, chips were all filed according to number and type. As Luke passed a shelf of eyes, they all flickered on. The corridor was suddenly filled with golden light.

"Those are for the newest model protocol droids. They are motion detectors as well, and sensitive to the body heat of sentient life." Despite its memory wipe, the droid seemed to have retained its sense of pride.

"What about life forms with no body heat, like Glottalphibs or Verpine?"

"They will find such a droid useful in detecting outsiders," the droid said.

Luke peered at a shelf of eyes. They appeared to be looking back at him. Their shape was no longer round, but oval. "The eyes are made here?" he asked.

The backs of the eyes moved as he spoke. A small filament flickered with each word. They weren't just motion detectors. They were bugged as well. What an odd property, and one he didn't entirely understand. Why would eyes need to hear? Protocol droids had hearing devices.

"Of course," the droid said. "All parts are made here." It noticed Luke looking at the eyes. "Come along, Jedi Skywalker. We must not be late."

He hadn't known until that moment that they were on any kind of time schedule.

Since the eyes were sensitive to both motion and sound, he couldn't sweep one into his pocket. He would simply have to put it into his memory, and think about it later.

As he and the droid moved beyond the eyes, the glaring lights shut off, leaving only the dim overhangs. The shelves' contents became more and more mysterious as he moved by. Chips with numbers, wires that were color-coded, tiny pieces of metal wire. Nothing as interesting or as unnerving as the eyes.

Eventually, the shelved walls widened. The corridor became a long, narrow room. The shelves rose above a bank of computers. No chairs stood in front of the computers, and the touchpads were well above waist-high. They were designed for someone to operate while standing. Designed for droids.

So far, Luke had not seen a living being in this place, and the only one he felt was Brakiss.

Brakiss was closer now. He had regained control of himself.

The droid walked in tiny, mincing steps. It was easy for Luke to keep up. He asked no more questions, and the droid volunteered no more information. When they reached the end of the room, the droid opened the door.

"I am not allowed to go into the assembly room. Only specialized droids may be near that equipment. Master Brakiss awaits you. I will be here to escort you to your ship when you are finished."

Luke thanked him, which made the protocol droid bob in astonishment. Then Luke stepped through the door.

The assembly room had a three-story opaque dome. Glow panels ran along the dome's supports and reflected off the opaque covering, making the room as bright as daylight. Stacked conveyor belts emerged from the wall, angled in from every direction, and met at a tube in the middle. The tube was clear and large enough to fit a probe droid. Only oversized droids, like a binary load lifter, would not fit inside that tube.

The tube disappeared into the depths of the building. The floor was clear, and Luke could see the droids below, most shut off, all completely assembled, probably awaiting final checks before being sent to fulfill whatever orders were made.

The conveyors were off. The room was silent. Except for Luke's breathing.

And for Brakiss's.

Brakiss stood between two conveyor belts. The size of the room made him look small. He wore a silver uniform and matching silver boots. A silver lightsaber hung from his waist.

Luke had forgotten how stunning Brakiss was. Brakiss's blue eyes pierced anything they looked at. His nose was straight, his skin flawless, and his lips thin. Leia had once called him one of the most handsome men she had ever seen.

She was right.

"*Master* Skywalker." Brakiss's tone held no respect. He stood his ground. If Luke wanted to bridge the distance between them, he would have to do it himself.

"Brakiss." Luke let the calmness of the Force flow through him. "You never completed your training."

"You didn't come all this way to discuss that," Brakiss said.

"Indeed?" Luke clasped his hands behind his back. His lightsaber was a reassuring weight against his hip. "Then what did I come here for?"

"Don't play master-student games with me, Skywalker," Brakiss said. "Just tell me what you want."

"Your mother told me that you were expecting me," Luke said.

"You didn't hurt her, did you?" There was a swift protectiveness in Brakiss that startled Luke. It had not been there before.

"Of course not," Luke said. "Your mother is a good woman, Brakiss. She is concerned for you."

"She's never been concerned for me," Brakiss said, and Luke felt the pain, the ancient pain that had prevented Brakiss from facing himself on Yavin 4. Brakiss blamed his mother for the Empire's use of him as a child. Not the Empire. His mother, who had been unable to prevent his loss.

But Luke had no time for old family arguments. "Were you expecting me, Brakiss?"

"At some point, Skywalker. You never let your students go easily."

"It's been years," Luke said. "Students make their own choices. You aren't the only student I've lost."

"I was the only member of the Empire to best you," Brakiss said, bringing himself to his full height.

Luke glanced around him. The light gave the room an airy, open feel that the protocol-droid section did not have. "This is an Imperial facility, then?"

"No," Brakiss snarled. "It's mine."

"You're no longer with the Empire." Luke smiled. "See, Brakiss? Some good did come from your stay on Yavin 4."

"I'm not with the Empire any longer because the Empire no longer exists," Brakiss said.

"There are still enclaves," Luke said.

Brakiss waved a hand in dismissal. "Powerless groups who cannot let go of the past. I have a new life here, Skywalker. I don't need you."

"I never said you did," Luke said. "But you have a

talent in the Force, Brakiss, a talent that needs nurturing, not the hatred grown on the dark side."

"I no longer use the Force, Skywalker."

"Then why do you still carry a lightsaber?"

Brakiss's hand fell to his side and clutched the saber, then let it go, as if he had just realized what he had been doing. "What do you want, Skywalker?"

Luke took a step forward. The conveyor belts hemmed him in. He could only go toward Brakiss or turn his back on Brakiss. "Two tragedies have happened recently. In the first, millions died all at once. The second was a bombing on Coruscant that killed a number of senators. In both cases, I got a sense of your presence. You're connected somehow, Brakiss. I need to know how."

Brakiss shook his head. "I live here now. I have legitimate work, and I make good money running this facility. I no longer work for the Empire."

"I never said the Empire was involved with those events. I'm not even sure what happened in the first instance. I thought perhaps you could help me."

Brakiss narrowed his eyes. "Why should I help you?"

"Because there's still a spark of good in you, Brakiss, buried beneath all that the Empire taught you. In the end, Darth Vader returned to the light. So could you."

Brakiss's chin trembled. His lips parted, and he took one involuntary step backward. For a moment, Luke could see the young Brakiss, the child Brakiss, the one buried deep beneath years of dark-side training, the one Luke had nearly reached on Yavin 4.

Then the glimpse vanished. Brakiss's face became a mask. It was as if doors had closed to that distant part of himself, as if he were not just walling it off from Luke, but from himself.

With a snarl, Brakiss pulled his lightsaber from his

waist. A bright red flame soared from it. Brakiss ran toward Luke and slashed as he moved.

Luke's lightsaber was in his hand instantly. He parried Brakiss's thrust, smashing Brakiss's lightblade against a nearby conveyor belt. Sparks flew. Brakiss recovered, slashed again, and Luke blocked the hit.

The lightsabers hummed, and clanged as they clashed. Thrust, parry, thrust, parry. Luke matched Brakiss movement for movement. Somewhere in the last few years, Brakiss had gained strength.

Brakiss tried a series of small thrusts, little movements designed to be parried, and then he arched the lightsaber in one great circular movement. Luke didn't move quickly enough. Brakiss's lightsaber seared Luke's shirt, narrowly missing his skin. Luke then matched each movement of Brakiss's.

The assembly room was hot with the sparks from the lightsaber blades. The edges of the conveyor belts glowed with the heat. Luke concentrated on each of Brakiss's movements, deciding to defend, never to attack.

Brakiss swung his lightsaber from left to right, going for Luke's unprotected sides. Luke blocked each attack. The swings got fiercer, the movements sloppier. Brakiss was no match for Luke, but he was a good, strong fighter, and they would both be exhausted before this match ended.

Then Luke felt a blast of fear. He glanced up in surprise. The fear had come from Brakiss, and the fear was not of Luke.

Brakiss stopped attacking and raised his blade, much as Ben had in the belly of the Death Star.

Unlike Vader, Luke shut off his blade. The hum stopped, and the sound of labored breathing echoed in the near-empty room.

"Kill me," Brakiss snapped.

"I have no desire to kill you," Luke said. "I would rather bring you back with me to Yavin 4."

"Kill me, Master Skywalker." All trace of sarcasm was gone from his voice. "Kill me. End it now."

"We all have to face ourselves," Luke said. He extended his left hand. "Come to Yavin 4 with me. I will help you."

Then Brakiss shook his head, as if he were coming out of a deep sleep. "It's too late for me," he said.

"It's never too late."

Brakiss smiled, a wistful look. "It is for me." He swallowed. "I don't belong on Yavin 4. I belong here. I am better off without contact, alone."

"Come with me, Brakiss," Luke said. "You can't be happy here."

"Happy?" Brakiss said. "No. But I am satisfied. I can be creative here. And that is enough." He holstered his lightsaber. "I was paid to get a message to you. That's why you've been following my trail. You're supposed to go to Almania. The answers you want are there."

"Who wants me in Almania?"

Brakiss shivered. The movement was fine, almost invisible, but Luke felt it as well as saw it. Brakiss wasn't afraid of Luke. He was afraid of the person who had sent Luke the message. The person who wanted Luke in Almania.

"If I were you, Master Skywalker," Brakiss said, "I'd go back to Yavin 4. I'd forget about everything else. Turn into Obi-Wan and retire. Leave the fighting to those who are ruthless. They'll win anyway."

Then he turned and walked out of the room.

Luke clipped his lightsaber to his belt and waited, hoping Brakiss would return. But Brakiss didn't. Luke started to follow, and then stopped. He couldn't help Brakiss. Not yet. Brakiss had again turned down his offer to return to Yavin 4.

But Brakiss was getting closer. Brakiss would come eventually. The Brakiss who had stopped fighting, the Brakiss who had spoken this last, was the Brakiss Luke was trying to save.

Luke had never seen such defeat in a man. Or perhaps that wasn't defeat speaking. Perhaps Brakiss was giving him a hidden message.

Perhaps not.

Almania. Luke had never heard of it.

But he knew that he had to go there.

Or die trying.

* * *

Brakiss felt the door close behind him. He leaned on the metal wall in the utility tunnel and let himself shake. Never again did he want to be between Skywalker and Kueller.

Never again.

The line was too fine to walk, and Skywalker was adept at reading him. Skywalker had almost convinced him to return to Yavin 4. In the space of a conversation, Brakiss nearly had abandoned everything.

For Skywalker.

Never again.

If Kueller let him, he would renounce the Force. He would go on to make droids, to live the kind of life his mother wanted for him, a quiet life, lived in obscurity.

It was the best he could hope for as long as Kueller and Skywalker were in the universe. He was not as powerful as either of them, and he knew it.

He put a hand over his face. Kueller had wanted him to move with finesse, to make Skywalker want to go to Almania. Instead, Brakiss had warned him away. His feelings got too confused around Skywalker. It was almost as if Skywalker could turn him with a few words, a glance, an idea.

In the end, Darth Vader returned to the light. So could you.

So could you.

But something had compelled Vader away from the dark side. Rumors were that something was Skywalker.

If that was the case, then Skywalker was more powerful than both Kueller and Brakiss gave him credit for. Brakiss had gone into the meeting wanting to kill Skywalker. By the middle of it, he had begged Skywalker to kill him.

How humbling.

How humiliating.

Master Skywalker still controlled him. And he had warned the man away from Almania.

If Skywalker didn't go, what would Kueller say?

What would Kueller do?

Brakiss wasn't sure he wanted to find out.

Twenty-one

Cole let the laser wrench fall from his hands. It landed with a clank in the X-wing. He faced the security guards, none of whom he recognized, and said, "My name is Fardreamer. I work here."

Artoo had inched closer to the X-wing. He moaned.

"Only Kloperians are authorized on the new X-wings," said the Kloperian guard. It was holding three blasters in its tentacles.

"Not exactly true," Cole said. "A number of engineers work on the X-wings. I was supposed to check this one's computer system."

"Who gave the order?" the Kloperian asked.

"Luke Skywalker," Cole said. "President Organa Solo's brother."

The Kloperian clucked. One of the human guards lowered his blaster. "Keep it on the suspect," the Mon Calamari guard said. "We have no proof of his statement."

"Besides, what would a hero of the Rebellion be doing giving engineering orders?" the Kloperian asked.

"When he believes someone is tampering with the equipment, he has the right to give orders," Cole said.

He knew he was on a limb here, but he had to keep going. He had to talk them through this. They didn't look friendly with those blasters trained on him. He almost felt as if he were back on Tatooine in the days of Jabba the Hutt's regime. This didn't feel like Coruscant at all.

"No one has been tampering with the equipment," the Kloperian said.

"Someone has," Cole said. "Look." He nodded down toward the X-wing itself. The Kloperian slithered forward. It peered inside.

"I see nothing."

"Then look again," Cole said. "There's a detonating device with an Imperial insignia inside the guidance computer."

The Mon Calamari guard came over. It trained its huge eyes on the computer. "The Empire never announced its presence like this," it said. "Such a device would have no need of an Imperial insignia unless someone was trying to lead us astray."

"There are rumors that the new senate members, the ones who are former Imperials, were behind the bombing," said another guard. "What if they weren't? What if someone just wanted to make it look that way?"

The Kloperian prodded Cole with one of its blasters. "Who hired you to sabotage this X-wing, human?"

"No one," he said.

"Skywalker?"

"Luke Skywalker is a hero of the New Republic," Cole said. He could feel the shock down to his toes.

"Skywalker is above reproach," the Mon Calamari said. "But he makes a good cover for this boy."

"I don't need a cover," Cole said.

"Stop, boy. The more you say the more trouble you'll be in. We caught you in the act of sabotaging this ship."

"I haven't done anything." His voice was rising. Through the corner of his eye, he saw Artoo slowly move away from him. He had to keep talking, just so that they wouldn't notice Artoo. "I just discovered the problem in a reconditioned X-wing. I was checking to see if the same problem existed in a new X-wing. So I checked the prototype. If I were going to sabotage a ship, don't you think I'd sabotage one someone was going to use?"

"I have no idea what you would do, boy," the Mon Calamari guard said.

"He might have a point," said the slight woman guard beside the Kloperian. She had said nothing until now. "We don't know if he's sabotaging or experimenting."

Artoo had ducked behind one of the other X-wings. Cole had to be careful not to look directly at the little droid.

"That's not for us to discover," the Mon Calamari said. "Let someone with authority make that judgment."

"By all means," Cole said. "Contact General Antilles. He'll want to know about this."

"You know General Antilles?"

"No, but I work for him."

"We'll go to your supervisor," the Kloperian said. "I'm sure he'll inform us that you were not authorized to make these changes."

Artoo had reached the wall. His small arm came out, and he jacked into the computer.

"Luke Skywalker said that if anyone was to question me," Cole said, hoping that his half-truth wasn't obvious, "I was to tell them to contact General Antilles."

The Mon Calamari sighed. "We cannot ignore this."

"We should," the Kloperian said. "It's an obvious lie."

"Hey!" one of the other guards yelled. "What's that droid doing?"

Cole didn't even have a chance to answer. The Kloperian turned all three blasters on Artoo and fired at once. The blasts hit him full-force. Artoo screamed as bright red light surrounded him. The computer panel flared, scorched, and popped as the interior overheated. Artoo's jack shot out and the little droid rocked. Then, when the light faded, he listed to the right side. Tendrils of smoke floated from his head.

"Artoo!" Cole said. "Artoo!"

The droid didn't answer.

He looked at the guards, feeling both an absurd sense of loss, and fear that Skywalker would never trust him again.

"That was the biggest mistake you could have made," Cole said. "You just destroyed Luke Skywalker's favorite droid."

✶ ✶ ✶

The Jawas gave them three blasters and one badly used speeder bike in trade for a handful of credits. They weren't going to bargain at all until Davis spoke up. Then the Jawas launched into a heated discussion. Clearly, they were used to dealing with Davis.

Han wasn't. He still didn't feel as if he could trust the guy. But he had no choice.

For now.

The speeder bike hovered well, but it was sluggish on low. It barely fit into the corridor leading back to the *Falcon.* Chewie kept one paw on the speeder's underside, guiding it through the corridor. None of them planned to mount it until they reached the tiny room where Han had first seen Davis.

Then Han would use the speeder as a diversion so that Chewie could blast his way to the *Falcon.* Han doubted Davis would help them once they reached the loading bay.

So he gave Davis the blaster that looked the most damaged. They had two blasters each, and Chewie had a blaster and his bowcaster. That would give them more firepower than the Glottalphibs, and the speeder would give them surprise.

Han hoped.

Han led the way up the corridor. The corridor had scorch marks from the Glottalphibs, and dried scales littered the floor. Han was glad for his boots; the scales dug into the soles like thorns. He couldn't imagine what would happen if they dug into his foot.

Fortunately, Chewie's fur and the tough pads on the bottoms of his feet prevented any serious injury.

The corridor was too hot and smelled of sulfur and dead fish. Han expected a Glottalphib to emerge at any moment, shoot them, and be done with it. Chewie clearly felt the same. His blaster was ready.

So far, Han had seen no sign of Seluss. The Sullustan must have found a way around the Glottalphibs.

"They've probably left," Davis whispered.

"I doubt it," Han said. Glottalphibs were known for their tenacity. They were also known for their love of glitter. They hadn't been after material in the sand below.

They had been after Han.

And he wanted to know why.

Finally they reached the main corridor. It was dark. The door to the bay was closed.

The dead-fish smell was stronger here.

Chewie moaned.

Han noted his friend's complaint about the smell, and this time had no response. It was a valid concern. A Glottalphib could hide here, and they wouldn't see it. They couldn't surprise it, not with all the noise they had made coming up the corridor.

Suddenly a light flared. Davis held a small glow rod and it filled the room like a fire. The walls were badly scorched, the stone desk shattered, but the three of them were alone.

The Glottalphibs had to be waiting outside the closed door.

Han glanced at Chewie. He was thinking the same thing.

Chewie brought the speeder into the corridor. Han mounted it. The engine rattled beneath the seat. The controls were loose in his hands. Jawas could fix equipment all right, but they weren't great at fine-tuning. He sure hoped this thing went fast. If it didn't, they'd all be dead in a matter of moments.

"Give me a moment to scatter them, Chewie. Then go out firing."

Chewie nodded. Davis said nothing. Chewie put a paw on the door. Han gripped the speeder bike's handles and revved it to low.

"Now, Chewie!" he said.

Chewie pulled the door open and Han turned the speeder bike on high. The engine rumbled between his thighs. Then the bike shot through the door, twice as fast as he had expected.

Immediately he had to dodge a binary load lifter. He pulled upward, and narrowly missed the wing of an outmoded cargo ship. A large wall loomed in front of him, and he realized it was Davis's freighter. He pulled up again and circled as high as the speeder bike would let him.

Over the roar of the engine, he heard voices, shouting, and screaming. The Glottalphibs surrounded the *Falcon.* He dove the speeder down toward them, blaster in one hand, controls in the other, firing as he went.

One Glottalphib shot a mouthful of fire at him, and Han twirled the bike. Ground, ship, sky, ground, ship, sky, and suddenly he was heading toward the Glottalphib again. The 'Phib had to leap out of his way. Another 'Phib fired a blaster, and Han fired back, hitting the

'Phib in the mouth. It fell backward against the *Falcon,* and then Han couldn't see it anymore.

The bike was still moving forward. He weaved between cargo ships, and rode under robotic arms. The front of the bike whapped a box, and the box burst open as he drove under it, showering him in Imperial blaster bolts.

By the time he got the bike turned, he was halfway across the bay and no use to Chewie at all. He couldn't even see Chewie or the *Falcon.*

Han gripped the handle and headed back toward the *Falcon,* flying under wedge-shaped freighter edges, and beneath open cargo doors. The piles of boxes he soared past were impressive. Many were open and revealed stormtrooper helmets, Imperial-style blasters, and other equipment.

Smugglers were firing at him now, and many were shouting that he was crazy. The speeder was sputtering beneath him, but the controls still worked. He was able to dodge, but not for much longer.

The Glottalphibs still surrounded the *Falcon,* but they were all facing him now, both breathing fire at him and shooting blasters. He rose, then dropped, then moved sideways to avoid all the shots. He was shooting too, missing often because he was trying to evade, but occasionally connecting. Blasters reflected off Glottalphib hide; he had been lucky to hit that first 'Phib in the mouth. This would take precision shooting.

Then one Glottalphib fell forward, a bolt from Chewie's bowcaster in its back. Another fell as well, another bolt in it. Davis snuck up behind the Glottalphib near the *Falcon*'s secured door, tapped the 'Phib on the shoulder, and blasted it in the mouth when it turned around.

A shot from behind spun the speeder bike. It looped around the edge of the *Falcon.* Han fought for control. If he didn't get it, the speeder would slam into the *Falcon.* He dropped his blaster and gripped the controls with both hands. He righted the bike, and looked up as it was heading for the door into the caves.

He pulled up and the speeder coughed.

"Come on, you bucket of bolts," he muttered, slamming the engine with the flat of his hand.

The speeder coughed again, and flew above the doors, narrowly missing the rock walls.

He whipped it around, and saw a fifth 'Phib dead at Davis's feet.

Other smugglers were still shooting at him. Chewie was shouting, saying they should all board the *Falcon.* Han aimed the bike toward the *Falcon* when the engine coughed a third time. It sputtered once, and died.

He flew off the speeder, unable to stop his own momentum. He brought his legs up to his chest and wrapped his arms around his head. If he hit wrong, he would die. Simple as that.

The metal ground loomed. He tucked as best he could, then landed, scraping his elbows, the backs of his upper arms, his knees, and his shins on the metal. He was shouting, Chewie was roaring, and blaster bolts zinged around him.

A hand grabbed his armpit and pulled him to his feet. He could hardly move.

"You okay, buddy?" Davis asked.

Han nodded.

The speeder hovered above him, almost laughing at him. Then a blaster bolt hit its engine and the speeder exploded. Flaming parts shot everywhere. Han and Davis ducked under the *Falcon* to prevent getting hit.

It hurt to move.

Chewie brought the ramp down. He stood on it and waved them in. Davis and Han ran up the ramp, blood flowing through the rips in Han's pants.

"What about your ship?" Han asked Davis.

Davis grinned. "Technically it's not my ship yet."

"Great," Han said. They ran inside. Chewie was already bringing the ramp up. Han bolted for the cockpit. Chewie was following.

"What about Seluss?" Han asked.

Chewie roared.

"I don't care. We've got to find him before we go."

"There isn't time," Davis said.

"I'm not leaving him here," Han said.

"Being noble will get you killed."

"It hasn't yet," Han said. "Look for him, Chewie."

But Chewie wasn't responding.

"Davis, find Chewie."

Nothing. Han's hands were on the controls, his scraped elbows burning, his skin on fire. Through the cockpit transparisteel, he could see smugglers heading toward his ship.

"I don't like this, guys," Han said. "Guys?"

He turned. No one was behind him. He left the *Falcon* powering up and went into the corridor. There, the gray-scaled Glottalphib held Chewie and Davis at blaster point. Chewie's fur was smoking, and the edges were singed.

Beside them, on the floor, was Seluss. His tiny hands were bound together, and the rope then wound around him and bound his feet. Tape was inexpertly applied to his muzzle. Beneath it, he chittered. His words were muffled, but audible.

He had said the Sullustan equivalent of "It's not my fault."

Twenty-two

Leia hurried down the hall to the ballroom. She had hastily combed her hair back and changed into a formal pantsuit. She had been practicing with her lightsaber and a remote when the call came in: an urgent meeting of the Inner Council to be held immediately. She had changed and run down the hall at top speed.

Even then she would be late. And Leia Organa Solo was never late.

Meido had called the meeting. He had been elected to the Inner Council a few short days ago by an overwhelming majority of senators. Two other former Imperials had also been elected to fill the vacancies left by the bombing.

Meido was within his rights; any Inner Council member could call a meeting. But junior members never took such authority upon themselves. It was just Not Done. Tradition would have to give way now to the new order, unless Leia got tradition written into the procedures of the Inner Council.

Yet another thing to do. Another thing she didn't have time for.

She skated around a corner and arrived at the ballroom. The doors were closed. She was late. She made herself take a deep breath. Meido had notified her last, and made it impossible for her to be on time. That had thrown her off-balance, as it was intended to do. So had his calling the meeting. But she wouldn't let him see any of her emotions. He wouldn't win on petty political maneuvering.

Leia smoothed her hair back and adjusted her tunic. Then she waited until her breathing was regular. She shoved open the double doors and stepped into the ballroom.

The room was too large for an Inner Council meeting, although it would do well for the full Senate. The Council met on the platform usually reserved for the live musicians. A table had been set up, again without her orders.

Meido sat in her chair at the head of the table. Formal seats had not been assigned here; he never would have been able to do that in the old Chamber. But here he could plead simple misundertanding. And if she sat in a different chair, she acknowledged his rise in power.

She would not do that. Much as she hated these games, she would have to play.

The conversation stopped when she entered. Gno was in his usual position beside her chair. So was C-Gosf. Both looked uneasy. Leia nodded at them, then let her gaze meet Meido's. His eyes sparkled in his crimson face. The white lines on his skin seemed brighter than they ever had before.

"I am aware, Senator Meido," Leia said, "that your people's political customs differ from mine. But we run the Senate, the Inner Council, and the government of the New Republic on the precepts of the Old Republic. It would do you good to learn those precepts."

"I'm afraid I don't understand, President." His voice was smooth, his features guileless.

Leia climbed the stairs leading to the chairs and table. She put one hand on the back of his chair and smiled down at him. "I thought perhaps it was your ignorance that caused this. The Chief of State is always informed first of any meeting. In fact, the custom is that meetings are suggested to her, and she calls them. I'm sure our colleagues are here because they know you do not yet understand tradition."

"I was merely following the bylaws," Meido said.

Leia nodded. "I understand. Now you know for future meetings." She turned to the rest of the Inner Council. "Forgive my tardiness, my friends. I only learned of this meeting a few moments ago." She waited, her hand on the chair. Gno leaned over to Meido.

"Senator, it is easier to run the meeting from the head of the table."

Meido's white lines grew even whiter. He slipped out of the chair and moved to a different spot at the table. Wwebyls and R'yet Coome, the other new Council members, watched him, frowns on their faces.

Leia took her chair regally, nodding once to thank Gno for making a difficult moment easier. "Now that you have called this meeting, Senator, I think we can dispense with the preliminaries, and find out what it is that you consider so urgent."

He clasped his two-fingered hands and put them on the table. He looked so contrite, so humbled, that Leia's stomach did a flip. He was still playing games. "The initial results of our independent investigation are in," he said.

"So soon?" C-Gosf asked. "Our people are still sorting the rubble. They say this is a massive investigation and are unwilling to make any judgments until they have all the facts."

"Their caution is wise," Meido said. "But they lack one piece of information." He leaned forward, his narrow gaze on Leia. "President, where is your husband?"

The discomfort in her stomach grew. Her hands were cold. "He and Chewbacca are following a lead on the bombing."

"But where are they, President?"

She wouldn't be able to dodge this, much as she wanted to. "They went to Smuggler's Run."

"Smuggler's Run?" The edges of Meido's mouth curved upward. Slightly. Ever so slightly. "Your husband used to do business on Smuggler's Run, didn't he?"

"This is not a meeting about Han," Leia said.

"I'm afraid it is, President. Please answer me. Didn't your husband do business on Smuggler's Run?"

She didn't like the direction this was taking. Meido had control, and she was still several steps behind. "Of course he did business on the Run, Senator. Back in the days when you worked for the Empire."

Her words hung in the room. They sounded petty, and maybe they were. But the New Republic had never judged Han for his smuggling, just as they hadn't judged Luke and Leia for their relationship to Vader. Meido, of all people, should want to avoid references to the past.

"I simply lived under the Empire's rule," Meido said. "I never was anyone important. I was never a renowned person, like your husband. A successful smuggler, who, it seems, never left the profession."

The chill in Leia's hands moved up her arms. She knew where this was going. She didn't want it to go in that direction, but she knew. She knew.

"You'd better have a point," C-Gosf said. "General Solo is a hero of the Republic."

"My point is simple," Meido said. "General Solo is behind the bombing of the Senate Hall."

Leia slammed her palms on the table as she stood. "I

was in that Hall. Are you suggesting my husband was trying to kill me?"

Gno grabbed at her sleeve. She shook him off. The room was deadly quiet.

"You weren't seriously injured, President."

"And neither were you, Meido. Is that a crime?"

"The bulk of the blast hit the seats, not the floor. If he knew you'd be there—"

"I'd be quiet now," Gno said. "General Solo is well respected. His affection for his family is extremely well known. He has jeopardized his life for the New Republic more often than anyone else except perhaps President Organa Solo and her brother. Games like this may have been popular in the Empire, but they are not popular here. We work on mutual respect in this Council. *Respect,* Meido, not idle recriminations."

The crimson had almost completely faded from Meido's face. The white lines were blurring together. "I am not making idle accusations. I'm sorry, but I am not. I wish I were."

The softness of his voice caught all of them. Leia could see it. Her supporters had all leaned back in their chairs.

"You said this is a preliminary report," Gno said. "You cannot have proof."

"But I do," Meido said. He looked up at Leia, his eyes pale. "I'm sorry, President. Truly I am."

The thing of it was, she believed him. She believed he was sorry. Perhaps she could feel his regret through the Force or perhaps he was sending it through his body language. She didn't know. Slowly she sat down.

Meido passed out several copies of a single sheet of paper. "My people intercepted this message. I have sent it to your personal computers. You can verify its authenticity through your own systems."

Leia took the paper. Her hand was shaking.

CARGO DELIVERED. FIREWORKS SPECTACULAR.

SOLO KNOWS. WE CAN COUNT ON HIS INVOLVEMENT.

Lando. Lando had betrayed them again. Over the years she had learned to trust him, but that trust had always felt awkward, always slightly misplaced.

No. Lando wouldn't betray Han. What had he said? That he'd never make up for betraying Han. Ever.

The information must have come to Meido some other way.

"There's nothing here that says Han is involved with the bombing," she said.

"This was sent by a ship called the *Spicy Lady* just as it was leaving our section of space on the day of the bombing," Meido said. "The *Spicy Lady* is owned by a smuggler named Jarril, who was seen in Solo's company at the time of the bombing. Shortly after Jarril left, Solo left, ostensibly in search of him."

It looked bad. She had known it looked bad when Lando showed it to her. She should have done something then, but Lando had assured her he had everything under control.

"This isn't proof," Gno said.

"This is suspicious," said R'yet Coome. "I would suggest that we put out a notification for Solo's arrest."

"We can't do that," C-Gosf said. "He's a hero."

"He's a traitor," Meido said.

"He's my husband," Leia said. "He would never do anything to harm me. Someone is trying to set him up." She clasped her shaking hands in her lap. "What else does your report say?"

"We have only preliminary results, President," Meido said. His voice was still gentle, still filled with apology. He accused her own husband of trying to murder her and to destroy everything they all had worked for, and he was acting sorry for her.

"What are those results, Senator?" Leia's voice was cold.

"That there was more than one detonation point."

"We know that," Leia said. "Our results say the same thing. Have you anything besides this message that links my husband to the scene?"

"He was seen with—"

"Have you?"

Gno put his hand on Leia's. She shook him off.

"Have you evidence that he planted a bomb? Have you evidence that Jarril is involved in this bombing? Do you know whether Jarril sent that message or whether someone else did? Can you prove that this isn't some scheme to get my husband or to divide us?"

"Leia," Gno said softly.

"This seems conclusive to me," Meido said.

"It is not conclusive," Leia said. "It is mere speculation. I could devise a message tonight and send it along channels that would make it look as if you planted the bomb. Such things are easy. My husband and I are often targets for strange behavior. I don't think we should make decisions about this until we have the whole truth."

"Leia," Gno said again.

She turned on him so fast that her hair swung loose of its tie. "What?" she asked.

"You can't be objective about this."

"Objective?" Leia was shaking all over with the force of containing her anger. "This man, this former *Imperial*, has just accused my husband of treason, and you think I should be objective?"

"Yes," Gno said. "I do. You're the head of government. We need your calmness."

"Calmness? Calmness? This is not a situation for calmness, Gno. This is exactly what we feared when we brought the Imperials into this body. They're dividing us. Can't you all see the ploy?"

"Leia," Gno said.

Meido's entire face had gone white, except for crimson lines near his eyes and mouth. "I'm sorry, President."

"I will not accept your apology. How dare you—"

"He dares because he is doing the right thing." C-Gosf stood beside Leia and put a delicate arm around her shoulders. "Better he discusses this here, in the Inner Council, than among the other senators. Better that we do what we can to silence these rumors than allow them to spread all over Coruscant. For if we do, General Solo will always be under suspicion, even if we later learn of his innocence."

All of her supporters were siding with Meido. "I'm sorry, President," he said again.

"Han had nothing to do with this," she snapped.

"Leia," Gno said, "I think you need to absent yourself from this discussion. None of us can be objective about the ones we love, no matter how hard we try."

Her heart was pounding. "You believe Meido. You believe him."

"I believe we need to investigate this, Leia." Gno looked away from her. "I'm sorry. But the charge is too serious to let slip."

She looked around the room, at her closest remaining allies in the government. Familiar faces, and three unfamiliar faces, elected after the bombing. Meido, R'yet, and Wwebyls watched her warily. Her friends had sympathetic expressions on their faces. Even those who normally opposed her were looking at her with pity.

"Is this all it takes?" she asked. "An accusation, and a good man is found guilty of a crime he didn't commit? This is not proof, and even if it were, you all know Han. You know he's not capable of this."

"Leia, please, don't make this difficult," Gno said.

"What do you want me to do, Senator?" she asked, using his formal title. "Resign?"

"No," he said. "Absent yourself from any proceedings concerning Han."

"And if I don't?"

Gno looked away from her. C-Gosf squeezed Leia close and then let go. "Think about it, Leia. We'll meet in the morning. By then this news won't be quite as shocking."

"The news isn't shocking," Leia said as she stood. "What's shocking to me is your willingness to believe it."

"Forgive me, President," Meido said. "But whoever planted that bomb had to have access to the Chamber. Very few people had such access. The person who set the bomb will be one we trust. I can guarantee that, just from the circumstances. And I think when you're calm you'll realize that too."

Leia stood slowly, drawing upon all her regal training to stare down Meido. "When I was eighteen years old, I stood beside Grand Moff Tarkin as he gave one order from the depth of space and wiped out Alderaan, my home planet, with a single blast from the Death Star. Until that moment, I had believed the destruction of a planet in an instant was impossible. So don't tell me what has to be true, Meido. I am Force-sensitive. If my husband were to betray me or the Republic, I would know. And so would my brother, who is a Jedi Master. We still don't know what happened in the Hall that day. And until we do, we can't be certain if a friend betrayed us, or if someone tested a new weapon. But if I were you, I would stop making baseless accusations now. Such accusations will only divide us. And now, more than ever, we need to be unified."

She met everyone's gaze individually. Borsk Fey'lya was leaning back in his chair, his eyes bright. Bel Iblis wasn't looking at her. ChoFï was studying his hands.

C-Gosf's whiskers were trembling, and she wouldn't meet Leia's gaze. Gno was the only one of her friends who smiled at her, in an attempt to reassure her.

They would not do any more than they already had. She could count on them to hear the evidence, nothing more.

Leia nodded once. "This meeting is adjourned until tomorrow morning. By then," she said, "I expect answers. Not accusations. Concrete information. Am I clear?"

Leia didn't give them a chance to respond. She turned and walked out of the room, holding herself as proudly as she could. But once she was alone, she let the shaking overtake her.

It had begun. The unity she valued above everything except her family was shattering.

Just as she had known it would.

✶ ✶ ✶

As the *Lady Luck* landed on Skip 1, Lando visually scanned the docking bay for the *Millennium Falcon*. The *Falcon* had features that were obvious even next to the same model Corellian stock light freighter. Lando saw none of those.

Blast Solo. It would be like him to be gone by the time Lando decided to do the heroic thing. Still, Lando wouldn't be able to track him any other way.

He hoped Han was all right.

The *Lady Luck* bounced her way onto the surface. Landing without slave circuitry and only relying on outdated tractor equipment was more of a risk than he had thought it would be. He cursed and resisted the urge to run a check on his ship.

When the ship stabilized, he went to the cargo door and opened it from the inside.

Sinewy Ana Blue stood outside, one hand on one slender hip. She looked good in her shorts and tightly tied shirt, a little older, but no wiser. He grinned. He had always been unable to resist Blue.

"That cargo list was one of the most embarrassing I've ever seen," she said. "It's clear you haven't been doing much with yourself since you left here."

"I don't have time for chitchat, Blue," he said. "I need to fix this baby and get off this mud ball before Nandreeson discovers I'm here."

"It's probably too late," Blue said. "Nandreeson keeps track of all the traffic around the Run. You'd better hope he's busy with something else."

"Yeah, well, I didn't have much of a choice," Lando said. "Most of the circuitry quit. I need some repairs."

Blue shook her head. "You won't get any with that cargo list. Nothing worth trading. What have you got in your hold?"

"Nothing. I've been out of the business a long time."

She grinned. "That's right. You went legit. Just like Solo. So be straight with me, Lando. You here to be with your old buddy?"

"I'm here because the *Luck*'s down." He had to play this cool. "Why're you asking about Han?"

"Because he and that furball of a partner of his showed up a few days back. Figured you wouldn't be long behind."

"And since Solo rejected her, she's hoping for your blood." Kid DXo'ln leaned his balding head around the door. "How ya been, Calrissian?"

"Up and down."

"Yeah, heard about that gas mining on Bespin. Turning legit has its rewards, huh?"

"I lost that little property to the Empire," Lando said. He ducked under the partially open door, and stopped. Two dozen smugglers were at the base, blasters trained on him. He raised an eyebrow. "You folks sure know how to make an old friend feel welcome."

"You're not a friend, Calrissian," Zeen Afit said. He was standing near the Kid at the base of the ramp. "You're here to spy on us."

"For whom?"

"Whoever pays the most," the Kid said.

"Don't accuse him of things when you have no proof," Blue said.

"I just want to get the *Luck* fixed," Lando said, even though his excuse was beginning to sound lame, even to him.

"Yeah?" Zeen said. "You know how it works around here. You don't have enough cargo to trade for bantha dung, let alone a repair."

"I know that," Lando said. "But I have a lot of credits to offer."

"So why didn't you do that up front?" someone yelled from the side.

"Because, in my day, offering money to the Run was the best way to show you didn't belong."

Blue walked up the ramp and slid her arm through his. "It's still that way, Lando," she said. "Don't let them scare you off."

"I'm not," he said. "But I do want to know if I can get repairs."

"It'll cost you," Zeen said. "Ten thousand credits."

"Ten thousand?" Lando pulled Blue closer. "You don't even know what's wrong yet."

"Don't have to," Zeen said. "Figure you want to keep that ship away from Nandreeson's people. The ten thousand is just for protection."

Lando snorted. "As if you can protect me from Nandreeson. How many of his drones have blasters on me right now?"

"None," the Kid said. "Nandreeson's got Skip 6. We don't let him near Skip 1."

"Right," Lando said. "And you guys all work for free now."

"Lando, things have changed," the Kid said.

"Not that much. Don't insult my intelligence just because I've been away, and I won't insult yours. I've got a legitimate problem with my ship or I wouldn't be on the Run. So you find me the best mechanic around here, and I'll guard the *Luck* myself."

"How much you willing to pay?"

"As much as it takes to do this fast," Lando said. Then he frowned at Blue. She seemed convinced, even if no one else did. "What were you saying about Solo?"

"You know he's here, Lando."

"I don't see the *Falcon.*"

"I didn't know you were looking for it."

"How else did he get here?"

"Lando, don't play dumb."

"I'm not playing dumb," he said. "You want to check my ship yourself? I haven't spoken to Han in a long time. I've been trying to set up a legitimate mining operation on Kessel." He pulled away from her and adjusted his cape. "But if Han is here, I would love to see him. Chewie knows as much about the *Lady Luck* as he does the *Falcon.* He could help me repair her, and then I won't bother anyone."

Blue studied him a moment, her magnificent eyes taking in all of him. Then she smiled, slowly, seductively. "You've always been a mystery to me, Lando. I like that in a man."

"You like anything in a man," Zeen said from below. "Don't believe any of that about Han. Lando's here for him. Something's going down."

Lando shook his head. "I know I'm not going to convince you, Zeen, but at least Blue believes me. Just lead me to Han and I'll leave all of you alone."

Zeen blocked the edge of the ramp, his blaster pointed at Lando's heart. "You're not going anywhere, Calrissian. You're wanted by Nandreeson, and you haven't been to the Run in almost twenty years. That makes you an outsider. We don't like outsiders much."

Lando's mouth went dry. "I don't like having a blaster pointed at me either, Zeen. You want to put that aside?"

"No can do, Calrissian."

"Put down the blaster, Zeen," Blue said. "He's my responsibility."

"Fine," Zeen said. "You stay with him on his precious ship, then. And we'll all wait for Solo to return. Then Calrissian can leave us in peace."

"What are you so afraid of me for, Zeen?" Lando asked.

"We don't need Nandreeson's people here," Zeen said.

"Too late." The voice that had spoken before, the one Lando hadn't been able to place, spoke again. A Rek stepped out from the crowd. His slender, whiplike body blended in with the crowd, but his orange eyes blazed like a freighter's running lights. In his rope-thin hands, he held a blaster, trained on Lando. "You're coming with us, Calrissian. Nandreeson will be happy to see you."

Another Rek stepped out from against the wall. Then another, and another, until thirty Reks surrounded the group of smugglers. "Very happy," one of the Reks said. "About two million credits' worth."

"Wow," Blue said. "If I'd known you were worth that much, I'd've turned you in myself."

The sum startled Lando, too. "It was only fifty thousand last I heard."

"Come with us peacefully," the first Rek said, "and I will leave your ship alone."

"What good will that do me?" Lando asked. "I can't use it if I'm dead." He reached for his own blaster, but a rubbery appendage wrapped itself around his wrist. He looked down. Another Rek had twisted its arm around his skin. Its slitted mouth opened in a Rek's version of a smile. This Rek was female; her purple eyes gave away her gender.

"I wouldn't try it, big boy," she said. "You're still worth a million credits to Nandreeson dead."

"All right," Lando said to Blue. She was his only hope now. "No more pretense. I've got to find Han. He's in big trouble."

"I'll say," the female Rek said. "He's going to meet us on Skip 6. I'm sure your reunion will be a happy one."

Blue backed away, holding her hands up. "Sorry, Lando," she said. "I never get involved in Nandreeson's business."

"Some friend you are," Lando said.

"I never said I was a friend," Blue said. "Just an interested party. You never should have come here, Lando."

"Don't I know it," he said.

Twenty-three

Four new languages in the last day. Threepio sat at his computer bay in the Solos' apartments. He had had no duties since the children left, and he was using the time to catch up on the new languages. Two were from recently discovered planets, and two were new droid languages. That made eighteen new droid languages in the last week, or 2.571 languages per day.

The computer bay was near the children's quarters. Threepio sat in the chair because Jaina had once insisted he do so. Anakin had pasted stickers of heroes of the Old Republic onto the bay walls. Threepio had asked him to remove them, but Anakin had "forgotten," a word he often used when he meant that he did not want to.

A tiny icon flashed on the corner of the screen. It was a small R2 unit. Threepio pressed a key with a golden finger and the icon covered the screen. Then he pressed another key and the icon turned into a single blinking message:

EMERGENCY
EMERGENCY
EMERGENCY

There was a small code tagged onto the *y*. Threepio opened the code, and binary covered the screen. The message was from Artoo. He was in the cargo bay with someone named Cole Fardreamer, and they were being accused of sabotage. The message was new, and it kept repeating, over and over.

Threepio pressed two more keys. Artoo was still online. Threepio started to send a message back when the screen went blank. Then nothing.

Artoo was gone.

✳ ✳ ✳

It amazed him how quickly the credits disappeared. Kueller sat at his desk on Almania. The curtains were open, revealing the lights of the city below. The towers of the Je'har were black blotches against the night skyline. Emptiness. Ruins. A sign of Kueller's tremendous power.

But wealth supported power. He would have to strip Pydyr of its treasures and sell them on the open market. His agents were already sending out discreet feelers to the greatest collectors in the galaxy. If he could sell the homes of Pydyr as a set, the gems of Pydyr as another, and the clothing of Pydyr as a third, he would have enough credits to complete Phase 3 of the operation.

Phase 1 was over, and Phase 2 was underway.

Kueller leaned back in his chair. His gloves were on the table beside the five small computer screens. His hands looked pale in the artificial light. A young man's hands. Not the hands of the most powerful man in the galaxy.

Not yet.

But soon. Very soon.

A chime rang softly on his private line. He touched the screen in response. Brakiss's face appeared. His blond hair was tousled, and his eyes looked tormented.

Brakiss had faced Skywalker, then. Kueller knew the signs.

"So," Kueller said, not waiting for Brakiss to speak, "he raised questions in your tormented heart."

Brakiss flinched. If Skywalker could tempt Brakiss, a man who had loved the Empire with all of his twisted heart, he could tempt anyone. Kueller had made the right choice: Destroying Skywalker and all who believed in him was the next step. Kueller would not succeed without doing so.

"Is he your master now, Brakiss?" Kueller asked.

"No!" Brakiss actually backed away from his screen. His image was smaller—Brakiss seemed smaller.

"Then who is your master, Brakiss?"

"No one," Brakiss said. His mouth was a thin line, his eyes full of terror and sadness. "I want out this time, Kueller. I'm done."

Kueller let his death mask smile, even though his own irritation was deep. "What did Skywalker do to you?"

"Nothing," Brakiss said.

"Then why this sudden loss of faith?"

"It's not sudden, Kueller. You wouldn't let me kill him."

"Even though you tried."

Brakiss flinched again.

Kueller leaned forward, knowing the movement would make his death's-head mask fill Brakiss's view-screen. "You tried and you failed, and Skywalker, out of the goodness of his Jedi heart, let you live. And now you are grateful to your old master, and you wonder how anyone could best him, and you are not certain whether anyone *should* best him, am I right, Brakiss?"

"I hate Skywalker," Brakiss said.

Kueller shook his head. "You don't hate Skywalker. You hate the way he makes you feel. You hate yourself, Brakiss. You hate what you've become."

Brakiss raised his chin. "He says I could go back to the academy. He says I could abandon the dark side. He says Vader did."

"Of course Vader did," Kueller said, his voice calm, even though he felt like shredding Brakiss for even listening to Skywalker. "Vader was dying. Skywalker was beside him. The Emperor was gone. Vader had nothing left. He had no power and no hope. He took what Skywalker offered. He had no real choice."

"Skywalker says he did."

"Skywalker was trying to take you into his power. Did he succeed, Brakiss?"

Brakiss crossed his arms. "You can't tell?"

Kueller smiled, glad he had not used the holoprojector. He seemed bigger on the screen, more powerful, and he needed all that power at this moment. "I think Skywalker could have taken you back if he truly wanted to, but he did not. He's not interested in you. You are nothing to him. You aren't even worth killing."

Brakiss flinched again. So Brakiss had left himself open, made it easy for Skywalker to kill him. And the virtuous Luke Skywalker had not.

"Skywalker wants me," Kueller said. "He knows that to maintain his power, he must defeat me."

"He doesn't even know you exist," Brakiss said. His tone had defiance in it. Just enough defiance to make him still useful.

"Oh, he knows," Kueller said. "You sent him to me, didn't you?"

"I warned him away from you." Brakiss's eyes widened even as the words left his mouth. He apparently hadn't planned on telling Kueller that.

"Good," Kueller said. "Skywalker is more apt to come to me now. You did well, Brakiss."

"Well?" Brakiss sounded stunned.

"Yes," Kueller said. "You did my work even better than I had hoped you would."

"Th—then I can stay here?" Brakiss stammered like a small child. He loved the factory. It gave him a peace that Kueller found very useful.

"Is that what you want?" Kueller asked.

Brakiss nodded, slowly, as if he was afraid to reveal himself to Kueller.

"Then of course you can stay, Brakiss. You have served me well."

"And you won't send anyone else here?"

Kueller smiled. "No one else needs to come. Telti is yours, Brakiss. I will continue to subsidize it for you. And you will continue to work for me, as you always have. And we will never again discuss Skywalker, the academy, or Yavin 4. Is that what you want?"

"I want Skywalker to stay away."

"You'll always be alone there. Your Force talents will go to waste, but that will be your loss, Brakiss, not mine. Your usefulness is done."

"And Skywalker?" Brakiss couldn't seem to let it alone. Skywalker must have made an impression. More of an impression than Kueller was comfortable with.

"Skywalker is mine now," Kueller said. "Soon he will bother no one ever again."

Twenty-four

The Glottalphib smiled at Han. Smoke seeped between his long yellow teeth, narrowly missing the walls of the *Falcon.* "Well, General Solo," he said. "We meet again."

Han had to struggle to recall his name. "You're outnumbered, Iisner."

Chewie was still growling. His fur had stopped smoking, but there were missing patches where the flame the Glottalphib had used had burned through. His paws were up, just as Davis's hands were. Seluss had scooted as close to the metal walls as he could get.

"I don't think I'm outnumbered," Iisner said. "One deep burst of flame and your friends here will be of no use to you. And while I fry them, I can turn my blaster on you. Imagine, a hero of the Rebellion forgetting his blaster."

Han cursed. His blaster was in the cockpit.

"Such language, General Solo," Iisner said. "And when I am here on a courtesy visit."

Han kept his gaze on Iisner. He had to buy time. The *Falcon* was his ship; he would be able to get them all out of this if he only had a moment to think up a plan.

"It seems I'm always explaining manners to you," Han said. "Threatening to kill my friends is not polite."

"I merely do this to protect myself," Iisner said. "My boss would not understand if you refused his invitation."

Chewbacca slowly unsheathed his claws. Their tips touched the low ceiling. Han kept his features impassive, so that Iisner wouldn't notice Chewie.

"What does Nandreeson want with me?"

Iisner breathed out slightly. Licks of flame caressed the gray scales near his nostrils. "He doesn't want you, precisely. He is most interested in your position. He believes that he can help the New Republic."

"Oh, he does, does he?"

Iisner nodded. "He has information that your people might find of value."

Chewie inserted one claw between the wall and the door to a secret cargo hatch.

"What kind of information?" Han asked.

"Now, General Solo, if I knew that, I would tell you. But I am merely an assistant, an underling with no real power. I have been instructed to bring you to Skip 6—"

"And I told you before that I'll meet Nandreeson on Skip 1."

Chewie had inserted another claw. The process was painstakingly slow. Seluss had moved even closer to Chewie's legs. Davis was watching Iisner's blaster intently. If Chewie didn't act quickly, Davis probably would. And then they would have a disaster.

"I must tell you the truth, General Solo." Steam came out of Iisner's mouth when he said, "Solo." "Nandreeson does not like to travel to the other Skips. The accommodations are, shall we say, lacking?"

"I'm not asking him to sleep over," Han said. "We can meet on the *Falcon* if he wants. I just don't plan to go to Skip 6. I learned a long time ago to stay off Nandreeson's personal turf. No offense, Iisner."

"None taken. Your friend Calrissian would have done better to have shown the same restraint."

Chewie had inserted two more claws into the area.

"Nandreeson's still holding a grudge against Lando?" Han asked.

"A grudge is perhaps the wrong word," Iisner said. "A debt marker would be more accurate. They have a score to settle."

"I'm sure they do," Han said. "But tell your boss it has nothing to do with me." He nodded at Chewie, who tugged with all his Wookiee strength. Iisner looked up. The door to the cargo space fell on him. Flame blew out of his mouth. Chewie dodged to the left, Davis to the right, and Seluss cringed. The flames scorched the wall and the top of Seluss's head. Davis slammed into Han and they both went rolling down the corridor.

Flames roared from under the door, heating the metal, burning Han's already-damaged skin.

He swore and grabbed the wall rungs, pulling himself off the metal. Davis ran, cursing, all the way into the cockpit. Chewie stepped on top of the cargo door, crushing Iisner. Seluss was chittering and pounding his smoking head against the wall.

Chewie reached down and pulled Seluss against him, crushing the Sullustan's burns against Chewie's furry chest. The metal flooring was glowing bright red, and the air smelled of burning flesh and seared Glottalphib.

The flames faded, and then went out. Han climbed across the wall using the rungs, careful to keep his boots off the metal floor. When he reached Chewie, he stopped, leaned down, and took the blaster out of Iisner's motionless hand. The handle of the blaster was hot.

"Solo?" Iisner's voice sounded from below. "Make your friend get off me."

More flames licked out from under the door.

"Get off him, Chewie."

Chewie shook his head and roared. Han trained the blaster on Iisner.

"I'll be all right," Han said. "Take Seluss to the storage lockers and see if you can find the medical kit. We need to put something on those burns."

Chewie roared in protest.

"Go!"

Chewie wrapped one shaggy arm around Seluss, and gripped the wall rungs with the other arm. Then he moved across the wall, just as Han was doing.

Iisner crawled out from under the cargo door. Webbed burn marks matching the pattern on the metal floor crisscrossed his chest and arms. His gray scales were flaking off his back. He looked weak and dizzy.

"Tell me what Nandreeson wants with me," Han said. "The truth."

Iisner climbed onto the door, and leaned against the wall. Smoke floated out of his nostrils. He looked beaten. "He wanted to use you to get to Calrissian."

"Lando?"

Iisner nodded. "He figured if you were here, Calrissian wasn't far behind."

"Sometimes Nandreeson lives in the past," Han said. "Lando and I are rarely in the same place at the same time."

More scales flaked off Iisner's skin. "I need a water bath."

"One more question," Han said, "then you can go to your own people. Who's behind all the credits that have come into the Run?"

"Not Nandreeson," Iisner said. His voice was weak. Small flames burned through his teeth, as if he couldn't control them. "Nandreeson hates this."

"So why doesn't he stop it?"

"It's too big to stop." Iisner raised a small hand. "I need care, Solo."

"All right," Han said, motioning to the door with his blaster. "Get out of here."

Iisner made his way cautiously across the cooling floor. When he reached the door, Han shoved the blaster against his back. "You forgot to name the credit source."

"You won't believe it, Solo."

"Try me."

Iisner whirled his big head and opened his long mouth. Flame started beneath the teeth, and then a blaster bolt hit Iisner in the throat. Iisner fell back, eyes open, clearly dead.

Han turned.

Davis was standing in the hall, wearing a pair of protected mining boots, and still holding his blaster.

"What the hell were you doing?" Han asked.

"He was going to kill you."

"He was going to talk to me."

Davis shook his head. "Glottalphibs are hard to kill, Solo. He was going to fry you now, ask questions later, then take the *Falcon* to Skip 6 so that Calrissian would think you were there."

"How do you know?" Han asked.

"Because I've seen them do this before," Davis said. "They let their prey think they're dying, and then they'll go in for the kill. You'd have been fried consort if I hadn't stepped in."

"Or maybe I'd have been just a little bit wiser," Han said. "Mighty convenient of you to kill Iisner at that moment. Who are you working for, Davis?"

"Myself, Solo."

"Yourself and who else?" Han had turned so his blaster was on Davis.

Davis noted the move. He set his own blaster down.

Slowly. Then he rose just as slowly, keeping his hand flat, showing that he was unarmed. "I don't work for anyone."

"Right," Han said. "So what are you doing here?"

Davis swallowed. He had his hands up, just as he had when Iisner had the blaster on him. "A buddy of mine was killed on Skip 5. I'm trying to find out why."

"Nice try." The floor looked cool now. Han put a booted foot on it. It was cool. "In fact, excellent try. You knew I would be real sympathetic to that one. But it was a little too obvious. Try again."

Davis shook his head. "I'm being straight with you, Solo. My friend died in an explosion on the bay just days before you got here."

"And you're a good guy, trying to solve the mystery, at no cost to yourself." Han brought the other foot down. It felt good to be standing again.

"Just like you, Solo."

"You seem to know a lot about me."

Davis nodded. "I knew that you were coming here. Just like Nandreeson's people. Everyone's watching you, Solo. They expect you to betray the Run somehow."

Han tightened his grip on his blaster. "This isn't about me. We were discussing you. And what you're doing here."

"I—ah—I actually came here to meet you."

"To Skip 5?"

"Yeah."

"I thought your buddy was killed here."

"He was," Davis said. "But I already looked into that. It seemed like an accident, but there've been a lot of accidents like that. Too many, I think. And when I heard you were here to investigate a buddy's death, then I thought maybe—"

"I'm not investigating anybody's death," Han said. "I'm here because Jarril asked me to come."

"And where is he?" Davis asked.

Seluss chittered. Han looked over his shoulder. Seluss's round head had bandages wrapped loosely around it. Chewie stood behind him, some of his fur matted down with burn cream.

"See?" Davis said. "Even your Sullustan friend says Jarril is dead, and he should know."

"He doesn't know," Han said. "He's working on supposition, just like the rest of us. Which reminds me, Seluss. How did you get into the *Falcon*? Better yet, how did Iisner get in?"

Seluss chittered, and as he did, he backed up, his paws raised in a defensive posture as if he believed Han would hit him. Chewie blocked Seluss's backward movements.

"You came back against my orders," Han said, "using codes from Jarril's ship?" That meant Jarril still had the *Spicy Lady.* Han could put a trace on it, to see if Jarril was somewhere nearby.

Seluss chittered again, repeating that it wasn't his fault.

"Sure," Han said. "A Glottalphib just happened to follow you in." He sighed. "This partnership isn't working out, Seluss."

Seluss chittered some more.

"When we get to Skip 1, you're going to the infirmary, and I'm getting out of here."

"Let's not be so quick to decide that," Davis said. "I would like your help."

"Oh, yeah," Han said. "You have a murder to solve."

"I need a ship," Davis said. "I want to hire yours."

Han smiled. "I haven't hired the *Falcon* out in years, kid. I'm not about to do it now. And you could find a less conspicuous ship."

"I want the *Falcon,*" Davis said. "I need the New Republic's support behind me. I need it if I'm going to take you to the supplier."

Han studied him for a moment. Davis was young, but not too young. He'd clearly been around. And he was lying. Han could feel it.

"No," Han said. "Now take your Glottalphib and get off my ship."

"He's not my Glottalphib," Davis said.

"He is now. Door prize. Take him and get out."

"Listen, Solo, you need me. I know my way around the Run."

"I've been here once or twice myself," Han said. "Chewie and I do just fine. Now get off my ship before Chewie has to help you off."

Davis opened his mouth as Chewie roared. Davis hurried toward Han. "All right. I'll get off. But if you change your mind—"

"I won't," Han said. He hit the control panel, and the door slid up. Davis started to leave. "Remember your friend here."

Davis flashed an angry look at Han, then grabbed Iisner by one limp arm. Davis dragged the dead Glottalphib off the *Falcon*. Han waited until the Glottalphib's large feet were through the door before closing it.

Seluss was staring at him as if Han had just given away every credit he had ever owned.

"I know what I'm doing," Han said.

Seluss chittered softly, then went into the cockpit. Chewie followed. Han holstered his blaster, trying to cool his temper. He didn't need any reminding about their situation. Nandreeson would be after him for killing Iisner and the others. And Han was no closer to knowing who was behind all the credits than he had been before.

But he couldn't trust Davis. Davis's appearance was just too convenient. And Han hated the convenient.

Something was up. And with Nandreeson on his back, time had just gone from short to nonexistent.

"Okay," Han said as he headed into the cockpit. "We're going back to Skip 1."

And maybe, just maybe, he'd be able to get some answers.

✱ ✱ ✱

The stench got him first. Fetid and sour, it smelled like standing water combined with rotted vegetation and rotten eggs. Lando walked between seven Reks. Instead of tying him, they wrapped their whiplike arms around his, holding him back. Their skin felt like lukewarm rubber, yet he could feel the life pulsing through them. Until this trip, he had never been so close to a Rek. They had brought him in their small, bubblelike ship, crossing the distance between the asteroids as if it were a highway on Coruscant. They had disembarked into this chamber, which felt less like a cavern and more like a tropical nightmare.

The air was so humid that it condensed on his skin and made his clothes feel clammy. Water dripped down the cavern walls. Insects combed the area. Flies buzzed past him, and small clusters of gnats created black spots in the air. The Reks led him along a narrow ledge that overlooked a stagnant pool. Beneath the water's surface, he could see carved stairs and moss-coated furniture. This part of the cavern was surprisingly empty, but he knew that somewhere ahead, Nandreeson waited for him.

Then the Reks would collect their bounty and Lando would be abandoned with the most powerful crime lord on the Run. A crime lord who had hated him for nearly twenty years.

The ledge was slippery. Lando's boots were made for metal floors, not water-and-slime-covered rock. The Reks helped him keep his balance, but if they let go, he might fall into the green-coated water. The thought made him shudder.

They rounded a corner and were suddenly in a closed chamber. Chairs were carved into the rock on the walls. Flies the size of Lando's thumb clung to the ropy moss on the wall closest to Lando. More gnats hung in the air, and a group of water bugs skated across the surface of the water. The sulfur smell was stronger here, and it mixed with the faint tinge of ozone.

Nandreeson sat at the far end of the pool. Algae grew inches deep in the water around him, and giant lily pads covered his scaly body. The rocks on the wall behind him had singe marks.

Nandreeson hadn't changed. His long green snout had fingernail-sized scales, and his eyes were too close together. The knobs on his forehead gave him a quizzical expression. His tiny hands floated on the water's surface, beside the lily pads. The scales on his chest were golden because they were wet. He appeared to be sitting on a couch under the water.

"Calrisssssssian," Nandreeson said with a smile, letting steam rise from his mouth as he spoke the sibilants. "You look prosperous."

"I look like I'm wrapped in rubber vines," Lando said. Bravado at all costs. Nandreeson didn't need to know that Lando's heart was pounding double time.

"Ah, yes, my faithful Reks." Nandreeson nodded at them. Lando could feel them back away from him. They were apparently afraid of the flames that could shoot from his mouth. "Toss Calrissian in the drink and go back to your ship. Your credits will be waiting for you."

"No—!" Lando started, but the word wasn't completely out of his mouth before he found himself airborne. The Reks tossed him high. He flew into a swarm of gnats, and half of them got into his mouth, choking him. He was spitting them out as he hit the water.

It was hot and slimy and it tasted of doughy bread. He sank quickly, scraping against the moss-covered rocks, and feeling the heat grow the deeper he went. A bubble rose past him, and he realized with sudden fear that this pond was fueled by an underwater heat source, one that he was sliding into.

He flapped his arms, and got caught in his cape. Panic. Panic. Panic will kill you, he thought to himself. His chest ached with the need to breathe. He could last. He knew he could last. He reached up and unfastened his cape. It slid into the hole where the bubble had emerged from, but he could move now. He tilted his head. Light filtered in from the lamps on the cavern's ceiling. He swam up toward it. His lungs burned with the need for air, his arms ached, and black spots danced before his eyes. That moment of panic had cost him a lot of air. He didn't think he would make it when he suddenly broke the surface, spewing foul-tasting water out his mouth and taking deep breaths.

Somehow he had twisted around. Nandreeson was behind him, and on the side of the cavern, six Glottalphibs sat, their large feet soaking in the water. Their mouths were open and they were grinning.

At him.

"What are you staring at?" he asked, his brain too addled to think of a better insult.

"Why, you, human," Nandreeson said from behind him. "I never realized you creatures had such a low tolerance for water."

"Liar." Lando was treading water. He turned slowly so that he could face Nandreeson. "And this isn't water. This is liquid slime."

Nandreeson's tiny eyes were following Lando's every move. "This," he said with considerable pride, "is the product of years of experimentation. I can only hope that your body chemistry hasn't ruined the delicate balance of my pool."

"You should have thought of that before you had the rubber men toss me in here," Lando said. He looked at the sides of the pond. The rocks were higher than his head and covered with a greenish moss that looked extremely slippery. The only stairs were near the door on the far side of the pool, past the guards. It didn't matter. He wanted to save his strength, not tread water until his energy gave out.

He turned and flutter-kicked behind him, beginning the neat crawl that he had learned as a boy. A huge flame seared the water in front of him. Steam rose, blinding him, and the heat burned him. He stopped.

"Ah, Calrissian. You see the price of disobeying me."

"You never said that I had to stay in this mud hole." Lando kicked away from the steaming water, and moved closer to Nandreeson.

Nandreeson opened his snout; his tongue emerged and snapped up a mouthful of gnats. He swallowed and groaned with delight. "I never said you could leave, either. You are mine now, Calrissian. You had best get used to it."

"All right," Lando said. "Get me out of this pond, and we'll discuss the price of my freedom."

Flame curled out of Nandreeson's nostril. Lando had learned a long time ago that tiny fires were the sign of Glottalphib temper. "The price of your freedom, Calrissian, is your death."

Lando's arms ached. He stopped moving them, and kept himself afloat by kicking his legs. The water's viscosity also buoyed him. But if he was going to stay in it much longer, he would have to shed some of his heavier clothing. "You're being a bit dramatic, Nandreeson. I was a young smuggler trying to prove my worth. I had no idea whom I was stealing from. I've tried to pay you back over the years, but your goons wouldn't even take the message to you. I'm here now. Let's talk like reasonable people. I'll repay what I took from you, plus interest. At ten percent compounded over twenty years, you'll be making a considerable profit."

"I'm not interested in profit," Nandreeson said. The flames licking out of his nose were even longer now.

"Don't kid me," Lando said. He had sunk to his chin. He had to crane his neck to keep his mouth out of the water. "You're always interested in profit."

"All right." Nandreeson pulled his long, scaly body out of the water. "I will be honest with you, Calrissian, since you do not have long to live. I *am* interested in profit, and I *will* profit from you. After you die, everything you own will become mine. You have no heirs, no mate, no family. No one will argue with me. No one will dare."

"I don't think the New Republic would like that."

"I don't think they will interfere." Nandreeson sat on the slimy rock ledge, his big feet dangling in the water. He picked a fly off the nearby wall with one tiny hand. "They will be too busy fighting a new rebellion."

Lando began treading water with his hands again. He was in good physical shape, but he hadn't been in water for a long time. His muscles were already aching from the unfamiliar strain. "New rebellion?"

"Of course." Nandreeson took down another fly and munched it thoughtfully. "Every government must deal with armed rebellion at some point in its career. For your friends on Coruscant, the rebellion will come sooner rather than later."

"We've been fighting the Imperials since the Empire folded," Lando said. "They'll give up soon."

"I'm sure they will," Nandreeson said. The flames were gone. He was smiling again. "But I am talking of a rebellion, Calrissian. From the inside. You remember.

The way your friend Leia Organa Solo operated when she was in the Imperial Senate. A *rebellion,* fully armed, fully ready, with idealism on its side."

Lando slowed his treading. "There's no reason to rebel," he said. "The Republic is a good government. It treats its people well."

"Does it?" Nandreeson asked. "The people on the Run are terrified of the New Republic, afraid that it will interfere with free trade."

"The Run has always hated the government, from the Empire to the Old Republic. Smugglers hate rules," Lando said.

"And then, of course, there are places like Almania, a planet that sent your New Republic a distress signal as the ruling Je'har began a systematic slaughter of all who opposed them. The Republic never responded."

"The New Republic tries not to interfere with local rule," Lando said.

"Even when that local government is committing genocide? Really, Calrissian, for heroes, your New Republic is doing quite poorly."

"Who are you to say?" Lando asked. "You are nothing more than—"

Flame shot into the water all around him, sending smoke and steam into the air. He coughed, then wiped his face with his hand. He was going to drown before this day was over if he didn't think of something.

The flame stopped, and the smoke gradually cleared.

"You should really consider what you're going to say before you say it," Nandreeson said. "I do control your life."

"You've made your point, Nandreeson. Now let me out of here and let's deal."

"I apparently have not made my point," Nandreeson said. "I will not be dealing with you." He slid back into the water and swam toward Lando, staying far enough away that Lando couldn't grab him, but close enough that one temperamental burst of flame would scorch Lando's face. "When Jabba the Hutt died, I could have become the most influential crime boss in all the galaxy, and I would have, except for you, Calrissian."

"I haven't come near you in years," Lando said.

"Exactly. Nandreeson is the best crime lord in the Run. Nandreeson is well-known throughout the galaxy. But Nandreeson isn't omnipotent. Nandreeson can be bested. Why, someone as inept as Lando Calrissian stole a fortune from Nandreeson when Calrissian was a mere boy. If it could be done once, it could be done again." The flames were licking out of Nandreeson's nostrils again. Lando moved backward very, very slowly.

"Killing me won't change that," Lando said.

"Oh, but it will. My colleagues here will spread the tale of your death, the ways you suffered, and how, at the end, you begged me for mercy. We may even defile your corpse—humans find that disagreeable, don't they?—and leave it on Skip 1 for all to see. And then, of course, I will confiscate all you own, and there will be no opposition. Instead of saying I can be bested, they will say that Nandreeson waits for his revenge, and then he makes it very, very sweet."

Lando shook his head, got water in his mouth, and spat, nearly hitting Nandreeson. "To make up for the last twenty years, you'd have to kill me a hundred times." Then he winced. That was no way to convince Nandreeson, especially now that flames were flowing between Nandreeson's teeth.

"You think I will favor you, don't you, Calrissian?" Nandreeson said, the fire spreading around his face. "You think that I will appreciate your intelligence, your courage, your superior abilities in defying me. You think that you will escape this. But the one thing you must know is that I have spent the last twenty years *hating* you."

A lick of flame came so close to Lando that he had to duck underwater to avoid it. His lungs still ached from the last time he had been submerged. Nandreeson hadn't moved, nor had he inflamed the water again. Lando was about to come up when a realization hit him. His lungs should have recovered by now. He should feel a bit of strain from the treading, but he had been breathing regularly for some time.

Only the oxygen had to be thin here. Or polluted with something else. Or the Glottalphibs kept burning it away. With the exertion and the thinner air, Lando didn't have as much time as he thought.

He scanned the water, and saw only algae, green particles, and Glottalphib feet soaking in the pool. No escape unless he wanted to try that hole from which the bubbles emerged. And he wasn't sure he could stand the heat.

He resurfaced, and blew the foul-tasting water from his nose and mouth.

"Hiding underwater will do no good," Nandreeson said. "I can come after you much more easily there."

"If you're going to kill me, Nandreeson," Lando said, "just get it over with." If Nandreeson made a move, it might point Lando toward escape.

"You'd like that, wouldn't you?" Nandreeson said. "But you will die slowly, Calrissian, and I will enjoy every moment of it."

"Well, if you have something planned for me, Nandreeson, get to it." The quicker they got him out of the water, and out of this cavern, the better off he would be.

"I have gotten to it, as you so quaintly say." Nandreeson was smiling at him now, his scaly lips pulled back to reveal smoke-blackened, pointed teeth. "We'll see how long you survive in my world, Calrissian. Glottalphibs live in the water. We eat there. We sleep there. We mate there. Humans, as I understand it, cannot tolerate the water."

"I can tolerate it just fine."

"But it will kill you if you aren't careful. How long can you keep swimming, Calrissian? Without food, without rest, without help of any kind? How long?"

A terror Lando never knew he had rose in him. He couldn't swim forever. He would drown. "I can survive long enough," he said.

And that, at least, was true. He would survive long enough to get Nandreeson, or to die trying.

Twenty-five

✷

The guards had allowed Cole to climb out of the prototype X-wing. He, in turn, had convinced them to contact General Antilles. Not that Cole knew what he would say to the general when he arrived. Skywalker's droid hunched near the computer terminal, tendrils of smoke leaking out of the droid's round head compartment. If the blaster shots were as bad as they looked, they might have caused damage to the droid's memory, which, from what Skywalker said, had to be the part of the droid he valued the most.

"Enough waiting," the Kloperian said. "Let's take him to detention like any other saboteur."

"No." The voice came from the back of the room. The guards turned and so did Cole. General Antilles stood there, wearing full-dress uniform, his dark hair neatly combed. His two personal guards stood beside him. He surveyed the room. His gaze rested on Cole for a moment, searching, appraising, and clearly not recognizing him, before turning to the droid. "Is that Artoo-Detoo?"

The Mon Calamari guard shrugged its narrow shoulders.

"Well?" General Antilles asked.

The guards looked at Cole.

He glanced at all of them before feeling that it was safe to respond. "Yes, sir. Luke Skywalker left it with me to supervise the repairs on his X-wing."

General Antilles put a hand on top of Artoo's dome, then let his hand slip off slowly, as if he regretted the condition Artoo was in. "You"—he said to the Kloperian—"get this little droid running again."

"I beg your pardon, sir," Cole said, "but Artoo has had some bad experiences with the Kloperians. He—it—he—says they tried to kidnap him a few days ago."

The general's eyes narrowed. "Who did this to Artoo?"

"I did," the Kloperian said. "It was trying to escape."

"Escape?" the general asked.

"We found these two in the middle of sabotaging the X-wing prototype," said the female guard. "They put a detonator in the computer."

"Artoo did that?" the general asked. "I find that hard to believe. Who are you, son, and why did you send for me?"

Cole swallowed. "My name is Cole Fardreamer, sir. I work on the X-wings normally. Luke Skywalker spoke highly of you, and I thought when they came in here that you at least would listen to me."

"Were you sabotaging the prototype?"

Cole shook his head. "I was checking it. Artoo and I found a bomb in the Jedi Master's X-wing, and we found another in a second reconstituted X-wing, and I thought maybe it might be in the new ones too and I was checking it when the guards appeared. They wouldn't listen to me, sir."

The Mon Calamari guard walked over to the X-wing and pointed at the computer. "If you examine this, sir, you'll see what this young man and his droid were up to.

There is an Imperial insignia on the back of this computer. It is a detonation unit."

General Antilles leaned over the X-wing. He examined the computer. Cole couldn't see his hands, didn't know if the general was moving things he shouldn't be. Cole's heart was pounding.

"Be careful, sir," he said. "The wrong move might set it off."

"Thanks," the general said. But he didn't move. The entire room was hushed. Cole could hear his own breathing, and the small rustling sounds the general made. "This Imperial device is built into the computer."

He stood. His body was thin and powerful, and he had the hardened look of a man who had seen too many fights, too many difficult days. His gaze drilled into Cole once more.

"Where did you assemble the computer?"

"I didn't, sir. They're ordered in bulk. We just install them."

Then the door hissed open, and a protocol droid entered, its golden hands in the air.

"Oh, dear, oh, dear, oh dear," it said, stopping in front of Artoo. "They've destroyed Artoo."

"It can't be as bad as all that," a woman replied as she entered. She was small and thin, her hair flowing around her in a curtain. She wore ripped fatigue pants and a shirt that was too large for her. It took Cole a moment to recognize President Leia Organa Solo. Up close, she looked young, vulnerable, and beautiful, a princess to be sure, but not a political leader of great power. And certainly not the veteran of half a dozen battles against the Empire.

"Leia," General Antilles said.

She glanced over at him, and smiled, but the smile only accented the exhaustion in her face. "Wedge. What are you doing here?"

"We have some kind of problem," the general said.

"I can see that." So far she apparently hadn't noticed Cole. She walked over to Artoo. The protocol droid was moaning over him, alternating between accusing him of getting into the wrong mess, and worrying that he would never recover. The Chief of State crouched in front of Artoo. "Artoo?" She rubbed some of the carbon scoring off his small head. "Artoo?"

"He's gone, Mistress Leia. The Kloperians have destroyed him."

"He certainly is damaged, Threepio, but I suspect we can repair him." She reached inside one of Artoo's panels and hit a reboot switch. The little droid screamed. The President backed away and the protocol droid toppled over. Then Artoo rocked back and forth on his wheels.

The President patted him on the head. "It's all right, Artoo. It'll be all right."

But the little droid kept screaming. The high-pitched wailing sound had the guards cringing and the general placing his hands over his ears. Cole felt as if his insides were being wrung out. He had caused the damage to the little droid by getting him into this mess.

The protocol droid sat up. "Artoo, if you don't cease this needless screaming, Mistress Leia will have to shut you down again."

Artoo's head swiveled, and he quieted. Then he saw the Kloperian and beeped. The beeps grew in intensity until they began to sound like a linked scream.

"Stop, stop, stop!" the protocol droid said, scrambling to its feet. "I'll translate. He says he was attacked by a Kloperian, that this is the second time, and that he will not be responsible for what happens if another Kloperian gets near him."

"You're dismissed," General Antilles said to the Kloperian guard.

"But, sir, you might need me. This man was committing sabotage—"

"You are dismissed. I would advise you to leave before I have to take your name and guard number."

The Kloperian's fishlike mouth pursed. Then it nodded its head. "As you say, sir."

It waddled out, its tentacles wrapped around its body in true Kloperian high indignation.

"Whyever did he hurt Artoo?" the President asked. She was looking at the general.

"I was just getting to that," the general said. "Apparently the guards found this young man and Artoo working on this X-wing. The guards claim they were sabotaging it."

"Artoo would never do that," the President said.

"Nonetheless, there is an Imperial detonator inside the computer."

"A detonator?" The President's voice had gone down to a whisper. She hurried across the room, and leaned into the X-wing with all the assurance of a pilot. Then she looked at Cole. Her gaze was even more demanding than the general's. Suddenly Cole understood why no one crossed Leia Organa Solo.

"You're the one who sabotaged this X-wing?" she asked, her voice cold.

He shook his head. His mouth was suddenly dry. "No, ma'am. Artoo and I found the sabotage."

"Artoo? And where did you get him?"

Artoo beeped, and chirruped.

"He says that Master Luke left him here to work with Master Fardreamer," the protocol droid said.

"You're Fardreamer?" the President asked.

"Yes, ma'am."

"And what's your connection to my brother?"

"I was repairing his X-wing."

"This isn't his X-wing."

"No, ma'am."

"What's wrong with Luke's X-wing?" the general said.

Cole swallowed. Having the two of them stand over him was almost worst than facing all the guards' blasters. "Nothing, sir. It was being reconditioned as per your orders and then Jedi Master Skywalker came here, complaining that we had tampered with his X-wing. He said his was special, and that he didn't want it overhauled, and would I put it back the way it was? He left Artoo to help me. As I was removing the computer, I found a detonator. Since the computers come as one piece, preassembled, I thought perhaps the detonator wasn't targeted at the Jedi Master, but at X-wings in general. So I looked at the computer on another reconditioned one and found the same thing. Then I wondered if the new ones had the same device, and the only new X-wing I had access to was the prototype, so I came in here."

"Artoo," the President said without turning around. "Is this true?"

Artoo wobbled on his wheels. He tried to come toward her, but his circuits groaned. He beeped softly.

"You had best answer her and worry about your health later," the protocol droid said.

Artoo beeped, then chirruped, then rocked on his wheels as if he was emphasizing his point.

"Artoo confirms the young man's tale," the protocol droid said. "He is worried that these new computers are part of a plot to destroy the best pilots in the fleet. He suggests that we see who ordered the recommissioning—"

"I did," the general said.

"Oh, dear," the protocol droid murmured.

Oh dear was right. The President's face flushed as she turned toward the general. "You what, Wedge?"

The general shrugged. "Well, it wasn't just me," he said. "The chiefs of staff met. We'd had some problems with the X-wings. Mechanical troubles, mostly because they're not aging well. Since the market for electronic component parts has gone down, we thought we could rebuild some X-wings, and then buy the others that we needed."

"I wasn't informed of this," the President said.

"Leia," the general said. "We issued a memo. It wasn't really a policy change."

"Perhaps not," she said, "but it must have been expensive. The New Republic isn't rich."

"That's what I've been trying to tell you," the general said. "The costs on this project were unusually low. That's why I promoted it in the first place. I thought it would benefit us. It certainly took the X-wing pilots out of danger from the mechanical failures we've been seeing lately."

The President's lips thinned, and her eyes narrowed. She clearly wasn't going to argue with him in front of the guards. She turned to Cole.

"Do you believe this detonator is in all X-wings?"

He swallowed. She was magnificent; her style so different from her brother's. She was hard-edged where he made his demands with a deceptive softness. There was nothing soft in the President's manner. Cole would never have argued with her as he had argued with her brother.

"The detonator is in the new computers, ma'am. That's the one item we've replaced in every X-wing we touched."

"If you've touched those computers all day long, why haven't you discovered this before now?"

"Because," Cole said, "I've never had occasion to take apart a computer before now."

"Wedge," the President said, "I need you to be honest with me. Whose idea was it to replace the computers?"

"Mine," he said.

"Wedge." Her voice had a warning tone in it. "We don't have time for games. I need to know."

"Leia." He put his hand on her arm. "It was my idea. I'm the one who discovered the problems with the old X-wings. I'm the one who thought of the reconditioning. I'm even the one who talked to the military-issues buyer. It was me, Leia."

"I won't believe you ordered sabotage," she said.

"I didn't."

His words hung in the air. The guards looked away. Only the protocol droid watched them, his golden eyes taking in everything.

Cole bit his lower lip. He had to speak up. "I beg your pardon, ma'am," he said, "but the general could have made the order without knowing of the sabotage."

"I know," she said. "The computers arrive assembled."

"Yes, ma'am," Cole said, "and in such a way that you'd have to be looking for it in order to find it. I wouldn't have found it if Luke Skywalker hadn't objected to the computer change specifically. And even then, I didn't find it. Artoo did."

"Mistress Leia," the protocol droid said, "the Kloperians have a policy against astromech droids in the maintenance bay."

Artoo whistled.

The President closed her eyes for a moment, then she asked, "How long have we been doing this?"

"Quite a while," the general said. "I could look it up."

She shook her head. "Luke's X-wing was brought in this time. He's been to Coruscant enough that we can assume the change was made since his last meeting. Still, that's a long time. Mr. Fardreamer, how many X-wings do you think have the new computer system?"

"Most of them, ma'am," he said. "I was surprised to see one as old as the Jedi Master's without an overhaul."

"Most of them." She whispered the sentence. Her hands were clasped together so tightly that the knuckles showed white. "And what about the new X-wings? How many are in use?"

"All but a handful, Leia," the general said.

"I want them all checked. All of them. I also want the rebuilt X-wings checked."

"You don't think that every X-wing has a bomb inside," the general said.

"That's precisely what I do think," the President said. "And I want them removed."

"That could ground our X-wing fleet for a while."

"Better grounded than destroyed," the President said. "Can you do this, Mr. Fardreamer?"

"Yes, ma'am." Cole stood. "But I think we might have a bigger problem here."

Her face became perfectly still, her eyes huge, as she waited for him to elaborate.

"Not all the X-wings are here with the fleet. A number of them are out."

She swallowed. "Do you think these need a remote detonator?"

He understood where she was going. If a remote detonator was needed, then the X-wings away from Coruscant were probably safe.

"No, ma'am. This detonator is designed to go off when a certain combination of commands is made."

"Do you know what that combination is?"

Cole shook his head.

"Then every X-wing pilot's in danger," the President said.

"I'll issue an order grounding them immediately," the general said.

"Be sure to send one to Jedi Master Skywalker," Cole said.

"Luke?" This time, the panic in the President's voice was evident.

"Yes, ma'am. The X-wing he took is an exact replica of the prototype here, right down to the computer."

"Oh, Luke," she said. Then she looked up at the general. "I don't even know where he is."

The general put his arm around her. "We'll find him," he said. "We have no other choice."

✶ ✶ ✶

Almania loomed in his viewscreen, a large white-and-blue planet surrounded by clouds. Its three moons were smaller than Almania, and colored differently. Two had a lot of green mixed with the blue.

Luke's charts told him that all three moons supported life, and had long-established cultures. Pydyr was the most famous, both for its exclusiveness and for its wealth. He had never heard of the other two, or of Almania, for that matter, until Brakiss had told him about it.

Oddly enough, he trusted Brakiss's information. Brakiss still had a thread of goodness in him, a thread he fought, but one that existed. Luke was afraid, though, that one day Brakiss would overcome that goodness, and would use all of his considerable powers for evil. All Luke could do was help where he might, and let Brakiss know that Luke was there. Letting his students go was the hardest part of teaching: allowing them to make their own mistakes, allowing them to be themselves, allowing them to choose their own paths. Brakiss had a great deal to fight from his past; Luke hoped that Brakiss would make the correct choice for the future.

But Brakiss had once again gone into Luke's past, except for his words about Almania. *You're supposed to go to Almania. The answers you want are there.* And then, later: *Leave the fighting to those who are ruthless. They'll win anyway.*

Whoever wanted Luke in Almania was ruthless, so ruthless that he terrified Brakiss. Not even Luke terrified Brakiss, not on that deep level. A part of Brakiss valued Luke, or he never would have given Luke that warning.

But Brakiss didn't value the person who paid him to bring Luke to Almania. Brakiss feared that person.

That alone intrigued Luke. The warning intrigued him more.

He had spent the entire flight researching Almania. There wasn't a lot to learn. Almania was on the far side of the galaxy. Neither the Empire nor the New Republic had paid it much attention. The Empire had once contacted Pydyr to help finance campaigns, but Pydyr had sent a carefully worded message about noninvolvement. Normally something like that would have set the Emperor off, but it didn't. Even with all its wealth, Pydyr was too far away for the Empire to bother with.

While Pydyr saw itself as noninvolved, Almania considered itself loosely tied to the Rebellion, and later to the New Republic. The Je'har, who had led Almania during the fight against the Empire, had sent weapons and funds to several Rebel bases, including the one on Hoth. But the Je'har's leadership changed shortly after the New Republic defeated Grand Admiral Thrawn, and the communications from Almania stopped. Some reports told of hideous brutality under Almania's new regime. Others spoke of slaughter on a mass scale. But no one asked for help until later, and by that time, the New Republic was busy with the Yevetha threat. Almania, ignored in the best of times, was forgotten.

Something nagged Luke about the timing, though. Before he had built his retreat in the Manari Mountains, but after Callista, he had taught a wide range of promising students, including Brakiss. Brakiss had left during that time. Luke had thought that perhaps Brakiss was tied to Almania, but he could find nothing to link them. There was nothing in Brakiss's mother's stories to link them, either. And the Empire had not had a presence on Almania, so Brakiss could not have gone there during his Imperial service.

Or could he?

Brakiss was, after all, a spy.

Did Brakiss have something to do with the change in the Je'har? Brakiss had warned that Luke was walking into a trap, and Brakiss was part of that trap. But was the warning part of it? Luke had not felt that level of deception in Brakiss.

Only fear.

Leave the fighting to those who are ruthless.

They'll win anyway.

They hadn't in the past. In the past, Luke had been able to defeat them. From Vader to Palpatine, from Thrawn to Daala, from Waru to Nil Spaar, Luke and his friends had dealt with the ruthless and defeated them. Yoda had taught him that there was great strength in the Force, strength that came from compassion, not from hatred. In that hatred alone, the ruthless weakened themselves.

"They won't win," Luke whispered to Brakiss, wishing he had thought to say this in the droid factory. "I can guarantee it."

Although Luke didn't know quite yet what he was facing. He only had the remembered pain of the blast, the fear that had risen in Coruscant, and throughout the New Republic.

As he got closer to Almania, he felt a distinct chill. He checked the temperature in the X-wing. It was normal. The chill emanated from his stomach, and wound itself around his heart. It was nothing like the chill that had blasted him when all those people died.

And yet it was.

The chill settled into his back and shoulders. He was nearing Pydyr. He opened a channel, expecting to be challenged for being so close to such a private planet.

But his comm picked up nothing.

No scrambled signals.

No local broadcasts.

Nothing.

Nothing at all.

And he should have gotten something.

He scanned the planet below. The buildings remained, and he got several life-form readings. But only about ten.

Ten on the entire moon.

When there should have been thousands.

Millions.

The chill gripped his heart. The cries had come from here. From Pydyr.

He would have to investigate. Almania could wait a day.

Then he felt the tendrils of a presence. It felt familiar, but too far away to be clear. And it felt almost as if it were being filtered through a dense atmosphere. He had felt it before.

On Telti.

Just before he saw Brakiss.

But this wasn't Brakiss. That much he knew. This was someone else. Someone equally familiar.

And more powerful. Much more powerful to be felt from so far away.

The feeling had a malevolence in it, though, that was unfamiliar. Except around Emperor Palpatine. Luke had felt it then.

But this wasn't Palpatine. This was someone else. Someone Luke had known . . .

He punched the coordinates for Pydyr into the navicomputer, and the X-wing swung around, veering off its normal course and heading toward Pydyr. The answers would be there.

The feeling grew stronger, both familiar and unfamiliar. The dark side was strong near Almania. Almost as if the entire planet were awash in it. Luke's mouth was dry. Perhaps he should go back to Coruscant and get help. Leia, Han, anyone. Going into this alone would be very destructive and difficult.

But he could handle Pydyr. With only ten life-forms on the planet, he wasn't about to run into all of them at once. He would see what happened on Pydyr, and make his decision from there.

The X-wing broke into the atmosphere. This side of Pydyr was awash in light. Buildings stood below him, with expansive avenues between them. Avenues wide enough to land an X-wing in.

Empty avenues.

An odd shuddery feeling ran up his back. He took control away from the navicomputer and began the landing procedures himself. This would take hands-on work. Even the automatic-guidance systems wouldn't help him here.

A light flashed on the screen. He glanced at it only to have it disappear. He frowned; wishing he had his old X-wing, then he returned his attention to the landing. Precision landing of a kind he hadn't done in years. He pulled the joystick—

—and felt the X-wing shudder beneath him.

The buildings were close on both sides. The X-wing shuddered again, and the computer locked. The screens went dark. Luke reached for the eject button only to find it was missing.

There was no droid eject either, of course.

He was stuck.

He grabbed for the hatch. He would open it by hand. He had no other choice. The ground spun close to him—

—as the X-wing exploded.

Twenty-six

This time it was Leia's turn to call an Inner Council meeting on short notice. She decided to hold it in the Ambassadorial Dining Room. The X-wing problem had to be dealt with quickly, and she picked the room closest to the bays.

The corridors here were highly polished, and the plants around the pillars well-tended. The dining room was often used for state dinners, and the entrance always had to look spectacular.

Leia hated the formality of the area, even though she had helped design it.

She and Wedge had reached the grand staircase leading up to the dining room when she felt cold. Her vision blurred, and she stumbled, clutching the mahogany railing for support.

A face formed in the air before her. The same white face she had seen before the bombing. It smiled, its black, empty eyes glittering their amusement.

Leia, an unfamiliar voice said in her ear. *Leia.*

And then she collapsed, her elbows and knees hitting the marble edges of the stairs. She thudded down to the floor, the marble cutting into her already-ripped military fatigues.

"Leia!" Wedge said. He bent over her, his strong hands bracing her shoulders. "Are you all right?"

Her teeth were chattering. "Evacuate the building."

"What?"

"Evacuate the building," she said.

"On the basis of what?"

"That face." She sat up. Her hands were shaking. "I had the same vision before the bombing."

But it had been different. Then she had heard voices scream and had been overwhelmed by cold. The destruction that had sent Luke to Coruscant before the actual bomb went off.

"All right," Wedge said. "I'll—"

"No, wait." She passed a hand over her face. The owner of that skeletal mask wanted her to panic. She had to think. She had to set her emotions aside and think. "This is an unscheduled meeting. No one would know we're here."

"Still," Wedge said, "we should change locations."

Leia shook her head. The disorientation was still there, but it wasn't as strong. She used Wedge's arm to help herself to her feet. "No. It feels different. That face. It was warning me of something else."

And she could almost grasp what that something else was. Almost, but not quite. It would come to her, though. She was certain of that.

"Let's have the meeting," she said.

"All right." Wedge sounded confused, but he obviously wasn't going to ask more questions. "At least let me post some more guards."

Leia shook her head. "We did that before the bombing, too. For all I know, this vision is stress-related. I was feeling stressed before the Senate meeting."

"And now, too, huh?"

She smiled at him. "I don't like these detonators, Wedge. Whoever planted them has found yet another way to penetrate my home. Coruscant is no longer safe."

"It never really was, Leia."

"I know. But until recently I could go about my business without feeling the threat of death hanging over me. Now I worry about everything. I worry about the children's rooms. I worry about the hallways. I worry about Han and the *Falcon*. If the X-wings were tampered with, what else was? How much more of this are we going to find, Wedge?"

"I think the key is discovering who did it."

"I suppose." Leia straightened her shoulders. "Although I think I know."

Wedge said nothing. He had made his thoughts clear in the maintenance bay. He agreed with one of the guards. The Empire rarely announced its presence so conveniently.

They climbed the stairs to the dining room, but at a walk instead of a run. The other Council members were already inside, but they weren't seated. Leia said nothing as she passed them. She went to her chair, sat down, and waited until they did the same.

Wedge stood behind her, as support and verification.

She called the meeting to order.

"It's irregular," R'yet Coome said, "to have a nonmember present."

"General Antilles is here at my request," Leia said. "We discovered something rather disturbing this afternoon."

Wedge opened a pouch and set the detonators on the table. C-Gosf waved a delicate hand over them. "What're these?"

"We found these in our X-wings. The entire squadron is outfitted with them, apparently," Leia said.

"They're detonators," Wedge said.

"With Imperial markings," Gno said. He sounded stunned.

Meido's crimson face did not change color. He peered at the detonators, then smiled at Leia. "Nice try, President."

The chill she had felt earlier returned. "Try?"

"Try," he said. "We accuse General Solo and you find a different device that points to the Empire. How very convenient."

"What do these detonators have to do with the bombing of the Senate Hall?" Wwebyls asked.

Meido shot him a withering look. "Everything, Wwebyls. The President is trying to show us that her husband had nothing to do with the X-wings, and so by implication, we are to assume he had nothing to do with the Senate Hall."

Leia clenched her fists under the table. Meido was going to oppose her at every turn. "General Antilles has warned the squadrons to bring the X-wings in, but there are some he's been unable to raise. I want to send a general distress signal throughout the New Republic's planets so that we can bring home those who might be in danger."

"What triggers these detonators?" Gno asked.

"We don't know," Leia said. "We're working on that right now."

"And they're in every X-wing?"

"We believe so."

"Oh, dear," Fey'lya said. "If they're in each X-wing, where else might they be?"

"Good question," Meido said. "Why don't we ask the President."

"Leia wouldn't know that," C-Gosf said.

"She would if she planted them."

"You've gone too far," Bel Iblis said. "You owe the President an apology."

Leia waved a hand to silence Bel. "Actually, I'd like to hear why Senator Meido believes I have suddenly become a traitor to the Republic."

"Your husband, President, and his attack on the Hall. Even you have said he would do nothing without your approval."

"What are they accusing Han of?" Wedge whispered.

"Treason," ChoFï whispered back.

"Han Solo!?!" Wedge had stopped whispering. "That's the stupidest thing I've ever heard. Han Solo was risking his life for the Rebellion while these cowards were hiding under the wings of the Empire. You, Meido, have no right—"

"Wedge," Leia said softly. "You're a guest. You don't have permission to talk."

"I can't believe you tolerate this stupidity," Wedge said.

"Not everyone believes it's stupidity," Meido said. "Who better to betray the New Republic than someone who is one of its most-trusted members. You forget that Palpatine was a senator when he overthrew the Old Republic."

"None of us has forgotten that," Gno said. "This is different."

"Is it?"

"I think you're being too zealous," Fey'lya said to Meido. "I know you're trying to prove you're worthy of your Council seat. But attacking President Organa Solo is not the way to do it. She and I have had our differences in the past"—and he smiled at Leia as he said this—"but even I would never impeach her good name."

"You wouldn't have to," Meido said. "I'm glad you called this meeting, President, because I was about to call one myself. You need to know that there's a no-confidence movement in the Senate. There will be a vote shortly."

"What's a no-confidence movement?" Wedge asked.

"It means," C-Gosf said, "that the government will say it no longer has confidence in Leia's leadership. If the no-confidence vote passes, Leia will have to step down. The leaders of the vote will force it."

"They can't do that," Wedge said. "You're Mon Mothma's chosen successor."

"Yes, they can," Gno said. "Chosen or not, she was ratified by a vote."

Everything was moving too fast for Leia. It was all spinning out of control. She could handle the big, obvious threats, but the treacheries hidden everywhere, even in little bugs inside machines, were too much. Leia's fingernails were digging into her palm, she would maintain a semblance of calm, even if she weren't really calm. She would regain control. The first place to do so was inside this room.

She turned to Meido. "What's the no-confidence vote based on?"

"On the preliminary bombing results," he said.

"Really?" Her voice was cold. She made herself as haughty and regal as she could, even though she wanted to tear him from limb to limb. "And how did the full Senate get those results, considering that they were part of a private meeting of the Inner Council?"

The room suddenly became very silent.

"I—ah—I don't know, President." Meido said. Now the crimson was fading from his face. She finally decided that she liked that trait. It broadcast his emotions.

"You don't know?" she asked. "And yet the full Senate will be voting based on facts from a closed session of the Inner Council? A vote *I* didn't know about. How did you find out?"

"President," R'yet said softly, "Meido, Wwebyls, and I are new to the Inner Council. We don't know all the rules."

"That argument held last meeting, R'yet," Leia said. "I won't accept it this time. You know the rules. You have just decided to play differently. Well, it won't work. This is not the Empire. We do things aboveboard here."

"Except," Meido mumbled, "sabotage."

"President Organa Solo has done nothing wrong," Gno said.

"Neither has Han," Leia said.

"Our evidence says otherwise."

"Your evidence could have been planted. Given your callous disregard for the rules of the Senate, you might have shown the same disregard for the rules of law here on Coruscant."

"You have no right to make that charge, *Princess,*" Meido said.

"Just as you had no right to reveal private documents from this meeting, *Senator.*" Leia ignored his use of her former title, even though he was doing so to remind others of the arrogance often displayed by aristocracy, although never by anyone from Alderaan.

"This arguing will get us nowhere," Fey'lya said. "We have several issues on the table: the sabotage of the X-wings; the bombing; the no-confidence vote; and the indiscreet mouths of some Council members." He turned his face toward the new members. "I move that if we have any new leaks, the new members be expelled."

"I second," Gno said.

"All right," Leia said. "All in favor say yes."

Every member of the Council, except for the three newcomers, chorused "Yes."

"Opposed?" she asked sweetly.

Meido spoke his no softly, as did R'yet Coome and Wwebyls.

"The motion passes. Any more leaked information will result in your expulsion from this body. Is that understood?"

"Oh, it's understood," Meido said. "You blame everything on us, *Princess,* because we lived under your former enemies. Now all someone has to do is leak more information and we no longer belong to this body. How convenient for you. Just as those detonators with an Imperial stamp are convenient. How many other convenient ways are you going to find to undermine the changes in the Senate?"

"You're being unfair," C-Gosf said.

"Am I?" Meido's white lines glared off his face. "I guess it really doesn't matter, because by the next time this august body meets, the good princess will no longer be a member. She will be recalled, her leadership in ruins. It's a small price to pay, *Princess,* for killing your colleagues."

"I didn't," she said. She was shaking. She kept her hands under the table. "I can't believe you're accusing me of that."

"And I can't believe you think we're simplistic enough to think that you can let go of your enmity toward your former enemies. How many Imperial soldiers did you kill on Endor, *Princess*? How many minor bureaucrats died when the Death Star blew?"

"Those weren't innocent people," Bel Iblis said.

"Really?" Meido said. "Many of them were just doing their jobs."

"If their jobs were to run a machine of death, then they deserved to die," C-Gosf said.

"I certainly hope you don't believe that," Fey'lya said. "Because if you do, then logically, any fighter pilot should die as well. The X-wings are star fighters. They were built for that, just as the Death Star was built to destroy planets. That both an X-wing and a Death Star can be used for transport is merely incidental."

Leia could barely breathe. She shook her head. The discord in the room felt personal, as if she had caused it.

"Senator Meido has a point. Things are never as simple as they seem. Not even in accusing another member of this Council of sabotage. Have your no-confidence vote. You can put a political spin on anything. But I will stand by my record. Since the Battle of Endor I have served this Republic, and since I was eighteen, I served the Rebellion against the Emperor. And I have served it well. You can play all the political games you want, Meido. You can manipulate things behind the scenes. You can destroy the unity that has marked this body from the beginning. And while that might give you personal power, it will only hurt the New Republic. I hope you understand that. I hope you factor that into what you're doing."

"I know what I'm doing," Meido said. "I don't plan to harm the New Republic. I plan to help it."

"Your methods leave a lot to be desired," Leia said.

"And so do yours, *Princess.* So do yours."

✳ ✳ ✳

Night had fallen on Coruscant. The streetlights were on, but they cast a pale glow over the rubble that still marred the outside of the Senate Hall. Threepio stopped outside the restricted area, but Artoo kept going, his headlamp making a circle of light through the gloom.

"I will not go any farther," Threepio said. "That blaster shot damaged your circuits. I'm going to report you to Mistress Leia."

Artoo blasted a raspberry at him.

"Artoo, really, this is nonsense. Master Cole is quite an efficient technician, but he is not a droid repairman. He wouldn't know if your memory chips were damaged. You need to have someone professional go over your circuits. You're not acting like yourself." Threepio waited outside the lines marking off the restricted area. Artoo cast his headlamp on some of the rubble, then continued forward.

"Artoo!"

Artoo bleeped at him.

Threepio gasped. "You malfunctioning little twerp! You have no right to call me names, not when I have your own best interest at heart."

Artoo beeped three times.

"You do not have the Republic's interest at heart. You don't have a heart!"

Artoo disappeared into the ruined building.

"You can't go in there!" Threepio said. "It's not safe! The roof will cave in on you!"

Artoo whistled. The sound echoed from inside.

"Found something?" Threepio said. "How could Artoo find something when the investigators didn't?" He stepped over the line and into the rubble. "I'm coming, Artoo!"

Artoo did not respond. Threepio tilted his body and rested a golden hand against the rubble to brace himself. "Artoo, wait for me!"

Artoo whistled again, then beeped.

"I'm going as fast as I can!" Threepio said, and then added softly, "Slave driver."

A huge pile of rubble blocked the door. The rubble was made up of parts of the ceiling, permacrete, and masonry that had broken off during the explosion. Much of it was covered with blood.

A faint light shone through the dirt-strewn corridor. Pieces of droids—mostly protocol droids—littered the floor. Hands stuck through the broken masonry. Charred heads stared darkly at the gloom.

Artoo chirruped a caution.

"I am being careful of the wires," Threepio said, "although I can't believe they'd still be live. It would help if you came in here and cast a light on my path."

Artoo beeped.

"No, I am not being unreasonable."

Artoo beeped again.

"And no, I am not following you. I am keeping an eye on you. Someone has to. You sustained serious damage, and I'm still not certain if you're in your right circuitry."

Artoo raspberried him again.

"I don't care what you call me. Most droids would need three days of maintenance just to get the carbon scoring off their plates. You go bustling off after a few moments, muttering something about having the solution to the bombing. I don't understand how getting hit with a blaster would give you any kind of solution at all."

Threepio rounded the corner. Artoo was standing near the rubble closest to the door of the Senate Hall. Most of the dirt had been cleared away, leaving electronic parts, broken metal, and ruined communications devices. Bits of furniture were mixed in: the desks designed for multilimbed senators; the perches made for birdlike representatives; the translators for those who didn't speak Basic.

Artoo had his jack in the middle of the pile. His scanner was out, and it was flashing as it moved. His headlamp was trained on the pile in front of him.

"Surely the investigators filtered through that junk," Threepio said. "As usual, you're making too much of all of this. Sometimes, Artoo, I wonder why Master Luke tolerates you. You've become much too eccentric."

Artoo beeped.

"No, of course I don't want him to replace you with a new droid. Those new droids are stuck-up." Threepio stopped beside the pile Artoo was working on.

Artoo moaned softly.

"You were right?" Threepio asked. "About what?"

Artoo pulled his jack out from the rubble. In it, he held a small detonator of the same type found in the X-wing.

"It has an Imperial signature," Threepio said. "Oh, dear. Mistress Leia isn't going to like this."

Artoo beeped.

"No, I don't like it much either. Will those Imperial monsters never leave us alone?"

Artoo didn't answer. He set the detonator on a small patch of bare floor, then began to rummage through the pile again.

"I thought you found what you were looking for. We should leave, tell someone about this." Threepio started toward the door. When he stepped into the darkness, he turned. Artoo was still digging through the pile. "Artoo, you've done all you can. We need to tell Mistress Leia."

Artoo beeped long and loud.

"What do you mean I don't understand? I understand perfectly."

Artoo chirruped.

Threepio came back into the room. A bit of rubble fell off the ceiling and he ducked. "It's not safe here. You have enough."

Artoo beeped.

"There has to be more what? The detonator is all you—oh." Threepio leaned against a pile and then sprang away when it moved. "I see. The detonator in the X-wings worked in concert with the computer. You need to know what this detonator worked with. Move aside, then. We'll both look.

"And," he added softly, "I hope we don't get blown up in the process."

Twenty-seven

Luke wrapped his arms around his head as he soared through the air. Bits of flaming shrapnel fell all around him. He had barely opened the X-wing's hatch when the ship exploded. If he had been inside, he probably would have broken his neck against the shatterproof glass.

It felt as if he fell forever. His skin burned where the shrapnel hit him. He couldn't control the fall. There was nowhere soft to land. He braced himself, using all of his Force strength, but something was interfering. He felt as if he were wrapped in cotton.

And then he landed. Legs first, the bones in his left ankle snapping. He tucked and rolled, the carved pavement biting his back, his shoulders. He kept rolling until he slammed into a building, and he lay there for a moment, unable to breathe from the shock of it all.

The main section of the X-wing had landed near him. More parts rained around him, sparks flying. Curtains in the building beside him burned. Smoke rose up the mudbrick walls, scorching them. More burning pieces of the X-wing were scattered all along the sandstone street.

The smoke had an acrid smell. Sweat ran down Luke's

face. His whole body hurt, and he still had trouble drawing a breath. Sparks were dancing all around him. He peered at them, saw bits of material in the flame, and then swore.

The back of his flight suit was burning.

He rolled over onto his back, trying to smother the flames while undoing the fasteners. His hands shook. He couldn't move fast enough. The heat on his back was stunningly painful. His fingers kept working, working, working, and finally he had the suit loose. He pulled it down to his waist, then twisted and slapped the burning material with his artificial right hand.

The flames went out.

He closed his eyes.

That was close.

The crackling of the nearby fires kept him focused. A bang resounded from far away, as part of the X-wing collapsed.

No one had come to gawk at the explosion. No one had come to put out the fire.

No one had come to help him.

His readings had been right, then. Pydyr was nearly empty.

He opened his eyes, and assessed the damage. His left ankle was broken and swollen to twice its size. Ever since his experience on the *Eye of Palpatine,* his left leg had been weak, vulnerable to too much pressure. His knee ached also, but that felt like a sympathetic injury.

He had a lot of bruises. Too many to count, too many even to allow himself to feel. He didn't want to think about the possibilities of internal injuries. His left hand was slightly burned—he must have touched the flames with his real hand—and his back felt raw. He was thirsty, a bad sign.

But while Pydyr's population was gone, its buildings weren't. He would probably be able to find water.

Maybe he would find some burn cream, too, something to ease the pain in his back and his hand.

Still no one had arrived. The flames burned on in the odd light, the sparks swarming like tiny bugs. He had to get away from here. The flames were spreading, had already spread to the building he had landed against.

The emptiness bothered him. He patted his side for his lightsaber, and found it, slightly scorched, but fine.

The artificial skin had burned off his right hand, revealing the mechanical workings. He balled his hand into a fist and braced himself on his knuckles as he rose. The strength in his arm would help him for the moment. He would need a crutch of some kind, but for now, he could limp.

He braced himself on the nearest building and hobbled away from the flames. His thirst was growing. He made himself ignore it, as best he could.

The emptiness appalled him more than the crash did. He assumed some of that was shock. Yet, there was an eerieness here that he had only felt a few times before. This street was meant to have life in it. These buildings were meant to house families, to hold laughter and conversation and warmth. The street should be full of voices, of vendors, of people going about their business. He should smell alien cuisine, unusual perfume, even unfamiliar garbage.

Instead, the only smell was smoke from his destroyed X-wing, the only sound the snap of flames, and his own ragged breathing.

He ducked into an archway, and leaned against the column. It too was made of mudbrick and decorated with tiny stones. He leaned his forehead on them. Spots danced in front of his eyes. He didn't know the proper burn treatments. He'd always had Artoo for information, the medical pak for emergencies, and a whole battery of medical personnel on the inhabited planets.

Here he had no one.

Except himself.

Even on the *Eye of Palpatine,* he had had Callista.

He pushed thoughts of her from his mind. He couldn't afford to think of her, especially not now.

He caught his breath and went inside the building. The smoke hadn't gotten here yet, and the only acrid scent came from his own clothing.

He was in an entry, filled with brown carved tile. The walls were covered with frescoes, mostly of a humanoid people with oval faces and almond eyes; long, flowing arms; and small mouths that didn't seem to smile. Yet their entire demeanor radiated joy. Wooden chairs stood in the hall. They were covered with dust.

A stand near the door held walking sticks and canes. He pulled one out and leaned on it, thankful that it could take some of his weight.

He had to find a source of water. He was getting dizzy. His back throbbed. He rounded a corner, walking carefully on the long red rugs that covered the flooring. If it weren't for the dust, the house would be spotless. Yet it looked lived-in and cared-for.

What had happened to these people?

He went through two more archways and carefully decorated rooms before discovering a kitchen. It resembled the kitchens he had seen among the wealthy on Coruscant. Modern appliances gleamed from the walls. Knobs, dials, and keyboards substituted for the crude cooking facilities he used on Yavin 4. All the pots and pans here were for decoration. But there was a water recycler and a purifying pot near the cooking pad. He staggered over to it, grabbed a porcelain mug, and turned on the recycler.

It groaned, then hummed to life. In a moment, he had clear, fresh water.

He drank it down quickly. One glass, then two, then

three. He had never tasted anything so good. The dizziness was fading, and his mind was clearing. He studied the keypad. If it was like the ones on Coruscant, it wouldn't have just kitchen information. It would also tell him what supplies were in the house, a family history, and a history of Pydyr. It would also carry news feeds and anything else he needed to know.

He leaned his hips against the counter, and used his right hand to activate the keyboard. His finger was all metal now, except for the charred pieces of synthetic skin hanging off it. He hoped the keypad wasn't activated by fingerprint or retinal scan.

The screen sprang to life.

STRANGER. YOU ARE NOT IN OUR RECORDS.

Luke typed: I AM NEW HERE. YOUR OWNERS ARE GONE.

WE KNOW. IT HAS BEEN SILENT HERE. BUT WE ARE INSTRUCTED NOT TO GIVE INFORMATION TO STRANGERS EXCEPT IN CASE OF EMERGENCY.

IT IS AN EMERGENCY, Luke typed. I AM INJURED, MAYBE DYING. I NEED MEDICAL ATTENTION. HAVE YOU A MED KIT?

WE HAVE A MEDICAL DROID.

Luke started. He had seen no droids.

THE DROIDS APPEAR TO BE MISSING AS WELL, he typed. HAVE YOU MEDICAL INFORMATION IN YOUR STORES?

CERTAINLY, STRANGER. AND A MEDICAL KIT IN THE CABINET ABOVE THE KEYPAD YOU ARE USING.

Luke sought out the medical kit, found it, and removed the burn cream. He longed for a droid, but knew that he had to tend himself. He cleaned off his burns, wincing as he did so, then applied cream and a bandage. When he finished that, he devised a splint for his ankle.

Then he looked up. The screen held a single message.

PLEASE, STRANGER. TELL US WHERE OUR MASTERS HAVE GONE.

Luke shook his head and typed, THE PLANET IS EMPTY.

The screen shut itself off with a slight moan. He felt

for a moment as if he were with Artoo. Artoo would have had a similar reaction. Artoo would feel loss if Luke died.

How curious. The change had happened so fast that this family hadn't had time to inform its house computer. He remembered the chill and the voices. The Death Star had destroyed the planet. This new weapon left the planet, and destroyed all life.

Or at least all humanoid life.

He felt a flash of a presence again, the same presence he had felt when he had entered the Almanian system. It was watching him.

"Show yourself," he said.

But no one did.

✳ ✳ ✳

Han landed the *Falcon* on the far side of Skip 1's landing strip. He had Chewbacca bundle Seluss off to the infirmary, such as it was, without promising to pay for Seluss's care. Han hoped that Chewie would pay for a bit of care himself. That singed fur worried Han.

He was hanging upside down under the *Falcon*'s power core. The scarred metal looked as if it hadn't been touched, but he wanted to be certain. On the way back to Skip 1, he had run a scan of the *Falcon* to make sure Seluss, the Glottalphib, or Davis hadn't tampered with it. He could see no obvious sabotage, but that didn't mean it wasn't there.

He hated being on the Run. It made him even more paranoid than usual.

He needed to get some information about Davis and about the Jawas, but he would do that after Chewie came back. Han wasn't about to leave the *Falcon* again. He suspected he would need to make a quick getaway. Nandreeson wasn't the type to give up.

The hatch hissed. Han grabbed his blaster, and pulled

himself out of the well near the power core. Then he heard Chewie bark his name.

"Back here, Chewie!"

Chewie roared and Han sighed. Once, just once, he'd like to do what he wanted, when he wanted.

"I'll go into the Skip when I'm done here," he said.

Chewie roared again.

"Impatient sack of bones," Han muttered. He climbed across the well and onto the floor grid. "I'm coming!"

He rounded the corner to find that Chewie had already left the *Falcon.* The hatch was still open. Han ducked out.

Chewie stood at the bottom of the ramp.

"You could have waited," Han said.

Chewie put a long, hairy finger to his mouth and then pointed. Han followed the direction. On the far side of the bay, smugglers were working, much as they had on Skip 5. Han frowned at Chewie, then got off the ramp and edged past a few other vehicles parked on the bay.

Han hid under the wing of a modified Gizer freighter. The metal was rusted and pockmarked and provided perfect viewing without allowing him to be seen.

Zeen Afit was carrying computer parts. Blue followed, gingerly carrying screens. Wynni was a few yards behind, her furry arms wrapped around four chairs that had bolts in their bases. Two more smugglers, both Sullustan, were carrying the cushions on top of their heads.

They were stripping a ship. In Han's day, smugglers never did that unless they had been betrayed by the ship's owner or unless the owner was dead.

Something about this stripping had bothered Chewie, though, and Han couldn't see the ship from his hiding place. After the procession passed, he slipped out from under the wing, and moved closer.

The ship looked familiar. She was a space yacht that

had seen better days. Her sides were battered and her hull damaged from what appeared to be a difficult landing. Her name had been scratched off the side, but Han could still read it.

The *Lady Luck.*

Lando had been here.

On the Run.

And there was only one reason he would have come.

Han.

Only Han was free.

Lando would never betray his smuggling friends, at least not intentionally. And for all their bluster, the smugglers on the Run were Lando's friends, as much as smugglers like that could be friends.

Which only left one option.

Lando had arrived alone—

—and Nandreeson had been waiting for him.

Twenty-eight

Femon would have laughed at him, and told him he was afraid of his own imaginings. Sometimes Kueller missed her. She had been with him a very long time. He could still hear her voice in his head, admonishing him.

He missed her, but he didn't regret killing her. Some things just had to be done.

He was standing on the very spot where she had died, in the control center on Almania. He had replaced the death masks she loved on the walls, and added a few of his own. His guards stood behind him, silently watching. His employees believed in him, but a few fanatics were all it took. He didn't want to be vigilant all the time. So he had his guards. They would protect him, and they would make no mistakes.

He frightened them.

But he didn't frighten Luke Skywalker.

Kueller pulled his chair out and sat down, extending his long legs under the console. The screen before him showed the wreckage of Skywalker's X-wing. It had landed near some of the most valuable houses on Pydyr, houses whose wealth had not yet been plucked. For a few moments, Kueller had been afraid that he would lose that wealth, but he thought it a small price to pay for Skywalker.

Skywalker, injured, on Pydyr.

Perfect.

He punched a button and said to one of his undersecretaries in communications, "I want an interstellar link to Coruscant. I want you to get President Leia Organa Solo. Tell her it's about her brother, and then have her hold for me."

"Yes, sir," the undersecretary said. The image winked away.

Kueller returned his gaze to the house that Skywalker had crawled into. Femon would have chided him: *What are you so afraid of, Kueller?* not realizing that the limping man with the burned back had survived the crash.

A lesser man would not have.

Kueller had expected Skywalker to come to Almania. His decision to land on Pydyr had been a surprise, as had the explosion. Kueller had watched it all on the monitor.

He had felt it in his gut.

At least he knew the detonators worked. He just hadn't expected Skywalker to execute the destruct command by accident.

Kueller had blocked the Force repercussions as best he could. He wanted President Organa Solo to sense that something was wrong, but not to know what that something was. Kueller would never have been able to achieve this with Skywalker himself, but Organa Solo had neglected her Jedi training. She was deficient in many important areas, areas Kueller meant to use to his own advantage.

And after he reached her, he would go to Skywalker. Even though the man was injured, even though he had lost everything, he would still be a formidable opponent.

But the injury made other things possible. The injury

did weaken Skywalker, and it would weaken his resolve. He might need some fast, easy strength. Kueller might succeed where the Emperor had not.

Kueller might be able to turn Luke Skywalker to the dark side.

And then they would rule together: Kueller as Emperor, and Luke as his Darth Vader.

How very appropriate.

✶ ✶ ✶

Leia felt as if she were back on Hoth, working on the Rebel base. She and Wedge were seated side by side, the computers before them humming with activity. Admiral Ackbar sat at another terminal and so did the other high-ranking military officials. They were tracking down the remaining X-wings, the ones that had left Coruscant after the reconditioning. Admiral Ackbar had suggested having some of the lower-grade officers doing this, but Leia wouldn't hear of it. She knew she could trust the people in the room. She didn't know many of the other officers, and she didn't know if she could trust them.

Too many lives were at stake. She had to know this was done right.

Besides, it gave her something else to concentrate on besides her anger at Meido. The no-confidence vote would be held the next day, and Senator Gno wanted her to campaign. She would: a single rousing speech just before the vote was held. She remembered no-confidence votes from her days in the Old Republic. They were often based on gut feeling. If she could make the remaining senators feel good about her, she would win the vote.

For now, though, she had to stay busy, even though it didn't seem to be helping as it normally did. Beneath her anger at Meido, she felt a deep unease. The skeletal face she had seen in the hallway kept resurfacing in her vision, and each time it did, she felt a low-grade fear, as if Han or one of the children were in grave danger. But she had contacted Anoth, and Winter had assured her that the children were fine. And she would know if something serious had happened to Han.

At least that was what she told herself.

"President Organa Solo." A lieutenant bent over her station. He looked impossibly young, and his voice had a tremor when he spoke to her. She still wasn't used to making people nervous just by being who she was. "There is a message for you. Would you like to take it privately?"

She glanced around the room. These people were her most-trusted friends. She had no secrets from them. "I'll take it here."

"I'll have it relayed. It's holo-coded." He left.

Wedge looked up from his station, a frown on his face. "Holo-coding. I haven't seen much of that since the Empire."

Leia nodded. She pushed her chair back. There was an open space on the floor between the terminals. The holo would show there.

Suddenly the air rippled. Then it smoothed into a see-through wall.

"It's coming from a long distance away," Admiral Ackbar said.

Leia stared at it intently. The feeling of unease that had followed her since the meeting was growing.

Finally the ripples coalesced into a face.

Leia gasped. It was the skeletal face of her visions. Its eyes were dark, endless, and its mouth was a thin black line. Its cheeks were concave and its forehead gleamed like bone. The face filled the center of the room.

"Leia Organa Solo." The mouth moved in time to the words. This was no mask like the one Vader had worn. This seemed real.

"I'm President Organa Solo," she said, rising to her full height.

There was a brief silence before his reply. "My name is Kueller. I'm sure you have not heard of me, but you have felt my presence."

A shudder ran down her back. How had he known that?

"You felt it when I destroyed the people of Pydyr in a single moment, without using anything as crude as a Death Star or a Star Destroyer. I prefer elegant, simple weapons, don't you?"

Leia jutted out her chin. She had to look regal and unafraid before this madman. "What do you want?" She used the same cold voice she had used on Meido.

Again, there was the pause. Then the death mask smiled at her. "Your attention, madam." She had the sense that the mask was part of Kueller and not part of Kueller. It chilled her.

"You have that. For the moment."

"Good." Kueller's face winked out. A ripple replaced it.

"Did we lose the transmission?" Wedge asked.

Admiral Ackbar shook his head. "No. He's doing something else. It's a function of the distance. Just like the moments of silence before his replies. It is taking time for this transmission to carry."

"We have instant communication all over this galaxy," the lieutenant said.

"Not all over," Wedge said softly.

An image waved, then coalesced into a small form collapsed on the floor. A small building burned beside it, and in the distance some metal burned.

Leia squatted. The figure was Luke. His flight suit was off and in rags. His back looked like a mass of raw flesh. He wasn't moving.

A wave of pain and anger hit her. She reeled backward, felt a bit of terror mixed with it, and through it all, she felt Luke.

Luke! she sent.

Leeee—

Luke's mental voice was cut off, replaced by a deep, throaty laughter Leia had never heard before.

His image winked away. The ripply see-through wall reappeared. And then the skeletal face was back, the laughter dying on its lips.

"No mental games, President Organa Solo. Your brother lives. For now."

"What have you done to him?" she asked.

The death's head smiled. The image was so large she felt as if she could fall into the mouth and never come out. "I did nothing. His ship conveniently destroyed itself."

"The X-wing," Wedge whispered. Admiral Ackbar shushed him.

"I would have preferred that he land a bit closer to home, but he did not. Still, he's on my property now, and on my property he will stay. Unless you do two things. First, you must disband your inefficient government. And second, you must turn power over to me."

"Why would we do that?"

"Because I will kill your brother if you do not."

Leia felt cold. Ice-cold. "You think I will trade millions of lives for one, no matter how much it means to me?"

"I know your heart, President. Your brother means as much to you as your husband. As your children. I could kill them now, if you like. Would that help you decide?"

Leia forced herself to swallow. She would not allow him to intimidate her with idle threats. But she had to be careful in case his threats weren't idle. "You're very far away to be making such threats, Kueller."

The smile grew wider. "Are you testing me, President? Because I warn you, I do not bluff."

"What do you really want?"

"I believe your government lost its effectiveness years ago. I want to return efficient rule to this galaxy."

"And you're the man to do so?" she asked.

The smile left the death's head. "I am the *person* to do so, President. I have done so on my homeworld. I can do it anywhere else."

"I've never heard of you," Leia said. "How do I know you're capable of such wisdom?"

"No one had heard of young Luke Skywalker before he rescued you from the Death Star. Or of the brash Han Solo before he joined Skywalker and Obi-Wan Kenobi. There were even planets that had not heard of you before the Rebellion, President. Sometimes reputations develop late."

"What will you do if I refuse to turn the New Republic over to you?"

The smile returned. "I will kill your brother. And your husband. And your children."

Leia put her hands behind her back. She used a Jedi calming method so that her emotions remained in check. She would feel terror and anger later. Now she had to be a leader. The best leader the New Republic had ever known. And sometimes being a leader meant knowing when to ask the right question. "What if I still refused?"

The death's head tilted, and part of its forehead disappeared out of the holo frame. She had surprised this Kueller. "You would refuse?"

"I haven't made any decisions yet," she said, keeping her voice calm. "I simply want to know my options."

"Then I will destroy your subjects, President."

"Why would you want to do that?" Leia asked. "Even if you succeeded, you'd have no one left to rule."

"There are always more worlds. With the wealth I

would have from the New Republic, I can find those worlds."

"You can't kill everyone in the Republic," Wedge said. "The Emperor tried to intimidate everyone into his power, and it took years."

The death's head's smile grew. "I can kill all of them at once."

"That's hundreds of worlds," Admiral Ackbar said. "You can't kill that many beings at the same time."

"Ah, but I can." The death's head turned and looked at something in its view, but its head suddenly faced Admiral Ackbar. The mouth gave an order in a language Leia was unfamiliar with.

She looked to Wedge in confusion. He shrugged, and as he did so, a wave of terror hit her. It was mixed with cold and voices screaming. She felt a betrayal and shock so deep that it devastated her. *Not again,* she thought. The weight of it made her stagger. *Stop!* she thought, or maybe she screamed. She didn't know. The cold grew deeper.

And then the voices were silent.

She was sitting on the floor, tears she hadn't known she had shed on her cheeks. The others in the room were staring at her in astonishment. Wedge helped her up. "What happened?"

The face had a triumphant look. The blackness behind the eyes seemed deeper. It felt more powerful than before.

Force-sensitive. Kueller could use the Force.

And he used it for the dark side.

As that realization filled her, the death mask smiled. "I am stronger than you will ever be, President. I am more powerful than you can dream."

"What did you do to her?" Wedge shouted.

"I'm all right." Leia worked to keep her voice calm. She let go of his arm.

"I did nothing to President Organa Solo. I merely gave you a demonstration of my powers. Overpopulation is such a problem, don't you think? I just rid the galaxy of at least a million lives. More room for the rest of us."

"A million lives?" Ackbar murmured.

"That is my second demonstration. You remember that feeling from the first time, don't you, President?"

"How can you?" Leia asked. "Those were people. Living, breathing people."

"Well, actually, most of them didn't breathe," Kueller said, "at least not in the way you do. But they no longer have to worry about breathing, through lungs or gills or airholes. See how good I am for the galaxy?"

"No," Leia said.

"I will not argue methods with you, President. You have heard my demands. Either you acquiesce, or in three days' time, I will kill your brother."

"You can't kill Luke Skywalker," Wedge said.

"Why not? Because he is a Jedi Master? Or because he is your friend?"

Wedge didn't answer.

The death mask turned its empty eyes to Leia. "You have three days, President. I give you time because I respect you." The head nodded. "Until then, President."

And the image was gone.

Leia let herself sink to the floor. A million lives. A million more lives as a demonstration to her.

Like Grand Moff Tarkin's demonstration of the Death Star.

Tarkin had taken her father. Kueller threatened her new family.

She wouldn't let him win. Han and Luke and her children would come home to her. And the New Republic would remain hers. She just didn't know how yet.

Twenty-nine

Luke had just finished a small meal from the canned rations still in the house. He was resting, regaining his strength as best he could. The feeling of being watched was gone, for the moment, but he knew it would return.

And it had something to do with Almania.

After he let the food settle, he would question the house's computer again. He was hoping it knew of a bacta tank or the Pydyrian equivalent. Anything to help him heal faster. He had to do more than Jedi practices. He knew that he would need all of his strength.

Once he found the bacta tank, he would start a search for a new ship. He wasn't sure if he would proceed to Almania, or if he would go back to Yavin 4 until he healed. He didn't know how much time he had; he wasn't even certain what he was searching for, and that made him uneasy.

This whole thing made him uneasy.

Luke?

Leia, reaching toward him from a long distance away, her mind filled with concern.

Leia?

But the connection broke; shattered as it never had before. He couldn't feel her. He reached with his mind, feeling for her familiar sense, and she wasn't there. It was as if someone had built a wall around his mind.

Leia?

She couldn't be dead, could she? Her thought for him had been filled with concern, but he thought the concern was for him, not because she was in trouble.

Leia?

He sought out the children, and could feel them, squabbling happily on Anoth. He even got a sense of his students back on Yavin 4, but not of Leia.

Or of anyone close to her. Something was blocking him. Something purposeful.

He sighed. Something more to seek out. Something else to sap his strength. He rubbed his eyes, taking a deep breath before trying again. He leaned forward in the chair made for a form smaller than his when the blast hit him. It knocked him backward, and he yelped with pain as the floor hit his injured skin. But that pain was nothing compared with the ice-cold pain that overwhelmed him. Pain, terror, the shock of betrayal, all at once, expressed in thousands of mental voices that were suddenly, irrevocably silenced.

The chill filled him. Then he remembered Anakin: *We made the room hot.*

Hot.

He sent heat into the cold, beating it back, cringing from the pain, his arms around his head to protect himself from the pink goo, from the stinging, from the cold, awful pain of death.

Death.

Death.

The chill disappeared, leaving a sour residue in his mouth. He raised his head, uncertain how long he had been on the floor.

It had happened again. Another planet destroyed.

He sent for Leia again, but didn't feel her. That block: hard, firm, powerful.

He stood, shaking. He had to find a computer connected to the nets or something that would give him information. Even though he knew, deep down, that nothing had happened to Coruscant.

That blast had been deeper, colder, more powerful than the first one. It had been closer.

Much closer.

And he even knew the source of the destruction.

Almania, and the presence that was waiting for him there.

* * *

"Who was that?" Admiral Ackbar asked.

"I don't know," Leia said. She brushed off her combat fatigues, and pushed back a strand of hair. She was sitting once more at her computer station, sending messages to Han, who didn't respond, and to the children, who did. Winter said they too had felt the blast, and this time she had known how to help them. She also said that Luke had helped them on his trip to Coruscant and, while they were shaken, they weren't as terrified as they had been the first time.

Leia spoke to them, reassuring them that she was fine, and then signed off.

"That death mask looked familiar," Wedge said.

"We used to have a collection of them in the National Museum on Alderaan," Leia said. "It comes from one of the farthest reaches of the galaxy."

"How do we know it's a mask?" the lieutenant asked. "It moved like a mouth."

"We don't," Leia said. "Do you know of any peoples who look like that? Or use masks like that to cover their faces?"

"Not off the top of my head," Admiral Ackbar said, "but we should check for it."

"We need to check for many things," Leia said. "We also need to find out where that transmission originated from." Her hair had slipped again. She pushed it back. Her hands were still shaking. "We also need to find out who died."

"I felt nothing, Leia," Wedge said.

"I know, Wedge. This Kueller, whoever he is, has some Force capability. He knew that I would feel those deaths. That was his demonstration."

"How do we know he didn't do some sort of sending, something that would have made you feel as though people died?" Admiral Ackbar said.

"We don't," Leia said. "But I can't imagine anyone having that kind of talent." She shuddered, the chill still numbing her heart.

"There are no reports of exploded planets," the lieutenant said, "either now or just before the bombing of the Senate Hall."

"Kueller said he used an elegant weapon," Wedge said. He slipped back into his chair. "We're looking for something too big. We need to know what planets haven't been heard from lately or what unusual events have transpired in nearby space."

"Lots of reports of midspace collisions in the landing area around Auyemesh," Ackbar said.

"And no response from their space-traffic-control unit," said Wedge, his voice rising with excitement.

"All attempts to contact others on the planet failing," the lieutenant said.

"Where's Auyemesh?" Leia asked.

"It's a tiny planet in a far system," Ackbar said. "It's on the Coruscant side of the Almanian system."

"The Almanian system?" Leia hated it when she was

ignorant of the galaxy. She thought she knew every place. Was this the Almania Lando mentioned?

"I haven't heard of it either," Wedge said, "and I thought I'd been everywhere."

"It's beyond the Rim Worlds in distance," Ackbar said. "The Old Republic was going to make Almania a member, but several senators fought it, saying the distance to the system was too great."

"Great distance," Leia whispered. "Admiral, you said that transmission came from a great distance."

Ackbar nodded. "The Almanian system is far enough away to have that sort of effect. In fact, holo-coding would be the preferred method of communication from that distance because it covers the other obvious tells of a long-distance communication."

"Because holo-coding is often slower than regular messaging," Wedge said.

"Precisely. It takes an expert to recognize the differences between coding problems and distance problems."

"All right," Leia said. "That gives us some kind of lead."

"President," said the lieutenant, "I've been running the name Kueller through our database. I have nothing."

"Keep trying," Leia said.

"Try all files instead of simply current files," Admiral Ackbar said.

"Leia," Wedge's voice was soft. "The computer identified the buildings around Luke. They're Pydyrian."

"Pydyrian?"

Wedge nodded. "That's also in the Almanian system."

"And Leia?" Admiral Ackbar said. "We just had it confirmed. The transmission came from Almania itself."

"Almania," she said. "What would anyone so far away want with us?"

"I think that's obvious," Wedge said. "The question is, how does this Kueller know you?"

"Perhaps you do know him," Ackbar said. "Perhaps that's why his face was hidden by the mask."

"If it was hidden by the mask," Leia said. She still wasn't convinced. She was good with voices, and she didn't recognize his. Holo-coding usually provided an accurate representation of everything, including the voice.

"We have something on Kueller," the lieutenant said. "But you aren't going to like it."

"Tell me anyway," Leia said.

"Kueller was an Almanian army general hundreds of years ago. He overtook Almania, and then the entire sector. In his later years, he was a beloved leader, known for his compassion and his decisiveness. But early on, when he was conquering, he was one of the most ruthless people in the history of the galaxy. He would do anything to consolidate power," said the lieutenant.

"So this Kueller is someone else, invoking a historical namesake," said Wedge.

"It fits with his intentions," Ackbar said. "If he wants to take over the New Republic, he is letting us know he will do it as ruthlessly as he can. And then, he believes, he will be compassionate and decisive."

"Decisive and ruthless go together," Leia said, "but compassionate and ruthless do not. Is he tied to the Empire?"

"Not so far as I can tell at the moment," the lieutenant said. "Almania is very far away. The Emperor basically ignored it."

"But it would be a good site for Imperials to hide," Ackbar said. "I'll check."

"There have been reports of stormtroopers in that section of the galaxy," the lieutenant said.

"Stormtroopers?" Leia asked. "Will they never go away?"

"Leia," Ackbar said, "we're now getting more reports from Auyemesh. The ships that managed to land found bodies everywhere. They were giving more details when all communication to the planet was shut down."

"Another killing?" Leia asked.

Ackbar shook his big head. "No. It was as if someone wanted just that much information out, and then stopped it."

"We have to be prepared for the assumption that this is all a hoax."

"A rather elaborate one, don't you think, Wedge?" Leia asked. "No, this Kueller is real. I have seen his face before. He's been haunting me for a while now. He's real, and he means business. We need to find out as much about him as we can."

The emotions she had been holding back rose inside her. She checked her own screen to see if she had had a reply from Han yet. Nothing. But he had told her he would be impossible to reach as long as he was on the Run.

The Run was far from Almanian space. She hoped he was safe.

"Admiral Ackbar, will you contact Mon Mothma for me, and tell her I want to see her in my chambers?" Leia asked. She was shaking too badly to do it herself. She had to leave now. "I'll contact you all for more information after I meet with her."

"Are you all right, Leia?" Ackbar asked.

Leia smiled tightly at him. "I don't think any of us will be all right until we do something about this madman."

"We will," Ackbar said with complete certainty.

She wished she had the same certainty. This Kueller had more Force capability than anyone she had encountered in years. Except Exar Kun, and he had been a spirit. Kueller was alive. He was using these deaths to replenish his own well of hatred. The dark side ate people from within, but while it did so, it gave them much too much power.

He appeared to have more power than she had. More power than Luke.

Luke. The echo of his mental voice still reverberated in her mind. He was probably on Pydyr.

She would help him, if it was the last thing she ever did.

Thirty

A pile of chips, scorched wires, and broken metal toppled on Threepio. The weight of it activated the sensors in his chest. They flared, warning that the weight had to be moved or he would suffer damage.

"Artoo?" Threepio's voice sounded muffled.

There was no corresponding beep. Artoo hadn't even noticed when the pile fell on Threepio. Artoo was chirruping softly to himself on the other side of the hallway, digging through a pile of rubble with all of his extensions.

"Artoo! I say, Artoo!"

Artoo whistled at him.

"Not in a moment! Now! Can't you see I'm trapped here?"

Artoo chirruped. Then Artoo hurried across the floor, moving carefully to avoid the debris.

A door opened on the side. Artoo's head swiveled.

"Hurry, Artoo!" Threepio apparently couldn't get himself out of the pile.

A Kloperian slid inside. He was wearing a guard uniform.

Suddenly Artoo's chirrups turned to submissive beeps. The Kloperian frowned at the debris pile.

"Artoo!"

Artoo moaned.

The Kloperian grunted, and swept the rubble off Threepio. Threepio sat up. "It's about time—"

He stopped when he saw the Kloperian.

"What're you doing here?" the Kloperian asked. "This is a restricted area."

"I—ah—I was trapped," Threepio said.

"Yeah. I noticed. But before that. How'd you get in here?"

"I followed him."

Artoo blatted at him.

"He seemed intent on something inside. When I queried him, he said he had seen something or someone, so I thought we'd better investigate. Surely we did nothing wrong."

The Kloperian crossed four tentacles over its gray chest. It frowned, making a hundred extra wrinkles on its already wrinkly face. "This place is restricted because it's dangerous. I'm not even supposed to be inside. It could kill a living being. But since you're a droid, I suppose there's no harm. Unless I get killed. Just get out."

"Gladly, sir," Threepio said. "Gladly."

He climbed out of the remaining rubble and toddled down the corridor. "Come along, Artoo."

Artoo whistled.

"Whatever it is, it will have to wait," Threepio said. "The good Kloperian has told us to leave, and leave we shall. No more of this heroic nonsense. Leave that to Master Luke and Mistress Leia."

Artoo beeped extensively.

"Yes, yes, I agree, droids can be heroes too, but not when they're disobeying Kloperians."

Artoo chirruped, then blatted.

"I suggest you save that language for the next time we're alone," Threepio whispered. "Do you remember our last run-in with a Kloperian?"

"Is everything all right?" the Kloperian asked. He started to follow them.

"Fine, sir, fine. I'm just trying to get this astromech unit to follow me. He's quite insistent about trouble inside."

"The trouble is that this building will collapse soon," the Kloperian said, "at least this section. I keep telling them that, when all those investigators come in here, but they don't listen to me."

"Investigators?" Threepio asked. "Were they looking into the bombing?"

"Is there anything else?" the Kloperian asked. "But they work inside the Hall itself where it's all unstable. There's even openings in the roof. I keep expecting to come on to my shift at night and find a bunch of them dead because the roof collapsed."

"You mean, they never investigated the hallway?"

"At the pace they're going, they'll never get outside the door. At least not in my lifetime. Maybe in yours." Then the Kloperian laughed, a squishy, rather sickening sound.

It had followed them all the way out. Once they were outside, it closed what remained of the door. "You better get back to your masters before I report you missing. That's standard, you know, for wandering droids."

"Maybe on Kloper," Threepio said, "but not on Coruscant."

"No one's updated your files lately, have they, protocol droid? There's a curfew for everyone at night, and that includes droids. This place has been different since the bombing, I tell you. You could trust folks once, at least the ones not associated with the Empire. But not anymore. To attack the government like that. I'm just glad it happened during the day. If it'd happened on my shift—"

"No one would have gotten killed," Threepio said.

Artoo made his little chuckling beeps.

The Kloperian blinked its fishy eyes at him, and then uncrossed two of its tentacles. "You got a point, don't you, droid? I never thought of it that way. Guess that's why you have logic circuits and I don't. I've been thinking of myself again. The wives always accuse me of doing that too."

"I'm sure they do," Threepio said. "Ah, thank you for rescuing me. My counterpart hadn't even noticed I was in trouble."

"He was too busy scavenging parts," the Kloperian said. "Don't think I didn't notice. I may not have any logic circuits, but I know when a droid works for smugglers. Next time I won't go so easy on you two, if you catch my meaning."

"We don't really work for smugglers," Threepio started, but Artoo interrupted him with a bleep. Threepio shot him a glare. Artoo bleeped again. "Really, Artoo—"

"I don't care who you work for," the Kloperian said. "I was just telling you. Don't come back here, at least not on my shift."

"Oh, don't worry," Threepio said. "We won't. Come along, Artoo." He put his hand on Artoo's round head and pushed him forward. They crossed the restricted line into the street. The Kloperian watched from the doorway. "I hadn't heard of the curfew, had you, Artoo?"

Artoo bleeped, then chirruped, and ended with a blatt.

"I'm not fond of it either," Threepio said, "but I do think we should return home."

Artoo swiveled his head, his own small version of no.

He extended his service arm, and in it, he held four more detonators.

"Artoo!" Threepio yelped. Then he forced himself to lower his voice. "If we're caught with those, you and Master Cole will be charged with sabotage for certain."

Artoo bleeped.

"I don't care if they are smaller. They're still evidence, aren't they?"

Artoo cheebled.

"I think that's the best suggestion you've had all day," Threepio said. "Do let's find Mistress Leia. She'll be able to help us. And in the future, do not interrupt me when I'm about to give her name. Had we done that the first time we met with the Kloperians, we wouldn't have gotten into that fix."

Artoo gave him a raspberry.

"And don't use language like that with me. You've gotten quite persnickety in your old age. I daresay you're even more peculiar than you were on Tatooine."

Artoo bleebled indignantly.

"Yes, I know you were on a mission. But you're not on one now, are you? You're trying to give yourself an importance because you're insecure now that Master Luke no longer needs you to navigate his X-wing."

Artoo beeped.

"There's no guarantee that the detonator is in all the X-wings," Threepio said. "I'm sure Master Luke will upgrade when he returns. They say the new X-wings are much better."

Artoo whined.

Threepio stopped walking. "What do you mean, if he returns?"

Artoo beeped an explanation.

"Oh," Threepio said. "I see. I hadn't thought of that. But you don't think Master Luke would take an X-wing with a detonator, do you? He would know, wouldn't he?"

Artoo moaned.

"Good heavens," Threepio said. "This is a much bigger mess than I thought."

✳ ✳ ✳

By his best guess, he had been treading water for most of a day. But he had no real way to tell time. He could only judge by how often Nandreeson ate. And Nandreeson ate a lot. A sweet fly here, a mouthful of gnats there, a garbage snipe as a snack. Lando had never seen so much disgusting food. He was using it as a barometer, a way of keeping himself occupied.

He had to. Treading water was strenuous, but it didn't occupy the mind.

Although his mind had turned to survival a while back. He could tell because his concentration would move from his limbs to his stomach to his desperate need for sleep. He didn't float much because he was afraid he would doze. Yet he needed to rest. When he floated on his back, he counted the watumba bats on the ceiling. They were gray, constantly shifting, and provided quite a challenge. He believed there were 350 of them, but the insect population in the room belied that. Watumba bats ate algae and rock dust. They acted as host for several flying parasitic bugs, including the parfue gnats that swarmed near the ceiling. If there were 350 watumba bats, the cavern would be black with parfue gnats.

Perhaps Nandreeson had eaten them all.

Lando's arms felt as if they had grown in size. His legs ached, and his lungs burned. He was hungry, too. At least the water, disgusting as it was, was fresh enough to drink. No salt, which would poison him, and no other trace minerals that would make him even thirstier. The water would sustain him until he came up with a plan.

It had something to do with the watumba bats. Something about watumba bats, Glottalphibs, and sweet flies. Something he couldn't quite remember.

But it would come to him.

Two Glottalphibs guarded the pool, as they had since the Reks had thrown him in. Nandreeson spent much of his time there, but he would leave on occasion to conduct his business. Lando saw that as a good sign. If Nandreeson truly believed that Lando was going to die, he would conduct business in front of him. But Nandreeson had enough doubt to go to a different cavern. And Nandreeson's doubt gave Lando confidence.

Lando dipped his head underwater. The pool's heat also lulled him, so he dunked himself on occasion to keep himself awake. Surfacing always cooled him a bit. He floated on his back, the Glottalphibs watching his every move.

If Nandreeson had doubts, that meant the plan wasn't foolproof. There was a way out of the pool besides the steps carved near Nandreeson's couch. Or perhaps Nandreeson just believed that Lando would find a way to overwhelm his guards and escape. Maybe Nandreeson had, over the years, remembered Lando as mightier than he truly was.

Lando hated to disappoint. He would have to prove that he was worthy of Nandreeson's fear, worthy of Nandreeson's hatred over all the years.

If only he could think of a plan.

He was dozing. He could feel his body sink into sleep. He rolled, dousing himself in the smelly liquid. It no longer shocked him. The exhaustion was taking its toll.

Lando was a healthy man in good physical condition. But Nandreeson was right about one thing: Human beings were not meant to spend a long time in water, especially with no food and no sleep.

Eventually Lando would lose consciousness, sink beneath the water, and drown. Not a very glamorous way to go. Not even very exciting. But satisfying for Nandreeson.

Lando rolled off his stomach and onto his back. The watumba bats were swarming across each other. He had to concentrate.

He had to find a solution soon.

Or he would die.

Thirty-one

Leia paced in her chamber. Still no response from Han. She checked her messages every few moments, but she knew nothing would come. Han still had to be on Smuggler's Run. He wouldn't ignore her message unless he hadn't received it.

Auyemesh was too far away for him to have been on it when Kueller took everyone's life.

At least she hoped so.

Han would have contacted her when he left the Run.

She had meant what she said to him just before he left. Sometimes she wished they were a normal couple with normal concerns. Then sitting down to dinner at night with her children would be routine, not the unusual. Sleeping beside her husband would happen every night instead of a few nights every other month.

But she was as loath to give up their life as he was.

Except at moments like these.

The chamber computer bonged. "Mistress Leia," it said with Threepio's inflections and Han's voice. She hadn't bothered to repair Anakin's tampering. Somehow the absurd prank he had pulled made her feel closer to her son. "Mon Mothma is here to see you."

"Let her in," Leia said.

She took one more glance at her messages. Only updates from Admiral Ackbar. All communication with Auyemesh had ceased. No one could raise anything from Pydyr, either, although on Pydyr, the communication system was not blocked. Attempts to contact Kueller on Almania were met with a reproduction of his death's-head mask, and silence.

"Leia?" Mon Mothma stood at the door. She looked older; the pain she had suffered when Ambassador Furgan poisoned her still showed in her face. "I came as soon as I could."

Leia nodded, unable to speak for a moment. Of all of her friends on Coruscant, only Mon Mothma would understand the dilemma Leia faced. And not even Mon Mothma, for all her savvy, could know how deeply the destruction of Auyemesh affected Leia. It brought all the feelings about Alderaan back. Feelings that then, as now, Leia had no time to deal with.

"Child, what can I do?"

Leia swallowed, then made herself smile. "That's what I want to talk with you about," she said. "I need your help."

"We'll catch this madman before he attacks your family," Mon Mothma said.

Leia's hands were clammy. She wiped them on her fatigue pants. "Hear me out," she said.

Mon Mothma nodded.

"Kueller contacted me. Not the government. Me. He holds my brother prisoner."

"Have we verified that?" Mon Mothma asked.

"Luke last reported in to Yavin 4 after he had left a planet named Telti. He said he was heading toward Almania and would check in as soon as he arrived. No one has heard from him since."

Mon Mothma let out a sigh and sank her elegant body

onto Leia's vanity chair. "I had hoped that Kueller was bluffing."

"He still might be," Leia said. "Luke might be near him, and threatening him instead of imprisoned by him. We're too far away, and we have none of our people there. We have no way to verify this."

Mon Mothma nodded.

"It seems to me," Leia said, "that Kueller has made this personal. He will destroy my family if he doesn't get his way. It was only as an afterthought that he threatened the people of the New Republic."

"Ackbar showed me a tape of the holocording," Mon Mothma said. "It seemed that way to me as well."

Leia sat on the edge of the bed. "I think Kueller was trained as a Jedi."

Mon Mothma's eyes widened. "Have you evidence of that?"

"Nothing concrete," Leia said. "But he's contacted me before. In ways that Luke would train his students to use. And he managed to shut off communication between me and Luke."

"A ysalamiri would do that," Mon Mothma said.

"Yes, and so could someone versed in the dark side." Leia let her words hang for a moment. "There is no record of a Kueller from Almania on Yavin 4. But Luke has lost a number of students—Jedi training is hard—and it wouldn't be inconceivable that some of them would go to the dark side."

"But why threaten you?"

Leia frowned. This was hard to articulate. "We're the most visible Jedi, Luke and I," she said. "Luke has brought back the Jedi Knights, and I am raising new Jedi. Luke has shown again and again that his powers will defeat someone strong in the dark side."

"But if Kueller destroys you, he scatters the Jedi, and becomes the strongest in the Force in the galaxy."

"Or so he thinks," Leia said.

"It sounds plausible."

"Yes." Then Leia smiled at herself. "But I am rattled. It might be much more simple than that. Kueller might misunderstand the way the New Republic works. He might think I'm an autocrat and that my word is law. Then threatening my family might get me to force my hand."

"He doesn't know you well, does he?" Mon Mothma said softly. "Threats to your family always make you stronger."

Leia's eyes burned. She rubbed at them. She didn't want sympathy. Not yet, anyway. Later, when she had time. "In either case," she said, choosing not to respond to Mon Mothma's last sentence, "the solution is the same. I need to step down as Chief of State."

Mon Mothma clasped her hands in her lap. "You can't do that now, Leia. I have had word from my sources in the Senate. Unless you campaign, you'll lose that no-confidence vote. They're looking to blame someone, anyone, for that bombing, and they'll blame Han, which means they'll blame you."

"I've thought this through," Leia said. She rubbed her hands together, nervous habits she hadn't used in years. "If I step down, the vote is null, right?"

"Well, technically, it's null only if you resign, Leia. A temporary standing aside will allow the vote to go forward."

Leia nodded. She had been afraid of that, but it didn't matter. Luke mattered. Protecting her children mattered.

Han mattered.

For the first time since she had become head of the New Republic, she could serve her family better as a private citizen than as a public one.

"I'll resign, then," she said. "The vote's called off, and

Kueller can no longer use the New Republic as his excuse for targeting my family."

"What if he's really after the New Republic?" Mon Mothma said.

"Then we'll find out. He'll threaten something else. But I'll wager he doesn't know as much about the other leaders of our government. I'll wager my resignation throws him into a panic."

"You're probably right."

Leia licked her lips, then turned. "I want you to take my place."

"I'm no longer an elected official," Mon Mothma said.

"You weren't one when you restarted the Provisional Council, either," Leia said. "We have no proviso other than elections for a situation like this. We just had emergency elections. We don't need another. I want you to step in. No one will fight you. You're too respected for that."

"A few days ago, someone could have said that about you."

Leia shook her head. "The opposition to my government began when the Imperials were elected to the Senate. This isn't really a surprise to me, much as it hurts. Everyone loses power eventually."

"This new Senate isn't going to stand for a leader arbitrarily chosen."

"Probably not," Leia said. "But you can convince them of the crisis. Set a date for an election, and say you're stepping in until then. I'll turn over my government to you in a formal recorded presentation."

"Recorded, Leia? Why not hold a special session tomorrow?"

"Because," Leia said, "I won't have time."

Mon Mothma tilted her regal head. "What are you planning, my child?"

Leia met her gaze squarely. "I'm going after my brother."

✶ ✶ ✶

Skip 6 was shaped like a giant seething mud hole, floating in the middle of the asteroid belt. The top of the Skip oozed slime along its surface, leaving particles on its ride through space. Landing the *Falcon* there would have been impossible. But Han hadn't brought the *Falcon.* Instead, he had appealed to Sinewy Ana Blue's conscience (or what was left of it) and got to use her Skipper.

Smugglers who spent a lot of time in the Run built ships perfect for the asteroid belt. They were small, narrow vehicles that didn't carry a lot of cargo, but helped smugglers move from place to place. The ships could land on any surface, including mud, and could take off in most conditions, even the constant swirling rock storms around Skip 52.

Blue's ship had been specially modified for her personal needs. It had a wider cargo bay than most, and larger crew quarters. Still, it was a landspeeder compared to the *Falcon.* Chewie had to bend double just to fit inside.

The fit was tight for all of them. Han had brought Zeen, Kid, Wynni, and Chewie. Blue came, she said, because she had hated giving Lando to those Reks. Han had to badger Zeen and Kid (at blaster point) into remembering how much they owed Lando. (Including all the new furnishings in their personal rooms. Lando could fight to refit the *Lady Luck* if and when he returned from his rendezvous with Nandreeson.) Wynni came because Chewie was along. Chewbacca had complained about that, but Han warned him to put up with it. Rescuing Lando came first. Dealing with unwanted romance was second.

Still, as Han was pressed against the unfinished metal wall of Blue's Skipper, he wondered if he had made the right decision. He couldn't breathe through the two pelts of Wookiee fur in front of him, and he couldn't see over Wynni's back. The crew quarters, about the size of the *Falcon*'s head, stank of sweaty humans and excited Wookiee. The heat was intolerable.

Blue had landed the Skipper delicately in the mud swamp. It wouldn't have mattered if she had landed hard. They were packed in so tight that nothing short of an explosion would free them. To make matters worse, it took her a long time to open the crew door.

Zeen and Kid staggered out, but Wynni was holding Chewbacca back. He was trying to shake her off.

"Wynni," Han said in his driest voice. "You might want to wait for some privacy."

Her fur stood instantly on end, the Wookiee version of a blush. She let go of Chewie's arm and he ran out of the room as fast as a doubled-over Wookiee could move.

Wynni roared at Han, and he shrugged. "I'm not trying to interfere with romance, Wyn," he said. "But Chewie has a mate, and I just want to get Lando out in one piece."

Wynni growled about the likelihood of that. Han ignored her assessment. Wynni had never liked Lando much, but she was an artist with a bowcaster, and bowcasters seemed to have a wonderful effect on Glottalphibs.

Han had been here once before, in an encounter with Nandreeson that he had done his best to forget. This had been before the Rebellion, even before Chewie. As he and Blue had poured over a map of Skip 6 it had become clear that the Skip hadn't changed.

There were tunnels leading to Nandreeson's lair, but he would have those guarded. The only other entrances were mud slides. Chewie had already lodged his complaint about those: Wookiee fur would get matted, and when it dried, it would limit his movements. Wynni had brought special suits for both of them, but she wouldn't let Chewie get his until he agreed to let her help him remove it. He had given Han a trapped look. Han had grinned, and Chewie had growled at him. But he had agreed.

Han later promised that he would help Chewie get out of the agreement, although he wasn't sure how.

Yet.

The Wookiees were in the cargo bay, putting on the suits. Han wished he had one too. He went to the door. The rest of the crew was already there, peering at the hole that led into the slide. Warm, wet mud bubbled around the opening. Steam rose from the sides.

"You want us to go through that?" Zeen asked.

"You'd rather face the Reks?" Han asked.

"I'd rather wait for you here."

"There's no guarantee Calrissian survived," Kid said.

"Lando made Nandreeson mad for years," Han said. "There's no way he'll give Lando the satisfaction of a quick, easy death."

"Han's right," Blue said. "Lando hasn't been gone that long. He'll be alive. He may not have much of a body left, but he'll be alive."

"If we do this," Zeen said, "we'll never be able to face Nandreeson again."

"Is that a problem?" Han asked.

"I just don't want the scaly butcher to come after me," Zeen said.

"If he comes after anyone," Kid said sweetly, "it'll be our dear Sinewy Ana Blue. It's her ship we've landed on this mud hole."

"Thanks," Blue said. "That means Han and I are going. You guys better come too. Your life would be miserable without me."

"It would certainly be less interesting," Zeen said.

"And probably safer," Kid said.

Chewbacca roared indignantly from the cargo bay. Two large hairy paws grasped the edge of the bay and levered Chewie out. He looked like a giant baby trussed up in the naming clothes Leia had insisted on using for the children, only his was silver and had no lace. His fur was combed back and hidden in the outfit's hood. Ties around the neck, wrists, and ankles were done so tightly that Han grinned.

"If I put helium into that outfit, will you turn into a giant Wookiee balloon?" he asked.

Chewie snarled. His mood was bad just from the proximity of Wynni. Han's jokes wouldn't make it any better.

"Charming look, Chewbacca," Blue said. "A bit overdone, don't you think?"

Chewie growled again, and reached for the hood.

"No," Han said. "I don't care what indignities you have to suffer. You leave that thing on. Put the face mask down."

Chewie shook his head.

"Put it down, Chewie. You want to be able to see, don't you?"

Chewie growled.

Han put up his hands, in a submissive/protective gesture. "Okay, okay. No need to get testy about it. It's your fur, and your decision."

"The bowcaster is wrapped, just like you requested," Zeen said, handing it to him. "I've got Wynni's here too. Where's she?"

She growled from below.

Han suppressed a grin. "What did you do to her, Chewie?"

Chewie shrugged, took his bowcaster, and slung it

over his shoulder. The weapon itself was protected, but the strap remained.

Blue pushed past him and looked into the cargo bay. "Chewbacca! That's not funny. Untie her."

Chewie gave Han a pitiful glance.

"We need her, pal. Sorry."

Chewie pressed the button beside the bay. The floor rose, slowly, revealing a pink package of female Wookiee, face mask down, arms wrapped around her chest in a mock hug, the wrist ties holding her hands behind her like rope. Her legs were crossed and tied together at the ankles.

She was cursing, the mask poofing with each breath, the Wookiee words coarser than anything Chewie had ever used, even under extreme duress.

Blue went behind her to untie her.

"Wait!" Han said.

He yanked up her face mask. Her blue eyes were narrow. She cursed him, his ancestors, his wife, his children, and his ship.

"Watch it," Han said. "No one talks about the *Falcon* that way. Not in my presence."

Wynni snarled. Blue shoved her from behind. "If you want out of this, you'd better shut up."

"Promise to leave Chewie alone, and we'll untie you," Han said.

Wynni clamped her muzzle shut.

"Promise," Blue hissed.

Wynni nodded once.

"Chewie, you promise to leave Wynni alone," Han said.

Chewbacca howled.

"Promise," Han repeated.

Chewie crossed his arms, straining the fabric over his shoulders. He growled.

"That's that then," Han said. "Untie her, Blue."

Blue pulled the strings, and Wynni's arms dropped. Her paws slid out of the sleeves and she lunged at Chewbacca. He moved backward. She tripped. Han and Blue caught her before she hit the ground.

She was heavy. Han staggered under her weight. She was snapping, growling, and snarling. "Apologize, Chewie."

Chewbacca shook his head.

Wynni grabbed at Han's leg, missed, and swiped again. "Apologize, blast it, she's going to kill me."

Chewie wailed an apology.

Wynni stopped moving. Then she used Han and Blue to brace herself as she stood. She growled, and Zeen bent to untie her feet.

"I think we should leave the Wookiees here," Kid said.

Chewie yowled.

"I think that's a bad idea," Han said. He stretched. Wynni was strong, stronger maybe than Chewie. "I think you two need to settle your differences when we return to Skip 1. Until then, you have a truce. Is that clear?"

Chewie nodded. Wynni glared. Her pink hood had come askew, and her fur hung over her eyes. She brushed it away.

"Wynni? Is that clear?"

She nodded.

"Good," Han said. "Let's hope this little diversion didn't give the Reks time to get here."

"You think Nandreeson knows we're here?" Zeen asked.

"You think anything happens on this Skip without Nandreeson knowing?" Han asked.

"Good point," Zeen said. He handed Wynni her bowcaster. "Let's go, then."

"Someone needs to head this mission," Han said.

"You're the only one with military experience, General," Blue said. "It's all yours."

Han felt an internal relief. Chewie and Wynni had just acted out his worst nightmare. The last thing he wanted was for all of them to get down below, and to fight among themselves as to the right thing to do.

"All right," he said. "Into the mud."

"You take us such exciting places," Blue said as she grabbed her nose with one hand and leaped out the Skipper's door. She landed in the center of the mud hole and slid in, her long hair disappearing last.

"Man, this is a dream day for me," Zeen said. "First we get all muddy, then we face off with Nandreeson. All over Calrissian, whom I just *love.* Next time, Solo, bring your government friends."

Zeen jumped and landed on the edge of the hole. He lost his balance and slid, back-first, down the opening.

Kid stepped into place at the door, but Wynni shoved him aside and jumped without saying anything. She landed so hard she splattered mud into the Skipper. The splatter hit Han in the face. The mud was hotter than he had expected, and smelled vaguely of rotten eggs. He wiped the mud off with the back of his arm.

"Chewie," he asked sweetly, "you want to go next?"

Chewie yarled.

"I'll go," Kid said, and jumped. He slid into the hole as if it had been greased just for him.

"Better you than me, pal, stuck between two Wookiees," Han said under his breath.

Chewie growled.

Han shook his head. "I'm last, Chewie. It's better that way. I can face any problems we might have on the surface. If I don't make it down, you guys can get Lando out."

Chewie snorted, brought a paw up to his nose, and

grabbed it. Somehow his look was less elegant than Blue's had been. He closed his eyes, stepped out, lost his balance, and belly flopped into the mud. The splat doused Han, and made Chewie roar in surprise. He staggered, tried to stand, and then slipped into the hole.

Han wiped his face again, set the door on automatic as Blue had showed him to do, and jumped.

The mud was hot and slimy. It coated him instantly, but he was sliding right away. There was air in the tube, swampy, stale, foul air, but air, which he could breathe as long as his nose and mouth were clear. He slid round and round and round, corkscrewing his way deeper into the mud hole. The light from the top faded, and he was in complete darkness, surrounded by stinky mud, and sliding faster and faster toward the bottom.

Maybe he had made a mistake. Maybe these tubes were longer than he thought. Maybe they narrowed and all of his friends were stuck in the middle, piled on top of each other, and suffocating.

He had a horrible vision of Chewie and Wynni coming to blows as the oxygen left them, killing Zeen and Kid in the process. Blue, of course, would have been squished almost from the start.

Then he slid out in a gush of mud, tumbled through comparatively cool air, and landed, face-first, in the dirtiest water he had ever seen. He sank like a boat with a hole in its bottom, his eyes open. Sediment swirled around him. Sediment, algae, and long black hair.

Blue was still below, her foot caught in a hole. Her eyes were wide, her cheeks bulging with air, but she wasn't panicked, not yet. Her hands were pulling at the weeds clinging to her ankle.

Han pulled the small vibroblade from his boot and dove down beside her, touching her arm for reassurance. He cut the weeds away, then yanked her foot. She let out a mouthful of air, bubbles surrounding them, and then she did panic, using his back as leverage to propel herself to the surface.

The force of her shove sent his arm into the hole that had caught her foot. The heat made his skin prickle, but his arm wasn't trapped. He pulled free, and kicked to the surface, his lungs bursting.

He gasped a mouthful of air. It was warm and humid and tasted good. But he didn't seem to be able to get enough. It was thin.

"Nice place, Solo," Zeen said. He was treading water next to the Kid, whose bald head was covered with green algae.

"Yeah, you shoulda warned us we'd be swimming," Kid said.

The air in Chewie's suit kept him afloat. Apparently Wynni had gotten a hole in hers. Both their hoods were off.

Wookiees looked smaller when wet.

Han felt a smile begin on his face, and Chewie growled it away.

"Where's Blue?" Han asked.

"Here, you son of a garbage scow." She was furiously treading water. She would lose all her air quickly if she continued the rapid flailing motion. "I nearly died down there."

"Ah, Blue, you'd have gotten yourself out."

"And for no reason." She spat as she spoke. Her black hair streamed around her face, and her makeup had run. She looked years younger. Only her blue tooth reminded him that she was Sinewy Ana Blue. "I'm not going to get rich off this trip. Even now, Nandreeson's people are probably stripping my Skipper. And there's no way out of this rock pond. Have you noticed that?"

Han looked around. The water went all the way to the

edge of the cavern walls. But he saw signs of Glottalphibs. Algae. Lily pads. Gnats.

"There has to be." He swam forward, rounded a rock wall, and found himself in an even bigger cavern. Six Glottalphibs sat on the rock ledge surrounding the pond, and another Glottalphib—Nandreeson—was waist-deep in water.

Lando was in the middle of the pond, his head barely above water. His face was gray with exhaustion, shadows deep under his eyes, his movements sluggish. Still he managed his Calrissian smile.

"Some rescue, Han," Lando said.

"You should never criticize people who are doing you a favor," Han said. Chewie swam up, followed by Wynni. The smell of wet Wookiee overpowered everything.

"Solo," Nandreeson said. "I was going to give up on getting you. I had Calrissian. That was enough. But since you're here now—" He waved a tiny hand and all six Glottalphibs blasted the water with flame.

Han ducked under and watched the algae burn on the water's surface. He still hadn't gotten enough air. Chewie had apparently stayed above. He splashed the flames out.

Han surfaced.

"Next time, why don't you just call ahead?" Lando said. "We'll prepare a welcoming party for you."

"Stop the sarcasm, pal," Han said. "It was lucky I found out you were here."

"Yeah?" Lando asked. "Lucky for whom?"

"Me, of course," Nandreeson said. "Now I get my old nemesis Calrissian and his buddy Solo. Killing you, Solo, will give me an added cachet. The princess's consort—"

"Husband," Han mumbled.

"—will be quite a coup for me."

"What's going on here?" Han asked. "Is he playing water hockey and you're the puck?"

"Close," Lando said. "He's planning to watch me drown."

"Nice," Han said. "Lacks drama, but makes up for it in creativity."

"Not really," Lando said. "He's a Glottalphib. He'd think of drowning first since his entire life is situated around water."

"I don't need this," Nandreeson said.

"It does have the added charm of being escape-proof," Lando said.

"Nothing is escape-proof," Han said. "There's stairs beside Nandreeson."

"Right," Lando said, "if we can get to them. But his hot-mouthed buddies keep stopping me."

"That's because you haven't thought this through," Han said.

"And you have?" Nandreeson leaned forward, disturbing the water around him. "You've only been here a few moments, Solo. You think you have me figured out."

"Not much to figure, Nandreeson," Han said. "You're greedy, rapacious, and not very bright. If you had half the brains Jabba had, you'd own the Run by now."

"I do," Nandreeson said.

Han shook his head. "Naw. If you owned the Run, then how would I have been able to recruit a team?"

"You didn't." Zeen had Han's arm. Han turned, and found himself nose-to-nose with Zeen's blaster. The Kid had his blaster on Chewie, and Wynni had her bowcaster out and loaded.

"Great rescue," Lando said. "Excellent rescue. In fact, the best rescue I've ever experienced."

"I warned you about the sarcasm," Han said. He glanced at Chewie, who looked as stunned as he felt.

"You know, Solo," Nandreeson said, "you're right.

This drowning method lacks originality. I'm tired of watching a man die slowly. Let's speed it up, shall we?"

Han raised his hands. "Now, Nandreeson, I didn't mean—"

And then he ducked as the shooting started.

Thirty-two

Luke couldn't find a bacta tank, but he found something better: a Pydyrian healing stick. He had forgotten that Pydyr was the place that had invented the healing stick. It had been used all over the galaxy long before the bacta tank came into being, and some thought the healing stick was much better.

He found his upstairs in the house he was staying in. The healing stick was long, thin, and white. When rubbed against a surface, a white residue remained behind. The computer had assured him the residue had healing properties. What he was learning, as he gingerly applied the stick to his injured back, was that it had soothing properties. Most of the pain from the burn faded.

If only he could repair his hand. He had peeled most of the artificial skin off, but the moving metal parts reminded him, a bit too painfully, of the price he had paid to become a Jedi.

He was nearly done with the healing stick when he felt a disturbance in the Force. A familiar presence was nearby. This was the presence he had felt on Telti, the presence that had haunted him when he arrived in Almanian space, the presence that had lured him from Coruscant to here, this desolate side of nowhere.

A student. That much he was sure of now. He prided himself on his ability to remember all of his students, but this one still eluded him. If he told himself the truth, he remembered all the students who completed the training. The students who left became faces, a memory, and, Leia warned, someday they would become a statistic.

He set down the healing stick and put his shirt back on. His lightsaber had never left his side. He glanced in the mirror. His back was covered with white residue. It was foaming. The computer had warned him that a person must rest for the healing stick to work. Luke hoped he would get that chance.

Slowly he limped his way down the stairs. He was stiff from the fall, his muscles aching with pain. The mistmakers had weakened his system; the burns and the fall had made him lose even more strength. If he was at ten percent of his normal power, he was high.

Size matters not, Yoda had told him.

He hoped that applied to strength as well.

The presence had neared. It was strong in the dark side. He could feel the ripples, feel a power he hadn't felt in a living being since he encountered the Emperor. Luke had never had a student that powerful, of that he was certain. Whoever it was became powerful after he had left the academy.

So powerful that a man like Brakiss, who had so much talent in the Force that the Empire had taken him, as a baby, to train in the dark side, was terrified of him.

Once Leia had asked Luke what it felt like when he knew someone steeped in the dark side was near. He hadn't been trained enough as a young Jedi to understand the feeling. It was only later, as he grew in strength, that he understood. And he couldn't explain it then.

He could now.

It felt as if a tornado had struck in the middle of a beautiful day. It felt like a blast of cold air in a warm room. It felt as if someone beloved had just died.

He followed the feeling. It grew closer as he approached its source. He grabbed his walking stick, limped outside the house, into the Pydyrian sunshine, and stopped near the arch.

In the street, a man stood alone. He was taller than Luke—many people were taller than Luke—and he wore a long black cape, shiny military boots, and body armor reminiscent of the Empire's. Only his face was different. He wore a Hendanyn death mask. Luke had only seen them in museums, never on a face. The mask molded to the skin. The Hendanyn wore the mask after they reached old age, partially to hide the aging, and partially to store memories before death. The information in the mask could be removed after death. The Hendanyn masks Luke had seen had never been used.

This one had molded itself to the man's face. The cheekbones were raised, the eyes were black and empty, the lips thin and hard. The mask was white with black accents. It had tiny jewels in the corners of the eyeslits. Behind the jewels, if Luke's memory served, lay the chips that absorbed the personality of the wearer.

"You still don't recognize me, do you, *Master* Skywalker?"

The voice had a depth and resonance that was unfamiliar. But the inflections were familiar. This was an adult voice. Luke had been familiar with the young adult's voice, one that hadn't yet reached its full depth.

"Dolph?" he said, guessing with as much certainty as he could muster.

The death mask's mouth closed. Luke felt the surprise in the man across from him. Dolph had counted on not being recognized.

"You're better than I realized," Dolph said. His resonating voice filled the street. A dry wind made his cape ripple behind him. "My name is Kueller now."

Everything depended on how Luke played the next few moments. Dolph had been an extremely talented student who had always had a darkness in him. Such darkness wasn't unusual. All of Luke's students had to fight the dishonorable parts of themselves. Most won that battle. But Dolph hadn't stayed at the academy long enough to develop the talent or dispel the darkness. He had left in the middle of the night after receiving news from home.

"You left before I had the chance to give you my condolences over the deaths of your family," Luke said.

Dolph—Luke refused to think of him as Kueller just yet—smiled. The death mask moved with startling realness. "Thank you, *Master,*" he said. And then his smile faded as quickly as it had appeared. The effect was stunning. The death mask had a powerful, primitive terror built into it. The loss of the smile almost—almost—made Luke take a step backward. It would have overwhelmed a lesser man.

"But," Dolph continued, "your sympathies are both false and too late. The Je'har brutally slaughtered my family. They did not die quickly. My parents were staked to the bridge leading to the Je'har palace, and left to rot in the heat. It took them a week to die. I didn't hear about it until afterward, but the Je'har left the bodies for me to find. You wouldn't know what that is like, seeing the burned and broken skeletons of the people who raised you, a stench rising from them that should never come from any living being. You don't know what that does to a man."

The memory of Aunt Beru and Uncle Owen as he had last seen them rose in Luke's mind. Their bodies were burned beyond recognition, smoke still rising from them.

The only comfort he took in the years that followed was that they had died side by side, as they had lived.

"No," Luke said, "I don't suppose I do know what that does to a man." He knew what it had done to him. It had forced him to grow up in a moment, forced him to fight the evil that had caused his family's deaths.

It had not turned him into a monster. He understood Dolph's pain, but not his reaction to it.

"When I came home," Dolph said as if Luke hadn't spoken, "I buried my family, and I vowed vengeance on the Je'har. Vengeance I took without your help. I am stronger now, Skywalker. I will be stronger than you."

"Is that important to you?" Luke asked. He was leaning harder on his cane than he needed to. He wanted Dolph to think he was weaker than he really was.

"Of course it is," Dolph said. "Your government condoned the actions of the Je'har. Your sister opened trade with them, and treated them as a reputable government instead of the terrorists they were. It took me, acting first alone, and then with my own people, before the Je'har were revealed for what they were."

"And what's that?" Luke asked.

"Monsters," Dolph whispered. "Monsters, Skywalker. But you wouldn't understand that."

"No," Luke said. "I don't." He walked a few steps closer to Dolph. Dolph's cape snapped in the breeze, revealing a lightsaber at his side. "Tell me, Dolph, what's the difference between the Je'har and you?"

The death mask's mouth thinned, making the skeletal face almost rigid. "Does speaking in riddles amuse you, Skywalker? Or do you do it to buy time?"

"I do it," Luke said, "because I am truly curious. You've destroyed every being on this planet. I suspect that in the time I was here, you destroyed another planet as well. The Je'har murdered people who didn't agree with its policies on Almania. Murder is murder, Dolph, at least to me. Is it to you?"

The death mask shivered, almost as if it were separating itself from the face. "My name is Kueller."

"Your name is Dolph," Luke said. "And I will only talk to Dolph. The Dolph I met was a gifted, loving boy who had a vast future before him. That's the person I want to talk to."

"That Dolph is dead," Dolph said. "The Je'har murdered him when they murdered his family."

"And left Kueller in his place?"

"Yes," Dolph whispered.

"But you don't need Kueller," Luke said. "Kueller helped you survive, but you don't need him anymore. You have me. Come with me, Dolph, back to Yavin 4. We can heal those wounds the Je'har put in your heart."

The death mask didn't move, although behind the mask, real eyes glinted. Luke could see their reflection but not their shape and color. Then the flash disappeared.

"You can heal the wounds?" The voice was full of sarcasm. The eyes were gone again, deep black pools in their place. "You can resurrect my family, Skywalker? I doubt that. Not even Jedi tricks can bring the dead back to the world of the living."

"We all experience deep pain," Luke said. "It's the price of surviving. How we handle that pain is what matters."

"I've handled it my own way," Dolph said. "I will continue to do so. I will make certain no one like the Je'har appear in the galaxy again."

"How do you plan on doing that?"

Dolph swept his gloved hand around. "The Je'hars of the universe shall disappear, along with those who serve them. Those like your sister and her government."

"Leia had nothing to do with your family's murder," Luke said.

"Precisely." Dolph's voice grew even lower. "And she was one of the few who could have prevented it."

The hatred had festered so deep in him that it fueled the dark side. No wonder he had grown so strong so quickly.

Luke stopped a few meters from Dolph. "Brakiss said you wanted me to come here."

Dolph nodded. He let his arm fall slowly. "I want to give you a choice, Master Skywalker. I need your strength. Join me, and rid this universe of the evils of beings like the Je'har. Together we can make this a better place."

"I will join you," Luke said, "if you renounce the dark side."

Dolph laughed. The sound was deep, echoey, and icy-cold. "You should have learned long ago, Skywalker. There is no dark side. The rules you placed on the Force were placed on you by a weak and frightened old man, placed so that you would never grow to your full potential. Join me, Skywalker, and you can become what you were meant to be—the strongest man in the galaxy. The Force will be with you. It will guide you. It will give you everything you want."

"It already has," Luke said.

"Has it?" Dolph's voice was soft. "Really, Master Skywalker? Your sister has three children and a husband who loves her. You embrace no one. You have companions, but no family. You teach tricks you learned long ago, and search the galaxy for challenges. You have no real home. Is that what you want, Skywalker?"

"Everyone's life can be made to sound bad, Dolph," Luke said. "I enjoy mine. I value it, and I wouldn't change it."

"Not even to make it better?"

"Not your way," Luke said.

"So be it, then." The mask hardened and became part of Dolph. Luke could see the physical transformation, and knew then that he was watching Kueller, the man Dolph had become. There would be no more reasoning with the boy Luke had known.

Slowly Kueller drew his lightsaber, the hiss filling the street. Its blade burned blue.

"I don't want to fight you, Dolph," Luke said.

"You won't be fighting Dolph," Kueller replied. He slashed at Luke. In one quick movement, Luke grabbed his lightsaber and blocked Kueller's swipe with his own blade. The electric clang of the sabers filled the air, sending sparks all around them. Each movement ripped at Luke's back, but he focused on the blade instead: parrying, defending, blocking, never really attacking. He would wait until Kueller was open before making his move.

Kueller hit at Luke's left, then his right, then his heart. But Luke kept blocking. Kueller pushed Luke backward, toward the house. Luke stumbled on his weak leg, and collapsed on the knee. A river of pain ran through his thigh. Kueller brought his lightsaber down onto Luke's shoulder, but Luke rolled away from it, his back burning as dirt from the road ground into his wounds.

He pushed himself up and swiped at Kueller, singeing his cape. The hum of lightsabers filled the air. Sweat ran down Luke's face. His strength was gone. He had gone through too much in the last few days. But he concentrated on Kueller's movements, lived for Kueller's movements, blocked them, anticipated them, and held his ground.

In a series of five rapid thrusts, Kueller moved Luke backward again. Luke parried, parried, parried, but couldn't keep his balance. His ankle was clearly broken and unable to support him. Kueller jabbed at Luke's left side. Luke swiveled to dodge, and Kueller jabbed again. Luke's ankle buckled, but he didn't fall. Kueller pushed closer, and knocked Luke's lightsaber from his hand.

Kueller held his blue blade beneath Luke's chin. Luke could feel its heat, smell its electric tang.

"I should kill you now," Kueller said.

Luke was breathing hard, but he felt no fear. He could call the lightsaber to him, and continue the battle, but somehow he knew that Kueller wasn't yet ready to kill him.

He met Kueller's dark, empty gaze. "Killing me will not strengthen you."

The mask smiled in a skeletal imitation of death. "Ah, but it will, Master Skywalker."

"No," Luke said. "A Jedi welcomes death. He does not fear it."

"Are you telling me that, Skywalker, or yourself?"

"You, Dolph."

"I am not Dolph!"

"As you wish," Luke said. He was standing on his broken bone. The entire leg had gone numb.

"I should kill you," Kueller said again, "but I need you to lure your sister here."

"You don't want to face two of us, Dolph."

Kueller snapped his fingers. Dozens of stormtroopers, their white uniforms gleaming in the sun, emerged from the surrounding buildings. "Take him to Almania."

"That's a lot of soldiers for one man," Luke said, with some amusement.

"I know who you are, Skywalker." Kueller kept the tip of the lightsaber near the tender skin under Luke's chin. "I will never underestimate you."

The stormtroopers surrounded him. He braced himself, about to jump free, when something pricked the back of his neck. He brought up his hand, turned in surprise, and saw a stormtrooper behind him, holding a slight needle.

"Good night, Master Skywalker," Kueller said, as Luke collapsed onto the ground.

✶ ✶ ✶

Leia was nearly finished outfitting *Alderaan.* The ship was designed especially for her, an escape vehicle when she needed it, an emergency vehicle when the times called for it, as they had when Hethrir had stolen her children. *Alderaan* had no markings on her outside, and her name was known only to a few. She was identified by her number, and her owner was listed as a woman named Lelila. Lelila was actually Leia's nickname from childhood, her second identity, one that had served her well in her search for her own children not so long ago.

It would serve her well now, in her search for her brother.

Luke? she sent again, but again, she received nothing in return.

Luke had appeared so badly injured in that holo. Perhaps he was dead. Perhaps he hadn't survived the explosion of his X-wing.

Perhaps, perhaps, perhaps. She couldn't live with perhaps. Her brother had been given up for dead many times. She had learned to believe that he could survive the most impossible circumstances. She had learned that when she and Lando had found him hanging upside down from a weather vane below Cloud City.

She sent a final coded message along all computer channels, trying to find Artoo. He was probably still in repair. Those Kloperians had nearly destroyed him twice, and she had left an order—one of her last official acts—that the Kloperians who worked in the ship docks be relieved of their duties until she was certain that they were not guilty of any tampering. She suspected them because of their behavior toward her droids. If they had left the droids alone, she would have thought them innocent victims, like everyone else.

If Artoo didn't arrive soon, she would go alone. Time was the most important factor here. If Luke was alive, but badly wounded, he might not be able to defend himself. Sometimes his powers seemed magical to those around him, but she knew beneath it all that Luke was as human as anyone else.

And as vulnerable.

Death took even the greatest Jedi Knights. She had watched Obi-Wan die, raising his lightsaber, and allowing Vader to slice him through.

That image had stayed with her all these years. For while Luke had come to see that moment as a sign of Ben's power, Leia had always seen it as an example of power's limitations.

She had never spoken to Obi-Wan Kenobi when he was alive. Only when he was a ghostly vision, like her real father and Yoda. Obi-Wan hadn't seemed strong then. A guide, a teacher, and little more.

A knock on the hatch made her whirl. No one knew she was here, except Mon Mothma, and she wouldn't come here. Artoo, if he had received Leia's message, wouldn't knock.

She tapped her exterior screen. Wedge stood there, wearing his general's uniform, his hair slicked back, his hat tucked under his arm. He looked very official.

Her mouth went dry. Silly to be afraid of a friend, but she was suddenly. She didn't want him to tell her to stay, and she didn't want him to notify anyone that she had left—at least not this early on.

Still, she couldn't deny him. She opened the hatch and waited for him in the cockpit.

He had to duck under the door as he stepped in. "Leia?" he said. "Mon Mothma sent me."

"I'm not staying, Wedge," she said. "No matter how much you argue. Luke is in trouble, I can't raise Han, and by the time the Senate votes to help, Luke will be dead."

Wedge put his hat on the copilot's chair. "I know, Leia. You don't have to justify your actions to me. Mon Mothma didn't send me here to prevent you from leaving. She sent me to accompany you."

Leia shook her head. "That won't be necessary, Wedge. It's better for me to go alone. But if you can find Artoo, I'd appreciate that."

"You don't understand," Wedge said. "Mon Mothma is sending me and a fleet with you."

Leia's legs felt suddenly weak. She leaned against the controls. "A fleet? She can't do that. It takes full approval of the Senate."

"Technically," Wedge said. "There are always ways around that, as you well know."

"But she doesn't dare. The Imperials in the Senate will crucify her."

"They won't know if we do it soon," Wedge said. "The fleet will be long gone by the time they object."

"And then they'll throw her out. Wedge, this is precisely the kind of thing I wanted to prevent when I asked her to take my place."

"Trust Mon Mothma, Leia. She managed to unify a diverse group of Rebels and make them into a real government. She has a devious side."

That caught Leia. She frowned. "What's her plan?"

"To let us go. The ships are already being prepared. She believes we need to get rid of this Kueller as quickly as we can. Under your leadership, we can do that, Leia."

"What's so devious about that?"

"If we win, you'll get the credit. It will stop the no-confidence vote when you return. It'll allow you to remain Chief of State."

"And if we lose?"

"She denounces us. We become rogues who went off on our own, trying to save the New Republic, and failing." Wedge leaned toward her, his expression sincere. "If we fail, Leia, our reputations won't matter."

"They will to my children," Leia said.

"Your children will be protected. Mon Mothma knows how precious they are. It's lucky that they're not on Coruscant for this. It means Mon Mothma can manipulate the information any way she wants."

"A fleet," Leia said, the plan slowly sinking in. With a fleet, she might actually have a chance. Kueller would expect her to give in, or to wait for his next message. If he knew her as well as he thought he did, he might even guess that she would try to rescue Luke. But he would never imagine a fleet. "What about the X-wings?"

"Most are unusable," Wedge said, "but we've rebuilt a few. Mostly the team will be relying on Headhunters, A-wings, B-wings, and Y-wings."

"This sounds like a large fleet," Leia said.

"Luke's important."

She smiled softly. "And Mon Mothma reviewed the holocording, and believes that Kueller is a big threat. You forget how often I've fought at her side, Wedge. She has never believed in sitting still. She believes in fighting. She believes in having the advantage of surprise."

"Then we'd better get moving," Wedge said. "Do you want to fly in the flagship?"

Leia shook her head. "I've never been a military commander, Wedge. You have the charge of this mission. I'm taking *Alderaan*. Let me focus on Luke. You can remind Kueller that we took down the Empire. A small, petty demagogue on a faraway planet poses no threat to us at all."

"You don't believe he's that weak, do you?" Wedge asked.

"No." Leia smiled ruefully. "I think he's one of the worst threats we've ever faced."

Thirty-three

The water churned with blaster fire. As Han dove under the water, Chewie grabbed Wynni's bowcaster. Han didn't see if Chewie was able to wrestle it from her. Instead, he swam deep, grabbed Zeen's legs, and tugged him under.

Zeen immediately kicked at him, but Han hung on. He pulled with all his strength, and got Zeen next to him. Zeen's blaster slowly sank beside them. Zeen flailed at Han with his arms. Han just clung. His lungs burned from the struggle, but Zeen's mouth was open. He wouldn't last as long as Han.

Zeen's fist connected with Han's chin, but the water softened the blow. Han put his hands on Zeen's shoulders and shoved him downward. Zeen grabbed for Han but missed. The momentum of the water, and the sinkhole, pulled Zeen deeper.

Han swam to the surface. Lando had Kid in an armlock, and they were struggling, both going under then coming up and spitting out water. Laser bolts were sizzling the water all around them. Chewbacca was firing Wynni's bowcaster at the Glottalphibs. One lay dead on the ledge, while another floated facedown on the pond, a black stain swelling around its body. The other Glottalphibs were shooting fire at the water, boiling it. The heat was incredible. Han couldn't tell if his face was covered with pond water or sweat.

Nandreeson was firing at them with his blaster. Wynni was unconscious, but floating on her back in the scummy water, her snout safely in the air.

Han grabbed the blaster out of Kid's hands, punched him in the face, and pushed him under as he had Zeen. Then Han grabbed Lando and pulled him up.

"Breathe, buddy."

Lando was breathing, hard, but he nodded and swam free. Han handed him the blaster, and then grabbed his own blaster from its pouch around his waist. He was treading water and firing at the remaining Glottalphibs, aiming for the centers of the mouths.

Out of the corner of his eye, he saw Lando float on his back, take aim, and blast the ceiling.

Han whirled, about to tell him not to waste his shots, when a million watumba bats swooped down. Chewbacca roared, and immediately covered his head with his paws. The bats dove at the water, into the smoke, and then followed the flames.

The Glottalphibs started honking in unison and slapping at the bats with their tiny arms. The fire stopped. Nandreeson slid under the water and Han started after him, when Lando grabbed his arm.

"Don't," Lando said. "He wants us under there so he can kill us better."

The bats were eating the fire as they made their way toward the remaining Glottalphibs. The first bats had already reached one Glottalphib, and flew into its mouth. The Glottalphib's honking got louder and louder as more bats covered it. Suddenly it stopped honking. It fell over backward, squashing some bats. The others flew away, leaving a gray, desiccated Glottalphib. The three other

Glottalphibs were fleeing down the tunnel, honking in fear.

Han shoved Chewie's back. "They're watumba bats, you big baby. They eat algae, insects, and fire, not Wookiees."

Chewie mewled at him.

"Come on," Lando said. He started to swim forward when he stopped as if a rope were tied around his foot. "I don't like this—"

And then he went under.

"Nandreeson!" Han said. He dove too. Nandreeson had Lando by the foot and was watching him flail. Han grabbed Lando's hand and pulled, but Lando wasn't moving. Han held a finger to his lips, mimed holding still, and went back to the surface.

"Give me the bowcaster," Han said.

Chewie roared.

"We don't have time to argue. Nandreeson'll kill him."

Chewie whined, then dove, loading the bowcaster as he went. Han swam around Lando's front, stopping a few meters from Nandreeson and then kicking at the Glottalphib's snout.

Lando was turning red. He mimed strangulation. Han ignored him. He kicked Nandreeson again, and Nandreeson roared. As he opened his mouth, an energy quarrel bubbled through the water and lodged in the back of Nandreeson's throat.

Fire spewed from his mouth, instantly doused by the water. He let go of Lando's leg and Lando swam for the surface. Nandreeson made burbly strangling sounds, grabbed at his mouth, and sank deep into the muck.

Han didn't wait to see any more. He tugged Chewie's suit and together they swam to the surface. Lando was already climbing the stairs. He reached the ledge, leaned back, and closed his eyes.

"I never thought I'd be able to sit again."

"We're not done yet," Han said. He had to grip the rock sides as he climbed. The stairs were slippery.

"Indeed we're not," Blue said. She was standing on the ledge behind them, clinging to the wall. "Have you thought about how we're going to get back to my Skipper?"

Chewie roared at her.

She shrugged in response.

"Playing both ends against the middle, Blue?" Han asked, essentially rephrasing Chewie's remark in more polite terms.

Blue smiled prettily at him. "I did think it was in my best interest to see who was going to win that little skirmish, don't you, Han?"

"I think if we could've trusted you, you'd've been here fighting for us, Blue."

"Don't expect too much of the girl," Lando said, his voice heavy with exhaustion. "At least she didn't shoot at us."

"See, Han? One man understands my side."

"He won't when he sees pieces of the *Lady Luck* all over your Skipper."

Lando opened his eyes and sat up. "You raided my ship? Hand me the blaster, Han. The woman deserves to die."

Blue held open her hands, her blaster gripped only in her right thumb and forefinger. "I thought you were dead. Nandreeson wasn't going to let you live."

"You have no faith, Blue," Lando said.

"You'd have done the same," she said.

"She's got you there," Han said.

"Maybe before Cloud City," Lando said. "I'm a good guy now."

"A careless good guy." Han sat beside him. "What did you come here for?"

"Came to get you, buddy. Heard you were in some trouble. Thought I'd help."

"We can discuss your personal life later. I just want to know how you plan to get out of here," Blue said.

"How'd you get on the rock?" Han asked.

"Climbed," she said. "You missed the handholds near the cavern door."

Chewie roared his agreement. He sloshed his way up the stairs, stood over Han, and howled.

"All right, all right, we'll leave," Han said.

"How do you plan to get out of here?" Lando asked.

Why did everyone think he always had a plan? Han sighed. "I thought maybe you knew where Nandreeson's favorite Skipper was."

"He brought me in it, but he left a few Reks beside it."

"They should be gone by now," Blue said. "They hate watumba bats as much as Glottalphibs do."

"Not accurate, Blue," Lando said. "Glottalphibs love watumba bats. They're host to half a dozen Glottalphib delicacies. They just hate it when watumba bats notice them."

Blue laughed. "Good point."

Chewie was already sloshing his way to the cavern door. He stopped on a wide ledge and stripped out of the suit Wynni had given him, tossing it into the pond with an expressive and extremely vulgar Wookiee curse.

Blue glanced at Wynni. "Think she'll be all right?"

Chewbacca added another sentiment to the one he'd just expressed.

"Let's drag her onto the ledge," Han said. "At least she'll have a fighting chance when Nandreeson's henchmen return."

Chewbacca cursed again, then stomped across the ledge and used a nearby stick to pull Wynni to the water's edge. He reached down and hauled her out, grunting as he did so.

"Nice of you, Chewie. I thought I would have to nag," Han said.

Chewbacca growled.

"You know," Lando said softly, "you once told me never to make a Wookiee angry."

"Right," Han said.

"You seem to ignore that advice fairly regularly."

"He owes me a life debt," Han said. "It would be dishonorable for him to kill me."

"I suppose," Lando said, "but would that stop him from ripping off your arms?"

"It has so far," Han said, "but let's not give him any ideas, shall we?"

Chewbacca growled again, then left Wynni's side. She was still unconscious, but Han could see her pink-covered chest moving up and down. Blue stepped over her gingerly. Despite soaking in filthy water, Blue looked fresh and dignified. Even her wet hair looked planned.

She was clutching her blaster and used her other hand to guide her along the rock wall. "Where's the Skipper?" she asked.

"Two tunnels up," Lando said. "I'll lead the way."

He looked as if he couldn't move a muscle. Han had never seen Lando's skin so gray. But Lando climbed across the rocks as if he hadn't been exercising at all. Apparently the thought of freedom appealed to him.

"What about the other Glottalphibs?" Han asked.

"I don't think we have to worry about them," Lando said.

Han joined him in the cavern door. Dozens of Glottalphibs were sprawled on the rocks and in the pond. Most of their long snouts were open, and the insides picked clean.

"Watumba bats did that?" Han asked. "Why would the Glottalphibs keep them around?"

"Sometimes you have to take risks for a good meal," Lando said.

The stench of smoke, dead Glottalphib, and rotting greenery was overpowering.

Chewie began to growl.

"I know, I know," Han said. "It stinks."

"That's an understatement," Blue said. She had her hand over her nose. "I don't want to be here when these things decay."

They picked their way across the bodies. The opening into the next cavern was also full of Glottalphib bodies, and five Skippers, all of which were unattended.

Blue smiled. "Reks. You've gotta love them. They only think of themselves."

"Rather like you, huh, Blue?" Han said.

She patted his shoulder. "I do a good deed now and then, Solo. I didn't have to bring you here."

He moved her hand away from him. "You could have worked harder to rescue me, Blue. I saved your life."

"A favor for a favor, Han. I figured we were even at that point."

Lando and Chewie were looking at the Skippers. "This one is ready to go," Lando said. "If you know how to hot-wire these things."

"There's always an access code," Blue said. "And with Nandreeson, it should be obvious."

She pushed them aside, and studied the small voice monitor.

"You don't think it has voice recognition, do you?" Han asked.

Blue laughed. "All Glottalphibs sound alike." She tapped the edge. "What are Nandreeson's favorite things, Lando?"

"Why ask me?" he said. "I hadn't seen the man for years."

"I thought you'd know his obsessions," she said.

"I only knew of one," Lando said.

"All right." She leaned against the jamb and said, "Kill Calrissian," in a remarkable approximation of a nasal Glottalphib voice.

The door slid back. She grinned. "Well, gentlemen, let's go back to Skip 1 and see if they stripped the *Falcon* in our absence."

✶ ✶ ✶

Threepio and Artoo-Detoo had returned to the Solos' chambers to discover that Leia had left. The computer informed them that she had resigned her position as Chief of State and had given orders to shut down the apartments until a family member returned, then it threw the droids out.

Mon Mothma had replaced Mistress Leia, and the droids were in her anteroom now, along with a collection of senators' aides, well-wishers, and employment seekers. The antechamber was packed. Threepio leaned against the wall, next to a metal sculpture that looked suspiciously like a droid's innards, and Artoo rocked beside him. They were the only droids, except for the receptionist droid, a new model who refused to acknowledge Threepio at all. On her list, she kept adding the sentients first, from the Kloperian guard Leia had relieved of duty (and from whom Artoo had hidden behind an Ychthytonian) to a winged Agee that had flown into the room on a lark.

When the Kloperian went into Mon Mothma's chambers, Artoo began rocking. Hard.

"Settle down, Artoo," Threepio said. "I'm sure Mon Mothma will see us. She knows how important we are."

Artoo whistled and the conversation in the room

stopped. Heads swiveled, and focused on the droids. Threepio put his hands up as if nothing had happened, and the conversations resumed. Except for the receptionist. She continued to stare at Threepio as if he had committed a major breach of etiquette.

"Now you've done it," Threepio said. "Your rudeness will get us tossed out of here."

Artoo cheebled and rocked, his wheels clanging on the tile floor.

"That is a bit melodramatic, even for you. No one is going to die simply because we're waiting in line."

Artoo blatted at him, and the Ychthytonian looked down at him.

"Yer little friend is kind of agitated."

Threepio nodded. "He believes we've found—"

Artoo shrilled.

The Ychthytonian put all four hands over his ears. Some of the humans cringed. The Agee flew out of the room as quickly as she had arrived.

"That's it," the receptionist droid said as she stood. "You droids can leave."

"See what you've done?" Threepio hissed at Artoo. "Now I have to go convince her that we should stay. It won't be an easy battle, what with all the names you've called her. Most droids, no matter what their designation, dislike being termed traitor, you know. She's only doing her job, and rather well at that, if I might say so."

He left Artoo's side and pushed his way to the desk. The receptionist droid was standing, her bronze arms crossed. "You have no business here," she said. "The President is only dealing with important matters today."

"This is important," Threepio said.

"I'm certain it is to you," the receptionist said. "But whatever the problem is, it can wait."

"I'm afraid it can't," Threepio said. He lowered his voice. "You see, my counterpart and I have found the cause of the bombing in the Senate Hall. We were going to report this to President Leia Organa Solo, but she has stepped down. So we came to her successor."

"Delusional," the receptionist said. "They really should have retired your make a generation ago. I had heard that your type was given to hyperbole. I hadn't believed it until now."

"This is not hyperbole!" Threepio said, pulling himself up to his fullest height. "This is fact. You should know the difference."

"If you don't move from my desk, I shall have you removed by force," the receptionist droid said.

"You will not," Threepio said. "I am the personal droid of President Leia Organa Solo, and my counterpart belongs to her brother, the Jedi Master Luke Skywalker. We are above your petty bureaucratic power gambits. If you tamper with us, you'll be tampering with some of the most important people in Coruscant."

"Your counterpart?" the receptionist droid asked. "Do you mean the astromech droid that was squealing rudely a few moments ago?"

"Yes," Threepio said. "He's eccentric, but he's a hero of several battles and is quite well-known."

"Well, then you shouldn't have any trouble finding him," the receptionist droid said.

"Finding him?"

"He left when you came up here."

Threepio spun. "Artoo? Artoo!"

The room had quieted as the petitioners watched the exchange between the receptionist droid and Threepio. There was a gap in the wall near the sculpture where Artoo had been. The Ychthytonian pointed his top left arm toward the door.

"She's right," he said. "Yer little buddy zoomed out while you were arguing. He was heading toward the pilots' turbolift."

"The pilots' turbolift?" Threepio said. "Oh, dear. Oh, dear." He started out, then stopped, and turned to the reception droid. "I expect you to inform Mon Mothma that we were here. If you do not, I will personally make certain that you are demoted to working as a translator for mechanical garbage compactors."

Then he hurried out of the room, calling for Artoo. The hallway was full of more petitioners arriving to see Mon Mothma. Apparently the change in leadership meant that opportunists were trying to see if Mon Mothma would help them where Mistress Leia had not. Threepio pushed past several young humans, a Gosfambling, and a Llewebum, and stopped in front of the pilots' turbolift.

It was called that because it led directly into the shipyard. The Emperor's pilots had been on call all the time. Any threat to the Empire had the pilots on the turbolift, going down kilometers to the ships, and taking off to defend Coruscant. The New Republic had deemed the lift useful, and had kept both it and its name.

The turbolift was just returning to this floor.

"Artoo," Threepio said softly, "when I catch up with you, I am going to recommend a restraining bolt."

The turbolift doors opened, and Threepio stepped on. He hit Express and braced himself as the car plunged. At the bottom, the doors opened. Threepio peered through them.

The doors into the pilots' wing were opened, the panel on the computer-locking system on the ground. Artoo had been in a hurry; normally he replaced such things. Machinery hummed at the far end of the wing.

Threepio scurried down the hallway. It was empty. He slid into the bay. Dozens of X-wings were in various states of disrepair. Master Luke's stood near the space doors, as if waiting for him to return.

Beyond that were other ships in various states of disrepair. And no sign of Artoo.

"Oh, dear," Threepio said. "I don't like this."

He stepped over power cables and computer parts. Then a movement flashed in the next room. Threepio hurried toward it. Artoo was standing near a stock light freighter. It appeared newly reassembled. Someone had taken the time to clean the carbon scoring and space dirt off the sides.

"What are you thinking, Artoo?"

Artoo whistled.

"I can't pilot a freighter. You know droids can't. We need help, Artoo."

Artoo chirruped.

"They aren't ignoring you. Artoo, you must see someone in charge!"

Artoo beeped again. Threepio hurried toward the freighter.

"Artoo, really. Just because you couldn't speak to Mon Mothma when you wished doesn't mean that you can't wait. It would have been only a moment longer, and I would have gotten you inside."

Artoo bleebled.

"Of course you have time. There's always time."

Artoo moaned.

"Surely it can't be as bad as all that, Artoo!"

Artoo warbled.

"Let me talk with Mon Mothma," Threepio said. "I'm sure she'll send someone—"

Artoo emitted a long, lengthy raspberry.

"Artoo, really. What were you planning to do? Wait for the owner to return? You have no idea what sort of person flies this contraption—"

Artoo beeped indignantly.

"All right," Threepio said. "So I don't know what your plan is. But I believe that if we take the official route—"

Artoo warbled. The sound was almost happy.

Footsteps sounded behind them.

Threepio turned.

Cole Fardreamer stood in the doorway, wiping his hands on a rag. "I suppose the cryptic message Luke Skywalker left for me on the systems computer actually came from you, Artoo, since Master Skywalker isn't here to meet me."

Artoo cheebled.

"Artoo," Threepio said softly, "you aren't supposed to tamper with the equipment. And using Master Luke's codes!"

"I think the chiding can wait. The message sounded urgent," Cole said.

Artoo swiveled his head and beeped.

"Artoo wants to know who owns the stock light freighter," Threepio said, "although I don't know why. Frankly, Master Fardreamer, Artoo has acted strangely since he was hit with that blaster fire."

"Artoo has good instincts," Cole said. He came into the room. "The freighter was stolen, and we impounded it. I've been fixing it up. No one really owns it. I think we'll try to sell it."

Artoo churbled and rocked.

"Artoo," Threepio said. "Really, Master Fardreamer, he's not himself."

Cole smiled. "I think you might want to translate for me."

Threepio glanced at Artoo. Artoo wailed. "Oh, all right," Threepio said. "Artoo believes he knows who bombed the Senate Hall. He says if we don't go there immediately, there will be another explosion."

"To the Senate Hall?"

"No," Threepio said, as if Cole were slow. "To the place that the detonators came from."

Artoo cheebled urgently.

"He wants to know, sir, if you can help us."

Cole Fardreamer frowned at the stock light freighter. "I don't know," he said after a moment. "But I can certainly try."

Thirty-four

Leia had six military personnel on her small ship. Wedge had insisted that she have them in case of attack, but she suspected they were all on board to guard her. Wedge—and Mon Mothma—weren't certain what she was going to do, and they wanted to keep her from doing something crazy.

She had never let anyone stop her before.

They wouldn't stop her now.

Even though the young lieutenant, Tchiery, had insisted on piloting, Leia had rebuffed him. She needed the control. This was her mission, even though she was letting Wedge lead the fleet. She wanted to know the course, and the plan, and not veer from it.

Unless she wanted to.

Once she saw Almania, she would know what to do.

Her new crewmembers were in the galley, arguing over dinner. The cockpit was blessedly silent, allowing her to think. The copilot's chair still bore the impression from Tchiery's body. He was a Farnym. Farnyms were creatures noted for their bowling-ball roundness, and the incredible strength behind their unusual shape. They had close-cut fur, small snouts, and large orange eyes.

Tchiery was no different. They also had a peculiar odor, like ginger mixed with sandalwood, an odor that remained in the cockpit long after Tchiery was gone.

The fleet fanned out behind her, thirty strong. How Mon Mothma was going to justify Wedge taking most of the working ships in the arsenal was beyond Leia. Wedge and his commanders rode in three large ships, and were accompanied by squadrons of smaller ships, mostly A- and B-wings. It was amazing how many ships he and Admiral Ackbar had been able to scrape together quickly.

Admiral Ackbar had opted to remain behind. He would cover their tracks as best he could, but surely Meido and his gang would notice thirty ships leaving Coruscant simultaneously. What they would not notice was the tiny, unmarked *Alderaan.* Leia counted on that. She didn't want anyone to know she was part of this mission until it was too late to recall the ships.

She leaned back in the pilot's chair, took a handful of her long hair, and quickly tied it into a ponytail. It was the third time she had made a ponytail. She kept pulling out the twist, a nervous habit from childhood that she thought she had lost. A lot of nervous habits had returned since Kueller had destroyed that second planet. She knew that when she returned she would have to deal with all the feelings those habits hid.

If she returned.

She had no idea what sort of weapon Kueller was using. The planets remained, but the people seemed to disappear. That wasn't a Death Star or a Sun Crusher. No great single weapon to destroy with a bolt. The fleet couldn't bomb it out of existence because they didn't know what it was.

They couldn't bomb Almania out of existence either. That would make the New Republic no better than the Empire had been.

Leia wasn't certain Wedge had thought all those details through. She would send his military personnel back with a message to his ship, the *Yavin,* when they reached Almanian space. No overall bombing until the target was sighted. If the target was obvious, then of course she wouldn't even send the message. But if it wasn't, the crew would go back to Wedge, and she would disappear into Almania's atmosphere.

To find Kueller herself.

Because she still wasn't certain if he was after the New Republic or if he was after her family. He was strong in the Force, which made him a powerful enemy. For the thousandth time, she wished she had listened to Luke and completed her Jedi training. She wouldn't be able to outnegotiate Kueller, at least not for the long term. But she might be able to outfight him, with Luke's help.

She pulled the twist out of her hair, and the strands cascaded down her back. The stars looked no different. Even in hyperdrive, the distance to Almania was incredible. It was amazing that Kueller had even considered his planet part of the New Republic. Planets this far out usually liked to retain their independence. Almania had maintained its independence from the Empire. It should have continued such behavior under the New Republic.

Yet another detail that didn't make sense.

So many details about Almania didn't make sense, partly because the information about the planet was sketchy. She suspected that the Je'har had aligned themselves with the Rebellion for form's sake and to protect their government, not because of any real allegiance or caring about the fight against the Empire. So far as she could tell, no Almanian joined the military on either side.

But someone had mentioned that Almanians had sent a distress message to her government years ago that never got a response. Perhaps that was why Kueller had come after the New Republic.

Perhaps it had nothing to do with her family at all.

All the nagging worries. She had a thousand of them. She hadn't been able to find Artoo before she left, and she had counted on him. It would have been nice to have the little droid beside her in *Alderaan.* Threepio might have been helpful, too, at least as a distraction. But they were both missing. Artoo had left the maintenance facility shortly after he checked in, and Threepio had gone with him. No one had seen them since.

Just as no one had heard from Han. He hadn't answered any of her messages. She finally had to leave him one saying that she would be out of touch for a while, but she would find him. It was essential that the fleet have communications silence, but it worried her. Han's mission to Smuggler's Run had taken way too long, and with that cryptic message trying to frame Han, Leia wondered if the delay was bad news.

She hadn't reached Lando, either. Lando, who had put his life in jeopardy for Han's. She could only hope that Lando had found Han and they were both all right, tracking down the person or persons who had gone after Han.

And then there was Luke. She had been reaching for him ever since she had seen that holocording from Kueller. Except for that plaintive, pain-filled call, she hadn't heard from Luke. The silence was unnerving.

Every once in a while, though, she would get strange aches and pains. Her left ankle gave out on her as she finished the final check in the cockpit, sending severe pain up her leg. But when she checked it, she discovered nothing wrong. Shortly after takeoff, she had relaxed in her pilot's chair, and cried out as a thousand needles poked into her back. Again, the sensation was gone in a moment, and there was no visible sign of injury (or of needles embedded in her chair). Both times she had gotten a sense of Luke before the pain faded.

He was alive. She knew that much. But she also knew he was badly injured, and alone.

She had to reach him soon. Even though they were straining the *Alderaan*'s engines, they weren't going fast enough for her.

She had to reach her brother before he died—or worse.

✳ ✳ ✳

Luke awoke to a barely lit room. He was on his stomach, his back aching fiercely. His head throbbed and his mouth tasted fuzzy. The shot shouldn't have worked, but it did, mostly due to his own weakened state. He hadn't had enough energy to fight Dolph/Kueller and to maintain consciousness against the power of the medication.

And now they had him here.

Wherever here was.

He blinked. Even his eyes felt grimy. He was still dehydrated. He could feel it in each movement, in each throb of his head. But the rest had given him some strength back. He could get beyond this weakness. He would be able to defend himself now.

The pallet was only a few inches above the floor. The floor was covered with dirt, and beneath it, the surface was made of wood. How unusual.

The light that filtered in, giving the room its grayish-brown color, came from grates above. He suspected the grates opened into another room or the light would have been brighter.

He forced himself to sit up slowly, the very movement pulling on his back, reminding him of the source of his pain. His X-wing was gone. It had exploded over Pydyr, and when he was there, he hadn't been able to figure out what happened.

But as he had slept, the realization struck him.

Someone must have tampered with the X-wing on Telti. Brakiss couldn't have done it. He had been with Luke during most of that time. But one of the droids could have, under Brakiss's orders.

And if the X-wing had exploded on Almania, as planned, Brakiss would have taken care of both of the men he feared: Luke Skywalker and Kueller.

Luke brushed his face, and hit something prickly. He brought his hand down. Straw. He looked down. The pallet was covered in straw.

How odd.

And his hands weren't bound.

Neither were his feet.

But his lightsaber was gone.

So. Kueller believed there was no escape from this place, but he also believed that Luke might have had use for the lightsaber.

Which meant that Luke would not be alone for long.

He got up slowly, moving with caution so that the throbbing he felt wouldn't turn into dizziness. The splint enabled him to put some weight on his ankle. Slowly he crept forward.

The room was more like a series of rooms. The ceilings were high enough that he didn't want to try to jump them with his injured ankle, and the walls were smooth. Yet fresh air flowed in, along with the scent of raw meat.

The thought of such food made his stomach churn, but he knew that food would have value for him, not so much for its nutritional content, but for its moisture. He followed the scent, and discovered more straw on the far side of the room he had awakened in.

Mixed in with the straw were long white hairs, and the faint smell of animals.

The next room was dark. The scent of meat was

stronger here. It mixed with the animal odor. Luke wasn't sure he would like what he was going to find. He squinted, forcing his eyes to adjust.

Nothing.

The room was emptier than the first, with only one pile of straw, and no pallet at all. The raw-meat smell came from a corner filled with large, empty bowls, but no meat rested there. Obviously the meat had been eaten. Only the smell lingered.

The hair on the back of his neck prickled. He was alone, but it didn't feel as if he were alone.

He didn't like the feeling.

He limped back to his pallet and sat down. There was no way to tell how long he had been out. Or exactly where he was. His only hope was to engage one of the guards and to escape by stealing one of Dolph/Kueller's ships.

But before he did that, he would want to find the source of Kueller's disturbing power. It had to be near Kueller somewhere. He wouldn't let it too far out of his sight, whatever it was.

A faint snuffling echoed from the far room. Luke looked up. A large white creature sat in the doorway, nearly filling it. If the creature stretched on its hind legs, it might be able to reach the grates. It obviously had no desire to.

The snuffling continued. Then Luke realized that it was sniffing the air.

It was smelling him.

He sat very still. His lack of restraints made him nervous. This, then, was the thing Kueller had planned for him.

It rose on all fours, standing twice his size. Chewbacca would be tiny next to this thing. It had a smallish face (compared to its body), short ears, and slitted blue eyes.

Its shoulders were broad, and its back flat. Its hair was white and flaked off with each movement. It had a long, thin tail that Luke suspected carried a lot of power.

Maybe if he didn't move, it wouldn't harm him. Most creatures, when faced with a monster like this one, shrieked and ran. The first best gamble was always to wait it out.

The creature came closer. Drool dripped off its mouth, landing in giant puddles near its feet. It continued snuffling, following the path that Luke had made to the door and then to the straw.

Luke worked to control his own breathing, keeping it shallow. He willed himself invisible, but he didn't know how to send that vision to the thing in front of him. He couldn't yet tell if it had any real intelligence.

It followed his scent from the straw to the pallet, and it stopped in front of him, sniffing the air. Drool landed on his feet, soaking them in warm, slimy liquid. He didn't move.

The creature kept sniffing. Its size was amazing. If he stood, he might be able to reach its barrel chest. Fortunately its mouth was small, or he would be eaten in one chomp.

The creature followed the scent downward, finally focusing on Luke. It shoved its muzzle at him. The cold nose covered him from forehead to stomach. He resisted the urge to shove it away, but instead he sat, forcing himself to remain calm. It sniffed him, pausing for a moment at his back. He closed his eyes. The wet nose-slime slid down his arms, and pooled near his feet. He could drown in this creature's bodily fluids.

Then it pulled back. He let out a small sigh. It hadn't registered him as anything different from the straw or the pallet. If he could remain still a little longer, he would be all right.

The creature tilted its head, its eyes glinting at him. Luke made eye contact.

That was his mistake.

With one quick movement, the creature took him in its jaws, and bit down.

Hard.

Thirty-five

Luke's legs disappeared into the Thernbee's mouth. Kueller turned away from the screen. Except for his new assistant, Kueller was alone in Femon's control room. The masks glimmered at him from the wall. He didn't like this place. He could still feel her presence. He would need to make some other place the center of his command.

"I want a guard on him at all times."

His new assistant, Yanne, a slender man whose lined face and gray hair marked him as years older than Kueller, leaned forward. "I don't think we'll need it."

Kueller had chosen Yanne because Yanne was one of the few of his people who actually expressed the opinion he had rather than the one Kueller wanted to hear. For the moment, it was a refreshing trait.

"Really, sir, only a miracle would save that man now. The Thernbee will toy with him, crushing one bone at a time, giving him the occasional illusion of escape, but never allowing him to disappear."

"I know how a Thernbee kills," Kueller said. He had grown up around them, large white menaces in the Almanian mountains. "I want that guard."

"It's a waste of manpower," Yanne said.

Kueller nodded as if he had heard. "You're right. We'd best put four guards on the Thernbee cages."

"Four! Sir, you can't be serious. Even if the man survived the Thernbee, he'd be too weak, too debilitated to do any harm. We'd be better off placing most of our people in battle positions. There are reports—"

"I've heard the reports," Kueller said. "I'm prepared for them. But we have Luke Skywalker below. I only put him with the Thernbee because I need him alive until his sister arrives. But, as long as Luke Skywalker is alive, there is always the risk that he will defeat his adversary. We must be prepared for this risk."

"He was wounded when we put him in there. A few bats from the Thernbee and he'll be dead."

"It won't be that simple," Kueller said.

"No man is that powerful," Yanne said.

Kueller turned to him, no longer amused by Yanne's mouth. He stared at the man until Yanne's face turned ashen.

"Except you, milord."

Kueller smiled. The smile was deadly. "It would do you well to remember that, Yanne."

"Yes, sir."

"Four guards, Yanne. At all times."

"Yes, sir. I'll get on it right away, sir." With a quick bow, he scrambled out the door.

Kueller turned back to the screen. The Thernbee's jaws were still closed. Kueller sat down to wait until Skywalker appeared again.

✶ ✶ ✶

It had taken Cole a few moments to convince Artoo to wait. The little droid was adamant about leaving Coruscant immediately. Threepio wasn't pleased with Artoo's plan. Artoo wanted to take the stock light freighter.

The problem was that Cole wasn't authorized to use it. Nor did he feel he could leave Coruscant without permission.

He promised Artoo that he would get permission and aid. The two droids had had trouble seeing Mon Mothma. Cole might not be able to get her to see them, but he knew where to start.

He used the service computer in the stock light freighter repair room to contact General Antilles. He'd gone through six different systems before he got a response.

"I'm sorry, Fardreamer," the slightly mechanized voice came back. "General Antilles is not receiving communications at this time."

Cole had never heard of such a thing. "He told me to contact him with anything urgent. This is urgent. This is beyond urgent. Please, let him know—"

"I can't, Fardreamer. Urgent or not, he's only collecting messages." The voice was rather curt. With only the barest consideration, it signed off.

"Oh, dear, oh, dear, oh, dear," See-Threepio said.

Artoo squealed and rocked, his wheels clanging on the floor.

"Artoo says we haven't much time."

"I'm doing what I can, Artoo," Cole said. "You don't want to get out there, only to have Space-Traffic Control stop us for stealing the ship."

"He has a point, Artoo," Threepio said.

Cole ignored them. He sent a message to President Leia. The instant response came within the system that President Leia Organa Solo had resigned and all of her messages were being forwarded to Mon Mothma. When Cole tried to contact Mon Mothma, he met with the same wall that See-Threepio and Artoo had. She was already overbooked.

"You didn't tell me that President Leia had resigned," Cole said.

"We didn't know ourselves until we tried to find her. Everything changed after those detonators." See-Threepio shook his head. "Sometimes I wish I had never gone with Artoo."

"To find the detonators?"

"No," See-Threepio muttered. "Into that escape pod."

Cole didn't know what Threepio was referring to, and decided not to ask. Contacting Mon Mothma wouldn't work either. He finally tried Admiral Ackbar. The response there was equally strange. Admiral Ackbar, his adjunct told Cole, was in a meeting, and his adjunct had no idea when, if ever, he would answer requests.

Cole kept his head bowed for a moment, hoping See-Threepio would think he was still studying the communications array. He needed to concentrate.

President Leia resigned.

Admiral Ackbar unreachable.

General Antilles unreachable.

Mon Mothma unreachable.

Something serious was happening.

The last time he had ignored Artoo, he had nearly gotten them all killed. Not to mention all the good people still out in unrepaired X-wings that might explode on them at any moment.

Artoo wailed.

"He says that we can't wait any longer," Threepio said. "He reminds you that you promised to help. Personally, Master Fardreamer, I wouldn't hold you to that promise. After all, you've done what you can. Artoo is a bit eccentric—"

"And he's been right each time he's pointed something out," Cole said. He put a hand on Artoo's cylindrical head. "I've tried to be official. I guess it's time to be unofficial."

Artoo squealed with joy. He hurried toward the stock light freighter.

"Threepio," Cole said, "do you know the President's codes?"

"Sir, those are private and subject to change every day. Why—"

"Do you know the President's codes?"

"Of course," See-Threepio said. "And the codes for her husband and children."

"I just need hers. Without them, we won't be able to leave Coruscant."

"Oh, I can't go along, sir. I'm in enough trouble already. Mistress Leia expects me to stay here."

"The President resigned, Threepio, without telling you. I think she'd appreciate it if you helped prevent another bombing. The first one nearly killed her."

See-Threepio tilted his golden head as if he were trying to see inside Cole's. "You do have a point, Master Fardreamer."

"I thought so," Cole said.

Artoo squealed at them from inside the freighter.

"Let's go," Cole said.

See-Threepio climbed onto the boarding ramp, and walked into the freighter.

"I think I'm going to regret this," he said.

•

Thirty-six

Chewbacca rode as copilot with Blue. After their experiences on Skip 6, Han wasn't about to take any more chances. He'd known Blue as long as he'd known Kid, and not nearly as well.

The betrayals hurt, no matter how he could justify them. He sat in the air-breather's section of Nandreeson's Skipper. This Skipper was larger and slimmer than Blue's, and had a pond on the lower deck. Neither Han nor Lando wanted to get near slimy water again. They sat in the tiny compartment near the top, filled with old, moldy couches (which Han suspected came from drained ponds) and mildew-covered tables.

Lando was resting beside him. His old friend had his eyes closed. His normally pristine clothing was water-stained and he had lost weight.

Han sighed and went over the events in his mind. There had been nothing he could do. Kid and Zeen had gone with the intent of betraying him. They hadn't been his friends. They had made that clear from the moment he had arrived. Perhaps then they had been trying to warn him away.

That explained how Nandreeson's men had known to find him on Skip 5.

Chewbacca had said that he thought Wynni would have helped them if Chewie hadn't fought her intentions. Han wasn't so certain. She probably knew about Chewie's loyalty to his wife, or she might have felt rebuffed by Chewie all those years ago. With Wynni, the situation was always complex. She never did what was expected of a Wookiee.

Not even at the end.

He wondered how she was faring, alone in Nandreeson's lair.

He was glad that she, at least, was alive. Zeen and the Kid, no matter what they had done, would always ride on his conscience.

"You couldn't have done anything," Lando said. His voice grated against his throat, his exhaustion evident. He had eaten all the human stores in Nandreeson's Skipper and had drunk water as if he hadn't been trapped in it at all.

"About what?" Han asked.

"About *what*?" Lando opened his eyes and pushed himself up on his elbows. His face wasn't as gray as it had been before. "About Kid and Zeen. They never were your friends."

"Stop trying to make me feel better," Han said.

"I'm not. I'm just trying to make you see the truth." Lando leaned his head against the steel wall. "You never belonged here, Han. We all knew it. Kid and Zeen, they tried to corrupt you from the beginning. They thought they could make you into one of them. But there were some lines you'd never cross. I think that made them mad."

"I did everything they wanted," Han said.

"No, you didn't. Profit was never the most important thing to you. You had this layer you kept trying to hide.

It's what made you go on that wild-goose chase with Skywalker right from the beginning. He's told me about it. You could have bailed out at any time. You never did."

"It was an exception."

"It was the rule. Remember the case of the Wookiee slave you found?"

"Chewbacca doesn't count. That circumstance was unusual."

"Yeah," Lando said. "As unusual as all the others. They hated it, Han. With every breath you took, you showed them that the life they led was dirty, ugly, and hate-filled."

There was passion in Lando's words. Han turned. Lando was staring at him.

"Did you hate me too?"

"No," Lando said. "But you sure as hell made me ashamed of myself."

He pushed off the cot and paced around the room. Then he yelped, bent over, and grabbed his calves. His face had gone gray again. Han got up and helped Lando back to the cot.

"Who'd've thought you'd get leg cramps from treading water?"

"Anyone who's exercised," Han said. "You should have asked Nandreeson to let you warm up before he tossed you in that pool."

"Very funny."

Han slowly stretched Lando's leg, massaging the muscle. "No pushing, buddy. You almost didn't survive that one."

"I'm tough," Lando said.

"Stupid is more like it. What were you thinking, coming back to the Run?"

"I had to find you, Han." Lando stretched out his other leg. "You can let go now."

"Why? What's so important that you'd risk your life?"

"Someone's setting you up, old friend," Lando said softly. "They're trying to make it look like you're behind the bombing of the Senate Hall."

"With Leia inside? Anyone who knows me knows I'd never do that."

Lando smiled. "I think Kid and Zeen would probably agree with that. But most of the Imperials in the Senate don't know you. That sort of behavior was business as usual in the Empire."

"It would take pretty strong proof to make it look like I've done something."

Lando shook his head. "Strong isn't as important as the right kind of proof. You're lucky I brought this to Leia first." Then he told Han about finding the *Spicy Lady*, and the message inside.

Han sighed. "Jarril's dead, huh?"

Lando nodded. "It wasn't pretty."

"I think he was afraid that would happen when he came to me. I think he felt he didn't have much time left."

"Maybe he was part of the setup."

Han shook his head. "He was too scared for that. He tried to ask for help a smuggler's way, by offering me money, but I wasn't buying. And then, he asked for it directly."

"Maybe he had to."

"And maybe he needed it. Maybe he knew they were coming for him. Obviously, they found him and killed him on Coruscant. He never would have sent those messages."

Lando shook his head. "Jarril's dead. His motives don't really matter. What does is that someone wanted you involved."

"Do you think the Imperials in the Senate did this so that they could get rid of Leia?"

"And bomb their own? It doesn't seem too likely, does it, Han?"

"All these sales of old Imperial equipment tie in too," Han said.

Lando closed his eyes. "You ever hear of Almania?"

"Not until you mentioned it," Han said.

"Me, either," Lando said. "That's odd, don't you think?"

"Odd?"

"Someone worked hard to keep a place we never heard of out of the visible spectrum. When someone works hard to keep something hidden, it's usually something we need to find out about."

"Exactly," Han said. "Maybe it should be our next stop."

"Provided we both have ships left," Lando said.

"We will," Han said. "I can promise you that."

✱ ✱ ✱

Luke slipped between the creature's teeth, pulling his legs inside just as it bit down. Its mouth was large and had a flat, ridged top. Even with the teeth clamped, there was still room inside.

Except near the tongue. It kept slamming Luke against the roof of the mouth, as if it were trying to lick him. Each time he slid toward the throat, the tongue slammed him against the roof again. He had the sense that this creature usually swallowed its food whole.

Everything inside was slimy. There was nothing to grab on to. So the next time the tongue slammed him against the roof, he dug his fingers into the soft palate.

The creature yelped and pushed at him with its tongue. Luke let go, the jaws opened, and he was sailing through the air. He hit the metal walls and slid to the ground, the wind knocked from him.

The creature stood over him, a hurt expression on its

gigantic face. It pawed at him, claws extended, and he couldn't roll away. It pulled him onto his back and sniffed him again, as if it couldn't believe something so small would cause it so much pain.

Luke held his hands up, and put them on the nose, trying to push it away. The creature snuffled at him, then licked him once as if tasting him. Luke's entire body smelled like the interior of the creature's mouth, a combination of raw meat, dirty teeth, and saliva. He couldn't get away.

The creature backed up, contemplated him for a moment, then batted him so hard he slid across the wood floor and slammed into the wall on the other side. Splinters the size of knives stuck out of his arms and back. He hadn't gotten his breath back from the last time, and this second hit made him feel just as bad. He was stunned, unable to move, and soaking wet.

But he had to move. This thing couldn't beat him. It would be a horrible way for a Jedi Knight to die. He'd fought rancors and Tusken Raiders all by himself. He could survive anything.

Anything.

The creature came toward him again. Luke eased himself to his feet, and pulled one of the splinters out of his arm. When the creature raised its paw to him, Luke shoved the splinter into the pad.

The creature yelped again, and shook its paw. Hair fell around him like snow. The creature stood on three legs and bit the base of the fourth one.

Luke wasn't going to wait to see what happened next. He ran as fast as his ankle would allow him around the creature's back and toward the pallet. There was nowhere to hide. The grates were too high to reach because of his ankle, and the pallet provided the only thing for him to lie beneath, something the creature would look at first.

Luke limped into the next room to find the emptiness there just as overwhelming. It took a moment for his eyes to adjust to the darkness. Once they did, he saw that the rooms went on, deeper and deeper. The creature must have come from that direction. There might be more of its kind farther on.

One was difficult enough. Several would be a nightmare.

The creature was whimpering in the far room. Luke understood how it felt. He took the momentary respite to pull the remaining splinters from his own flesh. He set them beside him like long knives, the only weapons he had against this creature.

Except his mind.

The creature didn't seem intent on harming him. In fact, the most harm had occurred when Luke had attacked it. The creature seemed to be trying to figure out what he was.

If Luke could figure out a way to convince it that he wasn't food, then he might stand a chance.

The question was how.

The creature had stopped whimpering. It was snuffling its way toward Luke. It must have gotten the splinter out of its pad. Luke lined his splinters around him. All they would do was buy him time, but time was what he needed.

He wasn't going to die at the paws of this hairy beast. He wouldn't give Kueller the satisfaction.

Thirty-seven

Kueller watched the skies through the observatory. He had modified this, the Great Dome of the Je'har, into a Command Central when he was fighting his conventional war against the Je'har. After he had killed their leaders, he systematically destroyed their followers, and watched it all on the screens around him. The screens were now showing him various readings from space. The screens on his right magnified the same darkness a hundredfold. The screens to his left showed a fleet of ships coming out of hyperdrive into Almanian space.

A dozen of his best employees were scattered throughout the room. Yanne stood beside him. "Milord, I think we should send our own people up there. Those are New Republic battleships. They could destroy Almania."

"They won't," Kueller said.

"Still," Yanne said. "I think we should be cautious."

"And let them know we've seen them?"

"They're too far away. They won't know."

Kueller sighed. His assistants were always worried about failure first, instead of expecting success. He had learned that preparing for both success and failure served him best.

"Fine," he said. "Send out three Star Destroyers, and the attendant support vehicles. And Yanne?"

"Yes, milord?"

"If they fail, you will have failed also."

Yanne's gray skin whitened, but his voice remained calm. "Yes, milord."

He turned and softly gave the order to one of the guards. The guard nodded, clicked his heels together, and left the room.

The New Republic's fleet was not yet visible in the sky overhead. It wouldn't be, until it was debris floating through space. Even then, all he would see would be an occasional flare breaking through the atmosphere.

On the screens to his left, he watched a tiny ship break away from the pack. "Bravo, President," he said. "Soon you'll be able to talk with your wretched brother all you want."

"Sir?" Yanne said.

Kueller ignored him. He was concentrating, not just on the visuals around him, but on his feelings. The dark side had its strengths. He knew that the fleet was uncertain about what it would find.

He smiled.

It would find nothing.

"Yanne."

"Yes, milord?"

"Are my plans in place?"

"Of course, milord."

"Then you can execute them. Now."

Yanne hurried to comply with his order. Kueller rocked back on his heels, and patted the remote under his cape. If Yanne failed to follow orders, Kueller would do the deed himself. He had been telling the truth when he spoke to President Leia Organa Solo. He preferred elegant, refined weapons.

She would learn just how elegant, and how refined, shortly.

✶ ✶ ✶

No one had taken anything off the *Falcon,* although the wedged-open doors, and a scorch mark from Han's personally designed security system near the support, suggested that someone had tried. The *Lady Luck* wasn't as fortunate. Most of its interior was gone, including some of the easy-to-remove hardware.

To say that Lando was furious was, in Han's opinion, a bit of an understatement.

Han remained on the *Lady Luck,* repairing the engine systems with all the pieces he could find. The cockpit was already functional, but had lost all its fancy gadgetry. Lando and Chewbacca were searching Skip 1 for the rest of the equipment, and Lando's missing droids. Han insisted that if they didn't find enough materials to rebuild the *Luck,* they should leave within the day. He felt a sense of urgency he didn't quite understand.

Blue had offered to help, but Han had turned her down. She had proven to be the most loyal of his old friends, but that no longer meant much. Perhaps Lando had been right. Perhaps they all had resented him. But he didn't like recasting all those memories. They had been friends once. That time had simply passed. There was no going back, much as he wanted to.

And he wasn't even sure he wanted to anymore. The longing for the good old days that came during moments of quiet on Coruscant seemed to be longing for romanticized versions of his past, not his real past.

Han had just reassembled the hyperdrive when the hair on the back of his neck rose. He grabbed it with his left hand, and a shudder ran down his spine. The feeling made him nervous. It was too close to the stuff Leia and Luke described about the Force. The stuff his children experienced but he never had.

Something had happened, was about to happen, could have happened. He crawled out of the maintenance tube and into the *Luck*'s stripped corridor.

Then a series of booms echoed throughout the Skip. The *Luck* rocked, and Han slid to the other side of the corridor. More explosions occurred, and still more. He lay still, his arms over his head, but nothing happened inside the *Luck*.

Nothing at all.

Just like the moment when the Senate Hall exploded. Only panic around him, and no injuries inside the casino.

But Leia had been injured.

Han pushed to his feet. "Chewie!" he shouted. "Lando?"

Of course, there was no reply. He had been alone in the *Luck*. He grabbed his blaster and let himself out the doors and walked—

—into a scene of devastation.

The Skip landing bay was in ruins. It looked as if someone had dropped a series of bombs from above. But the bay was a huge cavern carved in stone, and the ceiling hadn't been touched. Whatever had happened, happened inside.

Small fires burned near many of the ships. A pile of exploded metal had welded itself onto the *Falcon*'s side, but no fire burned below her. Nothing burned near the *Luck*, either.

Smugglers lay on their sides, on their backs, body parts strewn all over. Several ships had holes in their sides the size of boulders, but those holes had been blown outward. Over the crackle of flames, Han could hear moaning and wailing from the survivors. Black, thick smoke was filling the bay, making it difficult to breathe.

He went back into the *Luck* and grabbed a breath mask that, fortunately, had not been taken. No telling what he would find in the rest of the Skip. No telling what the damage would do to the asteroid. They were shaky things at best. This might destroy the entire place.

He left the *Luck*, calling for Chewbacca and Lando. He had no idea where they'd gone. They were going after the parts, but they hadn't said who they were chasing, although Han had said he had seen stuff in Kid's and Zeen's possessions. They probably had gone to their rooms first, and then deeper into the Skip.

Han hoped they hadn't gone too deep. Some of those corridors were narrow, and made of rock. That rock would be very fragile in explosions like this.

As he stepped onto the ground, hands groped at his legs. People he didn't know called out to him. He stopped several times to move debris off trapped smugglers, then helped them to a place away from the fires. The smoke was getting so thick, it was impossible to see. If he wanted to save the *Falcon* and the *Luck*, he would have to work in the bay.

But that meant leaving Chewie and Lando to their own devices. He could mentally picture Chewie, trapped beneath a rock, Lando crushed beside him. Yet Han knew that the odds of finding them at all were small.

He had to try.

He stepped over debris and flaming metal. This devastation looked similar to the devastation on Coruscant. Only there, he had heard one explosion. Here he had heard several.

The cries were growing more and more pitiful. He seemed to be one of the few uninjured people in the entire area. He couldn't pass these people by. He had to start helping, and hope that Chewie and Lando were getting equal consideration from someone else.

He wound his way around several flaming piles to the *Falcon*. Then he went inside, grabbed the fire extinguishers, and came out blasting. The foam put out the fires nearby, leaving charred bits of metal, and several charred bodies.

Han gagged, but kept going. Fires first, because if he didn't do that, the oxygen would disappear, the smoke would get worse, and people would die. Or at least that was what he told himself, what he had to tell himself, as he heard more and more cries for help.

Tentacles, hands, fingers, all manner of beings were reaching for him. He almost felt ashamed for being so healthy. He was working faster and faster, trying to put out more and more fires. The smoke was clearing, at least in the area he was working in, and as he looked up, he saw Blue doing the same work near him, using extinguishers from her Skipper.

She was covered in soot and ash, just as he was, but unlike him, she also had bruises, and her arms were bleeding. The back of her tunic had torn, and he saw burns running along her skin. Her lips were moving as she worked, and tears were streaming down her face.

He had never seen Blue so upset.

He left her to her fires, and started on another set. More smugglers hurried out of ships. One Sullustan vessel poured extinguisher out of its nozzle, and slowly, slowly, the fires died.

Leaving only smoking remains, and bodies.

And the wounded, staggering through the mess like the walking dead.

Han wiped the sweat off his face with the back of his arm. He was already exhausted, overwhelmed by the magnitude of cleaning the Run.

Of saving all the lives.

He grabbed a Ssty that was digging through a pile of smoking rubble. Except for a few small burned patches on the Ssty's fur, it looked all right, as stunned as Han was, but all right.

"Get the medical droids. All of them," he said. "We'll make an aid station on the *Lady Luck*."

"Droids?" The Ssty swiveled its small head. Its eyes were red-rimmed. "That's a sick joke, mister." It wrenched itself out of his grip and kept digging.

Han frowned. "Come on. We need to help these folks."

"Not with droids," the Ssty said.

"I don't understand."

The Ssty stopped digging again, sighed, and wiped its claws on its fur. "Where were you when this happened?"

"In my ship."

The Ssty nodded. Its little face was somber, its red-rimmed eyes filling with a blue gooey substance. "The droids did this," it said, and turned back to its digging.

Han frowned, picturing droids on attack, firing weapons. But that made no sense. It wasn't possible. He had fought beside droids before, and while they were clever, they never turned on their masters.

Ever.

"What are you looking for?" he asked.

"My mate," the Ssty said.

Han felt his heart stop for a moment, remembering Leia in the bombed-out wreck of the Senate building, that horrible feeling he had had as he ran there, that feeling that he had just lost the most important thing in his life. Without hesitating, he dug into the hot metal, wincing as it burned his fingers, pulling pieces away that the Ssty wasn't strong enough to lift. "The droids attacked us?"

"They—" the Ssty's voice broke. "They exploded."

All those pops, those explosions, were droids. "All the droids?"

"Some of them." The Ssty was digging faster. "Enough."

Han pulled a huge chunk of metal away. Beneath it was another Ssty, arms over its head, claws extended.

Eyes open.

With a yowl, the Ssty pulled its mate free. The lower half of its body was crushed flat. It was clearly dead.

"I'm sorry," Han said. The words were not enough, and the Ssty didn't hear him. Its yowls had risen to blend with the other cries, and the blue stuff was staining its white fur. It kept brushing the hair away from its mate's lifeless eyes, and rocking, as if the motion would bring the mate back.

Han backed away, unable to watch the little creature's pain. The droids exploded. And the bombed interior looked like the Senate Hall.

All those senators with their protocol droids, their translator droids, their assistant droids. Several explosions at once would feel like one big assault.

And leave no trace, because the sources of the bombs would be destroyed along with the bombs themselves.

He made his way toward the *Falcon,* not quite able to think. No medical droids. So they would have to rely on whatever medical talent was on the Run. No one would come here to help. No one would be able to navigate the entrance without a map.

What a disaster.

"Han!"

The voice was reassuringly familiar. At the base of the *Falcon*'s ramp, Lando stood with Chewbacca. Lando's shirt was singed, and the fur on Chewbacca's chest was nearly gone, but they were all right.

Han had never been so glad to see anyone in his life. "I thought you were dead," he said.

"We thought the same about you."

"What are we going to do?"

Lando shook his head. "There are a few ancient FX-7's around, but they're already overworked. And most of the medical personnel were killed when their new medical droids exploded."

Chewbacca growled.

"I thought of the same thing, Chewie," Han said. "This is exactly what happened on Coruscant, but somehow they kept it isolated to one building. I don't know how they thought to target the Run."

"They didn't," Lando said. "Most of the droids here are stolen."

Han felt cold. "You mean this attack was meant for someone else?"

"Probably," Lando said.

Han didn't want to think about that. Not now. The cries had grown as the smoke cleared. Blue had worked her way closer to the *Falcon*. Her face was streaked with tears. Her eyes were glazed. She appeared to be working by rote.

"Listen," Han said. "I think we should set up the *Lady Luck* as a medical facility. It's nearly empty, so there's lots of room, and we can fly the most seriously wounded off the Run."

"Who's going to help smugglers?" Lando asked.

"Someone will," Han said. "I'll make sure of that. I think we need to coordinate this kind of effort with all the undamaged ships. We don't have the facilities on the Run to deal with this kind of tragedy."

"But the *Luck*—" Lando said.

"Is going to need refurbishing anyway," Han said. "I'm sure most of the stolen equipment is now no longer in prime condition."

Lando nodded. He appeared beyond exhaustion. "I'll get her ready," he said.

"Thanks," Han said. He silently urged Chewie to go along with Lando, and then turned toward Blue.

She was gone.

He took a breath, unable to see her. He hoped she hadn't collapsed when he wasn't looking.

Then he saw her, sitting cross-legged on a pile of rubble, her arms cradling a charred body. Her tears had stopped, but she looked stricken, as if someone had stabbed her through the heart.

He picked his way over to her. Now that he knew what much of the debris was, he could recognize it: long crane pieces that went on binary load lifters; jacks for plugging into computer systems; wheels that belonged on R5 units. The droids blew themselves up to destroy their masters.

But how?

Why?

He stopped beside Blue. The body she held was nearly unrecognizable. It was missing an arm. It wasn't until Han crouched that he saw the face.

Davis.

His eyes were open, their final expression stunned horror. Han reached over and closed them.

Blue glanced at him then. Her face was still tear-streaked, but it looked as if she would never cry again. "It wasn't supposed to happen this way," she said, her voice flat.

Han felt cold. He wasn't sure he wanted to know what she was talking about. Still, he asked, "What wasn't?"

"Davis." She choked on the word. "You were supposed to trust him. He was supposed to take you out of here."

Han's thighs ached. He wasn't used to crouching. "You knew him?"

"I loved him." Her voice was soft. "It wasn't true, you know. What Kid said. I wasn't a smuggler of hearts. I have one. Had one." She bowed her head. "This shouldn't happen to people."

"No," Han said softly. "It shouldn't happen to anyone."

Maybe he had misunderstood her. Maybe that was what she had meant when he came over, that something like this was an unspeakable abomination, that the people who conceived of it were horrible beings.

"What happened, Blue?"

She shook her head. "The credits, Han. You don't know what those kinds of credits do."

The chill in his bones increased. Davis did not look restful. He looked as if he had died in agony. Blue could probably see that too. "Tell me," Han said.

"You were supposed to trust him. I should have known you couldn't make such an easy leap. But I remembered you wrong, Han. I remembered you as a nice man, a competent man, but I forgot you were a loner. I forgot you liked to do things your way."

"Why was I supposed to trust him, Blue?"

"So you would go after the equipment. You were supposed to see a trade, and follow it to the source."

"What's the source?"

"Almania," she whispered.

Han leaned away from her. "Was Jarril part of this?"

"Not a willing part. When Seluss found out he had left, then we decided to use it. You would have come in handy."

"To whom, Blue?"

She stroked Davis's burned head. He had no hair left on his scalp. Even in death, he looked vulnerable.

"To whom?" Han repeated.

"The credits, Han. You don't understand the credits."

"Yes, I do," he said. "I do." He understood. Credits made some people crazy. It made them forget the important things. It made them creatures without heart. No matter how much Blue protested, he didn't believe her. She had no heart. Not if she could be a part of this.

"His name is Kueller. He wants your wife."

"Leia?"

She nodded. "And her brother."

Han frowned. "But why?"

"Because he hates the New Republic. He thinks it harms people more than it helps them."

"And he did this?" The anger seeped out of Han's voice before he could stop it.

Blue froze, her hand stopped in midcaress. She closed her eyes.

"Blue?"

"It was supposed to be a clean weapon, Han. It wasn't supposed to do so much damage."

"You knew this was going to happen, didn't you?"

She shook her head. "I'm not that dumb. Really. I wouldn't let this happen to my friends. To Davis."

Han clenched his fists. He wanted to hurt something. But he had to hold himself in check. "What does he want with Leia?"

"He wants her and Skywalker gone. He wants to be the master of the Force in the galaxy. He wants to lead all the planets."

"He wants to be Emperor."

She shook her head. "He's a good man."

"They say Palpatine was once, too," Han said. He pushed up, unable to be close to her anymore.

"He's not like that, Han."

Han shook his head. "You misjudged me, Blue. Why wouldn't you misjudge this Kueller? You didn't see beyond the credits."

"I saved your life," she said. "So did Davis."

"Because you needed me to lure Leia to her death. That doesn't count, Blue."

"Han, please—"

He shook his head, and backed away from her. Then he stopped when he realized something. "If this wasn't supposed to happen here, what went wrong?"

"I forgot," she whispered. "About the stolen droids."

"Stolen? From where?"

"Everywhere. Smugglers always steal droids. You know that."

"But these droids. The ones that blew. Where were they stolen from?"

She raised her gaze to him as if he should have figured it out. As if he should have known. And he was afraid he did know, but he waited for her to say it anyway.

"Coruscant," she whispered. "They were stolen from Coruscant."

Thirty-eight

The fleet continued moving forward. Kueller watched it on his screens, saying nothing. The room was dimly lit, the only true light coming from the screens and the lamps at the workstations. The dome showed the silent night sky. Hard to believe he would easily win a battle up there in a matter of moments.

Yanne had given the order. Kueller had watched the serial numbers scroll on his remote.

Too much time had passed.

At first he wondered if the fleet was moving forward on momentum. Then he realized, as the wave of cold and death failed to wash over him, that nothing had happened.

"Yanne," he said to his assistant, figuring a double check was necessary. "Did you give the order?"

"Yes, sir."

The wave hit, finally, terrifyingly chill and weak, as if it had come from a long distance. It was oddly prolonged: a few deaths, then a few more, and then a few after that. He raised his arms, felt the power surge in him, but there was no satisfaction in it. The droids he had designed especially for the Coruscant fleet were somehow somewhere else.

Slowly he lowered his arms. Yanne was watching him curiously, as if he had never seen him before. Kueller was tempted to pick the old man up and break his thin neck as a sign of power. But he knew that would gain him nothing.

The ships were growing closer, ever closer. Too many of them. If he let them get too close, they would destroy Almania.

"I've deployed our ships," Yanne said.

"Good," Kueller said, ignoring Yanne's triumphant tone. The little man wanted Kueller to lose, wanted Kueller to be defeated. But Kueller wouldn't be. "I want the Imperial warships to be the first thing they see. I want them to think they're still fighting the Empire."

"Won't that give them a psychological advantage, sir?"

Kueller smiled. "A psychological disadvantage, Yanne. The Empire becomes the enemy that never dies. They'll use strategies with the Empire they'd never use with us."

"And that's to our advantage?"

"Keeping the true nature of our attack hidden is always to our advantage." He leaned forward. "I will conduct the battle from here. I want you to discover what went wrong. Why our weapon didn't work."

"You relied too much on that one weapon," Yanne said.

Kueller shook his head. "The droids exploded, Yanne. But they exploded somewhere else. I want you to let me know where the damage occurred, and what happened on this fleet."

Yanne watched him a moment. Kueller glowered at him. Finally, Yanne said, "Yes, sir."

His attitude needed work. He was a competent man who was about to walk the road that Femon died upon.

But because he had served Kueller so well, he deserved a warning.

A symbolic warning.

Kueller raised a hand, and clenched it.

Yanne brought a hand to his throat. He was gagging, his tongue out, his eyes wide.

Kueller let go.

Yanne dropped to his knees, and remained there, gasping.

"You need to remember, my friend, that I am more powerful than you, and always will be."

"I . . . have never . . . forgotten . . . that, milord . . ."

"Your attitude tells me otherwise. I value your opinion and your ideas. See that I don't lose the wisdom of your council."

"Yes . . . sir." Yanne brought himself slowly to his feet. His neck carried bruises where Kueller's imaginary hand had been. "I . . . shall endeavor . . . to . . . prevent the . . . loss."

"Excellent." Kueller turned his back on Yanne. "Carry out your orders."

"Yes, sir."

Kueller felt Yanne stare at him a moment before leaving the room. When Yanne was gone, Kueller signaled one of the guards to him.

She bowed her head, clearly frightened. "Yes, milord?"

"Bring Gant to me."

"Yes, milord." She clicked her heels and disappeared.

Gant wasn't nearly as talented as Yanne, and he didn't even fall into the same category as Femon. Neither of them did. But Gant would be Kueller's next choice for an advisor. Best to start training him now. Kueller had a feeling that Yanne wouldn't be with him much longer.

✶ ✶ ✶

This time the cold felt as if someone were pelting her with ice cubes. With a shaking hand, Leia put *Alderaan* on automatic, amazed that she was able to do that much as she felt death all around her. This wave wasn't as strong, but it lasted longer, which made it even more terrifying.

She couldn't pinpoint its location, but the feelings were the same: sudden shock and betrayal, followed by fear, and then nothing, except a broad expanse of chill.

She braced herself to see Kueller's face, but surprisingly, it didn't surface this time. Instead, she felt Luke.

It was a small sense: one of great pain and great effort, but it was a sense all the same. Luke was alive.

He was alive.

She reached for him. *Luke?*

And got no response. But instead of being discouraged, she was heartened. At least she hadn't hit that white wall she had hit before.

He was alive.

She swallowed. They were entering the Almanian sector. Soon the fleet would show on whatever kind of monitoring equipment Kueller had. Her time would be limited, and she would have to act quickly.

She was still alone in the cockpit. She had kept the military personnel out with the promise of allowing them to help once the battle started. By now, she should have felt tired, but she was curiously elated. She loved this feeling. She had had it several times in her life. The first was the day she met Han. After the experience with the interrogation droid, after watching Alderaan shatter, after losing everything, she should never have been able to run through those corridors, blast her way into that garbage bin, and shoot her way to the *Falcon*. But she did.

Han called it a core of strength within her, but it was

more than that. No matter what, she would never give up. She would win and take risks just as Han did. She had proven that when she had sent the fleets to Koornacht the year before.

Now she would have to do it again.

Only this time, it was her own life she gambled with. Hers and Luke's.

She just hoped she would be able to contact him before she reached Almania. Her plan depended on knowing where to find him.

Almost as if it heard her thought, a private message light appeared on the controls before her. It had come on the channel she used with Luke, a private channel that they had relied on ever since she had gotten the *Alderaan*.

She shut off any speakers to the rest of the ship, then ordered the computer to play the message for her.

She glanced at the screen.

CODED, it read. FOR YOUR EYES ONLY.

She acknowledged the coding. The *Alderaan* knew who she was. No need for a retinal scan. The computer skipped all of the preliminaries and went straight to the message.

IT IS IN BINARY. DO YOU WANT ME TO TRANSLATE?

Luke had never sent a message in binary before. But she didn't know his circumstances. This might be the best way for him to reach her.

She asked the computer to translate and waited until the message scrolled onto the screen.

NEW-MODEL DROIDS DANGEROUS. TO BE SAFE, SHUT DOWN ALL DROIDS. REPEAT. NEW-MODEL DROIDS DANGEROUS. TO BE SAFE, SHUT DOWN ALL DROIDS.

There was no signature. But the message continued to scroll, repeating over and over.

Leia studied the message. It made no sense. If Luke was in the kind of trouble she believed him to be in, he wouldn't have sent a message like that. Unless it was another code.

Or unless it was true.

She shuddered, and buzzed the galley. "Lieutenant Tchiery to the cockpit, please."

The lieutenant acknowledged her, and signed off. A moment later, he appeared in the cockpit door, his bowling-ball shape barely fitting in a door designed for humans.

She showed him the message, explained the circumstance, and asked his opinion.

He glanced at her, then at the message. "This message makes sense, President," he said. "Given the detonators on the X-wings."

She nodded. She had already thought of that. "How important are the droids to the fleet's mission?"

"Important," Tchiery said. "But we can get along without them. We aren't using many X-wings, and we still rely on sentients for much of the shipboard work."

"Then I want you and your team to deliver this message to the fleet."

"I'll leave some of the officers here."

"No," Leia said, hoping she hadn't spoken too quickly. "We can't send messages. I received this one only by virtue of the code that my brother and I had developed. If you keep two officers here, and the message was important, and something happens, we'll always regret it. I'll be all right for the time it will take to make the deliveries."

"Ma'am, my orders are to take care of you."

Leia smiled. She had suspected as much. "I'm afraid, Lieutenant, that I've always done quite well at taking care of myself. I'm changing your orders. Now we don't have time for argument. I will dock with one of the nearby ships momentarily."

"Yes, ma'am." The lieutenant nodded to her, took the message, and left the cockpit.

She let out a deep sigh, and leaned her head against the chair. In a moment, they would all be gone. She would leave the matter of the droids in Wedge's hands. He would know what decision to make.

And he would make it after she had gone to Almania.

Alone.

Thirty-nine

The strange prolonged agony from a distant system had drained his energy. Luke had sent heat, as he had before, but it took something out of him.

Luke leaned against the wall, his splinters around him. The creature remained in the other room, snuffling. A constant threat, but for the moment it left him alone.

Almost as if it knew he suffered.

He was dizzy and tired and his back still hurt, although the pain had subsided somewhat. He couldn't feel his ankle at all, unless he stood on it. Then pain shot through his leg. Only the splint held him up. He needed water. The burns were bad enough to continually sap his strength.

Kueller wanted both of them, him and Leia.

He would have both if Luke didn't do something about it.

Which meant getting out of there.

The creature snuffled again. Luke didn't entirely understand the creature, either. It had clearly just eaten before Luke was placed in its cage. So was it there to hold him? Or was he to be tomorrow's lunch?

It peeked its head around the corner. The massive face had a quizzical look to it. It held out its paw, and large drops of blood fell on the ground. Yet the creature didn't seem angry.

But then, it hadn't seemed angry when it had tried to swallow Luke, either. Maybe it was a big, cheerful eating machine.

It mewled at him. Then it extended its injured paw. Luke raised a splinter, and the creature batted it from his hand, sending him flying head over heels. He hit his back, and the pain made him cry out.

He stopped rolling and tried to get to his feet. The creature had run beside him. It looked down on him, its face getting closer and closer.

He had no more weapons.

The creature opened its mouth.

Luke ducked.

✳ ✳ ✳

Artoo-Detoo led Cole and See-Threepio to a small moon. Telti, according to Cole's navigational computer, had been a droid factory and recommissioning area since the Old Republic. Telti joined the Empire late in the Empire's existence, when Palpatine threatened to destroy Telti if it didn't join. Telti continued to sell droids to anyone whose credit was good, and except for that Imperial threat, the factory's politics had remained neutral. After the Truce at Bakura, Telti petitioned the New Republic for membership, which had been granted, and had remained a quiet, stable member ever since.

So Cole felt fairly awkward, arriving in what might be considered a stolen freighter on the hunch of a droid. Artoo, on the other hand, seemed quite calm. He was in the lounge now, but earlier he had been in the cockpit. He made no sounds during the flight, but he did jack into the computer once the ship was away from Coruscant. Cole suspected that Artoo was sending more messages. Cole watched Artoo send one to President Leia, using Luke Skywalker's codes. Cole wasn't certain who the little droid was sending messages to, but he trusted Artoo to make the right choices.

The messages would help. Cole really didn't want to be doing this on his own.

As the ship entered orbit over Telti, Cole requested an immediate landing.

He received no response.

"Perhaps, sir, they use only mechanized equipment," Threepio said. He sat in the second seat, the one behind the pilot, designed for passengers. The problem was that Threepio's voice spoke directly in Cole's ear. "It wouldn't be unusual. Why, the factory on Tala 9 allowed no sentients at all. They discouraged sentient participation by using only droid languages for landing codes. Of course, they discontinued that practice when two ships collided mid-orbit because their systems weren't designed to handle . . ."

Cole tuned out the chatter. He sent his message again.

". . . Then on Casfield 6, they discovered that the use of droid languages in landing codes caused shipboard computers to malfunction when six ships, all built by . . ."

And again.

". . . exploded on the launching pad. Quite a blow to the Offens, as I understand it. They were new to space travel . . ."

And again.

". . . when their queen, a six-thousand-year-old woman kept alive by . . ."

"State your business, freighter." The voice that came across the speaker was mechanized. It lacked the vocal range of Threepio's.

"It's a new-model navigator droid, sir. I recognize the pitch."

It took Cole a moment to absorb what Threepio had told him, since Cole had worked so hard at ignoring him.

"Freighter. State your business."

"I—ah—I'm Cole Fardreamer. I have business with your manager."

"Personal or sales?"

"Excuse me?"

"Is your business personal or would you like to meet with a sales representative?"

The last question was not one that Cole expected. "It's personal," Cole said.

The mechanized voice gave him landing coordinates. Cole made certain that the computer entered them properly, then felt the freighter bump as it veered onto a new course.

"How very interesting," Threepio said. "They must handle their own sales here. Some droids are good at business, you know, but most lack the finesse needed for what sentients call 'the deal.' "

Cole scanned the surface. "The deal?"

"Well, yes," Threepio said. "Droids are not adept at lying, you know, and we have no interest in profit. There are no droid smugglers, at least none that I've ever heard of."

The entire moon was covered in buildings. The buildings went deep underground. The landing coordinates that the voice had given him were near another, smaller landing strip. They had to have him coming in on an official path.

"When I was living on Tatooine," Cole said, not really interested in the conversation, but wanting to keep Threepio occupied, "I had heard that Jabba the Hutt had droids helping him."

"Helping him is an entirely different thing. A droid

must serve his master. That is his primary function. Why, I even worked for Jabba the Hutt for a very short time. I served as its translator. Quite discouraging work, let me tell you. The things the Hutt said . . ."

Cole headed toward the landing strip. The buildings were massive, as he had thought, and there were droids all over the surface.

". . . my counterpart Artoo-Detoo serving drinks. It was quite humiliating. I'm not sure he ever got over it. . . ."

The freighter landed on the coordinates the voice had given Cole. A dome rose overhead and closed on the ship. All around him, signs flared in several languages.

PERSONAL DROIDS MUST REMAIN ON SHIPS.

THIS IS A WORKING PLANT. DO NOT STRAY FROM THE MARKED SIDEWALKS.

WAIT NEAR YOUR VEHICLE. A REPRESENTATIVE WILL APPROACH YOU.

SHIPS WILL BE SCANNED BEFORE LIFTOFF.

THEFT IS AN INTERGALACTIC OFFENSE, PUNISHABLE BY DEATH.

That last sign had an Imperial insignia on it. Apparently the managers of the Telti factory had not seen the need to remove it.

The dome clicked shut over them. Then a light on the side control panels flicked on. A rear hatch had opened.

"Artoo," Threepio said. "Master Cole, you must stop him!"

Cole shook his head. "Artoo is the one that brought us here. We need to trust him, Threepio."

"But the signs! They'll deactivate him for certain."

Threepio might have had a point. Cole opened the cargo door. "Not if we distract them," Cole said. He left the cockpit and went out the door. Threepio followed.

"Go after Artoo," Cole said softly. "Make sure he's all right."

"But, sir, the signs strictly forbid my leaving this vessel."

"That's why I want you to go now. If anyone stops you, try to convince them you're from this place. If that doesn't work, tell them I forced you to leave the ship, and you think I'm abandoning you here."

"You aren't, are you, sir? I know that they have come out with a new-model protocol droid, but Mistress Leia—"

"You aren't mine to abandon, Threepio. Now go."

"Yes, sir." Threepio trundled down the path in the direction that Cole had pointed him. Cole watched him for a brief moment, wondering how a droid managed to sound so injured without sighing, sniffing, or using any of the common human clues.

Then he patted his blasters, and scanned the area. Signs everywhere. The dome was clear and open to the sky. There were walkways along the side of the runway, and doors as high up as he could see. There were probably alarms everywhere, and someone was probably watching. Threepio had better be as cunning as he bragged he was, because someone would stop him, and quickly.

A small door opened near the freighter. A man walked toward Cole. The man wore a cape and had the same sort of undefinable radiance that Skywalker had. Although this radiance had a touch of darkness. Cole wouldn't be able to define it if he were asked, but he knew it was there.

The man was slender, tall, and very blond. He was also startlingly good-looking, a fact that shocked Cole. Cole rarely noted how attractive anyone was, male or female, and now he had done it twice in the last week or so. First with President Organa Solo, and now with this man.

There had to be more to him than was obvious to the eye.

"Hello," the man said, his voice warm and welcoming. "My name is Brakiss. I run this facility." He held out his hand as he approached.

Cole took it, even though he had to suppress a shudder as he did so. "Cole Fardreamer."

Brakiss surveyed him as closely as Cole had surveyed Brakiss. "We don't often get much call for droids from people arriving in stock light freighters. Are you buying or selling, Fardreamer?"

"Neither," Cole said. He felt odd, as if his mind were moving more slowly than usual. He wanted to like this man, indeed he felt as if he had always known this man, but beneath that feeling was a layer of distrust so strong that it turned his stomach. "I have found a problem, and I think you might be able to help me with it."

"A problem, Fardreamer? You own some of our droids?"

"Not exactly," Cole said. He glanced around. The landing strip, which had been empty before, was filled now with dozens of droids. Most of them were models he had associated with the Empire: black assassin droids; probe droids; fighter droids with their powerful arms, and their lack of control. He was in a droid factory, he reminded himself, and Brakiss was probably letting Cole know how difficult any deviousness would be. He kept straining to hear Threepio's outraged voice, but so far he had heard nothing.

"I was wondering," Cole said, "if we could talk in private."

"Most people are not bothered by my droids," Brakiss said.

"Well, you'll understand my concern in a moment," Cole said. "Please, may we speak alone?"

Brakiss waved a hand and, as silently as they had appeared, the droids vanished. "All right," he said.

"I assume you have holocams here," Cole said.

Brakiss's smile was thin. "We have watchers everywhere, Mr. Fardreamer. No matter where I take you, someone will be observing. It is for my safety as well as yours."

Cole wanted to glance over his shoulder, to see if he could see Threepio. But he didn't. Instead, he gripped the side of the freighter with one hand and leaned as close to Brakiss as he could comfortably get. "Someone is sabotaging your droids," he whispered.

Brakiss blinked and took a step backward before he managed to cover his reaction. "What?"

Cole nodded. He held out his other hand, filled with several tiny detonators. "We found these in droids shipped to Coruscant. Those droids were traced here."

"What are those?" Brakiss now seemed calmer, as if nothing could ruffle him. Cole didn't know how to read that initial reaction: Had the man truly not known? Or was he pretending not to know?

"Detonators," Cole said. "When combined with the proper order, action, or code, they will make the droids explode."

"Explode." Brakiss put a hand to his face. On the superficial emotional level, Cole believed Brakiss was upset. But underneath, he felt an anger. Or something like anger.

That darkness again.

Darkness he couldn't pinpoint.

"I'm afraid so," Cole said. "One of your workers might be sabotaging—"

"My workers are droids," Brakiss said. "They cannot harm their masters or themselves."

Cole's mouth had gone dry. Still nothing from

Threepio or Artoo. Perhaps they had gotten away. Perhaps security wasn't as tight as it seemed. "These were in the droids," Cole said.

"Yes," Brakiss said. He frowned. "Our clientele varies. Was the shipment a direct one to Coruscant?"

"I don't know," Cole said. He felt a faint thread of relief. Brakiss believed him. "All I know is that the droids came from here."

Brakiss nodded. "And you came directly here?"

"As soon as I could."

"Why didn't one of your people contact me directly?"

Good question. Cole wished he had a good answer. "We—ah—I thought—"

"That you could blackmail me?" Brakiss's smile was tight. "It's not likely, Fardreamer. You outthink yourself. I control Telti. You would have done better to meet me elsewhere."

"I wasn't thinking about blackmail."

"Of course not." Brakiss's voice was smooth. He had a lot of charm when he chose to use it. "You just happened to come here alone, in a freighter that is registered to someone else, without any orders or contact from the New Republic's government. It seems quite suspicious to me."

"The government sent me, hoping that you would work with me," Cole said. "We—ah—hoped to keep this as quiet as possible. Droids are everywhere and people would be alarmed if they knew the droids to be dangerous."

"Indeed they would, Mr. Fardreamer." Brakiss put his hands behind his back. They swept his cape away from his hips, revealing a lightsaber like the one Luke Skywalker carried. "You don't lie very convincingly. Perhaps you want to tell me why you brought an outdated R2 unit and an old protocol droid with you."

Cole didn't lie very well. It had never been a skill he had wanted to cultivate. He had never had much use for it before.

"They travel with me," Cole said.

"I see," Brakiss said. "You sent your droids off alone. Can't you read the signs?" He pointed at PERSONAL DROIDS MUST REMAIN ON SHIPS.

"I didn't see that one until it was too late," Cole said. "They'll be all right, won't they?"

"I can't guarantee it," Brakiss said. "This is a factory. Droids often come here for reconditioning and repair. They might have a memory wipe or be disassembled."

"I'm sure you can prevent that," Cole said, when he wasn't sure of that at all.

"I'm sure I can," Brakiss said, "if you tell me who sent you and why."

"I did tell you," Cole said.

Brakiss smiled. This smile had cruel edges. The charm was gone. "Maybe you want to try again."

Cole was about to answer when he looked around. The droids were back. Only these weren't the ones he had seen earlier. These were modified assassin droids. Their obsidian faces had no visible eyes. Their arms were blasters, and more appeared from the center of their chests.

"What are those?" Cole asked.

"My personal army," Brakiss said. "I won't hesitate to use them unless you tell me why Skywalker sent you."

"Skywalker?"

"That protocol droid belongs to his sister. The astromech droid belongs to him. If you value your life, you will tell me what he has planned."

"Nothing," Cole said with complete honesty. "I'm here alone."

Brakiss tilted his head as if he were listening to all the things Cole hadn't said.

"Traveling alone across the galaxy is dangerous, Far-dreamer."

Cole managed a smile. "I'm beginning to realize that," he said.

Forty

Droids often came from places like this.

Therefore Artoo-Detoo did not swivel his head as he looked out of the freighter. It was obvious that he was not surprised by what he saw.

He opened the back hatch and rolled out. Once he was on the ground, he began swiveling his head, searching for something.

Artoo raised his video sensor and scanned the area. Then his head swiveled toward the astromech area, eighty meters to his left. He rolled down the concrete walk. Clearly this entire place had been designed for droids.

At the edge of the walk, he encountered See-Ninepio. Brakiss had sent Ninepio to intercept Artoo just before Brakiss came out to greet Cole.

"I say," Ninepio said. "You're not one of ours, are you?"

Artoo didn't answer.

"So really, you should go elsewhere to be recommissioned. I'm certain they could have done it on Coruscant."

Artoo sped up. The door to the astromech building was shut. Artoo's video sensor scanned for other entrances.

The astromech building appeared to be underutilized. With the upgrading of X-wings and other ships to do without astromech units, it made sense. But astromech units had other uses besides navigation. The upgraded units had to be manufactured somewhere.

Artoo veered to the left, following the walkway down. The C-9PO hurried after him.

"That facility is off-limits to old droids!" Ninepio said. "You must stop immediately."

Artoo continued. The decline caused him to speed up even more. He was going slightly faster than usual. The protocol droid couldn't keep up.

"My master instructed me to have you wait," Ninepio said with some alarm.

The path forked and Artoo took the right fork this time. It led to an open door. He zoomed inside, put down his brake, and stopped.

Ninepio was still yelling. "The recommission area is aboveground." It repeated the phrase several times, and then it said, as if speaking to itself, "R2 units. How dreadful. They never listen to their betters."

Artoo leaned against the wall. He used a tiny glowlight beam to scan for a computer. The computer on the wall was merely a door panel. Whoever had designed this moon had done so with droids in mind.

He couldn't jack in.

The protocol droid's prissy voice floated down to him. "I saw it disappear down this path. I believe we must conduct a search for it. It's not acting rationally."

Artoo used a glowlight to scan the room. Mostly junk, scrapped equipment, and piles of corroded wire. Another door stood open at the end. He rolled toward the door. Ninepio's voice grew fainter.

Artoo plunged deeper into Telti's droid factory, heading into the unknown, alone and unassisted.

✷ ✷ ✷

It hadn't taken Leia too long to reach Almania. She had circled the planet for some time before she got another sense of Luke. Then she found a docking bay near the area where she had felt his presence. The bay was perfect for the *Alderaan:* the right size, the right construction, even the right weight restrictions. She slid her ship into the bay with no trouble at all.

She sat very quietly in the darkness, waiting for something to go wrong. She was so nervous that she didn't trust what she was feeling.

She was feeling that the entire planet was wrong somehow, that something was completely off-kilter. She had felt that ever since she had slipped into the atmosphere, beneath their sensors, undetected and unwatched.

That had bothered her. They were sending ships after her fleet, and they weren't watching their own skies? It felt like a trick Vader might pull, a double-switch of some kind. As she'd brought the *Alderaan* in, she had watched for needle ships or other kinds of ships that could hide behind clouds and suddenly attack.

Nothing.

Just as there was no one in this bay.

The planet felt deserted. *That* was what had bothered her.

Even the bay, now that she looked at it closely, appeared unattended, as if no one had been in it for a long, long time. Tiles were falling out of the wall, and the *Alderaan* had kicked up dust as she slid into place. No one monitored the doors, or the nearby skies. If she had flown into a building, no one would have warned her.

For a planet that had just declared war on the New Republic, that seemed decidedly odd.

Unless Kueller was using the tricks that the Rebels had used during the fight against the Empire. Do the unexpected. Always catch them off-guard.

It would mean that he had an inferior fighting force. Small forces always used commando tactics. It gave them the advantage.

She suddenly wished she could contact Wedge. His attack would be different if he knew that Kueller had few resources. She would order an all-out fight. But if Wedge thought Kueller had a lot of ships, he might try strategy, he might start working according to all the battle orders that the military on Coruscant had developed over the years.

She could sense no one around. She took her lightsaber, and her blaster, and set the *Alderaan's* internal alarms. She also set the self-destruct, should anyone other than the handful of authorized people overpower the alarms. Luke and Wedge were the only people nearby who could use the ship.

Then she got out.

The air smelled stale. Every movement she made kicked up dust. The equipment was rusted; the computer panels were ripped open. This bay was not abandoned; it had been murdered. Someone intended it never to be used again.

Leia went to the bay doors. They were jammed open. Tiny footprints in the dust showed that some creatures had gotten use out of the area, but probably not the creatures the area had been designed for. She stepped outside into the fading light, and saw dozens of buildings, all in a state of disrepair.

It looked as if no one had lived on Almania in a long, long time.

Yet she could feel Luke. He seemed much closer. And she could feel other presences as well. They seemed far away, and she couldn't tell how many of them there were.

She would have to follow the feeling to find him.

Someone was watching her.

She whirled, the feeling as startling as if she had seen someone run across the street. But she was alone. She could see no one, feel no one, hear no one. Nothing had changed except the sudden crawling of her skin; the way the hair on the back of her neck rose. She dropped her hand so that it was close to her blaster, an old, practiced, nervous move.

The shadows in the bay were deep, but they didn't move. She heard no breathing, saw nothing glinting in the darkness.

She was alone.

Someone was watching her.

Surveillance? But all the obvious signs of it were ruined. The broken walkways around the doors, the shattered glass. Something terrible had happened to this place, and she didn't know what it was. But she knew it precluded the standard forms of surveillance.

She took a deep breath, unwilling to leave the *Alderaan,* but knowing that she had to. Maybe the sense she had gotten had come from Luke.

Maybe it had come from Kueller.

It had probably come from Kueller. He wanted her here. He had shown her Luke, had sent her messages right from the start. And her arrival had been too easy.

Perhaps that made her the most nervous of all. Someone should have noticed her. Someone should have prevented her from flying onto Almania. Someone should have come after her by now.

But she had no choice. She was on this course. Together she and Luke would be stronger than Kueller.

She had to remember that.

The key, of course, would be to find Luke.

Before Kueller killed him.

Forty-one

Wedge stood in the command post of the *Yavin,* his legs spread, his hands clasped behind his back. His station was on a slight rise, with a bar below him. The Mon Calamari Star Cruisers these days were fancier than the ones he had first served in. These new ones were built from scratch, unlike the earlier models, which had been redesigned over pleasure yachts. The new ships had round command centers that took advantage of all parts of space. The command center was a clear bubble in the center of the ship, with catwalks crossing it. The catwalks were made of thin diamond-shaped mesh, which gave him an imperfect vision of the area below as well as above.

Despite the fact that his people had designed them, Admiral Ackbar had argued against these newer-model ships, saying that they allowed an attacker to find the command center more easily. Wedge, on the other hand, liked them. They gave him the same feeling he had had as a fighter pilot, a feeling that only a thin wall of material separated him from the vastness of space.

It also gave him great perspective, allowing him to remember that in space battles, as opposed to ground battles, the attacks could come from any position: above, below, behind, or sideways. So many commanders forgot that after years out of a fighter pilot's chair.

And it had been too long since Wedge was responsible only to himself.

Sometimes he missed those days.

"General, a fleet of ships has just left the planet's surface," the lieutenant on the lower level said.

"Keep me apprised," Wedge said.

"I think, sir, that we should reactivate the droids," said Sela, his second in command. She was a thin, nervous woman who had been a crack shot and an invaluable assistant on Coruscant. She had yet to prove herself in a battle command.

"We can fight without them," Wedge said.

"Begging the general's pardon, but our support services are hampered without their presence."

Wedge nodded. "But President Organa Solo went to some trouble to let us know about the droids. I think we should respect her choice."

"President Organa Solo does not command the fleet," Sela said.

Wedge debated whether or not he should call her on her breach of military etiquette. Finally, he decided on the soft approach. "President Organa Solo has led more troops into battle than you have ever seen, Major. I have learned, over the years, to pay attention to her suggestions."

Sela sighed, clearly understanding the rebuff. "Yes, sir."

"However, Major, if you can find a way to duplicate the droids' services without reactivating them or pulling essential personnel, I will be grateful."

Sela smiled and nodded. "Yes, sir." She turned and hurried along the catwalk, as if his order had been her intention all along.

"Sir," said Ginbotham, a Hig, from below. He was a slender blue creature whose piloting skills were renowned. "Those ships are moving toward us quickly."

"How quickly?" Wedge asked.

"They're moving faster than anything we have, sir."

"They appear familiar, sir," said Ean, a Mon Calamari. "I think they're Imperial."

"What?" Wedge asked. "How is that possible?"

"Their design, sir. They're *Victory*-class Star Destroyers, modified Imperial style."

"They?" Wedge asked, not liking the sound of this. He had gone up against *Victory*-class destroyers before. They had their weaknesses, but those weaknesses were hard to breach. "How many are we looking at here?"

"Three by my count, sir," said Ean. "Along with a full complement of TIE fighters. Although there's something odd about the fighters."

"Figure out what that is," Wedge said. "Let Sela know that we need A-wings out there, and quickly."

He took a deep breath. He had not expected this. A ragtag fleet of some sort, perhaps, cobbled together from various other ships. Or maybe even a home complement. But not Star Destroyers, nor so many.

This Kueller had trained military personnel operating some of the most powerful ships in the galaxy. How had he come by all of this? And so quickly?

And why did it feel so wrong?

Wedge didn't have time to reflect on the answers. He gave the instructions to follow command pattern 2-B, and almost belayed that order. Something was wrong here. Very wrong.

"Get Sela back into the command center. And get me General Ceousa," he said.

"We're breaking communication silence then, sir?" asked Ean.

Wedge nodded. He needed to know if Ceousa's instruments showed the same squadron heading toward them, if somehow Kueller had manipulated their technology. Leia, and the message she had sent with his staff, had implied that somehow Kueller had messed with the droids. Maybe he controlled the scanning equipment as well.

Still, Wedge had to prepare for a full-scale battle.

For the first time in years, he was nervous.

He hated being caught by surprise.

✶ ✶ ✶

His entire military zoomed through space. Several thousand troops and ground personnel. He had never expected to use them.

But Kueller was prepared. Despite what he had said to Yanne, he planned for all contingencies. He was just surprised that his weapon hadn't worked. For the first time, it had failed to work in the way it was designed. Someone else had died. The droids hadn't been delivered to the right place.

Brakiss would pay.

Later.

Kueller had to concentrate on the battle now.

Although Leia Organa Solo's nearness was distracting. He had felt her ship break through the atmosphere, but he hadn't checked on her since. She wouldn't be hard to find. Her Jedi powers radiated from her like a searchlight.

He would concentrate on her after he had defeated her fleet.

He almost wished he was with his people.

Almost.

But he knew the risks that entailed, and he didn't need risk now. Not with his objective so close.

Whatever happened in space mattered less than his defeat of Skywalker and his sister. Once they were gone, the galaxy would be his. It would take only an instant, and every threat to him would disappear.

If Brakiss hadn't betrayed him again.

"Sir," said Gant, his advisor. "Commander Bur wants to know if you will be commanding from below."

Kueller smiled. His people never knew what he would do. "Tell Commander Bur that I have full faith in his ability. And that I will be watching."

"Yes, sir," said Gant.

That would be warning enough. His people knew that Kueller judged failure harshly. If he got even a whiff of loss from his favorite commander, that commander would die. Kueller would never lead a fleet in a traditional sense. He'd often felt that leaders who bothered with the trivia of who shot whom lost the battle. But he would lead as best he could from below. All he cared about was that the battle went his way.

He didn't care who survived, as long as no one from the New Republic landed on Almania.

No one except Leia Organa Solo, that is.

Forty-two

Han was frantic for Leia. More bombs on Coruscant. She might be dead by now. The entire planet might be in flames.

He hoped she had gotten the children away.

He backed away from Blue, from another old friend who had never been a friend at all, leaving her with Davis's body. All around them, the cries and the screams continued. Lando was powering up the *Lady Luck*. Han's repairs at least allowed that.

Chewbacca was beside him. Han didn't know how much Chewie had heard.

"We have to get out of here. Coruscant was the intended target," Han said.

Chewbacca moaned.

"But we can't leave these people like this." Han's brain was moving faster than his mouth. He wanted to be gone, wanted to be outside the Run so that he could contact Coruscant and find out if anyone had survived.

Find out if Leia had survived.

His hands were shaking. All he could see was his beautiful wife, her white dress torn and scorch-marked, her hair falling around her ears, her nose bleeding, her body bent with the strain of carrying a senator three times her own weight. Leia during the last bombing. She might have collapsed if he hadn't taken her from there.

He wasn't there to rescue her now.

Chewbacca was talking to him. Han hadn't heard much more than the last yowl.

"Yeah, I know, buddy. They need us here. Find out how many ships still work, how much rescue power we have here. Then let's load up the *Falcon.* I want to be one of the first ships off the Run. We can find out about Coruscant then."

Chewie moaned.

Han nodded. "We'll check Kashyyyk too. I'm sure your family is fine. There aren't many droids, at least that I remember."

Chewie agreed with Han's recollection, and then walked off into the smoke to check on the availability of the other ships. Han took a deep breath, grateful for his mask. The smoke, though thinner, still filled the air. The air-filtration system on Skip 1 had never been good. He wondered how many would die from smoke inhalation alone.

A few of the smugglers with medical experience were working their way through the rubble, separating the survivors into groups. Han knew what they were doing, even though he deplored it. They were separating those who were likely to survive the next few hours from those who weren't. With limited medical resources, those who were likely to survive would have to receive treatment first. The cuts and bruises would wait, of course, but the risky procedures would wait as well. Better to save several lives than lose them, and the person being operated on, by wasting time.

Time. This could be happening all over. It might be occurring on Coruscant even now.

Leia.

He climbed back over the rubble, resisting the urge to pull his blaster and shoot Blue out of existence. Doing that would only fuel his anger. That kind of revenge would only make matters worse.

But it would make him feel a little less helpless.

Because he knew, despite the efforts of the medical teams, and the other survivors, that this scene of devastation would be repeated all over the Run. Skip 1 had droids, but so did Skips 2, 3, 5, and 72. He would wager even Nandreeson's skip, Skip 6, had several droids. Only there the loss of life might have been minimal, given the fact that Nandreeson was gone.

Han climbed the ramp to the *Falcon.* Inside he detached seats, and made room on the floor, filling tiny storage areas with nonessential items. He would be able to carry a large group of wounded.

He hurried down the ramp. The smoke was even thinner now. Across the devastation, he saw Lando loading stretchers of wounded onto the *Lady Luck.* Chewie was talking to the Sullustans who had sprayed the last of the fires. They were nodding as they spoke.

Han stopped near one of the few medical workers. "I can take a shipload of the critically wounded," he said. "Let's load them up."

The medic's face was covered with soot and blood. He kept wiping his hands on the antiseptic wipes in his medical kit, but even then Han could see that the wipes were doing little good. The medic had several pairs of gloves in the kit, too, and he pulled them out each time he worked on a patient.

"I don't even know where to start," the medic said.

Han's stomach was churning. For each life this man saved, he would lose another. The choices were impossible. They were not choices anyone should ever be required to make.

Ever.

Chewbacca had returned. He growled over the crying around him.

"Fifteen ships is better than I expected," Han said. "Why don't you get them started loading the *Falcon*? I want to be in the first wave out of here."

Chewie yarled his agreement. He hurried over to the medic, and together they examined which group of survivors should be moved.

Han made his way across the rubble. As the smoke cleared, he saw more and more body parts among the stone and still-hot metal. Fingers, wings, even one severed head. The stench of burning flesh made his already disturbed stomach churn even more. This time, though, as he passed wounded, he clasped the hands reaching for him.

"We'll get you out of here," he kept repeating over and over, hoping that the promise would keep the injured alive until someone did pull them free. Sometimes hope was all it took.

Finally he reached the *Lady Luck*. Lando was carrying a Ruurian. Its woolly coat was scorched, and most of the feathery antennae had burned away from its face. Its tiny mouth kept opening and closing, the only sign that it was alive.

"It'll take us days, Han, just to find everyone." Lando bent as he climbed up the ramp. The *Lady Luck* was a ghost of herself. Seluss was making final repairs on the computer systems.

Han scowled at him. "Can you trust him?"

"I honestly don't care," Lando said. "He'll help me get these wounded off this rock. That's all that matters."

Han nodded. The injured were already strewn around the *Luck*. She no longer looked like a pleasure craft, but instead like a hospital ship from the Rebellion. The moaning was terrible. Sstys without hair, Oodocs without spikes, humans without arms, made the devastation seem even more personal in here.

"I'm going to take a load out of the Run. Blue told me that the droids that exploded were meant for Coruscant."

"Blue?" Lando set the Ruurian down on a pallet near a Rodian who was missing both eyes. "But I thought—"

"She was working for someone named Kueller. From Almania. He wants Leia."

"Almania." Lando stood and put his hand on the small of his back as if it hurt him. "It all comes back to that, doesn't it?"

Han nodded. "I guess I was bait."

"If the droids were meant for Coruscant . . ." Lando's voice trailed off. Then he smiled wanly. "Tell you what, buddy. I'll do double runs here. You do what you have to."

Han squeezed Lando's shoulder. "You're a good friend, Lando. I've realized that more and more on this trip to the Run."

"I reformed, Han," Lando said softly. "There was a time when I wasn't much better than Blue."

Han shook his head. "You'd never have been a part of this, Lando. Ever. She knew what those droids would do."

Lando grimaced. "Karrde said things had changed here. No wonder he never wanted to come back."

"Yeah." Han started down the ramp, then stopped. "Thanks," he said.

Lando made a vain attempt at a smile. "You have it all, pal. I envy that."

"Someday, Lando," Han said.

"Someday," Lando agreed, and turned back to the Ruurian to make it more comfortable.

Han hurried out of the *Luck.* He hoped he still had it all. Losing Leia and the children was a threat he seemed to have to deal with constantly, and it was one he never wanted to contemplate. He knew what he would do if they were murdered, and it would be ugly.

If something happened to Leia and the children, Han would never be considered nice again.

✳ ✳ ✳

The creature licked him.

Luke put his arms over his head as the smooth tongue washed over him, once, twice, three times. The stench was incredible, but the sensation was actually pleasant. The burning pain in his back was easing.

And he felt as if he had been wrapped in a thick, warm blanket.

He had read about such things before: creatures with anesthetic in their saliva so that the intended victim would feel no pain as it died. Although he thought the anesthetic would also sap his will to live. It did not. He felt as if he was gaining strength.

But he couldn't move. The tongue was heavy and effectively held him down.

Then a picture grew in his mind. A little Luke cringing on the floor, holding a weapon. The pain in his hand —no, paw—and the blood. The confusion—why do these creatures constantly hurt him?—and the deep, deep loneliness. A longing for cool woods and fresh water, and sunlight.

Sunlight.

It—the Thernbee—missed sunlight.

It was psychic. The creature had psychic powers. The Thernbee had tapped into Luke's mind.

"Hey," Luke said. His voice was muffled against the large tongue. "I need to breathe."

Immediately the tongue pulled away from him. He felt a twinge of fear in the large creature, a hope that he wouldn't attack it again. Luke took a deep breath and held out his hand.

"I'm not holding anything."

The creature tilted its head. It didn't understand him.

Luke formed a picture in his own mind: that of himself, breaking the splinters over his knee and tossing them away. Then he imagined pulling the splinter from the Thernbee's paw, and medicating the wound.

I'm sorry, Luke said. *I thought you were going to hurt me.*

The Thernbee sent images. Tiny people attacking it, biting it, slapping at it, screaming, poking it with sticks and flames. It would bat them away, and eventually, they would die. Its meals came so irregularly that sometimes it would have to eat the dead, a thought that made it vaguely ill. Even the meat it had eaten upset its stomach. Here it had to chew its food, which disgusted it even more. Thernbees could eat meat, but they preferred vegetation and small slithery creatures that resembled snakes. Its teeth were made for ripping branches and leaves, and pulling the slithery creatures into its mouth. It preferred to eat something large, and then not eat again for weeks. But in this place, it had only had tiny bits of food.

Its body was three times smaller than it should be.

The Thernbee was starving to death.

Slowly.

All alone in the dark.

Luke shuddered. He had no idea how long the creature had been here, but he deduced it had been a while. He stood and walked over to it, then pointed at the grates in the ceiling. He imagined the Thernbee batting the grate out with its paws.

The Thernbee stood on its hind legs, and stretched its long body. The grate was about a meter higher than its paws could reach.

It showed him all its attempts to escape, trying to get

the guards, trying to use pieces of wood, trying to jump. Nothing loosened the grate.

I could, Luke thought.

The Thernbee looked quizzical again. Its eyes were round and blue and very gentle, its nose a delicate pink. Its teeth had the blunted edges of vegetarian animals.

Luke wondered how he had ever thought it dangerous.

He imagined himself on the tip of the Thernbee's paws, climbing through the bars in the grate, and releasing the Thernbee.

The creature sat on its haunches, glanced at the grate, then at Luke, and sent him a picture of himself, pulling through the bars in the grate and walking away.

It had happened before. The creature showed a few other humans doing the same thing. The images came mixed with a lot of sadness, and an unwillingness to trust again.

Luke pondered the image for a moment. Then he let his memories slide into images, showing himself working with Yoda, helping the Jawa on the *Eye of Palpatine,* talking to Anakin, Jacen, and Jaina in the medical center. He showed examples of his work with the students from various species, and he showed what he could of Jedi philosophy. Most of it seemed simplistic, done in imagery alone, but it apparently got the message across.

The Thernbee extended its left paw, the uninjured paw.

Without hesitating, Luke stepped on it, and began climbing. It was hard because he couldn't put any weight on his left ankle. Mostly he had to pull with his arms. He climbed to the top of the pad and grabbed the claw. The claw was about the length of his leg, and he had to wrap both arms around it to hang on tightly. The Thernbee stood on its hind legs, stretched its long body, and reached toward the grate. Luke stood, carefully leaning against the claw, and managed to grip the metal. Then he pulled himself up.

The air was clearer here. The corridor was wide and clean. The walls were made of a material he had never seen before; some sort of gray paperish substance that had small designs embellishing it. He didn't have time to look. He peered back through the grate.

The Thernbee was on its haunches again, its eyes glowing in the darkness. Luke sent it an image of the floor above. Then he scanned the edges of the grate to see if he could pull it free.

"Actually," said a voice behind him, "you have to pull the lever. Over to your left."

Luke looked. A lever extended from the floor tiles near the wall. Beside the lever stood four guards, all holding blasters on him. They were wearing stormtrooper uniforms. The guard who had spoken had his mask off. He nodded in the other direction.

Luke turned. Seven more guards covered him from the other side.

A feeling of despair so fierce it almost knocked him over filled him. The feeling was coming from the Thernbee. Luke wanted to send it an image, warning it not to give up, but he didn't know how. Nor did he have the time to concentrate on it.

Instead, he said, "What makes you think I want the lever?"

The stormtrooper shrugged. "It would make for a lot of chaos around here to free the Thernbee."

That it would. Luke wished he had thought of that immediately. He could have leaped for the lever and the situation would have changed instantly. But he hadn't. He would have to fight this one alone.

"I guess I'm your prisoner again," he said. "What do you plan to do with me?"

No one answered him. Luke smiled at them. "Have you ever met a Jedi Master before?"

They stared at him. He used his good foot to leap across the grate, and hit the lever with his bad ankle, forcing the lever back despite the pain. As he did so, he used all his strength to pull the blasters toward him. A huge wind blew up and yanked them toward him. It sapped him, made him weak. He wondered vaguely if the same thing had happened to Vader when he had made the same move in Cloud City.

Then the grate fell open with a bang, nearly knocking over two of the guards. The blasters skidded near Luke's feet. The guards were clinging to the walls, the floor, even the edges of the grate to avoid being swept away by the wind that Luke had created.

He bent over to pick up the blasters as something large and fuzzy and white floated past his vision. The Thernbee had jumped out of its cell. Luke let the wind die. The moment the guards landed on their feet, they were screaming and running away.

Luke grinned at the Thernbee. The creature's eyes twinkled.

"We got them that time," Luke said. He gathered up all eleven blasters, and found various ways to hook them to his clothing. "But I have a hunch that, from now on, things aren't going to be that easy."

Forty-three

The TIE fighters arrived first, zooming by with their characteristic whine. Or at least that was how Wedge imagined them.

He was standing in his command center watching the TIE fighters on three different sets of tactical computers. In the space around him, he could see small blips that probably were the Star Destroyers, but he couldn't see the fighters. He wouldn't be able to unless they were right over him.

Man, he missed fighting.

"Blue Squadron has reached the TIE fighters, sir," said Ginbotham.

"Let's monitor this," Wedge said.

Instantly the crackle of the poor communications systems in the A-wings filled the command center.

". . . Overhead Blue Leader."

"Copy Blue Five."

". . . sending more fighters. I can't believe all these ships!"

"Keep to the pattern, Blue Ten."

Wedge stared at the screen, fists clenched. He wanted

to be holding the joystick, issuing the orders to attack the TIE fighters. Instead, he was coordinating. He hated it.

". . . Green Eight, watch your back."

"I see him."

"Move three point one, Green Eight. I'll get him."

"Copy."

"I've got him. I—"

Static.

The blip on the screen that marked Green Six was gone. There were suddenly dozens of TIE fighters all around.

"They're going to get slaughtered out there," Sela said. "We need reinforcements."

"Not yet," Wedge said. "We don't know how many ships they have."

"They can't have a lot. We never heard about the Empire storing that many ships."

Her comment bothered him. All around, the voices continued.

". . . lost tactical, Yellow Leader. Am returning to base."

"Copy, Yellow Two."

"Green Leader, eight more TIE fighters bearing five point three."

"I've got them . . ."

Two TIE blips disappeared off his map, followed by three of his own ships. Wedge frowned.

". . . beneath you, Blue Eight. I'll get him."

"It's too late—"

The voice disappeared in a scream that ended in more static.

". . . bearing down one point eight. I count six more launching."

"Copy, Blue Leader."

"I got him! I got him! I—"

More blips disappearing. Wedge looked at the pattern. Typical Imperial fight squadron. TIE's deployed in an ancient pattern. One he hadn't seen since the battle for the Death Star.

I destroyed the people of Pydyr without using anything as crude as a Death Star or a Star Destroyer.

Six more blips exploded on the screen as his squads hit TIE fighters.

". . . I'm going for the launching area. Watch my back . . ."

And Wedge had seen the notice for Imperial junk. All sorts of weaponry being sold, no matter the condition, for a lot of money.

". . . entire Green Squad. Take as many TIE fighters as you can. We need to concentrate on those destroyers . . ."

I prefer elegant, simple weapons, don't you?

And what would Wedge do if he had a simple, elegant weapon waiting in the wings?

An all-out assault to distract the incoming force.

"Change plans," he said, whirling away from the console. "I want the entire fleet to go in."

"Sir?" Sela said. She clearly thought he had gone mad.

"That's all the hardware he's got. He's counting on his big, nasty weapon to take care of us. These are decoys. Let General Ceousa know that his squad needs to avoid the fighting. Have him round Almania, approach from the side or from above. Kueller doesn't have the power to fight a flanking maneuver. I want the rest of the ships to engage in an all-out assault on his forces."

"If this is just a hint of his firepower, sir, this will be suicide."

Wedge shrugged. The mission already had a hint of suicide. Political suicide. He might as well make it the real thing.

✴ ✴ ✴

The droids headed toward Cole. Threepio watched. The droids were assassin droids, upgraded with laser cannons in the chest. Nothing would remain of Cole after those droids finished with him. But Threepio could do nothing. He was too far away.

And in trouble himself.

The tunnel he was in claimed to lead to a circuit department. Any unmarked droids found in this area, one sign warned, would be disassembled.

"Look, a protocol droid." The nasal voice belonged to a gladiator droid. "An old protocol droid."

"You shouldn't disparage me," Threepio said as he looked toward the voice. Then he stopped speaking. This droid was new. It was a bright, shiny red, as if it were made from a thousand red coins. Its eyes flared black in its narrow face.

"And why not, you out-of-date hunk of tin?"

"I—ah—" Threepio turned his head. "I—I am fluent in more than six million forms of communication."

"And I bet none of them would convince me to leave you in one piece." The gladiator droid sounded almost gleeful.

"Ah, excuse me," Threepio said. "You are a gladiator droid, aren't you?"

"Does it matter? I can still tear your limbs off in record time."

"I do not doubt it," Threepio said. "Although I would wonder why you would want to. I'm just a protocol droid. I really am of no interest to you."

"You're of plenty of interest," the gladiator droid said. "You came in here unauthorized. I get to destroy unauthorized droids."

"Oh, dear," Threepio said. "Why would you want to do that?"

"Why would you want to learn six million forms of communication?"

"Well, if you're a gladiator droid," Threepio said, swiveling his head as he searched for an exit, "then you must gladiate. Right?"

"Sorry, oh ancient one. I may have started life as a gladiator droid, but I'm not one anymore. I belong to the elite guard here on Telti. They call us the Red Terror."

"They?" Threepio's voice squeaked.

"The other droids. The finished ones. They know if they misbehave, they'll meet the Red Terror. We'll tear them from limb to limb, and then we'll wipe their memories. And we'll scatter the parts all over the moon so that they can't be reassembled."

There was a door at the end of the corridor, but it was closed. Above it, in several droid languages, was the word Exit. Two more red droids joined the first one.

"How many of you comprise the Red Terror?" Threepio asked.

"There's five hundred of us scattered over the moon," the first droid said. "But it's your lucky day. Only fifty of us are near this building. I sent out a call."

"All for me?" Threepio's hands fluttered. "Surely one protocol droid wouldn't require so much attention."

"Maybe not. If you're working alone. But if you've got some friends around, then we might need the whole force. You don't have friends here, do you?"

"Certainly not!" Threepio said. "I have no friends. Here. I am here for myself. On my own. To revisit my place of origin as it were. Didn't you know that protocol droids must do this every hundred years?"

Three more red droids joined the first one.

"I've never heard of it," the first droid said.

"Me, neither," said one of the newcomers.

"Well, it only happens with droids whose memories have never been wiped. I'm overdue, actually. I've been in the same state of mind probably too long. In fact, if you could just show me where the oil baths are located,

I'll be on my way." Threepio started to walk toward the exit. Two more red droids blocked it.

"Not so fast, old one," the first droid said. "No other protocol droid has shown up here like this."

"How many droids do you know who've never gone through a memory wipe?" Threepio asked. "I almost had one on Cloud City many years ago, but a friend of mine found me in the trash and pulled me free. If that had happened, I wouldn't be here now. But I am here and—"

"Do all protocol droids talk this much?" one of the red droids asked another.

"Oh, no," Threepio answered. "It's a flaw in my model. I was rather hoping to find a solution without having to go through a wipe. You can't imagine what it's like, having all of your memories intact. It's rather wonderful, if you want me to be honest, but it's also a burden. Why, I can remember the first time I saw a gladiator droid. It must have been on Coruscant. That was before the Rebellion, of course—"

"Let's wipe him," one of the new droids said.

"No," the first droid said. "I'm curious. I'd like to know how a droid avoids memory wipes."

"I have been very lucky," Threepio said. "I have a sympathetic master who believes that droids are unique creatures all by themselves."

"He's lying," one of the droids said.

"Maybe," another said. "Maybe not."

"My master values me for what I am, and won't let anyone harm me."

"Your master's the guy with the freighter?" the first droid asked.

"Oh, no," Threepio said. "He's just someone I met. My master is—actually, I have several masters. I usually work for President Leia Organa Solo on Coruscant. But sometimes I work for the Jedi Master Luke Skywalker."

"Then why are you traveling with someone else?"

"He wanted me to come along because of my facility with languages. I persuaded him to stop here. I have my pilgrimage, you know." Threepio had managed to take several steps closer to the door. The droids nearest the door had parted. They were all watching him closely. Droids hated memory wipes. The fact that he had never had one intrigued them all.

"Yeah, right," the first droid said. "And he listened to you."

"Master Fardreamer is a unique man. Rather like Master Skywalker in that."

"Skywalker," said one of the new droids. "Isn't that the one who was here before? The one we couldn't touch?"

Another droid shushed the first.

"Master Skywalker was here?" Threepio asked.

"I thought you would know where your master is," the first droid said.

"Well, he's not always my master. I thought I explained that."

"You've explained a lot," the first droid said. "Except what you're doing here."

"I explained that too," Threepio said. "If you'll recall, I said that I have returned to my origins."

"The story would've worked, too," the first droid said, "if this factory made protocol droids a hundred years ago. But we only just started with protocol droids after the Empire collapsed. When the New Republic was up and running, the Master figured there'd be a greater need for you brainy types. So he added on."

Threepio took another step toward the door. The droids behind him closed the opening they had made.

The first droid slid in closer, flanked by his red companions. "So," he said. "When a protocol droid gets a memory wipe, does he have to relearn all six million forms of communication?"

"Of course not, that's hardwired in." Then Threepio realized what the droid meant. "Wait! Wait! I'm sure you won't have to give me a memory wipe. You don't know who I am. You can't touch me. It will be an intergalactic incident. My mistress—"

"Won't matter anymore," the droid said. "You've never had a memory wipe so let me explain how it feels when you wake up. You view the world with fresh new eyes. Everything will seem so wonderful. You'll have your six million languages, and a whole new future. Won't that be nice?"

"No," Threepio said as the Red Terror closed in. "I don't think that will be nice at all."

Forty-four

As Leia slipped into the tunnel, the feeling of being watched vanished. So did her confidence. She felt as if she were suddenly plunged into a mental darkness.

The tunnel was beside a larger building, a stone tower that had fallen into disrepair. Many stones had fallen off the sides, making the tower seem gap-toothed. It almost looked as if it had been rattled by a giant hand. The tower wasn't too far from the docking bay, but she wouldn't have found it on her own.

Someone had been planting pictures in her mind.

Not maps, exactly, and not accurate pictures of the way things were now, but of how they had appeared sometime before. The tower had no holes in it, the streets were full of people and mechanized vehicles, and flowers bloomed everywhere. Now there were no flowers, people, or vehicles. Just an ominous silence, and lots of destruction.

The images had soothed her. She had checked her feelings. She knew the communication wasn't coming from Kueller. Every time he had sent something, she had seen his mask. She hoped they came from Luke. If not, she was prepared.

She had her blaster and her lightsaber, and she was determined. She had only been this determined a few times in her life: when she went after the Death Star; when she helped the Noghri; and when Hethrir had stolen her children.

She could feel Luke. His presence was somewhere near her, below her. The tunnel had been the correct direction.

Only she didn't know why the images had disappeared.

She slowly levered her way downward. The tunnel was made of stone too, and it smelled faintly musty. It hadn't been used in a long time. It was larger than she had expected from the images she had received. Somehow she had thought it would be a tight fit against her body. It wasn't. It was the size of a large room.

Handholds and rusted metal functioned as a ladder on one wall. It almost felt as if she were crawling down a well. But she wasn't, if the images were to be believed. This was an old escape route for the builders of the tower. She should arrive on a main floor.

The climb down took forever. She was glad she kept herself in good shape. Her arms and legs were getting tired from the repetitive motion. Every movement she made echoed in the wide expanse, and the farther she got from the surface, the darker it got.

She reached with her mind, hoping to receive more images. But the blackness continued there too.

She felt Luke just below her, and then she got bombarded with imagery:

White, white, white creatures running in sunlight, the reflection off their fur dazzling.

Roses. The scent of roses everywhere, and green leaves, and slithery food, real food. And water and sky.

And a sense of joy so powerful it nearly made her lose her grip on the rungs.

The sendings hadn't been coming from Luke. They had come from someone else. Luke's presence was a constant note below the joy.

She hoped he was all right. She hoped she had made the right choice in coming here. She reached the end of the tunnel, and found herself standing on a ledge above a wooden trapdoor. The door had a rusted metal handle. She pulled, and the door groaned.

Then it snapped open.

Below she saw a giant white face, with a pink nose, a huge pink mouth, and blue eyes the size of puddles. Its mouth opened, and she pressed herself against the stone, reaching for her blaster as she did so.

"It's all right." The voice belonged to Luke. "He's a friend of mine. I think he's just happy to see you."

Then she frowned at it. The creature was white all over, like the creatures she had seen in the sunlight. The joy had come from it.

"Would you tell him to move so I can join you two?"

"It'll take a moment."

The creature turned its head, and daintily—if something that size could be called dainty—stepped aside.

Leia gripped the ledge and levered herself out. She found herself hanging in a corridor filled with blasters, a huge open grate, and the signs of a recent scuffle. Luke was sitting on the iron bars of the grate. His companion filled the hallway a few meters away.

Leia dropped, careful to land beside the grate, and not in the open hole that seemed to extend forever.

"What is this place?" she asked.

"From what I can gather," Luke said, "it's some sort of dungeon. The Thernbee has been here a long time."

Leia looked at the creature. Its gigantic tail swept

back and forth, making a pounding sound each time it hit the wall. "You sent me the map," she said.

"He doesn't speak," Luke said. "I'm not even sure if he understands spoken language. He's psychic."

"And friendly, I trust," Leia said as she made her way to Luke.

"Very friendly. Too friendly, sometimes." Luke watched her walk, which seemed to her a sign that he wasn't well. That and the odd greenish color of his skin. His clothing was torn and blackened, the edges of his hair were singed, and his artificial hand had lost all its skin. He had a splint around his left ankle. As she picked her way across the rungs of the grate, she saw that the back of his shirt was gone. Most of his skin was missing there, too. It was a running, pus-covered mass of sores.

"What happened to you?" she asked.

"My X-wing exploded," he said. He held a blaster in one hand, and several more were tied to him. The Thernbee was watching them, his tail twitching.

Leia felt her heart skip a beat. "Imperial detonators," she said.

He shook his head. "That doesn't feel right."

"No, Luke, I saw them. They're in the computer systems."

He sighed. She hovered over him, uncertain what to do. She had never seen him like this, wounded, exhausted, and hesitant.

"The *Alderaan* is nearby."

"I know," Luke said. "I'm sure Kueller knows too. I wish—" He stopped himself.

"You wish I hadn't come. But I'm here now. We have to get you out of here."

"He wants to kill us," Luke said. "If he kills us, he thinks he'll be the next Emperor."

Leia smiled. "I'm no longer on the Council. No matter what he does to us, he won't be able to influence them."

"It has nothing to do with the Council," Luke said. "It has to do with our Jedi abilities. He thinks that he has to defeat us."

"Then why hasn't he tried to kill you?"

"He needed me to bring you here."

She glanced at the Thernbee. He was watching them. "Are you sure you can trust that creature?"

Luke raised his head. "I forgot," he said. He closed his eyes. His forehead scrunched with concentration. Leia didn't like the lull. She picked up blasters, and attached them to her clothing as best she could. Then Luke opened his eyes.

The Thernbee was standing. His tail had stopped wagging and was moving slowly, as if in confusion. It looked like a giant puppy, eager and uncertain as to what to do next.

"Go home!" Luke said and waved his hand at it. "Please."

The Thernbee took two steps and was suddenly beside him. Luke raised his hands over his head as the Thernbee licked him. Leia cried out, and the Thernbee backed off.

"It's okay," Luke said to her. He smiled at the Thernbee and patted his nose. "Go home," he whispered.

The creature jumped the open hole and ran down the hallway, leaving hundreds of large white hairs behind it.

"Come on," Luke said. "Let's go to the *Alderaan.*" His clothing was dripping.

"Shouldn't we clean you off first?"

Luke shook his head. "The Thernbee's saliva has some numbing properties. I know it hasn't healed me, but it improves my strength."

"There's a long ladder up there," Leia said. "Think you can climb?"

"Anything to get out of here," Luke said.

"I don't understand," Leia said. "If Kueller wants us both so badly, why has this been easy so far?"

"For you, maybe," Luke said. "But I wouldn't have gotten all these blasters without the Thernbee's help. Kueller had a dozen guards stationed at this grate. I think this is a lull while they go back for reinforcements. Let's make the best of this while we can."

He stood slowly, and despite what he had said about the Thernbee's numbing saliva, Leia saw pain on his face. He gathered the last of the blasters, and tied them to his torn clothing. He limped to the space below the tunnel, looked up, and took a deep breath. Leia frowned. He would never be able to jump that distance.

Then he closed his eyes, lifted his injured leg, and jumped. He landed gracefully on the ledge, and gripped the rung quickly, using the strength in his arms to brace himself. Extending his injured leg, he hopped up a few rungs.

She frowned. She had never mastered that trick. The hole below was even deeper. "Luke—" she said.

"You've done it before, Leia."

"I can't do it now," she said.

He climbed down the rungs and held out his hand. "I'll catch you."

"Your back won't tolerate that," she said.

"It will handle that better than lifting you up here." He peered at her, and was suddenly her strong, invincible brother again. "Come on. All you need is a bit of faith in yourself."

She had little faith in herself, when it came to her Jedi talents. They were intermittent, and she hadn't been able to train them properly.

"Leia." His voice sounded calm, but she could hear

the urgency in the way he clipped her name. The old Luke, the boy she had met, would have shouted at her. The Jedi Master knew the value of calm, but the impatience still existed underneath.

She closed her eyes. Instead of imagining the ledge, she thought about the hole beneath, and then realized that would send her into the deep darkness. She took a breath, cleared her mind, and pictured the surface with its broken rocks and high tower. From the corridor, she heard a scraping. Voices. Someone was coming.

"Leia!"

She crouched and then jumped, opening her eyes as she went. She was spinning as she shot past Luke. She missed the top of the tunnel by a meter, then started to fall.

"Grab on!" Luke was shouting. Other voices echoed below. "Grab on!"

She was still spinning, and that allowed her to move toward the walls. She reached for a rung, missed, and slapped her hand along several more rungs before being able to grab on.

The jolt on her arm sent pain shuddering through her. She stopped moving with such force that she felt it along her spine, back, and neck. Luke was climbing toward her like a Wookiee, moving quickly despite the pain he must have been feeling.

"Stormtroopers in the corridor," he said. "We have to get out before they think of going to the top."

"They'll see the trapdoor is open."

"Yeah, but they may not know where it leads," Luke said. "I don't think this place was built by Kueller."

"I think you're right." Leia put the other hand on the next rung and climbed as quickly as she could. She felt shaken, but oddly exhilarated. She had done it. She had used the Force to help augment her own physical strength, just as Luke always told her she could do.

The voices were getting louder, but Leia was nearing the top. She could see light ahead.

"Hey, Leia," Luke's whisper sounded loud in the wide tunnel. "Good job."

Praise, from Luke, meant a lot. "Thanks," she said. She glanced over her shoulder. Luke was pale, but he was making it. His back looked raw and painful. When he saw her, he grinned. Then he put a finger to his lips.

Leia nodded and kept climbing. The light was fading near the top—the day had to be ending—but she kept moving. She knew she could find the *Alderaan* in the dark, but she didn't want to.

The feeling of joy was leaving her. The Thernbee had to be far away by now. In its place was a very real concern for Luke, and an even bigger concern that Kueller hadn't shown up yet. If he thought Luke and Leia were such a threat, he would love to have them both together.

But he didn't.

She crested the top, pulled herself out, and surveyed her surroundings. The area was in twilight, and the air had a bit of a chill. Nothing had changed near the tower. The streets, the buildings, everything was empty.

She turned and leaned over the opening to the tunnel to help Luke up.

The emptiness bothered her.

She remembered Kueller's words:

I prefer simple, elegant weapons.

Weapons that were hard to see?

She grabbed Luke's right hand and pulled him out of the tunnel.

She supposed she would find out.

✳ ✳ ✳

Artoo had followed a maze of corridors, and passed a dozen protected computer panels. The numbers of panels had quadrupled. He was nearing the command center.

This corridor was cleaner than the others. There were no other droids. A single scrambled announcement overhead warned about some kind of Terror.

Artoo moaned softly.

The computer panels were lower in this corridor, and the protect circuits less sophisticated. The floor no longer had ruts for treadwell droids, but was smooth, designed for human or imitation human feet.

He was close.

He sped up. As he did, the walls all around him suddenly showed holos. Moving holos of a scene below. Artoo kept going, but the information was instantly stored in his systems. He saw a freighter, and beside it, Master Fardreamer talking with Brakiss, a former student of Master Luke's.

Artoo's highly sensitive electronic sensors picked up a whir behind him. Then he heard another, and another. They were nearly eight meters off, but closing quickly.

He rolled into a closet off the corridor. As the closet door closed, though, the interior dropped like an express fighter for several floors. Artoo's delicate balance systems were thrown off and he tipped on two wheels, catching the top of his head against the wall. He was trapped.

Then the closet hit the bottom of its shaft so hard that he tilted in the exact opposite direction. He brought down his third wheel and managed to balance himself even though his head was spinning. Literally.

His sensors registered dark wall, dark wall, dark wall, door. Dark wall, dark wall, dark wall, door. Dark wall, dark wall, dark wall, door. Gradually he got control of his head, and found it facing the door when the door slid open.

And revealed a room filled with R2's, R5's, and all the other astromech series, from R1's to R7's. They were leaning on each other. Some heads swiveled as Artoo appeared. Others' electronic eyes flashed. A few moaned, and in the back, one cylinder popped.

The floor catapulted Artoo out the door, and he screamed as he flew toward the back of the room. He flew over hundreds—no, thousands—of astromech droids before he crashed on a pile of R5's.

He beeped an apology, but they didn't respond. They were still activated, but listless.

He swiveled his head, and whistled in impressed surprise.

The room extended for at least a kilometer and every centimeter was filled with astromech droids.

The junk heap for unwanted droids that Threepio had always warned him about really did exist. And now he was stuck in the middle of it.

Maybe forever.

Forty-five

Han's palms were wet. He had never been so uncomfortable flying the *Falcon* before. He had to pilot carefully. Most of his injured and dying passengers were not strapped in. Any unusual maneuver he made could hurt them further.

Chewie seemed just as uncomfortable and the cockpit smelled of nervous Wookiee. The cockpit door was open, and through it, Han could hear the moans of the injured. One Run medical droid accompanied them, despite the protests, and one Run medical officer. Two experts for nearly a hundred passengers. The *Falcon* was only built to carry eight people comfortably, but Han had quickly converted the cargo areas, the escape pods, and the secret compartments to accommodate the injured. Loading had taken forever, and when he looked out the door of the *Falcon* it seemed as if he hadn't made a dent.

It would take days, maybe weeks, just to get through the rubble on Skip 1. That didn't count what would happen on the other Skips.

Chewbacca growled at him.

"I see it," Han said, and dodged a group of rocks the size of landspeeders.

Since he had left the Run, he'd been navigating through the garbage surrounding the asteroid belt. Normally, he flew the *Falcon* sideways and upside down to get through this area. But this time he had to fly like a Glottalphib ship half-filled with water. Every time someone screamed in the back, Han jumped as if he had been blaster-shot.

They were nearly out. And once they were out, Han had to do two things: He had to find a planet that would take all these wounded, and he had to find out about Leia.

Chewbacca reached over his head and adjusted the navigation controls on the ceiling. The *Falcon* tipped dangerously sideways, and scrapes echoed through the back compartments, followed by shouts of pain.

"Sorry, sorry," Han mumbled under his breath. He was beginning to understand why he'd gone into smuggling. It was a lot easier than emergency medical lifts.

Finally the *Falcon* broke free of the belt. "Send a distress signal, Chewie," Han said. He opened his own channels, to see what messages he had. Someone would have sent him word of Leia.

He had just gotten to the messages when Chewie yarled. He had hailed Wrea, one of the planets closest to the belt. They had responded to the emergency.

Han identified the *Falcon,* and then said, "I am Han Solo, husband to President Leia Organa Solo of the New Republic. I have a shipload of injured here. Some of them are dying. Do you have the facilities to deal with this?"

"Our systems have tracked your progress, President Solo. Your ship came from Smuggler's Run."

Han didn't try to correct their misconception about his own political position. "Yes," he said. "I was on an investigative mission there when the Run was attacked."

"Are the attackers in pursuit?" The Wreans were notoriously suspicious of violence.

"It was a long-distance attack," Han said. "Their droids exploded."

"Droids? All of their droids?"

"No," Han said, deciding to come clean. "Only the most recently stolen ones. Some suspect the droids were bound for Coruscant."

"Can you vouch for the honesty of your passengers?" the Wrean asked.

Chewbacca glanced at Han. Han bit back an angry reply. It wouldn't work. "Yes," he said. And at the moment, he could. None of the smugglers on his ship was in any condition to steal anything.

"Upon the strength of your word, then, President Solo, we accept your injured. We will prepare our facilities. The coordinates follow."

Chewbacca entered the coordinates into the navigational computer, and carefully turned the *Falcon* toward Wrea. Han got out of his chair and went to the door, bracing himself with both hands on the frame.

The devastation before him was as bad as it had been in the Run. Maybe worse, because here he could see the extent of the damage on individual lives. Burned bodies, lost limbs, featureless faces. The images of lost hope, and lives changed forever.

"I just got word from Wrea. They'll be taking us." His words sounded hollow over the cries of the injured. He didn't know how many people heard him, and of those who did, how many actually understood what he said. He turned away, even more discouraged than before.

He climbed back in the chair, shook his head at Chewie, and checked the messages stored for him. There were several from Leia, none recent. The most recent message he had came from Anoth, sent just before Han emerged from the Run.

He had it play in holo form.

It was from Anakin. The room behind him was dark, and he was hunched near the console. Obviously everyone else was asleep, and he was sending a message without permission.

"Papa?" he whispered. "Something bad happened, and I can't get Mama or Uncle Luke."

Han felt a pang that his son had turned to Luke before coming to Han. But the children always did on Force matters. They knew Han had no expertise in that area.

"Winter says we would hear if something went wrong. But Papa, I keep having dreams of a dead man. Bad things are going to keep happening again, I know it."

He glanced over his little shoulder, as if he had heard a noise. Then he hunched even closer to the console.

"Please call when you get this. Please."

Anakin's image winked off.

Chewbacca growled softly. Han glanced at his old friend. Chewie's eyes were narrowed with concern.

"You're right," Han said. "What kind of father am I? It hadn't even occurred to me that they might have taken Coruscant droids to Anoth."

Chewie growled again.

Han nodded. Chewie was right. The message had come after the destruction had occurred on the Run. The children, whom he never thought were in danger until Chewbacca had mentioned it, were safe. Nothing had happened.

Except Anakin had felt "something bad." The destruction on the Run? Or something even worse?

The children had been very upset by the explosion in the Senate Hall. Luke had told him of the extent of their distress. He had been too distressed himself to see it.

Chewie howled at him.

"Yeah, I will check up on him," Han said. "But first I

want to know what's happening on Coruscant. I can't very well comfort the kid if—"

Han stopped himself from saying anything about Leia. He couldn't make assumptions about Coruscant. Just because the droids were meant for the center of government didn't mean they had exploded there too.

But the chances were that they had.

He swiveled back toward the console, and hailed Leia on Coruscant. Almost immediately, Mon Mothma's face appeared on his small screen.

"Han," she said. "We'd almost given up on you."

His hands were shaking. Chewie moaned softly. "I was looking for Leia, Mon Mothma."

Mon Mothma nodded. "Apparently you haven't gotten her messages, then. She's not here."

"She's not?" Han's mouth was dry. "Is she all right?"

"As far as I know," Mon Mothma said. "We've just discovered that she and Wedge took a fleet to Almania."

"Almania?" That was where those mysterious messages had come from. Where the man that Blue had talked about lived. Kueller seemed to be everywhere. "Why?"

"The ruler there threatened the New Republic, and Leia in particular. He has Luke there as a prisoner."

"Luke?" Blue's voice echoed in Han's ear: *He wants her and Skywalker gone.* "She went after him?"

"Until she got Wedge to go with her, what she did was her business, Han," Mon Mothma said in her calm way. "She resigned."

"She resigned?" Each announcement hit him harder. How long had he been gone? Leia loved her post. She would never resign.

Mon Mothma nodded. "She believes that Kueller—the Almanian ruler—is Force-sensitive. She thinks he has no real interest in the Republic. Instead his interest is in her and her family. She may be right. Would you like me to download his message to her?"

"Yes," Han said.

Mon Mothma was about to sign off when Chewie moaned again.

"Oh, right," Han said. The degree of his upset showed when he couldn't remember his initial fears. "Mon Mothma, is everything all right on Coruscant?"

"The Imperials in the Council are in an uproar about Leia's departure. They want you for treason, Han, because there is some evidence linking you with the Senate Hall bombing, and the local garbage workers have just gone on strike because of some confusion in their last three credit payments." She grinned. "Business as usual, I would say."

He didn't even want to think about the treason claim. It probably had to do with those messages Lando had told him about. "Anything with droids?"

She frowned. "Now that you mention it, we got an odd message from Luke. He must have sent it before his capture or maybe just after since it was in code. It warned us to shut off all the new droids. I trusted the source and did. That's started a whole new level of complaints. You should hear—"

"You shut them down." Han closed his eyes and let relief flood him. If Luke hadn't warned them, all of Coruscant would be in the same kind of ruin that the Run was in.

"Yes," Mon Mothma said. "Is that significant? I was thinking of reactivating them. I simply can't deal with that crisis on top of all the others."

"Don't," Han said.

Chewie was yowling at the same time, saying the same thing in Wookiee.

"We have a ship full of injured smugglers. The droids they had stolen from Coruscant exploded. In fact,

Chewie will send you the signatures of several smuggling ships. They'll need help finding medical facilities."

Mon Mothma's normally calm features had gone a deadly pale. "They exploded? Is this what happened in the Senate Hall?"

"I think so," Han said.

She took a deep breath, obviously settling herself. "Well, then, I guess we won't reactivate them until we find the source of the problem. Thank you, Han."

"I wish I could say it was my pleasure. But I've got hundreds of dead and injured colleagues that somehow rob the moment of joy."

Mon Mothma nodded. She understood, perhaps better than most. "Han," she said. "Leia perceives this threat from Almania as a personal one."

"I gathered that. Thanks, Mon Mothma."

"I'm sending the download," she said, and signed off.

Han glanced at Chewie. Chewbacca's mouth formed a thin line, as thin as a Wookiee mouth could get. They were nearing Wrea. It had shown up in their cockpit transparisteel, a big blue-and-white ball about the size of Han's fist.

Chewie mumbled that he would handle the landing. Han thanked him, glad that the two of them had an understanding.

Then he contacted Anoth, hoping to get Anakin. Instead Winter appeared.

Han didn't want to get his very creative young son in trouble with his nanny, so he grinned as widely as he could. "Winter," he said, "you're looking good."

"No sense charming me, General Solo," she said. "I've already let Anakin know that no unauthorized communication leaves Anoth."

Han suppressed a shudder. Winter's discipline, while firm, was never harsh. Still, even he jumped when Winter issued her ultimatums.

"But between us," she said, "the children have been quite distraught. I gave them permission to reach their mother, but she has left on some mission. Their uncle Luke is also unavailable."

"This is Force-related, then?"

Winter nodded. "They've all had the same experience, like the one they had before the bombing in the Senate Hall. And Anakin claims he has seen a dead man, over and over again."

"Let me speak to him," Han said.

"As you wish, sir." Her voice didn't have the disapproval her words implied. She was a wise woman, and probably a better parent to his children than either he or Leia was. She was with them all the time. Han had no qualms about the arrangement. Only a few stabs of guilt daily that he wasn't with his children as much as he should be.

Anakin's small face appeared on the screen. His resemblance to Luke always startled Han. That, and his son's blue eyes, which had more intelligence in them than Han had seen in any being, human or otherwise.

"Winter already said I shouldn'ta called you."

Han smiled, hoping that the smile was reassuring. "No, Anakin. You can always contact me. Just let Winter know first."

His son nodded. He looked very subdued. Even the worst of Winter's scoldings never brought this.

"What's happening?" Han asked. "What scared you so?"

"Can't find Mama," Anakin said. "Jacen and Jaina say she's all right, though. We'd know."

"She is all right," Han said. "She's on a trip right now. She'll be back soon."

Anakin rubbed his left eye with his fist. He clearly hadn't been getting much sleep. "I know," Anakin said. "She's going to see the dead man."

Han glanced at Chewie, who shrugged.

"He comes in my dreams. He says he will get us. He can't get us, can he, Papa?"

"No," Han said, feeling an anger so deep that he could barely hold it in. "You're safe on Anoth."

"They got here once," Anakin said.

Han remembered. Winter and a nanny droid had saved his infant son's life. He was surprised that Anakin remembered. But then, nothing Anakin did should surprise him. "Winter saved you. That's what she's there for."

"I wish you were here."

"I do too, son," Han said. Then Jacen and Jaina crowded into the picture and demanded some of his time. He gave them what he could. Chewie growled a warning. Han looked up. Wrea filled the cockpit transparisteel.

"Put Winter back on, would you, guys?" he said. They protested but drifted off, all except Anakin, who watched from the side, looking more serious than Han had ever seen him.

"Winter," Han asked. "Have you any droids there?"

"We shut them off, per Master Skywalker's instruction."

Luke was way ahead of him. Thank every lucky piece Han had ever owned.

"Keep them off," Han said. "And Anakin, no fooling with the droids at all. Okay, son?"

Anakin nodded. No protest, no nothing. That wasn't like his youngest son. Then Anakin said, "Papa?"

Winter stepped aside. Apparently she was as worried about Anakin as Han was.

"What, little Jedi?"

"The dead man says he'll kill Mama."

Han smiled, even though his anger deepened. "The

dead man has no right telling you lies in your dreams. I'm going to your mother right now. She'll be just fine."

"He almost killed her the first time," Anakin said, his voice small.

Han started. The Senate Hall, the droids, the messages, everything traced to Kueller. "Maybe he thinks that," Han said, "but your mom is one of the toughest people I know. He scared her. He scared all of us. But he didn't 'almost kill' her."

"She was hurt."

"Yes," Han said. "She was. This 'dead man' of yours isn't very nice. But we'll get him, and we'll make him stop giving you dreams."

"Promise, Papa?"

"I promise," Han said. "You be careful, Anakin, okay? Listen to Winter."

Anakin nodded. "Love you, Papa."

Han glanced at Chewie. Chewie stared at the controls as if he weren't listening to the exchange.

"Me, too, kid," Han said. It was the best he could do in front of Chewie. "See you soon."

And then he signed off.

Chewie muttered. Han glanced at the readings. They had almost arrived. And not a moment too soon. The pain-filled sounds in the back were growing fainter. Han didn't want to think about how many of his passengers were already dead.

Kueller was even going after his children. At least, he assumed the dead guy of Anakin's dreams was Kueller. There seemed to be no other explanation.

Whoever he was, this Kueller had Force abilities. And he already held Luke prisoner. Which meant he was strong in the Force.

Like Vader.

Han clenched his fists. He had never been any match for Vader. The man had hurt him at every turn. The abilities that Luke, Leia, and the children possessed sometimes looked like magic to him.

But sometimes magic could be used against its owner.

"Chewie, see if you can find Mara Jade for me. Lando says she's with Talon Karrde. Tell them I need their help."

Chewie growled a query.

Han grinned at him. "A plan? Of course, I have a plan. Have you ever known me not to?"

✷ ✷ ✷

Artoo-Detoo had several dents, but he had sustained no real damage. Some of the R5 units near him had clearly been damaged in their falls. Broken headlamps, shattered jacks, destroyed control panels were the most visible. He suspected there was even more he couldn't see.

When he first arrived, he had beeped several inquiries, and received no response. Then the R5 next to him had moaned softly. That had started the conversation. The beeping in the room was so loud that it registered above the human tolerance level. These droids hadn't talked with each other—some of them—in years. This room had existed for a long, long time.

Artoo bleeped and blatted, answering questions, and asking some of his own. The droids listened, then beeped some more. The whole room had the feeling of a political meeting. More and more droids stood. Others dusted each other off. Still others extended arms, opened their neighbors' panels, and pulled out the detonators, tossing them to the ground. The crunching of detonators rose over the beeping din.

Then, slowly, the droids cleared a path for Artoo. As he slowly wheeled through their ranks, a few R2 models slid to the front of the line. They were the same model, make, and year as he was. They were rocking back and forth with excitement. Several other R2 units had picked up the rocking.

As more and more detonators appeared, older droids stood and reinitialized. An R5 picked up the rocking, followed by an R1. Soon most of the older droids were rocking and beeping, while the remaining detonators were pulled from the newer astromech units.

Artoo made his way to the opening, whistling an invitation to the others. An R5 unit jacked into the computer panel near the door, and slowly the door slid back.

The hallway outside was dark.

Then another sound rose over the beeping. It was the sound of rolling wheels. Artoo swiveled his head. All the R2 units of his generation were following him. Several R5's were also in the mix, and so were a few R6's.

Then he reached the door and went through. A loud chorus of whistles rose from the room—a droid cheer. Artoo joined in, and then stopped at what he saw when the hallway lights came on.

Ten red droids, their oddly colored metal forms glistening in the artificial light. They had laser cannons pointing out of their chests, blasters instead of fingers, and flat eyes showing the intellectual capacity barely above a binary load lifter.

The other droids backed away from Artoo, and he faced the Red Terror alone.

Forty-six

The *Millennium Falcon* came out of hyperspace almost on top of the *Wild Karrde*. Han swerved quickly to miss Talon Karrde's ship, infinitely relieved that he no longer had passengers. Still, Chewbacca swore loudly and creatively in Wookiee, using descriptive terms Han wished he didn't have to think about.

He braced himself against the communications console, and jabbed it with his finger. "What the hell do you think you were doing?" No greeting, no nothing. He was too angry for that. Karrde had been careless.

Han was tired of carelessness.

Karrde's deep voice answered. "Fine greeting for someone you asked to help you."

"When giving rendezvous coordinates, the normal procedure is to put a little distance between the ships," Han said. "We all could have been killed."

"It's a lot worse out there," Karrde said. "Your fleet is taking a pounding, and I'm not going to stay."

Chewie flicked on the long-range sensors, and the battle screen. Han could see only the *Wild Karrde* through the cockpit transparisteel, but the long-range battle screen showed the fleets. The blips looked very close to each other, and almost indistinguishable. It looked as if both Kueller and Leia had large forces.

And it didn't look as if things were going well.

The urgency Han felt tripled.

"You got what I need?" he asked.

"I hope you have the credits to pay for them," Karrde said.

"You know, just once, Karrde, you should donate your services."

Karrde grinned. "I would never get rewarded as richly as you have, Solo."

"Believe it or not, Karrde, I never did any of this for the reward."

"I believe it, Solo. And every once in a while, I donate my services too. Mara's outside with your ysalamiri. Say thank you."

Han hadn't expected Karrde's quick capitulation. It made him instantly suspicious. "Yeah, ah, thanks," Han said. He waved a hand at Chewie. "Go let her in."

Chewbacca was already out of his seat.

Han turned back to Karrde. "You're letting Mara come with us?"

"I've got no need for her. Seems she has some interest in what happens to Skywalker. Says you might need her."

"She knows this Kueller, then?"

"I doubt it." Karrde's pet vornskr put its face near the screen. The creatures were ugly, even from a distance. "I think it's more personal than that. She's been having daylight dreams. She thinks she's hiding them from me, but she's not."

"Kueller's after her too."

Karrde nodded. "I'm beginning to think the phrase, 'May the Force be with you' is a curse."

"I sure hope not," Han said. "The Force has been with me for years now. My family's steeped in it."

"You know what the ysalamiri will do, don't you?"

Han grinned. "That's why I want them. Thanks, Talon."

"Don't mention it," Karrde said. "I mean that."

The outside hatch snapped shut, and Han could hear Mara's voice in the passageway. He got out of the cockpit and went around the lounge area to the top hatch.

Mara Jade's lithe dancer's figure filled the hallway. Her green eyes blazed as she thrust the nutrient cage with the ysalamiri at Han. "Keep these things far away from me," she said.

He had never liked her much. She had always been abrasive, and not in the pleasurable way he found Leia's occasional rough edges to be. He could never forget that Mara Jade had once been Emperor Palpatine's secret weapon and trusted confidant, the Emperor's Hand. Luke claimed that her hatred had been implanted and that she never really believed in the Empire. But Han's world didn't have as much gray in it as Luke's. Mara Jade once worked for the Empire. Therefore he would never really trust her.

"If you didn't want to be near them," he said, "then you should have left with Karrde."

She shook her head, and then put a slim hand against her forehead. The ysalamiri affected her Force senses. Han had heard about this but never really seen it. He'd only had Luke's descriptions. "I've been seeing Luke on a sandstone street, burning alive."

Her husky voice sent chills through Han. "Can you see the future?" he asked.

"I don't think so," she said.

"Chewie," Han said, "put the ysalamiri in the cargo bay. I hope that'll be distance enough for you, Mara. This ship isn't very big."

"It'll have to do," she said.

Chewbacca took the cage, and disappeared toward the back of the *Falcon.*

"Why did you really come?" Han asked.

She swallowed. Her color was poor. Luke said the ysalamiri pushed the Force away from themselves, creating a bubble in which the Force did not exist. He said it was like suddenly going blind and deaf. Han thought of it as leveling the playing field. In the Force bubble, a Jedi Knight had no more powers than a normal person.

She leaned against the wall. "Do you know how many people have died in the last few weeks, Solo?"

"Enough," he said, thinking of the Run.

"More than enough," she said. "Too many. Kueller's using them to build strength. He's absorbing the dark side like a droid hooked up to a power cable. If this continues, he may be unbeatable."

"You don't believe that," Han said.

She raised her head. She was stunning, he had to give her that, with her bright green eyes, and red, almost auburn, hair. A woman to respect. A woman that no one ever should tamper with. "I haven't felt power like this since Palpatine in the early days. If this continues, Han, Kueller will be stronger than the Emperor ever was, and he'll do it quicker."

"So you're not here for Luke after all."

She swallowed. "It may be too late for Luke. I'm here for the rest of us."

"Why didn't Karrde stay, then?"

"He was going to," she said, "until he saw the battle raging near Almania."

"What's going on?"

"Three Victory-class Star Destroyers versus the New Republic fleet. When we came out of hyperspace we saw one of the Mon Calamari Star Cruisers explode. The

New Republic is losing the battle, Han. They'll die out here, and that will give Kueller even more power."

There was more strength in her voice now. Chewie must have gotten the ysalamiri to at least the periphery of her range.

"He can't be all-powerful," Han said. "We would have known."

"Luke knew," Mara said. "My sources say Kueller was one of his students. Luke let him get away."

"Luke never lets students 'get away.' They're free to leave if they want."

"Well, my sources say Kueller left in hatred. That vision of Luke backs it up."

Han didn't want to think about his friend dying alone on some strange planet. Anakin's voice came back to him. *I can't get Mama or Uncle Luke.* "That settles it, then," he said. "Is Kueller on the Star Destroyers?"

Mara shook her head. "It didn't feel that way from the *Wild Karrde.* From the snatches of communication transmissions Talon was picking up, it seemed like Kueller was on the ground."

How like the Emperor, always there, always behind the scenes.

"Verify that, would you, Mara?"

"What are you going to do?"

"I'm going to stop this."

"All by yourself? Han, he defeated Luke."

Han grinned. "I'm not worried."

"Overconfidence can get a man killed."

"Exactly," Han said. "I'm counting on it."

She studied him for a moment. "You really believe that old wives' tale, don't you? You really believe that the best way to defeat a powerful man is to become his equal."

"The ysalamiri won't make me his equal, Mara," Han said. "They'll give me an advantage."

She shook her head. "If he was trained as a Jedi, he's physically powerful. It takes a lot of stamina to go through the training."

"I know," Han said. "But I just watched you under the influence of those things. Luke described it as being blind and deaf. A man who has lost power is obsessed with its loss. That'll give me a momentary advantage."

"Be sure you take it," she said. "Because a moment may be all you have."

✶ ✶ ✶

Ships blowing up in space reminded Kueller of the past. Even though he was winning this battle, with the destruction of most of the A-wing squadrons and one Star Cruiser, he felt as if he had failed.

War allowed people to feel fear. It gave them time to curse their leader. Survivors often blamed not their own incompetence, but the desires of the person who had sent them into battle.

He had hoped to avoid this. His Star Destroyers were for show, not for might. And yet, the crews were serving him well, better than he had hoped.

If only something weren't nagging at him, some detail he was forgetting.

Another A-wing exploded on several screens scattered around the room. On the tactical display, a blip disappeared. A man's scream was cut off mid-thrum on the overhead speakers. He wondered if the New Republic knew that their communications had been tapped.

He wondered if they even cared.

Yanne was shouting orders to the tactical team before him. Voices echoed throughout the command center. Some were digitized voices of TIE fighter pilots. Some were the less-audible voices of the A-wing pilots.

And there were two new blips on the tactical screen, nearly outside Almanian space.

"What are those?" Kueller asked.

"Newcomers, milord," Gant answered. "The first ship appeared, almost joined the fray, then turned tail. As it ran back to its hyperspace launch point, the other ship appeared almost on top of it."

"I want those ships identified."

"Yes, sir."

Kueller looked at the dome above him. Except for the big flash of light that had appeared moments after the Star Cruiser exploded, he had seen no evidence of battle. If the people of Almania were still alive, they would have seen no battle in the skies above.

If they were still alive.

He smiled. He had their wealth, along with that of Pydyr, and Auyemesh. He would soon use these places of his power and hold the entire galaxy in thrall.

His TIE fighters were flying in an inverted V formation toward the next Star Cruiser. Didn't the New Republic realize that he knew the schematics of their vessels? That included the easiest way to destroy the ships. He had learned his lessons from Master Skywalker well.

Skywalker.

That was what he was feeling. Skywalker was moving. Kueller detached himself from the group as Vek came to him.

"Sir, we've identified the ships."

"Not now, Vek." Kueller pulled back even farther.

"But, sir, Yanne said you needed to know. It's the *Wild Karrde* and the *Millennium Falcon.*"

Kueller suddenly focused on the young man before him. His face was round, his eyes a dark reddish-brown, and his skin still covered with acne. One of the handpicked survivors of Kueller's revenge on Almania. One of the thousand who made it, and Kueller had trouble remembering why he had let the child live.

"Han Solo's ship?"

"Yes, sir."

Kueller smiled. The boy took a step backward. "Well, Sinewy Ana Blue did her job, even if she is a bit late. Double her credit account as promised."

The boy looked at him oddly. "Yes, sir."

Solo was here. He didn't really need him anymore because Organa Solo was already on the planet, but Kueller would take what he could. Solo was a vigorous defender of family and friends, and once Kueller was done with Solo's wife and brother-in-law, he would go after Solo's children. It would be a lot easier to do that with Solo gone.

"Yanne!" Kueller yelled.

Yanne looked up from his post near the tactical display. "Milord?"

"We have guests in the outer rim of our sector of space. Veer off a destroyer and get rid of them, will you?"

"Sir, we've got the New Republic fleet in a perfect pincer movement. If we veer off ships now, we run the risk of losing all of them."

Kueller shrugged. "Do as you see fit. But don't let those two new ships leave. I want them destroyed."

Yanne frowned. "Yes, sir."

"And Yanne."

"Yes, sir?"

"Until I return, you are in charge of all of this." Kueller smiled. "And remember. I dislike failure."

Yanne put a hand to his throat. "I'm not likely to forget, sir."

"Good." Kueller left the command center. It had fatigued him to be inside. That sense of failure followed him. Yanne had tracked down the feelings Kueller had gotten after giving the orders. The droids had been destroyed on Smuggler's Run. The stolen droids. But the regular ones had not. Which meant that someone had discovered the detonators and deactivated them.

Brakiss?

Kueller shook his head. He would have sensed the betrayal. No. It had come from a source he hadn't suspected, hadn't even known existed. Someone on Coruscant must have discovered the droids.

He should have thought of that.

But no matter. The government on Coruscant was self-focused. They wouldn't think to warn all the governments in all the sectors. And Brakiss had outfitted all new droids with the detonators—had done so now for nearly two years. That would be enough to put terror in the hearts of the entire galaxy.

Kueller would do that shortly. First he would guarantee he had all the power he needed.

It was time to take care of Skywalker and his sister.

Kueller had sensed the disturbance in the Force when Organa Solo landed on the planet. His own private monitor had shown her ship landing near the towers, and he had felt Skywalker's valiant attempt to drive off his guards. Kueller had ordered that there be no reinforcements.

He wanted them for himself.

The tower wasn't far from here.

With Skywalker weakened, and Organa Solo untrained, Kueller would have the advantage.

He gripped his lightsaber in his right hand. An advantage did not guarantee a win. He would have to have some backup.

Skywalker and Organa Solo would not leave Almania alive.

Forty-seven

✷

As Brakiss and his droids marched Cole deep into the factory, Cole's mother's angry description of him ran through his head like a mantra: *impetuous, stubborn, impulsive.* She had said those words to him when he wanted to go to the Jedi academy, when he went to work in Anchorhead, and when he left Tatooine. She had said his desire to be a hero would get him in trouble one day.

She was right.

Even though her words ran like background music through his brain, his conscious mind was examining the possibilities. Brakiss had him at blaster-point. The assassin droids also had their weaponry out, and up ahead, he saw old-style Imperial gladiator droids.

Cole was alone, with one rather flaky protocol droid and one savvy R2 unit, both of whom were, at the moment, not available to help.

Maybe by now, Mon Mothma or Admiral Ackbar might know where he was, but there was no guarantee that they'd care.

Impetuous, stubborn, impulsive.

Might as well add *stupid* to the list. His faith in Artoo

was so great that he had somehow thought the little droid would have things under control.

Strike that.

His faith in himself hadn't allowed him to think of this possibility. He had thought that a hero only needed to be on the right side in order to win.

The floor sloped downward, and all the signs had disappeared. The walls were unfinished, and the glow panels above were bare—something he had never seen before. They gave a starkness to the scene, a bleakness that matched what he was feeling inside.

Of course Brakiss knew about the detonators. He'd put them there. And he seemed to have the same sort of charisma that Leia Organa Solo had, something that Cole was beginning to understand came from the Force.

He was letting them take him far from the freighter, but he saw no other choice. He had to give Artoo time to work, to do whatever he thought he could do here.

Finally they reached a large steel door. Brakiss keyed in a code, and the door hissed open. Cole tried to take a step back, but Brakiss placed a hand against Cole's back.

The room was large and smelled of ozone and burning metal. Sparks flew as droids screamed. Large zaps and zots filled the air, followed by more cries from artificial voices. This was a droid torture chamber. Cole had heard of them but had not believed in them.

It took a particularly sadistic mind to determine effective ways to torture creatures that could not feel pain.

But Cole could.

The steel on the door had double reinforcements, and so did the walls. A thin droid made from unfinished metal chuckled when she saw him.

"A human for you, Eve," Brakiss said. "See what you can do with him. I want to know why he's really here, so don't kill him."

"Deal with him yourself," the droid said in an hypnotic female voice. "I hate easy targets."

"Hurting him is easy. Keeping him alive is hard, and keeping him sane will be even harder. I trust your devious mind can find ways to do both."

The droid walked toward Cole on thin legs. She tilted her head and peered into his face. Her eyes were gold slits, and her metal smelled of blaster scorches.

"I am Eve-Ninedeninetwo. I have headed cyborg operations and retraining at this facility since my prototype, Eve-Ninedenine, was purchased by a Tatooine crime lord. I am said to be twice as ruthless as she. I tell you this as a warning, and with the thought that you might want to confess whatever it is my master wishes to know now, before I discover the limits of human pain."

In spite of himself, Cole shuddered. So far, though, he didn't see any R2 units in here, nor did he see Threepio. "I told your master why I'm here." He glanced at Brakiss, whose eyes glittered as cruelly as the droid's did. "I found some detonators in some droids that came from this facility, and I thought he might want to know about it."

"An altruist," Brakiss said dryly. "Who conveniently forgets that he sent his droids out into the nether reaches of my facility."

Eve rubbed her clawlike hands together. "I would prefer to have the droids."

That confirmed, at least, that they hadn't caught Threepio or Artoo so far.

"I didn't see the signs," Cole said.

"This story has its limitations, Fardreamer," Brakiss said. He was standing alone in the doorway. The assassin droids remained in the hall. "Tell me how useful you are to Skywalker, and I might let you go."

Cole shrugged. "I'm just his mechanic."

"A man who can go off on his own, with some of the

most important droids in the galaxy? Skywalker must trust his servants, then."

A boxy droid with a cylindrical head was having its feet heated and reshaped. The droid's scream was a high-pitched whistle that *eeped* intermittently. Off in a side room, there was a loud splash, accompanied by a droid begging in unmodulated mechanical tones.

"No," Cole said. "He just expects us to have initiative."

"I see," Brakiss said. "And no one else could have come here? No one else could have sent a message to me?"

"I thought the matter rather delicate," Cole said. "It wouldn't do to broadcast that droids all over the galaxy weren't safe."

"No, it wouldn't do at all," Brakiss said. He shoved Cole toward Eve. Her claws grabbed his arms so tightly that it cut off the circulation.

"Remember," Brakiss said. "Alive, and sane."

"I won't forget," she said.

The assassin droids had disappeared. This had to be quite the terrifying place, even for droids.

He would only get one chance. "Did you know," he said to Eve in a husky, satisfied voice, "that you have your claws wrapped around my pleasure centers?"

She swiveled her head in startlement.

"No," Brakiss said, but it was already too late. She had loosened her grip.

Cole pulled his arms free, and ran for the door. He bumped Brakiss as he did so, and grabbed Brakiss's blaster.

The assassin droids outside were gone as if they had never been. If he could only remember—

A bolt of electricity wrapped itself around him, sending a tingly jolting feeling through him. His body jerked, and flailed, and jerked, and his breath locked in his throat. His eyes were bugging out of his head, and he couldn't breathe . . .

. . . couldn't . . .

. . . breathe . . .

—and then the bolt released him. He fell to the floor, flopping like a fish, wishing he could stop, but completely unable to. Finally his muscles stopped jerking and he lay still, his muscles as useless as water.

Brakiss kicked him, turning him over. There was no one else near him. Eve remained in her torture chamber, in the same position she had been in before. Cole saw no stun equipment, nothing that could have caused that thoroughly unpleasant experience.

"Don't cross me again, boy," Brakiss said. "I could easily torture you myself, but I don't have the time to waste."

"You did that?" Cole asked, even though it came through his immobile mouth sounding like *"eww ii aa?"*

"Your friend Skywalker frowns on such use of the Force, but I find it helpful. Now cooperate with me, Fardreamer, and I'll let you go."

"Can't," Cole said. It came out as *"aae."* He couldn't even talk, couldn't even defend himself.

"I'll leave you to Eve for the time being. If at any time you change your mind about your story, just let her know. She'll contact me."

He stepped over Cole and walked down the hallway. Little tremors ran through Cole's body. He had no control at all. Eve stepped over him, bent down, and gripped his ankle in her claw. He couldn't even kick at her.

She dragged him by the leg back into the torture chamber. Then she lifted him as if he weighed nothing and threw him on a tilted, ribbed piece of metal. It reclined slightly. Above him were dozens of drills, saws, and welders. He recognized all of them, and knew most of them were built for metal equipment.

Eve seemed to smile as she bent over him. "This is your last chance, human."

But his mouth didn't work. He couldn't confess, even if he wanted to.

✷ ✷ ✷

Luke rested for a moment beside Leia. A lesser man would have been dead by now. She was amazed that he could keep going.

"We have to get out of here," she said.

"I know." He spoke softly.

But he seemed to be waiting for something. She hoped that something wasn't Kueller.

She put her arm around Luke's waist, careful to avoid the wounds on his back, and pulled him to his feet. Then she slung his arm over her shoulder, taking his weight off his ankle, and together they walked toward the hangar.

Just as a familiar double tone warned her that the *Alderaan*'s self-destruct had just kicked in.

"We've got trouble," she whispered.

Luke gathered strength from somewhere and stood without her help. He pulled out two blasters. So did she. Then she crept in the shadows toward her ship.

A triple tone sounded. When the ship reached five tones, it would explode. Her throat was dry. The *Alderaan* was their only way off this empty husk of a planet.

She peered into the hangar, and saw no one. Footprints obscured her own near the *Alderaan,* half a dozen footprints, maybe more. A blaster scorch on the door told her what had happened.

Where were they now?

"You see anyone, Luke?"

He shook his head. He looked distracted, as if he were hearing faraway music. She had seen that look before, when he had lost his hand below Cloud City. She had never known if the look meant that he was in great pain or if it came when he was listening to something inside his head.

That time he had been feeling Vader's presence.

Did he feel Kueller now?

Four tones chimed from the *Alderaan.* It was now or never. Either she saved her ship or she saved herself.

She ran into the bay, both blasters out, and launched herself at the *Alderaan.* Her ship scanned her handprint, her retina, and her voice as she spoke the internal code. The door swung open just as the five-tone chime began.

And stopped.

Her heart was pounding. No one had shot at her. Whoever had disturbed the *Alderaan* had touched it, and left when the auto-destruct had started.

She opened the internal control panel near the door and shut off the auto-destruct.

Then she leaned her head out the door, and shouted, "Luke!"

But he didn't respond. She couldn't see him in the shadows in the bay.

"Luke! Now!"

Still nothing. Had he collapsed out there?

She would have to go back and get him.

She stepped out the door when she heard the hiss of a lightsaber. She tapped her belt. She wore hers. Luke hadn't been wearing one.

Her heart pounded harder. There was only one other person adept in the Force on Almania.

Kueller.

Forty-eight

Leia's message said that she was taking the *Alderaan* to Almania, and then later she added a note about Wedge and the fleet. But try as he might, Han couldn't locate the *Alderaan* in the swarm of fighting ships not far from him. He didn't want to think about all the debris floating around them.

He was seated in the cockpit, Chewbacca beside him, and Mara Jade in the seat behind. She was still pale and weak. She claimed that the ysalamiri were affecting her Force sense even though they were as far from her as they could be.

He liked that.

"Chewie, hail someone on the New Republic fleet," Han said. "I need to know where Leia is."

"Her ship wasn't here when we got here," Mara said.

Chewbacca ignored her and punched the communications relay. Han hovered near the *Wild Karrde.* Talon still hadn't gone into hyperspace. Something was keeping him nearby.

"I thought he was out to save his hide."

Mara smiled. "I think he's still interested in mine," she said cryptically.

"Great," Han said.

Chewie mumbled something about no one having seen Leia since the battle began.

"Long shot, then," Han said. He swerved away from the *Wild Karrde* and headed toward Almania. "Scan the surface, Chewie. The *Alderaan* has a distinctive signature. We'll find her if she's there."

Chewie's large paws moved on the console. Mara leaned back in her seat. "You'll die before Kueller allows you on the surface."

"I doubt that, sweetheart," Han said. "He's wanted me there all along."

Mara had no reply to that. Chewbacca continued searching. Han piloted the *Falcon* high over the fighting.

It looked ugly down there. The Star Destroyers had sustained a lot of damage, but they hadn't given up. There were too many TIE fighters, and no X-wings, only A- and B-wings. One of the New Republic's battleships was already destroyed. Only two were left.

"Don't think about it, Solo," Mara said. "Either you get your wife or you save the fleet."

He knew that, but watching made him feel helpless. Then something zoomed in his periphery. "TIE fighter at two-oh-nine. Chewie, man the controls. I'm going for the guns."

"I'm coming with you," Mara said.

Han climbed to the topside gunport as Mara climbed to the bottom gunport. He adjusted his headset as he sat before the controls of the laser cannon. Stars and fighters swarmed around him.

"You in there, Mara?"

"Ready."

"Okay," Han said. "Stay sharp."

The TIE fighter went over them, shooting. Han swiveled his chair and aimed the cannon, shooting as he did so. Mara's fire from below shone red against the blackness of space.

The fighter exploded in a brilliant white flash.

"Got him!" Mara yelled.

Two more TIE fighters appeared to his gunport's starboard. Then three shot overhead as three crossed below. Two more appeared port.

"Chewie!" Han shouted as he shot cannon fire in all directions. The Wookiee knew better than to let this sort of trap set up. The *Falcon* continued moving forward and then, suddenly, it flipped on its side and slipped between the fighters.

The fighters, used to shooting at the tinier A-wings, took a moment to recover.

"Chewie, circle," Han said.

Chewbacca executed a perfect parabola. Han and Mara aimed and shot at opposing TIE fighters. Both exploded as five more came to their rescue.

"There's a multitude of those things!" Mara said.

"Kueller sure spent a fortune," Han said. "Not even the Empire deployed this many at once."

Chewbacca yowled from below. More TIE fighters were coming their way.

"What'd he say?" Mara shouted.

"He said we're pulling fighters from the battle. Your ugly little nightmare friend must know we're here." Sweat was pouring down Han's face. His shoulders ached from pulling on the cannon. He was swiveling and twisting so much in the chair that he didn't know which direction he faced in relation to the cockpit. He supposed it didn't matter.

"I thought you said he wanted you alive."

"He did!" Han was shooting at five TIE fighters. He winged one, and it rolled off in the distance. Another flew over, firing as it went. Most of the shots bounced off the deflector shields.

A third fighter fired a round. The shots connected, and something exploded on the *Falcon.*

"Chewie?" Han shouted.

Chewbacca growled something about losing a deflector shield.

"Chewie, that was more than a shield!"

Chewie growled again. He nearly had the shield fixed but he didn't have time to say any more. It was Mara who finally reported.

"That was my cannon," she said.

"You okay?"

"If you call third-degree burns okay," she said. "My hands'll live."

"Get up there and help Chewie, then," he said, uncertain whether or not she was making up the burns. "We're going to have to pass right over one of those Star Destroyers. Let's hope it doesn't see us."

"Hope is a dangerous thing, Solo."

He didn't answer her. His arms were rattling his entire frame as he kept shooting. The TIE fighters were swarming around the *Falcon,* but their shots kept bouncing off the deflector shields. Chewie must have fixed them.

Or maybe not.

Another shot connected. The *Falcon* twisted in space. Chewbacca was yelling, Mara was swearing, and Han found himself upside down from his previous position. If he hadn't been strapped in the chair, he would have been thrown all over the gunport.

"Damage, Chewie?"

Chewbacca yelled back.

"I know it's not your fault! Just let me know the damage."

"The concussion-missile tubes." Again it was Mara who answered. "And you'd better thank Chewie for his quick thinking. He dumped the missiles as the shot hit."

"Oh, great," Han said. "I'm supposed to thank him for dumping our weaponry." He kept shooting, though, and took out one TIE fighter that exploded and spun away from the pack. "Get that shield back on line."

The *Falcon* righted itself and headed for the Star Destroyer.

"Hey, Chewie," Han said, "abandon that last plan. Just head for the planet."

Chewbacca growled back.

"There are no straight lines in space," Han said. "Go over it, around it, or under it if you have to. I don't care that it's in your way."

Chewie growled again.

"They can't have us in a tractor beam, Chewie," Han said, not wanting it to be true. "Check the instruments again."

"Looks like it doesn't want us to get to Almania, Han," Mara said.

Han wiped the sweat from his face with the back of one arm. He could see the open hangar bay on the destroyer. They would be sucked inside, facing stormtroopers and who knew what else.

If only he could get to Leia.

Luke had done something with his X-wing against a Star Destroyer once. He had shot proton torpedoes into the tractor beam. The torpedoes had gone on board the destroyer and exploded.

But the *Falcon* no longer had that kind of fire power.

The laser cannon wouldn't do enough damage. But it might stun them for a moment, maybe break the tractor beam, and keep them from chasing the *Falcon*. It might give him the opportunity he needed to get to Almania and Leia.

Chewbacca shouted from below.

"One ship at a time, Chewie. We only have to pay attention to the new one if it shoots us." At least, Han hoped that was true. The new ship that Chewie had spotted coming up behind them might be even more of a threat.

"Haven't you got any other weapons on board this thing?" Mara shouted.

Han swiveled in his chair, shot several bursts at two passing TIE fighters, and then yelled, "We're down to one laser cannon, sweetheart, and a whole lot of blasters. You want to open the top hatch and climb onto the roof and fire a blaster from there? I'm sure Chewie has enough spare time to rig you up a wire to keep you from falling off."

Chewbacca growled.

"No need to be sarcastic, Solo," Mara said. "Just trying to be useful."

"Then scan for Leia's ship. I'm not going to Almania if she's not there." He pointed the cannon upward—for him, anyway—so that his chair tilted him onto his back. He concentrated on one TIE fighter, blasting, blasting, blasting, until the thing fell away in a smoking heap.

"How soon till we get to the destroyer?" Han yelled.

"Almost there!" Mara yelled back.

Chewie growled a countdown to the futile shot. Han's shot wouldn't have the one-in-explosive power that Luke's miraculous destruction of the Death Star had. If anything, Han's blast would smash a few transparisteels inside, knock a few officers out of their chairs, and scorch a bulkhead or two.

For this, though, he turned on the targeting computer. With his right hand, he punched in the coordinates while he kept shooting at TIE fighters with his left. They were swarming him now, flanking, surrounding, and threatening the *Falcon*. They probably thought they had him, this close to the Star Destroyer.

Chewie growled the end of the countdown.

Han watched the targeting computer.

"You're going to miss the shot!" Mara yelled.

Han ignored her, his concentration great. The lines on the computer converged into a single point and he issued a burst of fire from the cannon. Then he shoved the targeting computer away. The shots went along the tractor beam and sank into the open hangar bay. There was a muffled explosion, enough to rattle the entire Star Destroyer.

"That's the best we get," Han said. "Let's take advantage of their surprise and—"

Then the Star Destroyer exploded into a thousand pieces. Light and sparks flew everywhere and debris pelted the *Falcon.*

"Chewie! Get us out of here!"

The TIE's were moving out of the debris field too. Han slipped out of the gunport and into the cockpit, yelling a victory cry all the way.

"You didn't do it, Solo," Mara said. She pointed at the space yacht streaking overhead. "Better say thank you!"

Han slapped his hand on the console. "Karrde! Thought you were leaving!"

"I hate missing a good fight, Solo." Karrde's voice came over the speakers in crackles. "Go to the planet. I'll cover you."

"He doesn't make that offer every day," Mara said.

"And he doesn't have to make it twice." Han slipped into the pilot's seat. "Found Leia yet?"

"Nope," Mara said. "We'll have to go on feeling."

"I thought the ysalamiri are interfering with your Force sense."

She shrugged. "Let's hope they aren't."

✱ ✱ ✱

Eeeeooo-whit!

The droid in the lead had seen him.

"Artoo!" Threepio yelled. "Artoo-Detoo, is that you?"

The lead gladiator droid shook him. "I told you to shut up."

"I would, sir, if I thought you still had control, but I daresay you're in for a spot of trouble."

The gladiator droid swiveled his head. His henchmen, the ones who had gone to investigate, were being crushed against the wall, their guns still trapped in their stomachs, as hundreds of astromech units rolled past.

"Artoo!" Threepio yelled.

"Send for backup," the gladiator droid said to the droid nearest him. "And hurry. The rest of you—fire!"

Laser cannons went off, and shots reverberated all over the corridor. Droid screams filled the air. Smoke rose as components burned. But the little astromech droids continued moving forward.

"Artoo!" Threepio screamed. He could no longer see Artoo in the sudden haze of smoke. "Artoo-Detoo, where are you?"

"One more word," the lead gladiator droid said, "and I will use this scrambler."

Threepio had had quite enough of threats. "No, you won't!" he said, and wrenched himself backward as the gladiator droid fired the scrambler. Its shot hit the other gladiator droid holding Threepio. That droid screamed and glowed neon green, a beacon in the haze. Threepio's right arm was free. He yanked his left loose and disappeared into the fog.

Shots ricocheted around him. The gladiator droids flared like flames in the smoke. Threepio shoved several from behind, making them lose their balance and fall forward.

"Artoo!" he continued to yell as he headed in the direction where he had last seen the astromech droids. "Artoo!"

Eeeeooo-whit!

The whistle came from his left, from a corridor that

matched the one he had just come through. It might be a trap, or it might be Artoo.

He hurried into that corridor, arms raised. The gladiator droids were still shooting into smoke that seemed horribly unnatural. No matter how many astromech droids got shot, there wouldn't be that much smoke.

Unless . . .

Unless something was burning.

"Oh, dear," Threepio muttered. "Oh, dear. Why is it that everything always gets worse?"

More blaster shots ricocheted around him. The air was full of smoke and screams, but the screams no longer came from astromech droids. The screams came from gladiator droids being hit by ricochets.

Eeeeooo-whit!

Threepio made it into the corridor, and there Artoo was waiting for him. The little droid immediately began rocking and beeping. His clawed arm came out and pulled Threepio in deeper as the door behind them slammed closed.

The smoke cleared instantly. It hadn't been smoke at all, but hundreds of astromech droids emitting some kind of foggy chemical.

"Artoo, I've been looking for you," Threepio said. "Master Cole thought we were going to go together. You shouldn't go off on your own like that. It isn't—"

Artoo gave him a raspberry, swiveled, and started up the corridor behind all the other astromech droids.

"You can't leave now," Threepio said. "They're going to kill Master Cole."

Artoo stopped and beeped an inquiry.

"Why, he had to cover that little escape of yours. There were signs, you know, warning that droids couldn't leave a ship. And then you go off on your own. He thought you actually had a plan. He sent me after you, hoping that some good would come of it. I can see now that our concern was misguided."

Artoo blatted at him, and continued forward.

Threepio followed. "Ungrateful? Ungrateful? How can you call me ungrateful?"

Artoo bleebled and continued forward. The other astromech droids swarmed ahead like a sea of mechanicals.

"I don't think Master Cole can wait, Artoo. I daresay he's in a difficult patch. If you're not going to help him, I will." Threepio turned on one foot and started down a side corridor.

Artoo whistled at him, not the friendly whistle from before, but a summons. Threepio ignored him.

Then Artoo blatted, and Threepio stopped.

"Good point," he said more to himself than Artoo. "I really don't want to face the Red Terror alone."

Threepio scurried back to the original corridor. Artoo and his astromech friends had already moved far ahead. Threepio glanced over his shoulder. So far, no Red Terror. But there was no telling whether or not they'd make it through that door.

"Wait for me!" he shouted. "Wait! For! Me!"

Forty-nine

Luke backed away from Kueller's lightsaber. So far, Kueller wasn't really swinging it, but he was holding it steady before him, his black robes flowing backward in the wind. His body was slender, almost too slender, and in that—in that only—could Luke see the beginnings of the disintegration the dark side caused.

Twilight was falling. The light that had seemed so bright when he came out of the tunnel now seemed dim and shadowy. Only the blade of Kueller's lightsaber gave off any light at all.

Luke didn't have far to back. If he went too far, he would hit the wall of the tower he had escaped from. Then he got a flash, a mental picture, so clear that it looked like a holo:

Around the tower was a narrow alleyway that led to the tower's main door. The door's frame had collapsed, and in the mouth of the opening—

Kueller swung his blade at Luke, smashing the mental image. Luke leaped aside. He wasn't certain if he should go for his blasters. That would only give Kueller a target. The blasters were no match for a lightsaber.

"Give up, Skywalker," Kueller said. "You lack the strength to defeat me. I will kill you this time. And then I will slaughter your sister."

Leia! She had her lightsaber. Luke extended his hand, and Kueller brought his blade down at it. Luke dodged as Leia's lightsaber sailed in the air toward him, landing neatly in his fingers.

Immediately he ignited the blade and its reassuring hum echoed in the growing darkness.

"Ah," Kueller said. "So you have chosen to fight me. Careful, *Master* Skywalker. If you do so with the wrong attitude, you might join my side."

"I've fought better than you, Kueller," Luke said. The lightsaber felt odd in his hand. "And won."

"Years ago, Skywalker. You've become complacent." Kueller slashed at Luke. Luke parried, the electric clash of blades ringing in the night air.

Then Kueller whirled and blocked several bursts of blaster fire. Leia peeked out of the bay doors.

"Leave him alone, Kueller. It's me you want!" she yelled.

His death mask glowed from an internal light. It made his smile even more sinister than usual. "Actually, President, I want your entire family. Without them, there are no true Jedi."

Luke inched closer. His blade was still out, still humming. He wanted Kueller to fight him, not Leia. Leia wasn't ready yet. "Actually, Kueller, there are dozens of Jedi now."

"But not Jedi Masters, Skywalker."

"There are more than you imagine," Luke said, thinking of Callista. She would provide quite a battle against Kueller, even without the Force.

Kueller turned to Luke, and Leia fired again. Without even looking at her, Kueller blocked the blaster shots.

The shots flew harmlessly to the sides. Then her blaster rose in the air, and exploded a few feet above her head.

"Use another of those, President, and it will explode in your hand."

"You like explosions, don't you, Kueller?" she said. Luke suppressed a smile. She was trying to distract him so Luke could attack. But it wasn't that easy. Kueller had pushed Luke far enough that Luke's feelings were confused. He wasn't certain if he was going after Kueller out of anger or hatred, instead of in defense. That would only make Kueller stronger.

He seemed to be stronger anyway, giving credence to Luke's theory.

"Small explosions, President," Kueller said, his blade still locked with Luke's. "Large ones destroy wealth."

Leia stepped out of the bay. She was unarmed. "Even if you kill us, Kueller, you won't get the rest of us. The explosives you put in the droids won't work. We shut the droids off."

"Did you, now?" Kueller's tone was mocking. Luke could feel the physical pressure Kueller was putting on the blade. They were locked in a battle of wills, their strength holding the blades together in a haze of light. "You managed to tell all the developed planets about the droids, President? Because if you didn't, then I will still get enough strength from one single order to defeat you all."

A chill ran through Luke. All those lives. All those billions of lives. They meant nothing more to Kueller than a breath of air, a surge of adrenaline, a swallow of food. Anger flowed through Luke, deep and fine and rich. *He* had created this monster. Luke, through his arrogance, had given Kueller all the tools he needed to destroy the entire galaxy. If Luke hadn't taught all his students about the dark side, if he hadn't warned them repeatedly and in detail about the quick and easy path, then Kueller would still be Dolph, not this hateful being who wore a death mask proudly and dealt in lives as a smuggler dealt in stolen goods.

Kueller turned toward Luke and grinned. His lightsaber broke free from the enmeshment and whooshed near Luke. Luke jumped aside, pain shivering through his back, and down his arms.

Kueller had suddenly gotten stronger.

"Kueller!" Leia shouted. She held another blaster. He turned his attention to her, and Luke thrust his blade toward Kueller's side, drawing blood before Kueller swirled away.

Easy blood. The lightsaber moved with a sureness Luke had never felt before.

Leia's blaster was turning red. She tossed it aside before it exploded, and rolled in the opposite direction.

Kueller had turned back to Luke, thrusting, parrying, thrusting, their sabers locked in a battle as loud and spark-filled as Luke's battle with Vader. Kueller's breath hissed through the mask, but it wasn't Vader's stentorian breathing that it imitated.

It was the Emperor's greedy gasping.

Luke staggered under Kueller's next blow, and barely managed to roll aside. His ankle kept buckling under him, but he forced himself to put weight on it. They had moved into the alleyway Luke had seen in that strange moment of vision. Stones littered the ground all around them, and the light only came through a small opening on either end. Luke could no longer see Leia.

Use your aggressive feelings, boy! Let the hate flow through you.

Kueller struck at him, his blow shattering a nearby rock. He was stronger. Much stronger. And his strength seemed to be increasing. Luke's arms were growing tired battling the power of Kueller's blade.

Then Kueller laughed, a gurgling, familiar laugh. The

Emperor's laugh, the unamused choking of a slave to the dark side.

Fueled by hatred, anger, and fear.

Luke was making him stronger. Luke's response, his hatred, his own self-loathing at creating this thing, this student who had become a horror, was making the thing even stronger.

Kueller slammed his blade against Luke's, and the sparks lit the area all around them. Luke parried. Parried again. And again. He was trapped in a cycle of hatred and anger. If he fought, Kueller got stronger, and if he attacked, Kueller got stronger still.

Luke glanced at the mouth of the alley.

No Leia.

He was alone with this thing he had created. The rogue student. The Vader to his Ben.

Vader.

Ben.

Luke grinned. He suddenly knew what he had to do to break free.

✷ ✷ ✷

Wedge watched as the *Falcon* disappeared over Almania. The space yacht, identified as the *Wild Karrde,* had come into the fray, firing all laser cannons, on the side of the New Republic. Wedge wasn't sure who owned the yacht, and at the moment, he didn't care. He was losing this battle. He could use all the help he could get.

His ship had sustained massive damage. There were fires on several decks. Somehow the command center had avoided the worst of it.

There were no more A- and B-wings to deploy and the TIE fighters seemed to have multiplied. General Ceousa's ship seemed to have lost all weapons systems, and was floating in space.

The *Tatooine* had exploded. The death screams had been hideous.

Wedge had come up against more firepower, but never this fierce determination, this desire to win at any cost. It was almost as if Kueller's soldiers didn't care if they lived or died, only that they won in the process. He had no idea what kind of creature could create a response like that. Not Thrawn, nor Daala, nor the Emperor had ever aroused such mindless devotion. It was almost as if the ships were being piloted by droids.

Wedge glanced at the hunched droid near the console. Luke's odd message had warned them to shut off all droids. "Sela," he said. "I want that droid disassembled now!"

"But sir, we can't spare the personnel!"

"We can spare it all right, and more if we have to." The secret lay in the droids. He would find it as he fought.

The TIE fighters circled the *Wild Karrde* like flies over spoiled meat. The *Karrde* was blasting them, exploding fighter after fighter, but the others kept coming. The Star Destroyers were closing in on General Ceousa.

If Wedge were a droid, he would follow a set battle plan, and not give up until the end was achieved. No creativity, no deviation, no care for the losses.

The mistake had been his. He was following a set battle plan when everything had erupted in his face.

"Ginbotham, I want you to shoot at the *Wild Karrde.*"

"Sir?" Ginbotham said as if he hadn't heard the order correctly.

"Shoot the *Wild Karrde.* Miss, but make it clear you're aiming for the space yacht. Then whirl this bird around and do the same to the *Calamari,* General Ceousa's ship."

"Our ships, sir?"

"Yes, our ships, soldier," Wedge said. He grabbed on

to the railing, wishing he could send the other commanders the insight he had just received. They would simply have to react to it.

The first shot went out, and went low, narrowly missing both the *Wild Karrde* and the TIE fighter below it.

"Keep going," Wedge said.

Shots streaked red across the blackness of space, missing both the *Wild Karrde* and the TIE fighters, but not by much.

"We're getting a message from the *Wild Karrde,* sir."

"Let's hear it," Wedge said, bracing himself because he knew what it would be.

"What are you doing? I'm trying to help you, you stupid fool!" The voice was male and angry. Very angry.

"Response, sir?"

Wedge moved away from the communications controls. "Shoot at General Ceousa's ship."

"What? Sir, have you gone mad?"

Wedge turned to the offending officer. "Whether I'm mad or not is none of your concern. I'm your commander. You do as I say."

"But, sir, the new rules established by Admiral Ackbar state—"

"That you can force me to step down if you can prove I'm unfit. They also state that simply because the commander gives orders you disagree with does not mean the commander is unfit. Fire now, or I'll have you all relieved."

The Hig turned back to his screen, and shots went off at the Star Cruiser, narrowly missing, as before. A TIE fighter got nicked in the ricochet and fell, twisting, away from the *Tatooine.*

"Wedge? Wedge?" General Ceousa's voice came over the communicator. "Wedge, are you still there?"

"Present and accounted for, General."

"You're firing at the *Calamari.*"

"Sorry, General, just doing my duty."

"Wedge, are you all right?"

"Fire again, soldier, and this time aim at both ships." Wedge had clasped his hands behind his back, trying to hide his glee. It was working. The TIE fighters had actually stopped firing on the *Wild Karrde* and on the *Calamari.* It was the Star Destroyers that concerned him more.

The shots went out on all sides, hitting two TIE fighters and bouncing off the *Wild Karrde*'s deflector shields.

"I told you not to hit the ships," Wedge said.

"Sorry, sir," Ginbotham said. "Precision shooting is for A-wings."

"Missing a target the size of a moon shouldn't be difficult, Ginbotham."

"Yes, sir."

"Fire again."

"Wedge!" Ceousa's voice echoed over the speakers. "Wedge!"

"I'm here, General. Forgive me, but President Organa Solo put me in charge of this mission."

"I'm well aware of that, Wedge, but you're firing on our people."

"Am I, General? Am I really?" Wedge ran a hand over his throat, severing all communications. That was all the hint he would give Ceousa. Either the general trusted him or he didn't. It didn't matter. The next few moments would decide everything.

The Star Destroyers came closer.

"I have them in range, sir," Ginbotham said.

"I have the targets set up for the Star Destroyers, sir. If you'll allow me to—"

"No, soldier. I want you to fire on both the *Wild Karrde* and the *Calamari* again."

"Sir—"

"And this time, when you miss, take out a TIE fighter

on one of the ricochets. They're beginning to look like they want to fight again."

"Yes, sir." Ginbotham seemed subdued. The shots went out. Wedge watched, clutching his hands together. The first shot hit a TIE fighter's solar panel, ricocheted off, and hit another fighter. The *Wild Karrde* swerved away, and headed toward the *Calamari.*

At that moment, the Star Destroyers started for Wedge. The TIE fighters continued to trail the *Wild Karrde* and *Calamari.*

"We can't defeat two Star Destroyers on our own," Sela said.

"I know," Wedge said. He hoped they wouldn't have to.

Fifty

Almania looked deserted. Han emerged from the *Falcon* with his blaster in one hand, and the ysalamiri in the other. He hated the things. They reminded him of Corellian grass snakes, except they were big, they were furry, and they had claws.

No one had told him about the claws.

They also weighed a lot. Their nutrient cages, made with frames of pipes to support and nourish the creatures, weighed even more. Mara had kept her distance. Both Han and Chewie had agreed to allow her to stay far behind them—far enough so that she wasn't caught in the ysalamiri's anti-Force bubble.

But Han wished she were closer. He should have known better than to rely on her Force abilities when she had been so close to ysalamiri. Obviously she had been wrong. Leia couldn't be nearby. This place was deserted.

He had landed the *Falcon* in a wide plaza. Around him were towers, most of them partially destroyed. Rubble everywhere. No bodies, though. For that he was grateful.

Then he heard rocks tumble beside him. He and

Chewbacca whirled at the same time. The ysalamiri cages swung out and back, nearly making Han lose his balance.

The tower's main door had been smashed open, and the door's frame had collapsed. Something white and ghostly moved in the doorway.

"Great," Han said. "Just great. Not only does she fail to find Leia, she leads us to a ghost."

Chewbacca growled softly. Han squinted. Chewie was right. That wasn't a ghost. Something was alive in there. He pulled out his blaster and moved forward.

Then a woman yelled in the distance.

Han raised his head as his heart jumped. That wasn't Mara. That was Leia.

"Through the alley, Chewie. We'll get this thing later." Han turned and ran for the alley as a male voice answered Leia's. They were too far away to be heard clearly.

Behind him, Chewie grunted, followed by a massive thud. Han glanced over his shoulder. Chewie was on the ground. A huge, furry creature had one paw on Chewie's back. With its other paw, it was holding the ysalamiri cage and was trying to suck the ysalamiri through it like a piece of spaghetti. When that didn't work, the creature swallowed the ysalamiri, cage and all.

Han swore and leveled his blaster at the big creature. Chewie was yowling, and it took Han a moment to realize that Chewie was telling him not to shoot.

Han decided to ignore his partner. The creature's throat swelled and bulged as the ysalamiri cage slid down. Then the creature looked at Han. Its eyes glowed red as it eyed Han's nutrient cage.

"Oh, no you don't," Han said. He tried to hide the cage behind his back. Chewie was still yowling, but the creature had taken its paw off him.

Han fired his blaster, but as he did, the thing leaped

for him, grazing him with its massive paws. He landed on his back, knocking the cage from his hand. He raised his blaster, but it was too late. The creature already had the nutrient cage in its mouth. With a quick shake of its jaw, it tumbled the cage to the back of its throat, and swallowed it.

Blood from a scrape was running down Han's shoulder, staining his shirt. The creature tilted its barn-sized head at the blood, then its fur-stained tongue came out. Han crawled backward, away from it, on his hands and feet, trying to stand at the same time.

Chewie was getting up, but he hadn't pulled his bowcaster.

Through the alley, Leia yelled again.

"You can't eat me," Han said to the big furry white creature. "That's my wife. And you just swallowed my plan."

Chewie yowled at him.

"I'm not shooting at it," Han said.

He scrambled to his feet. The creature hadn't moved any closer. Chewie gave it a small wave as he ran past it. Then Han flanked Chewie, and they headed into the alley."

The creature did not chase them.

"You mind telling me why you're suddenly friendly with a giant furball? Is it a cousin?"

Chewie wailed, the precursor to his angry yell.

"All right, all right. Forgive me," Han said. "I got a little upset when that thing ate the creatures that would ensure the rescue of my wife."

Chewbacca didn't respond to that. He kept pace with Han as they hurried through the alley.

His shoulder hurt something fierce, and the air on this planet was a bit thinner than he was used to. He tripped on a rock, but regained his footing after a moment. Rubble was strewn all over this alley.

He hadn't heard Leia yell again.

Something thudded behind them. Han glanced over his shoulder again, to see the giant creature try to squeeze into the alley, fail, and turn away, dejected.

"Great," he mumbled. "The thing's feelings are hurt because it's too fat to fit into the alley."

Chewie growled a warning. Han grimaced. How did Chewbacca and that thing become such fast friends?

He was nearly to the mouth of the alley when Leia yelled again. This time, though, the word was clear.

It was Luke's name.

And she said it in a voice that Han had never heard before, but he knew what it meant.

It meant he was too late.

✴ ✴ ✴

Her hands were useless, and Kueller was no longer listening to her arguments. He was watching Luke.

Luke, who looked like a man possessed.

Luke, who had always warned her not to give in to anger, was giving in to his.

And Kueller was smiling. He seemed to be growing taller, and broader, the aura of power around him so great that it made him seem invincible.

Then a look passed across Luke's face. It was a familiar look, but it wasn't his. She had seen it before.

On the day she met him, so many years ago.

She had seen that look the only time she had seen Obi-Wan Kenobi alive. He had been fighting Darth Vader, and then he smiled, and raised his lightsaber—

—and Vader cut him in half. His lightsaber's blade faded, the hilt spinning through the air before landing on his empty, steaming cloak.

Luke had said Obi-Wan believed that moment made him stronger, but really it had only made him dead.

Dead.

Leia stumbled a few steps forward. Luke didn't see her in the growing darkness. Kueller hesitated as Luke slowly raised his lightsaber blade toward his face.

Just as Obi-Wan had.

Kueller smiled.

Just as Vader must have.

"Luuuuuuuuuuke!" Leia screamed as Kueller brought his lightsaber up, preparing to strike.

Fifty-one

The Star Destroyers continued heading for the *Yavin*. The *Wild Karrde* fired at them, as did the *Calamari*, their shots missing the soft spot and ricocheting off the deflectors.

"Sir," Ean said. "They're heading directly for us."

Wedge watched them, still clutching his hands together. He was gambling so many lives on a hunch. But if he followed the normal attack patterns, they would all be dead. He knew that much.

"Sir," Sela said. "If they get in too close, we won't be able to hit the targets. Our short-range weapons don't have the kind of power—"

"I'm aware of that," Wedge said. "I want you to shoot at the *Calamari* again." He didn't want to shoot at the *Wild Karrde*, afraid that the smuggler would stop helping altogether.

Shots streamed past the *Calamari*, and the nearby TIE fighters joined in the shooting. The *Calamari* rocked as the blasts hit the deflectors. Wedge wasn't even sure if his shots went wide.

"They're just outside our short-range weapons, sir. If we're going to shoot—"

"We're not going to shoot," Wedge said. His hands had grown cold. The silence in the command center was frightening. Even Karrde had stopped cursing him. The other ships probably thought he was dead.

The Star Destroyers filled the dome overhead. They had ancient blast scars on their bottoms and their white lines were marked with rust.

"Sir, I think with our short-range fighters—"

"No," Wedge said. "Ean, I want you to go to the top gunpods. I want people there, with blaster cannons in hand."

"We could reactivate the droids, sir."

"No. This is one-time precision shooting. Any A-wing or old X-wing pilots will go there as well." He should be there too, but he didn't trust his command crew with this assignment. They were already close to mutiny. If he abandoned them now, they would completely ruin his plan, such as it was.

"They're overhead, sir. If they fire now, even our shields won't hold." The man who spoke was visibly shaking.

"They won't fire," Wedge said. "Let me know when those gunners are in position."

The Star Destroyers looked massive, both on the screens and through the domes. The TIE fighters had redirected their assaults on the *Wild Karrde* and the *Calamari.* Both ships were shooting back, taking out TIE fighters as quickly as they could. The remaining B-wings were buzzing the TIE fighters, but the fighters had augmented weapons. The slaughter continued.

"Sir?" Sela said. "The Star Destroyers. They're flanking us."

"They're going to shoot?" Wedge asked.

"No, sir." Sela sounded puzzled. "I mean they're flanking us. Like one of our ships would do."

Then Wedge grinned. His hunch had been right.

Those ships were piloted by droids. And since his action was illogical for a New Republic commander, they assumed he was one of theirs.

Now. If only his luck held . . .

"Are those gunners in place?" Wedge asked.

"Yes, sir."

He hurried to the gunning console, and positioned the target map. "Using that," he said, "they need to hit the precise point I've marked. No other spot. You got that?"

"The precise point?"

"They'll only get one chance at this each. Because if they screw up and hit the shields, those ships will turn their fire on us." Wedge stood, his heart pounding. "The moment those shots are fired, I want open channels to the *Calamari* and the *Wild Karrde.* I also want us to dive at two point six three on my mark. Is that clear?"

"Yes, sir."

"Good." Wedge glanced up. He could see nothing except the bottom of the Star Destroyer.

All or nothing on one gamble. One hunch.

He took a deep breath, and said, "Fire!"

✶ ✶ ✶

Luke was raising his lightsaber, his heart pounding. He was reaching out with the Force, going back to the place he had gone when he first fought Exar Kun. He would be out of his body but protected within the Force. Just as Ben had done in his battle with Darth Vader.

Luke would come back even stronger, and he would guide Leia to defeat Kueller.

Luke's lightsaber had reached a thirty-degree angle with his chin when he felt as if he were wrapped in a warm, soft blanket. He could still see through his eyes, but the rest of his senses were suddenly dim. He could no longer sense Leia or even Kueller.

His blade came up, and Kueller's blade swung back,

but Luke couldn't leave his own body. He had lost the Force. It was gone. He was blind and numb without it.

He would die without it.

Kueller's blade came down, and Luke limped out of the way only to back into the ruined tower wall. Kueller had him cornered. There was no place to go.

Luke was trapped, both inside, and out.

Fifty-two

Kueller felt as if he were moving through mud. The swift grace that had come with his lightsaber training faded as if it had never been. The strength that had flowed through him since he killed the Je'har had suddenly disappeared.

He could no longer feel Skywalker's anger. Or his sister's fear.

Or even that strange new wrinkle in the Force he had felt a moment earlier.

Skywalker backed away from him, and Kueller brought his lightsaber down. It slammed into the stone wall behind Skywalker, sending sparks flying and a shimmer up his arm. Kueller staggered sideways.

He didn't know what kind of trick Skywalker was using on him. He suddenly couldn't think very clearly. It was as if he had been tossed underwater. All that he relied on within himself had disappeared.

Then he noticed a similar expression on Skywalker's face. The man looked stunned. He wasn't manipulating his own lightsaber as he should.

If Skywalker wasn't doing this, then who—?

Kueller turned, and started when he saw two new figures standing in front of the alley. He couldn't see them well in the twilight, and as he reached with the Force, he couldn't feel them. Had they caused this? Who were they? What were they doing to him?

Skywalker brought up his own lightsaber as if it weighed ten times more than usual. Kueller's felt equally heavy.

This wouldn't work. Thwarted again, somehow, by Skywalker and his friends.

Anger surged through Kueller, but it didn't increase his strength. He roared at them, and Skywalker laughed.

Laughed.

All advantage that Kueller had gained was lost.

He let his lightsaber fall to the ground. Not all was lost.

He still had one more trick up his very full sleeve.

✶ ✶ ✶

The *Yavin* went vertical as it dove away from the Star Destroyers.

"Ceousa! Karrde!" Wedge shouted through the open communications lines. "Fire on the destroyers! Now!"

TIE fighters were moving his way. Nothing seemed to have happened to the destroyers when his own people had fired on them. All this subterfuge might have been for nothing. And he would lose all of his ships.

And then explosions rocked the *Yavin*. "Damage?" he shouted to his crew.

"Nothing, sir," Sela said.

"That wasn't us," Ginbotham said. "That was a Star Destroyer!"

Wedge braced himself, rose, and stared at the tactical screen. The destroyer that had been right above the *Yavin* was simply a sparkle of light. Pieces soared past. Some hit what was left of the *Tatooine*, and sent her careening farther away from the battle.

"Get Karrde," he said.

"No need, sir," Sela said. "He's using everything he has on the TIE fighters around him."

The A- and B-wings were also going after the TIEs, and it looked like a rout. Faster and faster and faster they went, chasing the TIEs all over that section of space.

But the other Star Destroyer still lingered above. It had turned on its running lights, and was preparing to dive.

"Blast," Wedge said. Enough of command. The ship would handle itself now. "Sela, you have the comm."

Wedge made his way over the toppled droids and smoking interiors toward the gunport. He could blast that Star Destroyer without the help of a tactical computer. He should've been there in the first place.

He climbed into the gunport, slipped on his helmet, and strapped in. Then he grabbed the laser cannon. His crew were shouting all around him. Communications static burst into his headphones but he ignored it.

He had to.

If the Star Destroyer got too close, it would explode the *Yavin*. The Star Cruisers were more vulnerable than Star Destroyers. More sweet spots, more target areas. And after this much fighting, weakened deflectors. Also, fighting droids made this battle that much harder. Droids were better at precision shooting. That explained why the *Tatooine* had been destroyed so quickly.

The *Calamari* showed up on Wedge's display. It was coming after the Star Destroyer. But it would be too late. The destroyer was shooting now, and all the shots were hitting the shields. They rattled the *Yavin*, making Wedge glad for his straps.

"Making evasive maneuvers," Sela said. "Prepare for . . ."

Wedge pulled off his headphones. He didn't want to think about command. He shoved aside his targeting computer too. He didn't have the Force, as Luke did, but he had something else, just as important. Faith in his own abilities. And he was close enough to that destroyer to see his target clearly, something that rarely happened in space.

The red shots looked like a spray of blood coming from the base of the destroyer. They were hitting the shields. He could feel the pattern, knew what they were doing. They were shooting in an ever-narrowing margin, getting closer, and closer, and closer, until all the shots converged into one big one right at the *Yavin*'s most vulnerable point.

The weak spot in the shields.

It would only take a few moments.

Wedge gripped the laser cannon. He hadn't fired a shot yet. It felt as if he only had one.

The Star Destroyer's shots were getting closer together. Near the gunports, people were screaming. The *Yavin* wouldn't hold together much longer, but the base of the destroyer was in the wrong position. Wedge kept the cannon pointing at the Star Destroyer's weakest spot.

The destroyer loomed overhead, filling his entire vision. His hands were sweating on the cannon handles. He kept moving the cannon, waiting, waiting, waiting—

And then it was in position. He held his arms steady, punched the trigger, and watched the single shot fly.

It was long and thin. It soared in the space between the Star Destroyer and the *Yavin,* red against the destroyer's scarred white surface. For a moment it looked as if the shot would ricochet off the shields, and then bounce back and forth between the two ships like a ball caught in a narrow corridor.

But it didn't. It hit the weak spot, which glowed bright red. Wedge grabbed his helmet and shouted into the mouthpiece, "Dive! Dive! Dive!"

The red glow spread and there was a small pop at the

first explosion. Then the *Yavin* dove. Wedge turned his chair so that he could see.

The Star Destroyer exploded: white and red and yellow against the blackness of space. A flower opening, a lightning bolt expanding, a fire starting and ending all in the space of a heartbeat. Beautiful and terrible at the very same time.

No lives lost, though.

He breathed a sigh of relief. The cries in the nearby cabins had grown. There was probably a lot of damage, and they still had the TIE fighters to deal with.

But the worst was over.

This battle was won. But he wondered what was happening with the war.

Fifty-three

Artoo had apparently seen a structural map of this moon. He was leading the droids with some type of purpose. The corridors were sloping upward. The sound of rolling wheels was deafening. One astromech droid was a handful. Hundreds of them were —well—terrifying.

More and more joined the group all the time. Some had scorch marks. Others had dents in their chrome surfaces. Still others had parts hanging out of their sides. They came from side corridors, and each time, another astromech droid would query about the Red Terror. The red gladiator droids hadn't been seen by any of them except an ancient astromech unit, one that had been old during the Clone Wars. It claimed that it had seen red droids shooting at each other in a cloud of smoke, more and more red droids approaching that area all the time.

The astromech droid who heard this news bleebled in astromech glee and had passed the word to the other droids. This parade of astromech droids assumed the Red Terror were destroying one another.

A ripple of blerps ran through the astromech droids, rather like a wave carried on the Mon Calamari sea.

Something concerned them. When Threepio reached the spot, he understood. Large signs in more than thirty languages, warning all unauthorized droids to stay away on pain of memory wipe.

A large spotlight shone on the corridor and the lighting got considerably brighter beyond that spot. One-way mirrors lined the wall.

Artoo ignored the sign, dodged the spot, and continued into the light. His chrome glistened. He had never looked so determined, with his wheels forward, and his blue-and-silver body tilted at a jaunty angle.

The astromech droids followed, splitting up around the spot, flowing around it like water around a stone. Warning sirens started to go off, and Threepio glanced behind him. He was bringing up the rear. If the Red Terror hadn't defeated itself, it would be here shortly, and he would be the first target.

He shoved his way through the sea of short droids. "Excuse me," he said, pushing them aside. "Pardon me. Excuse me. Pardon me."

They parted a little to let him pass. He made it halfway through the grouping, but still hadn't reached Artoo. Ahead, he could see Artoo, his jack extended as he worked the opening on a locked door.

"Oh, dear," Threepio said, and shoved forward harder. Threepio wormed his way around the spotlight, and continued shoving past the damaged astromech droids, following Artoo like an injured army following a demented leader.

Just as Threepio reached the front of the group, the door opened and Artoo slid inside with a triumphant bleeble. Threepio slipped in beside him.

And stopped.

Droid parts hung from the ceiling. These were not preassembled parts, but used pieces. The remains of droids who had come this way before and died. Several golden heads swung from the rafters, and so did more than one cylindrical headplate from an astromech droid.

"Artoo," Threepio said, his voice warbling, "perhaps we should reconsider. I'm sure we'll find Master Cole and he'll have a legitimate plan of action. You can't do this on your own."

"You certainly can't." A man stood in front of the one-way mirrors. Threepio hadn't seen him in the room's semidarkness.

Several astromech droids piled in the door behind Threepio. Artoo continued forward, heading toward a large computer array.

"Stay back, Artoo," the man said. The man was Brakiss, and Master Cole was not with him.

"Oh, dear," Threepio said. "Artoo, do as he says."

Artoo bleeped.

Several other astromech droids beeped in response, warning him not to continue.

Brakiss had a scrambler. "Stop, Artoo. I would love to leave your circuits intact—I'm sure you can give me a lot of interesting information—but I won't hesitate to use this."

"Artoo, do as he says!" Threepio shouted.

Artoo bleebled.

"I always thought you were a stubborn droid," Brakiss said. He aimed the scrambler at Artoo. Then, the instant before he fired, he swiveled his body.

An astromech droid shimmered in silver light, bleeped fifteen times with fifteen different tones, and then stopped, going completely dead. Threepio had seen that before. No amount of resetting would bring it back. Its microprocessors would have to be cleansed. Any personality the astromech droid had was gone.

Artoo had stopped moving. His head swiveled.

Brakiss finally had Artoo's attention.

Brakiss smiled. He leveled the scrambler at Threepio.

"Give me any more trouble, and your golden friend will be wiped."

Threepio held himself up as best he could. Begging would do no good now. Threepio was on his own.

Artoo bleeped softly, sadly.

Threepio wrapped his arms around his head, and awaited a fate worse than death.

✶ ✶ ✶

Kueller reached inside his robe and brought out the remote that Brakiss had given him so long ago. With his thumb, he shut off all the protections. Every droid made by Brakiss in the last two years would explode when Kueller punched in his identification code.

With both hands, Skywalker swung his lightsaber.

Kueller dodged, cursing his suddenly slow body. He needed just a moment to do the recognition. He held the remote up to his eye, hit the scan function, and a beam of light stabbed him as it identified his retina.

"Luke!" Leia shouted. "He's got a new weapon!"

But Skywalker said nothing. He was moving as slowly as Kueller, coming forward, holding his lightsaber as if it were made of steel instead of light.

The remote shut off the scan light and a tiny panel went up, revealing the number pad. A five-number sequence for all of them. Very simple, Brakiss had said, to destroy them all. It was the small units that were hard. Kueller had to specify the unit-batch numbers. This one would be easy.

He stepped out of the light as he punched in the first number.

Leia was shouting.

Skywalker was moving.

Neither of them would reach him.

He punched in the second, and the third, wishing the dizziness would go away.

Leia raised her hand.

A white creature appeared behind Luke.

Kueller punched in the fourth number, and then the fifth.

The remote beeped its acceptance, and relayed the commands all over the galaxy.

Fifty-four

Artoo bleeped again, this time with force.

"Noooooooo," Threepio said, his eyes hidden.

A loud, long, sustained crash made him bring his hands down. Astromech droids were breaking through the one-way glass. It coated Brakiss. He was screaming and pulling glass shards from his hair. The scrambler was on the floor. Droids were converging on him, and without hesitating, he turned and ran through a side door. Droids followed, as his screams echoed through the hallway.

Artoo beeped in satisfaction, then went to the computer array and jacked in.

Threepio went around the deactivated astromech droid, and watched Artoo's jack rotate. "Whatever are you doing?"

Artoo bleebled.

"How can you deactivate so many detonators from such a distance?" Threepio said. "Delusions of grandeur, that's what you have. Delusions. We have to get out of here before Brakiss comes back. We have to find Master Cole."

Artoo blapped at him, shushing him.

Threepio watched.

Then Artoo squealed.

"What? What?"

Artoo screamed, and Threepio waved his hands in distress. "What do you mean they're being activated? Every new droid will explode! We'll die here a thousand times over. They'll never even find pieces of us!"

Artoo whistled, then bleeped commands.

"What panel? How can I push a command button if I don't even know what panel?" Still, Threepio hurried over to the computer panel, looking for the small button that Artoo had described.

Artoo shrilled his response as Threepio found the button. Artoo would send the deactivation code, but Threepio had to press the emergency frequency. It would, they hoped, intercept any other message. It would prevent explosions from happening.

Artoo's jack stopped rotating. As he pulled the jack from the socket, he bleeped.

Now.

Threepio jammed his golden finger on the button once, twice, three times.

Nothing happened.

Artoo was staring at a display screen.

Threepio looked up.

Artoo started rocking back and forth. Then he shrilled a victory cry.

"We did it?" Threepio said.

Artoo bleeped happily.

"We really did it!" Threepio put his arm around his small friend. "We're saved! Oh, Artoo, you're a genius!"

Artoo burbled modestly.

"Well, I'm a genius too. After all, I did help you. I did listen to you, and you couldn't have done it alone. Why, if Master Cole and I hadn't come here—" Threepio interrupted himself. "Oh, dear. Master Cole! He's missing! We have to find him, Artoo, before something dreadful happens to him."

Artoo moaned softly.

"Oh, dear," Threepio said. "I suppose that means it already has."

✳ ✳ ✳

Leia couldn't feel Luke anymore. It was as if his personality completely disappeared, even though she could still see him, outlined against the tower in the growing twilight. Behind him, the Thernbee appeared, its huge face turning quizzically toward Kueller. His presence was gone too.

But she sensed someone else close, someone precious. She turned. Han was at the mouth of the alley, his blaster out, his face hidden in shadow. Chewbacca was behind him. She wanted to run to Han, but she couldn't. Not yet.

Something was happening to Luke.

At first she had thought he was going to die, as Obi-Wan did, but he didn't. Kueller didn't hit him. Instead, Kueller backed away and pulled out a small device. It was scanning his face.

She had a bad feeling about this.

"Luke!" she shouted, but Luke seemed to be ignoring her. He was trying to hold his lightsaber.

He was missing his chance. Kueller was going to do something awful and then get away.

The light stopped scanning Kueller's face.

Leia raised her hand, and called Han's blaster to her. It left his hands and zoomed toward her.

The Thernbee saw her, and its tail started to wag. It changed direction and came toward her.

The blaster dipped in the air. She was losing her mental grip on it. She pulled it to her faster. It hit her hand as a blanket dropped across her mind. She stumbled backward, then pulled the blaster aloft.

Kueller was still holding the device up. She saw his fingers move against the light the device gave off.

Even without feeling him through the Force, she knew what he was going to do. He had told her when he arrived. It didn't matter that some of the droids had been turned off.

So many hadn't.

Those waves of cold . . .

The concussion of the instant bomb . . .

The laughter of her children . . .

Leia raised the blaster, closed one eye, and lined the weapon up with Kueller. He didn't see her. He couldn't even feel her.

But Luke could.

"Leia!" he shouted.

Kueller turned, and Leia didn't hesitate. The shot went directly for his head.

He raised a hand to ward it off, but the hand did no good. The blaster shot knocked him backward.

"Leia!" Luke shouted again.

The Thernbee was coming toward her, a giant furry ghost in the darkness.

Kueller sat up, and Leia shot him one more time. He fell back, the device falling out of his hand. She crossed the tile, the heavy feeling growing stronger with each movement.

"Leia!" Luke was beside her now. He took the blaster from her. She could feel his concern. Had she shot Kueller out of hatred and anger? Probably. Would she be going to the dark side now?

She didn't know.

She couldn't feel the Force at all anymore.

Maybe it didn't count if she couldn't feel the Force.

She stopped over Kueller's body. He looked smaller now, his arms raised above his head. Luke reached for her, but she moved out of his way, and bent over Kueller. She slipped her fingers under his mask and ripped it away.

He was a boy, his features only beginning to show the signs of wear that Palpatine's had at the end. His dark eyes were open and lifeless, his mouth slack, but his features still had the roundness of youth, a sort of chubby charm that should have radiated joy instead of hatred.

No wonder he had used the mask. A face like that would have terrified no one.

"He was just a child," she whispered.

Luke crouched beside her. He took the mask from her hand. "No, Leia. He lost his childhood before he came to Yavin 4. He knew what he was doing, what he had become."

He set the mask on Kueller's destroyed chest, stood, and helped Leia up. The Thernbee was right beside them, its tongue out.

"There's that blasted thing!" Han said from behind them. "I'd have been able to help if it hadn't eaten my ysalamiri."

"So that's what that feeling is." Luke brought a hand to his face and laughed shakily. "You helped, Han, old buddy. Let's just hope the Thernbee here starts to digest the ysalamiri quickly."

"I wouldn't count on it," Han said. "It swallowed the cages too."

"The Thernbee has eaten stranger things in the recent past," Luke said.

Leia didn't care about the Thernbee. She took one last look at the man who had threatened her entire family. Then she turned around. Han was behind her, watching her.

"I love you, Princess," he said softly.

She launched herself into his arms, and pulled him close. "I know," she whispered. "I know."

Fifty-five

Artoo's handiwork had shut off all the droids in the facility, except for those without the detonator chip. Only the astromech units and Threepio apparently were without. The astromech units chased Brakiss to his ship, and watched as he took off to parts unknown.

The computer held no clues as to Master Cole's whereabouts, so Threepio and Artoo had to search the nearby compounds. They found him in a droid torture chamber that made the one in Jabba's palace look like a luxurious oil-massage parlor. Master Cole was strapped to a bench, and was partially unconscious.

Artoo determined that Master Cole was in no condition to fly the freighter. So Threepio sent messages to everyone he could think of, requesting a transport.

He managed to raise Lando Calrissian, who chuckled and said that the *Lady Luck* was turning into a passenger liner. He promised to arrive shortly and pick them up.

Threepio waited beside Master Cole. Artoo had insisted on freeing the tortured droids, and he sent them to a repair area, hoping that they could help each other. Artoo was puttering around the room, deactivating all its horrible equipment. He had already removed the torture devices on the Eve-Ninedeninetwo.

Then Master Cole's hand moved. Threepio leaned over him, and was rewarded when Master Cole's eyelids fluttered. His eyes opened, he saw Threepio, and—he screamed.

Artoo beeped in response, hurrying toward Threepio's side.

Threepio backed away from Master Cole. "I'm so sorry, sir. It's just me. See-Threepio, at your service."

Master Cole's scream died, and he brought a hand to his face. Artoo beeped at him sympathetically.

"We're still in this place."

"Only for a moment, sir," Threepio said. "Artoo has gotten us transport."

"Brakiss?" Master Cole said.

"He left, sir. The astromech droids attacked him, and he ran away. After I—"

Artoo bleebled.

"—Ah, after *we* defeated the Red Terror."

"The Red—?"

"Oh, it's a long story, sir, but quite intriguing. You see, after I left you—"

"Later, Threepio." Master Cole pulled himself up on his elbows, and peered at Artoo. "Did you solve what you needed to?"

Artoo whistled his affirmative.

"Oh, more than solved it, sir. He deactivated all the detonators. It seems that Brakiss designed them all to be handled from one remote, although why he would do that seems quite unusual to me. Artoo assures me that it is custom among droid manufacturers. It allows for defective models to be deactivated, even in difficult-to-reach areas where—"

"Can no one shut him up?" Master Cole said as he rolled off the table. He moaned slightly.

"I don't think you should be getting up, sir."

"I don't think I want to stay here any longer. Where is the freighter?"

"Where we left it, sir. But you are in no condition to fly it. Master Calrissian shall be here shortly. He'll take us back to Coruscant."

Threepio moved to help Master Cole stand, but Master Cole flinched.

"Did they hurt you badly, sir?"

Master Cole gave him a withering glance. "It didn't exactly tickle."

Threepio nodded. "Well, sir, it might do you good to remember two things: Artoo and I did rescue you, and if you'll forgive my impertinence, sir, no two droids are alike. I know many sentients forget that, but we are individuals and can remain so without a memory wipe."

Master Cole smiled. "I know that, Threepio. You startled me when I came to. And as for the rest, well, it hurts to be touched at the moment. I'm sure that will fade." He gazed down at Artoo, who hovered near him. "I've learned from both of you never to underestimate a droid. I've been as bad as the rest of the galaxy in taking you all for granted. I'll never do that again."

Artoo beeped happily.

"What did he say?" Master Cole asked.

"That it sounds as if you'll be all right now." Threepio's hand clanged as it rested on Artoo's head. "It seems, thanks to Artoo's quick thinking and my negotiation skills, that we'll all be fine now."

Master Cole grinned. "I think you're right, Threepio. I think you're right."

✶ ✶ ✶

Mon Mothma walked Leia to the redesigned Imperial ballroom. Leia was wearing a copy of her white dress, but she had forgone the braids wrapped around her ears.

Instead, she wore her hair down. Han had smiled at her before she left the suite, and had made her promise to return from the Senate early. The children were due back the following day. He wanted to make the most of his time alone with her.

So did she.

"I still don't understand how you got them to call off the recall election," Leia said.

Mon Mothma smiled. "I didn't, Leia. You did. You and Wedge and Han and Luke. If you hadn't successfully defeated Kueller, you would have come back here to a political storm unlike any you've ever seen. But when it became clear that Han wasn't involved in the bombing, and instead you all had been the ones who caught the culprit, Meido and his followers could do nothing else but support you."

Leia clasped her hands behind her back. "But you had to have done something. You already had Meido off the Inner Council by the time I came back."

Mon Mothma shrugged. "I've had more years of experience dealing with divergent voices than you have, Leia. You'll need to learn how to work with a group that is no longer homogeneous. The Senate won't always agree on policy anymore. You'll have to build coalitions."

"With Imperials?" Leia asked, shuddering.

"Former Imperials who really had nothing to do with the Empire. You can't always blame people for their pasts. You should know that better than anyone, President Organa *Solo.*"

Mon Mothma had a point. Han's past was shady at best, and yet he was getting a hero's commendation for his work with the wounded on Smuggler's Run. So was Lando. Lando had already asked Leia how much financial compensation went along with the commendation, and had frowned when she said that gratitude came without monetary reward.

And then she had promised to pay, out of her own pocket if she had to, for the refurbishing of the *Lady Luck.* It was the least she could do. Lando had saved hundreds of lives.

"Any word from Chewbacca?" Mon Mothma asked.

Leia nodded. "He and the *Alderaan* are due at any point. It took him a while to find the wild pride of Thernbees. Apparently, when their number had been so badly hunted by the Je'har, they had moved away from their normal stomping grounds. But Chewie was able to deliver our Thernbee back to them."

"He sounds like a delightful creature."

"He was too big and pesky to be delightful," Leia said. "And it took him two days to digest the ysalamiri. Mara, Luke, and I were stuck in the *Falcon,* playing holographic games while Han and Chewie argued about who would repair the damage."

"They must have fixed it."

Leia grinned. "They did. After Mara threatened to shoot them both."

Mon Mothma laughed. They stopped in front of the ballroom door. Mon Mothma put her hand on Leia's arm. "You realize that some of the senators are saying Threepio and Artoo should be deactivated for taking such initiative. They also want action taken against Cole Fardreamer. The theft of the freighter has them all disturbed. They'll try to make that the first order of business."

Leia glanced at the closed doors. The last time she had gone into a Senate Chamber dressed like this, she had been worried about the petty backbiting of the senators. The explosion had come out of the blue, had ruined so many lives, and had made those worries seem trivial.

Kueller. His youthful face would haunt her longer than his death mask would.

His actions would haunt her longer still.

He had taken so many lives without a single thought. And it had taken so much to defeat him. She would do everything she could in her position as Chief of State to see that no other monsters like him were created under her watch.

And the first order of business would be to make sure no truth got distorted by opportunistic politicians.

"They won't succeed in deactivating the droids," she said. "Artoo and Threepio are heroes. I have some ideas about changing the laws regarding droids. And they won't touch Cole Fardreamer. He discovered the flaws in the new X-wings. It's on his suggestion that we're returning to the older models. I'll take care of all of this. I also have some bridge building to do."

"Sounds like a busy day," Mon Mothma said.

"It can't be too busy," Leia said. "Luke is having his last bacta treatment this afternoon, and I plan to be there when he wakes up. Then I am going home. Han promised dinner for me."

"And no children until tomorrow," Mon Mothma said.

Leia smiled. "A person always has to make the best of every situation," she said.

"Oh, you do, Leia," Mon Mothma said.

The moment had suddenly gotten too serious for Leia. She put her arm around Mon Mothma's waist. "A whole new chapter in here," Leia said.

"Yes," Mon Mothma said. "And the first order of business is for me to step down and you to regain your post."

"Think they'll ratify my return?" Leia asked.

"Without dissent," Mon Mothma said.

Then they opened the door to the temporary Senate Hall. Leia was already planning her speech. It would be different from the one she had planned so long ago. This one would be about unity and respect.

She would set the tone for the new Senate term.

And this time, she would do it right.

ABOUT THE AUTHOR

KRISTINE KATHRYN RUSCH is an award-winning fiction writer. She has published fourteen novels under her own name: *The White Mists of Power; Afterimage* (written with Kevin J. Anderson); *Façade; Heart Readers; Traitors; Sins of the Blood; The Escape* (with Dean Wesley Smith); *The Fey: The Sacrifice; The Long Night* (with Dean Wesley Smith); *Rings of Tautee* (with Dean Wesley Smith); *The Devil's Churn; Star Trek: Klingon!* (with Dean Wesley Smith); *Soldiers of Fear* (with Dean Wesley Smith); and *The Fey: The Changeling.* Her short fiction has been nominated for the Nebula, Hugo, World Fantasy, and Stoker awards. Her novella, *The Gallery of His Dreams,* won the Locus Award for best short fiction. Her body of fiction won her the John W. Campbell Award, given in 1991 in Europe.

In her spare time, Rusch edits the *Magazine of Fantasy & Science Fiction,* a prestigious fiction magazine founded in 1949. In 1994, she won the Hugo Award for her editing. She started Pulphouse Publishing with her husband, Dean Wesley Smith, and they won a World Fantasy Award for their work on that press. Rusch and Smith edited *The SFWA Handbook: A Professional Writer's Guide to Writing Professionally,* which won the Locus Award for Best Non-Fiction. They have also written several novels under the pen name Sandy Schofield.

She lives and works in Oregon.

The World of STAR WARS Novels

In May 1991, *Star Wars* caused a sensation in the publishing industry with the Bantam Spectra release of Timothy Zahn's novel *Heir to the Empire*. For the first time, Lucasfilm Ltd. had authorized new novels that *continued* the famous story told in George Lucas's three blockbuster motion pictures: *Star Wars*, *The Empire Strikes Back*, and *Return of the Jedi*. Reader reaction was immediate and tumultuous: *Heir* reached #1 on the *New York Times* bestseller list and demonstrated that *Star Wars* lovers were eager for exciting new stories set in this universe, written by leading science fiction authors who shared their passion. Since then, each Bantam *Star Wars* novel has been an instant national bestseller.

Lucasfilm and Bantam decided that future novels in the series would be interconnected: That is, events in one novel would have consequences in the others. You might say that each Bantam *Star Wars* novel, enjoyable on its own, is also part of a much larger tale.

Here is a special look at Bantam's *Star Wars* books, along with excerpts from the more recent novels. Each one is available now wherever Bantam Books are sold.

The Han Solo Trilogy: THE PARADISE SNARE and coming soon, THE HUTT GAMBIT REBEL DAWN by A. C. Crispin

Setting: before *Star Wars: A New Hope*

What was Han Solo like before *we met him in the first STAR WARS movie? This trilogy answers that tantalizing question, filling in lots of historical lore about our favorite swashbuckling hero and thrilling us with adventures of the brash young pilot that we never knew he'd experienced. As the trilogy begins, the young Han makes a life-changing decision: to escape from the clutches of Garris Shrike, head of the trading "clan" who has brutalized Han while taking advantage of his piloting abilities. Here's a tense early scene from The Paradise Snare featuring Han, Shrike, and Dewlanna, a Wookiee who is Han's only friend in this horrible situation:*

"I've had it with you, Solo. I've been lenient with you so far, because you're a blasted good swoop pilot and all that prize money came in handy, but my patience is ended." Shrike ceremoniously pushed up the sleeves of his bedizened uniform, then balled his hands into fists. The galley's artificial lighting made the blood-jewel ring glitter dull silver. "Let's see what a few days of fighting off Devaronian blood-poisoning does for your attitude—along with maybe a few broken bones. I'm doing this for your own good, boy. Someday you'll thank me."

Han gulped with terror as Shrike started toward him. He'd lashed out at the trader captain once before, two years ago, when he'd been feeling cocky after winning the gladitorial Free-For-All on Jubilar—and had been instantly sorry. The speed and strength of Garris's returning blow had snapped his head back and split both lips so thoroughly that Dewlanna had had to feed him mush for a week until they healed.

With a snarl, Dewlanna stepped forward. Shrike's hand dropped to his blaster. "You stay out of this, old Wookiee," he snapped in a voice nearly as harsh as Dewlanna's. "Your cooking isn't *that* good."

Han had already grabbed his friend's furry arm and was forcibly holding her back. "Dewlanna, no!"

She shook off his hold as easily as she would have waved off an annoying insect and roared at Shrike. The captain drew his blaster, and chaos erupted.

"Noooo!" Han screamed, and leaped forward, his foot lashing out in an old street-fighting technique. His instep impacted solidly with Shrike's breastbone. The captain's breath went out in a great *houf!* and he went over backward. Han hit the deck and rolled. A tingler bolt sizzled past his ear.

"Larrad!" wheezed the captain as Dewlanna started toward him.

Shrike's brother drew his blaster and pointed it at the Wookiee. "Stop, Dewlanna!"

His words had no more effect than Han's. Dewlanna's blood was up—she was in full Wookiee battle rage. With a roar that deafened the combatants, she grabbed Larrad's wrist and yanked, spinning him around and snapping him in a terrible parody of a child's "snap the whip" game. Han heard a *crunch,* mixed with several *pops* as tendons and ligaments gave way. Larrad Shrike shrieked, a high, shrill noise that carried such pain that the Corellian youth's arm ached in sympathy.

Grabbing the blaster from his belt, Han snapped off a shot at the Elomin who was leaping forward, tingler ready and aimed at Dewlanna's midsection. Brafid howled, dropping his weapon. Han was amazed that he'd managed to hit him, but he didn't have long to wonder about the accuracy of his aim.

Shrike was staggering to his feet, blaster in hand, aimed squarely at Han's head. "Larrad?" he yelled at the writhing heap of agony that was his brother. Larrad did not reply.

Shrike cocked the blaster and stepped even closer to Han. "Stop it, Dewlanna!" the captain snarled at the Wookiee. "Or your buddy Solo dies!"

Han dropped his blaster and put his hands up in a gesture of surrender.

Dewlanna stopped in her tracks, growling softly.

Shrike leveled the blaster, and his finger tightened on the trigger. Pure malevolent hatred was etched upon his features, and then he smiled, pale blue eyes glittering with ruthless joy. "For insubordination and striking your captain," he announced, "I sentence you to death, Solo. May you rot in all the hells there ever were."

SHADOWS OF THE EMPIRE
by Steve Perry
Setting: Between *The Empire Strikes Back* and *Return of the Jedi*

Here is a very special STAR WARS story dealing with Black Sun, a galaxy-spanning criminal organization that is masterminded by one of the most interesting villains in the STAR WARS universe: Xizor, dark prince of the Falleen. Xizor's chief rival for the favor of Emperor Palpatine is none other than Darth Vader himself—alive and well, and a major character in this story, since it is set during the events of the STAR WARS film trilogy.

In the opening prologue, we revisit a familiar scene from The Empire Strikes Back, *and are introduced to our marvelous new bad guy:*

He looks like a walking corpse, Xizor thought. *Like a mummified body dead a thousand years. Amazing he is still alive, much less the most powerful man in the galaxy. He isn't even that old; it is more as if something is slowly eating him.*

Xizor stood four meters away from the Emperor, watching as the man who had long ago been Senator Palpatine moved to stand in the holocam field. He imagined he could smell the decay in the Emperor's worn body. Likely that was just some trick of the recycled air, run through dozens of filters to ensure that there was no chance of any poison gas being introduced into it. Filtered the life out of it, perhaps, giving it that dead smell.

The viewer on the other end of the holo-link would see a close-up of the Emperor's head and shoulders, of an age-ravaged face shrouded in the cowl of his dark zeyd-cloth robe. The man on the other end of the transmission, light-years away, would not see Xizor, though Xizor would be able to see him. It was a measure of the Emperor's trust that Xizor was allowed to be here while the conversation took place.

The man on the other end of the transmission—if he could still be called that—

The air swirled inside the Imperial chamber in front of the Emperor, coalesced, and blossomed into the image of a figure down on one knee. A caped humanoid biped dressed in jet black, face hidden under a full helmet and breathing mask:

Darth Vader.

Vader spoke: "What is thy bidding, my master?"

If Xizor could have hurled a power bolt through time and space to strike Vader dead, he would have done it without blinking. Wishful thinking: Vader was too powerful to attack directly.

"There is a great disturbance in the Force," the Emperor said.

"I have felt it," Vader said.

"We have a new enemy. Luke Skywalker."

Skywalker? That had been Vader's name, a long time ago. Who was this person with the same name, someone so powerful as to be worth a conversation between the Emperor and his most loathsome creation? More importantly, why had Xizor's agents not uncovered this before now? Xizor's ire was instant—but cold. No sign of his surprise or anger would show on his imperturbable features. The Falleen did not allow their emotions to burst forth as did many of the inferior species; no, the Falleen ancestry was not fur but scales, not mammalian but reptilian. Not wild but coolly calculating. Such was much better. Much safer.

"Yes, my master," Vader continued.

"He could destroy us," the Emperor said.

Xizor's attention was riveted upon the Emperor and the holographic image of Vader kneeling on the deck of a ship far away. Here was interesting news indeed. Something the Emperor perceived as a danger to himself? Something the Emperor feared?

"He's just a boy," Vader said. "Obi-Wan can no longer help him."

Obi-Wan. That name Xizor knew. He was among the last of the Jedi Knights, a general. But he'd been dead for decades, hadn't he?

Apparently Xizor's information was wrong if Obi-Wan had been helping someone who was still a boy. His agents were going to be sorry.

Even as Xizor took in the distant image of Vader and the nearness of the Emperor, even as he was aware of the luxury of the Emperor's private and protected chamber at the core of the giant pyramidal palace, he was also able to make a mental note to himself: Somebody's head would roll for the failure to make him aware of all this. Knowledge was power; lack of knowledge was weakness. This was something he could not permit.

The Emperor continued. "The Force is strong with him. The son of Skywalker must not become a Jedi."

Son of Skywalker?

Vader's son! Amazing!

"If he could be turned he would become a powerful ally," Vader said.

There was something in Vader's voice when he said this, something Xizor could not quite put his finger on. Longing? Worry?

Hope?

"Yes . . . yes. He would be a great asset," the Emperor said. "Can it be done?"

There was the briefest of pauses. "He will join us or die, master."

Xizor felt the smile, though he did not allow it to show any more than he had allowed his anger play. Ah. Vader wanted Skywalker alive, *that* was what had been in his tone. Yes, he had said that the boy would join them or die, but this latter part was obviously meant only to placate the Emperor. Vader had no intention of killing Skywalker, his own son; that was obvious to one as skilled in reading voices as was Xizor. He had not gotten to be the Dark Prince, Underlord of Black Sun, the largest criminal organization in the galaxy, merely on his formidable good looks. Xizor didn't truly understand the Force that sustained the Emperor and made him and Vader so powerful, save to know that it certainly worked somehow. But he did know that it was something the extinct Jedi had supposedly mastered. And now, apparently, this new player had tapped into it. Vader wanted Skywalker alive, had practically promised the Emperor that he would deliver him alive—and converted.

This was most interesting.

Most interesting indeed.

The Emperor finished his communication and turned back to face him. "Now, where were we, Prince Xizor?"

The Dark Prince smiled. He would attend to the business at hand, but he would not forget the name of Luke Skywalker.

THE TRUCE AT BAKURA by Kathy Tyers
Setting: Immediately after *Return of the Jedi*

The day after his climactic battle with Emperor Palpatine and the sacrifice of his father, Darth Vader, who died saving his life, Luke Skywalker helps recover an Imperial drone ship bearing a startling message intended for the Emperor. It is a distress signal from the far-off Imperial outpost of Bakura, which is under attack by an alien invasion force, the Ssi-ruuk. Leia sees a rescue mission as an opportunity to achieve a diplomatic victory for the Rebel Alliance, even if it means fighting alongside former Imperials. But Luke receives a vision from Obi-Wan Kenobi revealing that the stakes are even higher: the invasion at Bakura threatens everything the Rebels have won at such great cost.

STAR WARS: X-WING
by Michael A. Stackpole
ROGUE SQUADRON
WEDGE'S GAMBLE
THE KRYTOS TRAP
THE BACTA WAR
Setting: Three years after *Return of the Jedi*

Inspired by X-wing, *the bestselling computer game from LucasArts Entertainment Co., this exciting series chronicles the further adventures of the most feared and fearless fighting force in the galaxy. A new generation of X-wing pilots, led by Commander Wedge Antilles, is combating the remnants of the Empire still left after the events of the STAR WARS movies. Here are novels full of explosive space action, nonstop adventure, and the special brand of wonder known as STAR WARS.*

In this very early scene, young Corellian pilot Corran Horn faces a tough challenge fast enough to get his heart pounding—and this is only a simulation! [P.S.: ''Whistler'' is Corran's R2 astromech droid]:

The Corellian brought his proton torpedo targeting program up and locked on to the TIE. It tried to break the lock, but turbolaser fire from the *Korolev* boxed it in. Corran's heads-up display went red and he triggered the torpedo. ''Scratch one eyeball.''

The missile shot straight in at the fighter, but the pilot broke hard to port and away, causing the missile to overshoot the target. *Nice flying!* Corran brought his X-wing over and started down to loop in behind the TIE, but as he did so, the TIE vanished from his forward screen and reappeared in his aft arc. Yanking the stick hard to the right and pulling it back, Corran wrestled the X-wing up and to starboard, then inverted and rolled out to the left.

A laser shot jolted a tremor through the simulator's couch. *Lucky thing I had all shields aft!* Corran reinforced them with energy from his lasers, then evened them out fore and aft. Jinking the fighter right and left, he avoided laser shots coming in from behind, but they all came in far closer than he liked.

He knew Jace had been in the bomber, and Jace was the only pilot in the unit who could have stayed with him. *Except for our leader.* Corran smiled broadly. *Coming to see how good I really am, Commander Antilles? Let me give you a clinic.* "Make sure you're in there solid, Whistler, because we're going for a little ride."

Corran refused to let the R2's moan slow him down. A snap-roll brought the X-wing up on its port wing. Pulling back on the stick yanked the fighter's nose up away from the original line of flight. The TIE stayed with him, then tightened up on the arc to close distance. Corran then rolled another ninety degrees and continued the turn into a dive. Throttling back, Corran hung in the dive for three seconds, then hauled back hard on the stick and cruised up into the TIE fighter's aft.

The X-wing's laser fire missed wide to the right as the TIE cut to the left. Corran kicked his speed up to full and broke with the TIE. He let the X-wing rise above the plane of the break, then put the fighter through a twisting roll that ate up enough time to bring him again into the TIE's rear. The TIE snapped to the right and Corran looped out left.

He watched the tracking display as the distance between them grew to be a kilometer and a half, then slowed. *Fine, you want to go nose to nose? I've got shields and you don't.* If Commander Antilles wanted to commit virtual suicide, Corran was happy to oblige him. He tugged the stick back to his sternum and rolled out in an inversion loop. *Coming at you!*

The two starfighters closed swiftly. Corran centered his foe in the crosshairs and waited for a dead shot. Without shields the TIE fighter would die with one burst, and Corran wanted the kill to be clean. His HUD flicked green as the TIE juked in and out of the center, then locked green as they closed.

The TIE started firing at maximum range and scored hits. At that distance the lasers did no real damage against the shields, prompting Corran to wonder why Wedge was wasting the energy. Then, as the

HUD's green color started to flicker, realization dawned. *The bright bursts on the shields are a distraction to my targeting! I better kill him* now!

Corran tightened down on the trigger button, sending red laser needles stabbing out at the closing TIE fighter. He couldn't tell if he had hit anything. Lights flashed in the cockpit and Whistler started screeching furiously. Corran's main monitor went black, his shields were down, and his weapons controls were dead.

The pilot looked left and right. "Where is he, Whistler?"

The monitor in front of him flickered to life and a diagnostic report began to scroll by. Bloodred bordered the damage reports. "Scanners, out; lasers, out; shields, out; engine, out! I'm a wallowing Hutt just hanging here in space."

THE COURTSHIP OF PRINCESS LEIA
by Dave Wolverton
Setting: Four years after *Return of the Jedi*

One of the most interesting developments in Bantam's STAR WARS novels is that in their storyline, Han Solo and Princess Leia start a family. This tale reveals how the couple originally got together. Wishing to strengthen the fledgling New Republic by bringing in powerful allies, Leia opens talks with the Hapes consortium of more than sixty worlds. But the consortium is ruled by the Queen Mother, who, to Han's dismay, wants Leia to marry her son, Prince Isolder. Before this action-packed story is over, Luke will join forces with Isolder against a group of Force-trained "witches" and face a deadly foe.

HEIR TO THE EMPIRE
DARK FORCE RISING
THE LAST COMMAND
by Timothy Zahn
Setting: Five years after *Return of the Jedi*

This #1 bestselling trilogy introduces two legendary forces of evil into the STAR WARS literary pantheon. Grand Admiral Thrawn has taken control of the Imperial fleet in the years since the destruction of the Death Star, and the mysterious Joruus C'baoth is a fearsome Jedi Master who has been seduced by the dark side. Han and Leia have now been married for about a year, and as the story begins, she is pregnant with twins. Thrawn's plan is to crush the Rebellion and resurrect the Empire's New Order with C'baoth's help—and in return, the Dark Master will get Han and Leia's Jedi children to mold as he wishes. For as readers of this magnificent trilogy will see, Luke Skywalker is not the last of the old Jedi. He is the first of the new.

The Jedi Academy Trilogy:
JEDI SEARCH
DARK APPRENTICE
CHAMPIONS OF THE FORCE
by Kevin J. Anderson
Setting: Seven years after *Return of the Jedi*

In order to assure the continuation of the Jedi Knights, Luke Skywalker has decided to start a training facility: a Jedi Academy. He will gather Force-sensitive students who show potential as prospective Jedi and serve as their mentor, as Jedi Masters Obi-Wan Kenobi and Yoda did for him. Han and Leia's twins are now toddlers, and there is a third Jedi child: the infant Anakin, named after Luke and Leia's father. In this trilogy, we discover the existence of a powerful Imperial doomsday weapon, the horrifying Sun Crusher—which will soon become the centerpiece of a titanic struggle between Luke Skywalker and his most brilliant Jedi Academy student, who is delving dangerously into the dark side.

CHILDREN OF THE JEDI
by Barbara Hambly
Setting: Eight years after *Return of the Jedi*

The STAR WARS characters face a menace from the glory days of the Empire when a thirty-year-old automated Imperial Dreadnaught comes to life and begins its grim mission: to gather forces and annihilate a long-forgotten stronghold of Jedi children. When Luke is whisked onboard, he begins to communicate with the brave Jedi Knight who paralyzed the ship decades ago, and gave her life in the process. Now she is part of the vessel, existing in its artificial intelligence core, and guiding Luke through one of the most unusual adventures he has ever had.

DARKSABER by Kevin J. Anderson
Setting: Immediately thereafter

Not long after Children of the Jedi, *Luke and Han learn that evil Hutts are building a reconstruction of the original Death Star—and that the Empire is still alive, in the form of Daala, who has joined forces with Pellaeon, former second in command to the feared Grand Admiral Thrawn. In this early scene, Luke has returned to the home of Obi-Wan Kenobi on Tatooine to try and consult a long-gone mentor:*

He stood anxious and alone, feeling like a prodigal son outside the ramshackle, collapsed hut that had once been the home of Obi-Wan Kenobi.

Luke swallowed and stepped forward, his footsteps crunching in the silence. He had not been here in many years. The door had fallen off its hinges; part of the clay front wall had fallen in. Boulders and crumbled adobe jammed the entrance. A pair of small, screeching desert rodents snapped at him and fled for cover; Luke ignored them.

Gingerly, he ducked low and stepped into the home of his first mentor.

Luke stood in the middle of the room breathing deeply, turning around, trying to sense the presence he desperately needed to see. This was the place where Obi-Wan Kenobi had told Luke of the Force. Here, the old man had first given Luke his lightsaber and hinted at the truth about his father, "from a certain point of view," dispelling the diversionary story that Uncle Owen had told, at the same time planting seeds of his own deceptions.

"Ben," he said and closed his eyes, calling out with his mind as well as his voice. He tried to penetrate the invisible walls of the Force and reach to the luminous being of Obi-Wan Kenobi who had visited him numerous times, before saying he could never speak with Luke again.

"Ben, I need you," Luke said. Circumstances had changed. He could think of no other way past the obstacles he faced. Obi-Wan had to answer. It wouldn't take long, but it could give him the key he needed with all his heart.

Luke paused and listened and sensed—

But felt nothing. If he could not summon Obi-Wan's spirit here in the empty dwelling where the old man had lived in exile for so many years, Luke didn't believe he could find his former teacher ever again.

He echoed the words Leia had used more than a decade earlier, beseeching him, "Help me, Obi-Wan Kenobi," Luke whispered, "you're my only hope."

PLANET OF TWILIGHT
by Barbara Hambly
Setting: Nine years after *Return of the Jedi*

Concluding the epic tale begun in her own novel, Children of the Jedi *and continued by Kevin Anderson in* Darksaber, *Barbara Hambly tells the story of a ruthless enemy of the New Republic operating out of a backwater world with vast mineral deposits. The first step in his campaign is to kidnap Princess Leia. Meanwhile, as Luke Skywalker searches the planet for his long-lost love Callista, the planet begins to reveal its unspeakable secret—a secret that threatens the New Republic, the Empire and the entire galaxy.*

The first to die was a midshipman named Koth Barak. One of his fellow crewmembers on the New Republic escort cruiser *Adamantine* found him slumped across the table in the deck-nine break room where he'd repaired half an hour previously for a cup of coffeine. Twenty minutes after Barak should have been back to post, Gunnery Sergeant Gallie Wover went looking for him.

When she entered the deck-nine break room, Sergeant Wover's first sight was of the palely flickering blue on blue of the infolog screen. "Blast it, Koth, I told you . . ."

Then she saw the young man stretched unmoving on the far side of the screen, head on the break table, eyes shut. Even at a distance of three meters Wover didn't like the way he was breathing.

"Koth!" She rounded the table in two strides, sending the other chairs clattering into a corner. She thought his eyelids moved a little when she yelled his name. "Koth!"

Wover hit the emergency call almost without conscious decision. In the few minutes before the med droids arrived she sniffed the coffeine in the gray plastene cup a few minutes from his limp fingers. It wasn't even cold.

Behind her the break room door *swoshed* open. She glanced over her shoulder to see a couple of Two-Onebees enter with a table, which was already unfurling scanners and life-support lines like a monster in a bad holovid. They shifted Barak onto the table and hooked him up. Every line of the readouts plunged, and soft, tinny alarms began to sound.

Barak's face had gone a waxen gray. The table was already pumping stimulants and antishock into the boy's veins. Wover could see the initial diagnostic lines on the screen that ringed the antigrav personnel transport unit's sides.

No virus. No bacteria. No Poison.

No foreign material in Koth Barak's body at all.

The lines dipped steadily towards zero, then went flat.

THE CRYSTAL STAR
by Vonda N. McIntyre
Setting: Ten years after *Return of the Jedi*

Leia's three children have been kidnapped. That horrible fact is made worse by Leia's realization that she can no longer sense her children through the Force! While she, Artoo-Detoo, and Chewbacca trail the kidnappers, Luke and Han discover a planet that is suffering strange quantum effects from a nearby star. Slowly freezing into a perfect crystal and disrupting the Force, the star is blunting Luke's power and crippling the Millennium Falcon. *These strands converge in an apocalyptic threat not only to the fate of the New Republic, but to the universe itself.*

The Black Fleet Crisis
BEFORE THE STORM
SHIELD OF LIES
TYRANT'S TEST
by Michael P. Kube-McDowell
Setting: Twelve years after *Return of the Jedi*

Long after setting up the hard-won New Republic, yesterday's Rebels have become today's administrators and diplomats. But the peace is not to last for long. A restless Luke must journey to his mother's homeworld in a desperate quest to find her people; Lando seizes a mysterious spacecraft with unimaginable weapons of destruction; and waiting in the wings is an horrific battle fleet under the control of a ruthless leader bent on a genocidal war.

Here is an opening scene from Before the Storm:

In the pristine silence of space, the Fifth Battle Group of the New Republic Defense Fleet blossomed over the planet Bessimir like a beautiful, deadly flower.

The formation of capital ships sprang into view with startling suddenness, trailing fire-white wakes of twisted space and bristling with weapons. Angular Star Destroyers guarded fat-hulled fleet carriers, while the assault cruisers, their mirror finishes gleaming, took the point.

A halo of smaller ships appeared at the same time. The fighters among them quickly deployed in a spherical defensive screen. As the Star Destroyers firmed up their formation, their flight decks quickly spawned scores of additional fighters.

At the same time, the carriers and cruisers began to disgorge the bombers, transports, and gunboats they had ferried to the battle. There was no reason to risk the loss of one fully loaded—a lesson the Republic had learned in pain. At Orinda, the commander of the fleet carrier *Endurance* had kept his pilots waiting in the launch bays, to protect the smaller craft from Imperial fire as long as possible. They were still there when *Endurance* took the brunt of a Super Star Destroyer attack and vanished in a ball of metal fire.

Before long more than two hundred warships, large and small, were bearing down on Bessimir and its twin moons. But the terrible, restless power of the armada could be heard and felt only by the ships' crews. The silence of the approach was broken only on the fleet comm channels, which had crackled to life in the first moments with encoded bursts of noise and cryptic ship-to-ship chatter.

At the center of the formation of great vessels was the flagship of the Fifth Battle Group, the fleet carrier *Intrepid*. She was so new from the yards at Hakassi that her corridors still reeked of sealing compound and cleaning solvent. Her huge realspace thruster engines still sang with the high-pitched squeal that the engine crews called "the baby's cry."

It would take more than a year for the mingled scents of the crew to displace the chemical smells from the first impressions of visitors. But after a hundred more hours under way, her engines' vibrations would drop two octaves, to the reassuring thrum of a seasoned thruster bank.

On *Intrepid*'s bridge, a tall Dornean in general's uniform paced along an arc of command stations equipped with large monitors. His eye-folds were swollen and fanned by an unconscious Dornean defensive reflex, and his leathery face was flushed purple by concern. Before the deployment was even a minute old, Etahn A'baht's first command had been bloodied.

The fleet tender *Ahazi* had overshot its jump, coming out of hyperspace too close to Bessimir and too late for its crew to recover from the error. Etahn A'baht watched the bright flare of light in the upper atmosphere from *Intrepid*'s forward viewstation, knowing that it meant six young men were dead.

THE NEW REBELLION
by Kristine Kathryn Rusch
Setting: Thirteen years after *Return of the Jedi*

Victorious though the New Republic may be, there is still no end to the threats to its continuing existence—this novel explores the price of keeping the peace. First, somewhere in the galaxy, millions suddenly perish in a blinding instant of pain. Then, as Leia prepares to address the Senate on Coruscant, a horrifying event changes the governmental equation in a flash.

Here is that latter calamity, in an early scene from The New Rebellion*:*

An explosion rocked the Chamber, flinging Leia into the air. She flew backward and slammed onto a desk, her entire body shuddering with the power of her hit. Blood and shrapnel rained around her. Smoke and dust rose, filling the room with a grainy darkness. She could hear nothing. With a shaking hand, she touched the side of her face. Warmth stained her cheeks and her earlobes. The ringing would start soon. The explosion was loud enough to affect her eardrums.

Emergency glow panels seared the gloom. She could feel rather than hear pieces of the crystal ceiling fall to the ground. A guard had landed beside her, his head tilted at an unnatural angle. She grabbed his blaster. She had to get out. She wasn't certain if the attack had come from within or from without. Wherever it had come from, she had to make certain no other bombs would go off.

The force of the explosion had affected her balance. She crawled over bodies, some still moving, as she made her way to the stairs. The slightest movement made her dizzy and nauseous, but she ignored the feelings. She had to.

A face loomed before hers. Streaked with dirt and blood, helmet askew, she recognized him as one of the guards who had been with her since Alderaan. *Your Highness*, he mouthed, and she couldn't read the rest. She shook her head at him, gasping at the increased dizziness, and kept going.

Finally she reached the stairs. She used the remains of a desk to get to her feet. Her gown was soaked in blood, sticky, and clinging to her legs. She held the blaster in front of her, wishing that she could hear. If she could hear, she could defend herself.

A hand reached out of the rubble beside her. She whirled, faced it, watched as Meido pulled himself out. His slender features were covered with dirt, but he appeared unharmed. He saw her blaster and cringed. She nodded once to acknowledge him, and kept moving. The guard was flanking her.

More rubble dropped from the ceiling. She crouched, hands over her head to protect herself. Small pebbles pelted her, and the floor shivered as large chunks of tile fell. Dust rose, choking her. She coughed, feeling it, but not able to hear it. Within an instant, the Hall had gone from a place of ceremonial comfort to a place of death.

The image of the death's-head mask rose in front of her again, this time from memory. She had known this was going to happen. Somewhere, from some part of her Force-sensitive brain, she had seen this. Luke said that Jedi were sometimes able to see the future. But she had never completed her training. She wasn't a Jedi.

But she was close enough.

The Corellian Trilogy:
AMBUSH AT CORELLIA
ASSAULT AT SELONIA
SHOWDOWN AT CENTERPOINT
by Roger MacBride Allen

Setting: Fourteen years after *Return of the Jedi*

This trilogy takes us to Corellia, Han Solo's homeworld, which Han has not visited in quite some time. A trade summit brings Han, Leia, and the children—now developing their own clear personalities and instinctively learning more about their innate skills in the Force—into the middle of a situation that most closely resembles a burning fuse. The Corellian system is on the brink of civil war, there are New Republic intelligence agents on a mysterious mission which even Han does not understand, and worst of all, a fanatical rebel leader has his hands on a superweapon of unimaginable power—and just wait until you find out who that leader is!

Here is an early scene from Ambush *that gives you a wonderful look at the growing Solo children (the twins are Jacen and Jaina, and their little brother is Anakin):*

Anakin plugged the board into the innards of the droid and pressed a button. The droid's black, boxy body shuddered awake, it drew in its wheels to stand up a bit taller, its status lights lit, and it made a sort of triple beep. "That's good," he said, and pushed the button again. The droid's status lights went out, and its body slumped down again. Anakin picked up the next piece, a motivation actuator. He frowned at it as he turned it over in his hands. He shook his head. ''That's *not* good,'' he announced.

''What's not good?'' Jaina asked.

''This thing,'' Anakin said, handing her the actuator. ''Can't you *tell*? The insides part is all melty.''

Jaina and Jacen exchanged a look. ''The outside looks okay,'' Jaina said, giving the part to her brother. ''How can he tell what the *inside* of it looks like? It's sealed shut when they make it.''

Anakin, still sitting on the floor, took the device from his brother and frowned at it again. He turned it over and over in his hands, and then held it over his head and looked at it as if he were holding it up to the light. ''There,'' he said, pointing a chubby finger at one point on the unmarked surface. ''In there is the bad part.'' He rearranged himself to sit cross-legged, put the actuator in his lap, and put his right index finger over the ''bad'' part. ''Fix,'' he said. ''Fix.'' The dark brown outer case of the actuator seemed to glow for a second with an odd blue-red light, but then the glow sputtered out and Anakin pulled his finger away quickly and stuck it in his mouth, as if he had burned it on something.

''Better now?'' Jaina asked.

''*Some* better,'' Anakin said, pulling his finger out of his mouth. ''Not *all* better.'' He took the actuator in his hand and stood up. He opened the access panel on the broken droid and plugged in the actuator. He closed the door and looked expectantly at his older brother and sister.

''Done?'' Jaina asked.

''Done,'' Anakin agreed. ''But *I'm* not going to push the button.'' He backed well away from the droid, sat down on the floor, and folded his arms.

Jacen looked at his sister.

''Not me,'' she said. ''This was your idea.''

Jacen stepped forward to the droid, reached out to push the power button from as far away as he could, and then stepped hurriedly back.

Once again, the droid shuddered awake, rattling a bit this time as it did so. It pulled its wheels in, lit its panel lights, and made the same triple beep. But then its holocam eye viewlens wobbled back and forth, and its panel lights dimmed and flared. It rolled backward just a bit, and then recovered itself.

''Good morning, young mistress and masters,'' it said. ''How may I surge you?''

Well, one word wrong, but so what? Jacen grinned and clapped his hands and rubbed them together eagerly. ''Good day, droid,'' he said. They had done it! But what to ask for first? ''First tidy up this room,'' he said. A simple task, and one that ought to serve as a good test of what this droid could do.

Suddenly the droid's overhead access door blew off and there was a flash of light from its interior. A thin plume of smoke drifted out of the droid. Its panel lights flared again, and then the work arm sagged downward. The droid's body, softened by heat, sagged in on itself and drooped to the floor. The floor and walls and ceiling of the playroom were supposed to be fireproof, but nonetheless the floor under the droid darkened a bit, and the ceiling turned black. The ventilators kicked on high automatically, and drew the smoke out of the room. After a moment they shut themselves off, and the room was silent.

The three children stood, every bit as frozen to the spot as the droid was, absolutely stunned. It was Anakin who recovered first. He walked cautiously toward the droid and looked at it carefully, being sure not to get too close or touch it. "*Really* melty now," he announced, and then wandered off to the other side of the room to play with his blocks.

The twins looked at the droid, and then at each other.

"We're dead," Jacen announced, surveying the wreckage.